ALSO BY PETRA DURST-BENNING
IN THE GLASSBLOWER TRILOGY

The Glassblower
The American Lady

The Paradise of Glass

The Glassblower Trilogy

PETRA DURST-BENNING

Translated by Samuel Willcocks

amazon crossing

This is a work of fiction. Names, characters, organizations, places, events, and incidents are either products of the author's imagination or are used fictitiously.

Text copyright © 2006 Petra Durst-Benning
Translation copyright © 2015 Samuel Willcocks
All rights reserved.

No part of this book may be reproduced, or stored in a retrieval system, or transmitted in any form or by any means, electronic, mechanical, photocopying, recording, or otherwise, without express written permission of the publisher.

Previously published as *Das gläserne Paradies* by Ullstein in Germany in 2006. Translated from German by Samuel Willcocks. First published in English by AmazonCrossing in 2015.

Published by AmazonCrossing, Seattle

www.apub.com

Amazon, the Amazon logo, and AmazonCrossing are trademarks of Amazon.com, Inc., or its affiliates.

ISBN-13: 9781503945050
ISBN-10: 1503945057

Cover design by Marc Cohen

Printed in the United States of America

IN MEMORIAM

Alfi

IN MEMORIAM

Samuel Willcocks

People who dream in broad daylight
learn about things which are never
revealed to those who dream at night.

Dante Gabriel Rossetti

PROLOGUE

September 18, 1911

Wanda walked toward the railway station, her back straight, her face expressionless. As always at this time of day the station was busy. Glassblowers from nearby Lauscha who had delivered their wares to a wholesaler in Sonneberg mingled with housewives from Steinach and the surrounding villages who had finished their shopping in town and were hurrying home. Solemn businessmen stood around, important-looking briefcases in hand. Many of them tilted their faces upward to catch the last warm rays of sunshine.

But Wanda didn't feel the sunshine, even though it was unusually warm for mid-September. Nor did she notice the tempting scent of grilled sausages wafting through the air from a nearby stall.

When she finally reached the platform, the tension drained from her face. Over. Finished. She didn't have to put on a brave face any longer. Nobody would care if she howled or screamed, if she sobbed and sniffled and her nose ran like a child's.

But she didn't howl. And she didn't scream.

She didn't even feel her own sorrow.

Because she'd lost everything.

She had let down her nearest and dearest. She was a failure, utterly and completely.

Hadn't she always known that?

She gazed down at the railway track. Oh, how well she knew the train ride from Sonneberg to Lauscha! She knew its every curve, the corners where the motion of the train pressed her against the side of the hard bench, the spot where the engine began to huff and puff and slowed down. She knew where the shadows lay on the steep mountainsides, when the compartments would be invaded by sudden gloom.

She'd always considered it such a romantic ride! And she'd always thought that Lauscha, where she got off the train, was romantic too. The little town nestled into its high valley, the very heart of the paradise of glass . . .

Wanda groaned. The thought of all those people waiting for her at the station made her stomach cramp. There must be a welcoming committee there already, probably ready to greet her with wine and song—why else had they all insisted on staying behind in Lauscha, today of all days, instead of coming along with her to Sonneberg? And now she had to face these dear, sweet souls—the people who had trusted her with everything they had and who wanted to celebrate her return—and she would have to look them in the eye and tell them that—

No, never! She'd never take that train again; she'd never ride the railway to Lauscha.

She had reached the end of her journey. What a strange feeling it was.

How different everything had felt yesterday, during the consecration service for the new church in Lauscha!

She heard the train pulling in behind her. There was already a hint of coal in the air. The closer the train came, the stronger the smell of soot would become. Right now the people on the platform were gazing up into the sunshine, enjoying the warmth, but soon they would begin to cough and wrinkle their noses.

Only last winter a young woman had thrown herself in front of a train as it came into the station. Her appalling death had been headline news in all the papers. At the time Wanda could not imagine the depths of despair that could drive a person to do such a thing. She had said that it was cowardly to end your life that way. She could still remember talking to Eva about it right after it had happened—they had ended up arguing about it. Eva claimed she understood why the woman had committed suicide, she understood her despair, and that she would never say that a person who did such a thing was a coward. After all, it wasn't an easy death to be torn to pieces on the rails, to have your limbs ripped apart by several tons of metal and your whole body crushed . . . Wanda hadn't wanted to listen.

You and your self-satisfied arrogance! You always thought you could take care of everything on your own. Imagined that you were better than the rest of them. That you were smarter, cleverer, braver.

The piercing sound of the braking train grew louder and louder. Wanda turned around, saw the black colossus approaching, belching out smoke.

Over. Finished. She'd lost it all.

She took a step forward.

CHAPTER ONE

Late May 1911

"Pardon me for asking again, young lady, but am I really to put down 'Father: Unknown'?"

The registrar leaned across the desk toward her, his eyebrows raised, and pushed the birth certificate away almost as though it revolted him. The sunbeams falling through the window behind him seemed to cast a halo around his head, which didn't at all suit the tone of voice in which he said "young lady."

Wanda and Johanna both noticed the judgmental tone in his voice, but neither of them reacted to it. What could they have said?

When Wanda didn't answer straightaway, the man added, "The shame of illegitimate birth stays with a person her whole life long, surely you realize that? Do you really wish to do this to your daughter?" He made no attempt to disguise his disapproval.

Wanda blinked.

She had never been so tired in all her life.

Her gaze fell on the little baby in her arms. She was sleeping peacefully now, but had cried all through the night. Just as she had every night since they had got back to Lauscha five days ago . . .

"Yes," she said, struggling to keep her voice firm.

The registrar sighed. "I have to say that your story is rather far-fetched. An American citizen is visiting her family in Lauscha, but happens to be in Italy just when her child is born . . ." He waited, almost expectantly, sharpening a pencil as he stared across his desk.

A tired smile flitted across Wanda's face.

Far-fetched? What on earth would the man say if he knew the truth? He would certainly drop that pencil that he was sharpening with such care and attention.

Because the truth was that the baby in her arms wasn't hers at all, but rather her Aunt Marie's.

Aunt Marie, whom she, Wanda, hadn't been able to save. Marie, who had died such a dreadful death.

Marie, who had followed her great love, Franco, to Genoa, only to discover when she got there that her husband was not just a liar but a murderer as well.

Marie, who had been locked away for what she knew. Franco's family had shut her up behind bars. Oh, it was a gilded cage, of course. But that didn't change the fact that she had spent the last few weeks of her pregnancy alone, her mind swirling with fear and worry, her heart burdened by the lies she had been told. Marie's sisters had known nothing about this terrible turn of events. Nor had Wanda—Marie had not been allowed any contact with the outside world. Franco had been arrested by the police in New York once it had come to light that the de Lucca family was heavily involved in smuggling human cargo from Italy to America and that men had died in the course of these operations. The knowledge that her husband was a murderer had been almost enough to kill Marie as well.

Wanda shuddered. *Pull yourself together, just make sure that you get that birth certificate,* said an urgent voice inside her, but the memory of those dreadful events in Genoa was stronger.

Wanda had simply wanted to visit her aunt—she hadn't been expecting bad news of any kind—and had walked into a hell such as she had never even imagined in her worst nightmares.

She looked up at the registrar, who was just beginning to sharpen another pencil.

Take a deep breath, fight off the exhaustion, fend off the memories— then she'd give the man all the answers he wanted. So that she could get what she so urgently needed—a legal birth certificate for Sylvie.

It was what Marie had wanted.

Marie . . .

If she wasn't careful she would burst into tears at the thought of her aunt, and if that happened she knew she wouldn't be able to stop crying.

Anything but that. Not here, in this stuffy registry office in the Sonneberg city hall, where dusty shelves and folders held the records of life and death.

When Marie came down with childbed fever after the birth, there had been nobody there to help her but the de Lucca family doctor, who spoke neither German nor English. Wanda hadn't been able to talk to him at all. She had pleaded over and over again with Franco's mother, the Countess Patrizia, that they had to get Marie to a hospital, that perhaps there would be better treatment available there, some way to fight the infection and the fever that had resulted. But the countess had vehemently refused, insisting that only the family doctor was allowed to see the patient.

Wanda swallowed. Should she have been more demanding? Shouldn't she have been able to free Marie from the palace single-handedly, and drag her off to a hospital? And if she had, would her aunt still be alive? But as it was, Wanda hadn't even dared leave the palace herself for fear that she wouldn't be allowed back in.

She hadn't trusted Franco's parents any more than she had trusted Franco himself.

Franco . . . the very thought of him made Wanda shudder.

Was he still in America? Or did the de Lucca family have enough influence to free their son from an American prison? Did Franco know by now that he had a daughter, and that Wanda had rescued the child from the clutches of his terrible parents?

Marie had kept a diary, and the de Luccas had insisted that the book was not to leave their palace at any price. They had offered to give Sylvie over to Wanda in exchange for what Marie knew about their shameful family secrets, and Wanda had agreed to the deal. She could never have left Marie's daughter behind in Italy.

"You must take Sylvie back to Lauscha!" Marie had implored her. "My daughter must grow up among glassblowers, not among murderers." Her eyes already had that strange gleam that frightened Wanda so. As though Marie were burning up from inside. A short while later, she had closed her eyes for the last time.

And so Wanda had carried out Marie's dying wish. But what about the baby's father? Once Franco found out what had happened, he would surely not let his child grow up anywhere but in his family's ancestral palace.

Wanda sat up with a start. She nestled Sylvie in the crook of her left arm and fished out a crumpled sheet of paper from her bag with her other hand.

"This is my daughter's Italian birth certificate."

The registrar frowned as he took the document from her. "Why didn't you give me that straight away? Not that foreign papers are a great deal of help here . . . But if this document has been properly issued by the Italian authorities, then of course it makes my work a great deal easier. Let's see, what does it say?" He glanced at the child and then picked up Wanda's passport. He unfolded it and peered at the details. Johanna and Wanda could practically see the wheels turning in his mind.

Johanna cleared her throat. "You are quite right in your assumption," she said in a low voice. "My niece was already . . . expecting when she came to visit us in October. My sister Ruth thought that the best thing to do was to let us take care of her for a while. If she had stayed in New York, it would only have led to needless gossip. I'm sure you understand. I told her, 'Ruth, these things happen even in the best families, don't fret!'"

Johanna forced a smile.

Wanda glanced over at her aunt. Wasn't she laying it on a bit thick?

The man curled the corners of his mouth in disapproval.

"And you took care of her by allowing her, a pregnant girl—unmarried and still a minor—to travel to Italy all on her own? I've heard some stories in my time, but this . . ."

The registrar looked at Johanna in astonishment.

She feigned a furious expression.

Wanda smiled to herself. At least her reputation wasn't the only one being ruined here . . .

"America—well, that explains the matter of the child's father," the registrar muttered, and wrote something on the form in front of him.

Wanda sighed with relief. Soon they'd be done. Perhaps she could ask the man to open the window a little? Some fresh air would do her good, and—

"And your mother? Where is she?"

Johanna cleared her throat. "We are expecting Wanda's mother in the next few weeks. She can hardly wait to take her daughter in her arms again. She is also very much looking forward to seeing her granddaughter—so we may enjoy a reconciliation in our household. I'm sure you understand."

The man bent forward over the birth certificate once more and muttered something about "moral laxity." A moment later, he pushed the document across the desk to them.

"Sylvie Miles, mother Wanda Miles, father unknown—that will be three marks forty pennies, payable in the room next door, they'll give you a receipt."

CHAPTER TWO

They had spent so long in the Sonneberg city hall that they missed their train to Lauscha. Since the next one wasn't due for an hour, Johanna suggested that they go to a nearby café. Wanda would rather have waited on the platform, but in the end she agreed. Although it was a sunny day, there was an easterly wind blowing. It was too cold to stand around on the windy station platform with a newborn.

"Well, we did it!" Johanna said, gripping her coffee cup as though it held the elixir of life. "What a dreadful man! That sneering tone in his voice—I would have loved to give him a piece of my mind! Ah well, what can we do . . . ?" She waved a hand dismissively. "At least we got what we came for. You're officially a mother now, though I really don't know whether I should congratulate you! Dear Lord in Heaven, and you're still a minor . . ." She heaved a great sigh.

"I'll come of age next year!" Wanda said. After checking on Sylvie, who was sleeping peacefully in her carriage, she picked up her own coffee cup and took a sip. She had never been able to stand the stuff in America, but it had grown on her since she had come to live with Johanna and her family. Over the past few months coffee had become more than just a hot, black, rather bitter brew—it was a little bit of luxury in a house where luxuries were few and far between. Wanda shut her eyes for a moment. When she opened them again, she saw that Johanna was weeping quietly.

"If only Marie had never run off with that dreadful man!" she said suddenly. She pressed a hand to her lips and blinked rapidly.

"Oh, Auntie . . ." Wanda said helplessly. She missed Marie so much that it hurt, and sometimes she wanted to scream aloud at the injustice of fate. Why did she have to die like that?

Marie, the glassblower, whose face always sparkled with a hint of glitter. Marie, with her lust for life! Walled up in a stony niche in a cemetery in Genoa.

There had only been a handful of people at the burial. The whole thing had happened at breakneck speed. The countess had told Wanda that this was the law in Italy, but more likely Franco's family had just wanted to avoid any awkward questions that the local authorities might ask when they buried Marie.

"And then this business today! There's no turning back now, you realize that?" Johanna interrupted Wanda's thoughts as she wiped her eyes. "To be quite honest with you I would have preferred to wait for your mother to get here before going to the registry office. I mean, she's entitled to a word or two in the matter, isn't she?" She rolled her eyes. "Oh dear, Ruth is going to rake me over the coals for this, I can tell already."

"No she won't," Wanda replied, tired. She patted her handbag where it sat next to her on the padded bench. "This birth certificate will protect Sylvie from Franco and his family. Nobody can come and take the child away now. And that's exactly what Marie wanted. Mother will understand that I had no choice."

Johanna shook her head. "There's always a choice. Peter and I could have taken the girl. I am her aunt, after all!" Her lower lip trembled again as she said these last few words.

Wanda put her hand on her aunt's arm. "Little Sylvie needs all of us, and we'll all look after her! But the fact is that I have more time for her than you do. And once Richard and I are married, Sylvie will have her own family."

Johanna snorted. "Well that's another thing! You know that I think the world of Richard; he's an excellent glassblower. But will he be such an excellent husband? I don't know . . ." She fell quiet as the waitress set down two plates of apple cake. As soon as the woman left, Johanna spoke up before Wanda could get a word in edgewise. "Richard is so . . . single-minded! I mean, yes, we work with glass all day, every day as well, that's our life, and sometimes I feel that we need it to be able to breathe, the way other people need air." She shook her head. "But Richard . . . he really does love glass more than anything else. Does he have time for a wife? For a family? Can he give you the love you need?"

Wanda raised her eyebrows. "Of course! Richard is the most loving man I know! You should see how he fusses over Sylvie and me. And as for his work—would you rather I had fallen in love with an idle do-nothing? He's very focused, that's all. And ambitious. What's wrong with that?"

Johanna waved the question away. "There's nothing wrong with it. All the same—I don't think your mother will be pleased to hear that you want to get married this summer. You've hardly known each other six months! You know what they say, marry in haste, repent at leisure. Look what happened to Marie . . ."

"Really, there's no comparison!" Wanda replied hotly. "Richard is an honorable man and he'll always be there for Sylvie and for me. He wanted me to name him as the father—that shows he feels responsible for us. He was almost offended when I rejected the idea."

Johanna muttered something that might have been an apology and prodded at the apple cake with her fork.

Wanda took another sip of coffee. She felt exhausted all over again. Perhaps it was a good thing that she was so tired—otherwise she might have gotten into a full-blown argument with Johanna. Instead she ate her apple cake without really tasting it.

Johanna looked up from her plate. "And then there's the fact that you're living in your father's house, not with us. That will lead to trouble as well. How am I supposed to explain to your mother that you didn't bring Sylvie to live with us?"

Wanda felt a twinge of anger despite her exhaustion. Not this again . . . She hadn't known what to do—she had simply gone with her feelings, following her conscience as well as she could—was that a crime? It wasn't as though she had a handbook where she could look these things up! Nobody had doubted her decisions in Genoa, and when she had gotten out of there, they all said that she had done the right thing—Johanna, her father and mother on the telephone, Richard. They had all praised her bravery. But ever since she had returned to Lauscha, everybody had been telling her what to do. She wished she could tell Johanna to keep her ideas to herself.

"It's best for everybody that I live with my father," she said, fighting to keep her voice calm. "Eva likes looking after Sylvie and she's a great help to me. And there's plenty of room. Father wants to let me have the whole second floor of the house. He's even begun to stoke the stove again." She laughed.

Johanna smiled as well. Thomas Heimer had never been a man of many words, but the fact that he was willing to burn firewood in late May to warm the house for his daughter showed how much he loved Wanda.

"Still, we would have found somewhere for you to stay, perhaps in Marie's old room. I could have thrown Magnus out—I don't quite know why he's still living with us, actually. It was one thing when he and Marie were together, but he can't just stay in her room forever after!"

She was frowning now.

Wanda made a face too. She knew her aunt well enough to realize that Magnus's days were numbered in the Steinmann-Maienbaum household.

"Leave the poor fellow alone. He suffered enough when Marie left him for Franco. And now he's grieving . . . He's in no state to go looking for somewhere else to live just now," Wanda said.

Johanna snorted. "Well, perhaps you're right. Don't listen to your old aunt! Maybe I'm just finding fault today so that I don't burst into tears. In any case . . ." She sat up straight, as though to lend weight to her words. "You're a mother now, and I really do wish you the very best!" Then she sighed again. "If only . . ."

Wanda interrupted her, laughing. "Oh, Aunt . . ."

A little while later they set off back to the station. The chestnut trees on either side of the street were shedding their petals, which drifted down through the air. As Wanda tried to pick some petals out of her aunt's hair, Johanna stopped abruptly and took Wanda's hand.

"It's almost exactly seven months since I came to meet you at the train." She laughed. "I can still remember it like it was yesterday. It was ice-cold and your train was late, so I went and waited in a café. I was so impatient to see you again! To take you in my arms after all those years . . ."

Wanda smiled. "Seven months . . . It seems more like seven years since then!"

Had that really been her? The naive child who had arrived in Germany from America in October last year with a mountain of luggage, a head full of dreams, and a heart full of longing, waiting for the moment when she would meet her biological father? She had desperately wanted to be taken seriously, wanted to belong. She wanted to be important, and more than just the pretty, useless daughter of Ruth and Steven Miles.

Shortly before that, her Aunt Marie had decided not to go back to Lauscha after visiting her sister and niece in New York, but instead to move to Italy with Franco. When Wanda's cousin Anna, Johanna's daughter, sprained her ankle around that time, Wanda had seen her chance: if she went to Lauscha, she told her mother, then she could help Aunt Johanna. Ruth had been against the voyage from the start and would far rather have kept her daughter in New York. But Wanda was adamant that she wanted to cheer her aunt up and that she was keen to be of help.

Wanda to the rescue—ha!

Instead, she had fallen horribly ill upon arrival and been nothing but a burden for Johanna's family . . .

Wanda shook herself, upset. What was wrong with her today? She had spent the whole day looking back . . . as though there would be no tomorrow.

Her real reason for coming to Lauscha had been to meet her father. She wanted to find her place in the world, a place that she had never been able to find in New York.

"Everybody has a mission in life . . ." All of a sudden she remembered Marie's words. It had been during their last conversation, just before her aunt had set out for Europe with Franco. As they had so many times before, they had been sitting on the roof of the skyscraper that housed the Miles family's apartment. How earnestly Marie had spoken then!

She glanced at the baby carriage. Sylvie had opened her eyes wide and was making little mewling noises.

And now she, Wanda, really did have a purpose in life—thanks to Marie. Wasn't that a dreadful, ironic twist of fate?

The truth was that she was terrified of motherhood, but she would never have admitted such a thing to Johanna.

She had Richard by her side, though. He would always be there for her, and his love made her strong, invulnerable.

Wanda took another deep breath. Then it was time to board the train that would take them home.

To Lauscha.

CHAPTER THREE

When Wanda opened the front door to her father's house later that afternoon, she could hear voices from the kitchen; Richard, her father, and her uncle Michel all seemed to be there. Had the men already finished work for the day? That would be good news, Wanda thought.

With the last of her strength she maneuvered the bulky carriage into the front hall. Her back was slick with sweat, her dress was plastered to her armpits, and strands of hair clung to her forehead. Wanda groaned softly as she lifted Sylvie up.

Once upon a time Wanda herself had lain in this carriage, her father had explained after he had fetched it from the lumber room and dusted it off. He had also mentioned that back then—twenty years ago now—it had been most unusual to see a woman taking her baby out for a walk in a carriage. But Ruth had always insisted on keeping up with the very latest fashions, and she had had her way in the end.

Oh, Mother, did you have just as much trouble coming up the hill from the station?

Wanda changed Sylvie's diaper, then she went to freshen up. She looked longingly at her bed. How good it would be to lie down and rest for an hour, to shut her eyes and think of nothing at all, to not have to answer anybody's questions . . .

But Richard was sitting down there in the kitchen and he would certainly want to know how things had gone at the registry office. Richard . . . Wanda felt her fatigue vanish at the thought of him, and she hurried downstairs with a light heart.

"Wanda! We were just talking about you!" Thomas Heimer said when she appeared in the doorway with Sylvie in her arms.

Michel, Richard, and her father were all seated at the table, which was covered with drawings. Yellow bars of sunlight from the window fell across the papers.

"We need your advice," Richard said, beckoning Wanda to come closer.

Whenever Wanda went into the Heimer family kitchen these days, she was always quietly surprised by how much it had changed. It was no longer the cold, unwelcoming room it had been the first time she had visited last winter. Back then the light had struggled to penetrate the dirty panes, and it was only after Wanda had persuaded her father to chop down the two huge fir trees in front of the window that the room had any light. And with light came life: the kitchen was now the center of the house. Before, Eva had been the only one to spend any time in the kitchen, clattering and banging about with a grim look on her face, but now the family gathered here to drink a glass of beer or talk about business. The table was clean and so were the dishes drying by the sink. Eva and Wanda had found an old rocking chair and set it by the table, so that Wilhelm Heimer could sit in comfort when he felt strong enough to get out of bed. Her father had more orders coming in these days, and the pantry was always full—the days when Eva had to boil up squirrels instead of chicken to make the soup were over.

Wanda made a face at the thought. She could still remember the fusty smell of those days—dreadful!

"What are you plotting now? And where's Eva?" she said, as she sat down on the bench next to Richard. She kissed him quickly, just once, since Richard didn't like it when she was too affectionate while her father was around.

"Here I am!" Eva called a moment later. "And there's my little angel . . ." Before Wanda could say anything, Eva had taken the baby and put her over her shoulder. "Now we'll have a nice bit of warm milk, and then your Auntie Eva is going to take you to Steinach!" She grumbled at Wanda, "You're very late! What kept you so long? The poor child is half starved!"

"The whole business with the birth certificate was much more complicated than I expected," Wanda said. She had already silently prepared a dramatic speech to tell them all about what had happened at the registry office, but nobody asked. The men had bent their heads together over their papers and carried on talking to one another.

Wanda frowned. Did nobody care what had happened to her?

"Do you still want to go to Steinach?" she asked Eva instead. "Sylvie must be tired; she might need a little peace and quiet—"

"Nonsense!" Eva cut in. "Fresh air never did a child any harm. Anyway, I told my sisters that I would come by to have a look at some old baby things—I'm sure there's something there for our little darling!" She looked at Sylvie, her eyes shining.

"But I—" *I don't want Sylvie wearing scratchy and moth-eaten old clothes,* Wanda wanted to say. *I'd rather buy her some nice new clothes!* But she held her tongue.

"If you're hungry there's still some potatoes left, and cottage cheese!" Eva called. A moment later, she was gone, taking the baby and the bottle with her.

Richard looked up from the papers. "What's got into her? Is she really the same woman who used to be such a dreadful nag?"

"Richard," Thomas Heimer said in a tone of gentle reproach.

Wanda smiled. She leaned back for a moment and relaxed, shutting her eyes.

It wasn't just the kitchen that was different. Eva, who lived with Wanda's grandfather as his wife, also had changed almost beyond recognition. In the old days she had walked around with a sour look on her face all the time, but now she was more relaxed, almost cheerful. She had wanted to have a child when she was younger, but she had had to forget that dream, along with so many others. It meant a great deal to Eva that fate had brought a baby into the house, even if wasn't her own.

Wanda wasn't entirely happy with the way Eva treated Sylvie. Was it really good for a child to be wrapped up so tightly swaddled that it could barely move? And wouldn't it be better to warm the water before giving the baby a bath? But since Wanda didn't know any better herself, she mostly kept quiet. Besides, having Eva to help meant that she could relax a bit from time to time. Like now . . .

"I just don't want her getting too used to Sylvie," Richard grumbled. "Otherwise she'll be all the more upset once we get married and the house is quiet again."

Wanda sat up. Since she'd only been following the conversation with half an ear, she felt she owed him an answer.

"Well then, Eva will come to see us often enough, won't she? You only live a few houses down, after all."

Wanda tried to ignore the queasy feeling that suddenly gripped her stomach. Of course she was looking forward to the day when she and Richard would stand at the altar and say "I do." She couldn't wait be with the man she loved day and night, to spend all her time with him—no more hasty kisses and whispered endearments.

But she was also scared of having to take responsibility for her own household. What if it turned out that she was utterly unsuited to being a housewife? If she had any talent at all in that realm, she certainly hadn't noticed it so far . . .

She shook herself involuntarily, like a cat caught out in the rain. She picked up one of the sheets of paper to give herself something else to think about.

"Another bird figurine?" She had trouble keeping the disappointment from her voice. Why couldn't she persuade her father that there was simply no demand for his glass animals these days?

"That's supposed to be a cuckoo—don't you recognize it?" Thomas Heimer said.

"We've had an order from Karl-Heinz Brauninger." That was Michel, who hadn't said a word until now. That wasn't unusual in itself. What was unusual was that he had come out of his room. Yes, quite a few things had changed in the last few months . . .

"A hotel in the Black Forest wants us to send them some designs for wine glasses, water glasses, fruit bowls, and large serving dishes. And apparently every piece has to have a cuckoo on it."

Richard held a sketch out to Wanda. "I think that we should engrave the images into the glass, or possibly even use chemical etching, but your father wants to paint them on the old-fashioned way. What do you say?"

Wanda looked at the fine detail of the sketch and thought hard. She could see now that Richard had drawn it. A cuckoo? An order from the Black Forest? Didn't they have enough glassblowers of their own down there? Before she could say anything, Richard took the sketch back from her.

"Perhaps we should begin by making a few sample pieces in each style . . ."

"Yes, then we could see for ourselves . . ." Thomas Heimer said.

Disappointed, Wanda looked from face to face.

Of course, she was pleased about the new order, and pleased that her father and Michel were so enthusiastic about it. It wasn't so long ago that the flame had almost gone out here in the Heimer workshop. The fact that Karl-Heinz Brauninger kept coming back with new orders showed how good Thomas Heimer really was.

But . . . was nobody interested in how she felt? In what had happened at the registry office? Why were they sitting here debating a cuckoo? Marie was dead and had left Sylvie in her care! How could the men simply ignore such a thing?

"You're all so heartless!" Wanda burst into tears. She sobbed as she hurled accusations at them.

Her father and Michel looked at one another.

Michel cleared his throat. "Don't we have urgent business elsewhere, brother of mine?"

Thomas nodded quickly.

A moment later, Richard and Wanda found themselves alone. He took her in his arms and rocked her back and forth as though she were a child having a nightmare. Slowly she calmed down.

"You're quite right," he murmured in her ear. "We really are a bunch of heartless fools. But . . . you see . . ." He sighed.

She looked at him, her eyes blurry with tears. "Yes?"

"Here in Lauscha we've learned that bad news doesn't ever go away if you spend all your time talking about it. Quite the opposite, the pain only fades once you begin looking to the future! You must try to forget your sorrows as quickly as you can."

"What if I can't?" Wanda asked in a low voice. How could she ever forget Marie? She didn't *want* to forget Marie!

She was tired from crying and felt like she couldn't breathe. She struggled for air but could do no more than yawn.

"You still have all your wonderful memories of the times you spent with Marie! Remember New York, all those adventures I've heard so much about! Your eyes shone like stars when you told me those stories. Nobody can take those times away from you, can they?"

"Of course not." It was a comforting thought, but she was nonetheless still disappointed by Richard's and her father's lack of interest.

Richard lifted her chin and looked into her eyes. "Once we're married you won't have time to sit around feeling weepy." He smiled at her. "Then you'll have your own little family, you'll have a house to look after, and Sylvie. As for this man, Franco . . . don't you worry. Nobody will ever take Sylvie away from us, I can promise you that!"

Wanda chewed on her thumbnail, lost in thought. Richard meant well, she knew that, but his words did nothing to ease her pain. In fact, instead of reassuring her, they scared her a bit.

"And what if I can't manage?"

"What's not to manage? My house is small enough; it's easy to keep clean. And as for food, well, I'm not fussy there. My goodness," he laughed, "I'll be happy enough just to have something warm to eat! Anyway, it's not as though you have anything else to do. Your father and Michel can manage well enough on their own. And you won't need to help me with my work. When I visited the art fair in Venice with Gotthilf Täuber, we made some useful contacts. I have no doubt the orders will start coming in soon. As long as I can work in peace without interruption, everything will be fine. So you can concentrate on Sylvie and taking care of the house. And who knows? She may even have a little brother or sister soon enough."

Wanda nodded, embarrassed. The way Richard described it, it all sounded so simple, but . . . Something he said disturbed her, like a splinter wedged under her skin. She couldn't say quite what. Perhaps if she weren't so tired . . .

"Tell me, when is your mother arriving, exactly?" Richard asked after a minute's silence—but by then Wanda had fallen asleep.

CHAPTER FOUR

Sylvie woke up many times over the next few nights and screamed relentlessly until Wanda fed her, changed her diaper, and whispered to her. At some point, the little one would fall asleep again as suddenly as she had woken up, but Wanda would lie awake for hours, her head swirling with thoughts of Genoa and Marie, of her mother's visit and the preparations for the wedding. The next day, she always felt utterly worn out and was only too happy to let Eva take the baby for a few hours. Another baby after Sylvie? She would have to talk to Richard about that.

The days began getting longer and brighter. The sun was high in the sky above the steep mountainsides, and its beams reached into every corner of Lauscha. There had been plenty of rain that spring, and the weather had been so warm the past few weeks that the trees had grown full. The pale-green treetops sprinkled among the darker growth gave the forests a cheerful look. People opened their windows wide and hung their laundry up to dry on long clotheslines, and they put furniture out in front of their houses to air.

Thomas and Michel Heimer had put a wooden bench outside their front door, so that Wanda could enjoy the fine weather with the carriage next to her. She spent many hours sitting on the bench with her grandfather while he named the birds they could hear sing-ing in the woods and the flowers the bees were visiting in their search for nectar. He explained that the shrieking, chattering sound she heard at dawn in the bushes behind the house was the call of the pine marten. Wanda breathed in the astringent scent of the elder flowers and marveled at how much Wilhelm Heimer knew, how close he was to nature. He told her that everybody who lived here in the forest knew these things, that there was nothing special about it. Anybody who spent their every working hour blowing glass at the flame and the lamp felt the urge to get out in the open air when-ever they had any free time to enjoy God's creation. Many of the villagers in Lauscha spoke of the woods as "Doctor Forest" because so many of the plants that grew there could be turned into useful salves and tinctures. But her grandfather said that even a walk in the woods had healing powers, that a man could find himself again in the peace and quiet. They had even founded the Thuringian Forest Club more than twenty-five years ago, which was still going strong.

Wanda wished that she could find the same peace. But despite her best soul-searching efforts, she couldn't locate that feeling inside her. For her one bird was just like any other—she couldn't even hear the difference between their songs. And the one time she had tried to set out with Sylvie for a longer walk in the woods, the carriage's wheels had promptly gotten bogged down in the damp earth, mak-ing it almost impossible to go on. After that Wanda had sworn that she would only ever stroll around in the village.

I never learned any of this in New York, she thought.

People were constantly coming by to visit and admire Sylvie and to hear Wanda tell the tale of how Marie had died. She and Johanna invented a different version of events for the villagers, telling them that the baby's father had died while on a trip and then that Marie had died of childbed fever. They said that it had been Marie's dying wish that Wanda should take the child to Lauscha. Only the closest family members knew anything about Franco's crimes and the way Marie had suffered at the hands of his dreadful family. Not even Magnus, Marie's partner for many years, knew that part of the story.

Wanda was touched by how fondly people remembered Marie. Every visitor tried to come up with an anecdote or a little recollection about her. She knew it wasn't easy for them—her Aunt Marie had been a loner who didn't often take part in village life.

When Joost Steinmann was still alive he had kept a close eye on his three daughters. Marie, Ruth, and Johanna had never been allowed to go to the village dances or other celebrations. Later Marie had dared to break the centuries-old restriction that dictated that only men were allowed to blow glass, while the women painted and decorated the finished baubles and dipped them into the silver bath. She had worked alone, learning the craft in her own house. Of course people were proud of Marie, whose Christmas ornaments were now sold all over the world! Wanda could hear the pride in their voices. But she could also hear the suspicion that some of them had felt all the same. Marie's tireless creativity and stubborn determination to go her own way had left their mark.

Wanda resolved to play a more active part in Lauscha village life than her aunt had, though she had the troubling feeling that she wouldn't succeed in doing so. Back in March, Eva and many of the other women had thrown a charity bazaar for the new church, but Wanda had been thinking only of Richard at the time and had excused herself from getting involved, claiming that she was no good at handicrafts. By the time the church was half-built and the new bells arrived in mid-May, she and Richard were in Italy, in a warm haze of wine and lovemaking.

Of course, the visitors asked about Ruth as well. The older villagers still remembered how the middle Steinmann sister had left Lauscha eighteen years ago with Wanda to begin a new life in America with her lover, who was assistant to the great Mr.

Woolworth. They also remembered how her husband, Thomas, had drowned his rage and despair in beer and schnapps. What a scandal it had been!

And now they had heard that Ruth was coming back. Their eyes gleamed as they asked exactly when she would arrive, and Wanda knew that many of them were hoping for another scandal.

Their excitement shook Wanda out of her lethargy. She had to do everything she could to ensure that Ruth's visit to Lauscha was a success. So that her mother would understand why it was that Wanda had lost her heart to the paradise of glass. And to Richard, of course.

Over the next few days Wanda hurried down the steep street from her father's house to Johanna's countless times. Her mother was to sleep in Cousin Anna's room—was everything ready there? Couldn't they find a new embroidered bedspread to liven up the room instead of the faded old thing they had now? And would that little wardrobe be enough for all of Ruth's luggage? If Wanda knew her mother, she'd be bringing a mountain of clothes along with her—perhaps Magnus could fit another rail in between the window and the wardrobe to hang things on?

Wanda flurried around the room, wrinkling her nose. Was she mistaken or was there a whiff of mothballs in the air? Perhaps they should put out some bowls of dried rose petals . . . She got on her knees and peered under the bed—had all the dust balls really been swept away?

Finally Johanna had had enough. She declared that Ruth had spent her childhood and youth in this house and that if it was good enough for her then, it was good enough for her now. Her sister knew perfectly well that she wouldn't be staying in a palace. And no, they wouldn't eat in the front parlor; they would eat in the kitchen just like they did every day. Nobody in the Steinmann-Maienbaum household had time for fine table linens and other such frivolities. Johanna finished up by saying that Wanda was flapping about like a startled hen and that if she didn't calm down, her aunt would happily wring her neck just like a chicken's . . .

Half-laughing, half-offended, Wanda had to concede that Johanna was right.

Well then, she would go and take care of Richard's house. Wasn't that far more important, after all? She wanted her mother to have a good impression of her future home!

On her way through town, Wanda tried to see everything through Ruth's eyes.

Thank goodness it was spring! The houses' dark shingles didn't seem so gloomy in the sunshine; in fact, the play of light and shadow, bright and dark, looked rather cheerful. Tender shoots of kohlrabi and carrot tops were peeping out of the soil in the little front gardens, and the flowerbeds were neatly weeded and raked. The cherry tree in Karl Flein's garden was covered with tiny cherries—yellow at the moment, but perhaps they would ripen by the time Ruth arrived. Karl would be delighted to give her a bowl full—Mother loved cherries. In New York she had to go to one of the city's specialty shops to find them. Wanda wanted her mother to understand why she preferred this simple country life to life in the big city.

Wanda sighed happily. Yes, that's what she would tell her mother.

But what was this? She stopped abruptly and frowned.

Did old Widow Grün have to put her trash out in front of the house? And did the neighbor's skinny goats really have to graze the dandelions like that? The yellow flowers would give a lovely splash of color to the street scene . . .

A few houses down she stopped again and lifted her nose into the air like a dog catching a scent. Was she mistaken, or could she really smell somebody's outhouse all the way out here on the street?

Wanda itched to go into every house and tell people, *Put flowers in your window! Repair those dilapidated garden fences! Tidy the place up a bit so that Mother will like it!* Instead she hurried on to the top of the village. Perhaps—if she just made sure to keep her mother distracted as they walked through town—she might not notice all its little faults . . .

Richard looked on as Wanda put a vase of meadow flowers onto the table. She hadn't been able to find a tablecloth anywhere in the house. She warmed some water and washed every single piece of glass that Richard had gathered like trophies on long shelves around the room, while he watched her like a hawk. Once every piece was free of dust and grime, Wanda looked around and spotted a plain old metal tin hanging over the stove. That was . . . it was a baking pan, which must have belonged to Richard's mother! Wanda took it down from the hook and polished it until the copper gleamed red-gold. Satisfied, she hung it back up over the stove. She took up all the rugs from the floor and put them over the frame behind the house, then whacked them with the carpet-beater until she was drenched in sweat. At least the carpets were clean now, though the colors were still faded and the edges still frayed.

Ruth wouldn't be bothered by a few old carpets, though, would she? Richard put every penny that he earned right back into his business—and besides he had more important things to do than to prettify his house. Surely Mother would realize that a woman's touch would work wonders in this little cottage—wouldn't she?

CHAPTER FIVE

"How big it's all become—I hardly recognize our old workshop!" Ruth swept her hand around in an all-encompassing gesture. The elaborate pleats and ruffles of her sleeve came perilously close to a gas flame as she did so, and she hastily drew her arm back.

Wanda sighed quietly to herself. Wasn't it typical of Mother that she should wear such fancy clothing on her first day here? The dress, with its lace and ruffles, would have been perfect for a theater premiere in New York, but it was completely out of place in a workshop where there was an open flame and where people hurried about with arms full of glassware, cardboard boxes, and wrapping paper. The room smelled strongly of chemicals and unwashed bodies.

Ruth clapped her hands, and the gold bangles on her wrist chimed together. "You can't imagine how happy I am to be back after all this time! The atmosphere . . . I'm home again . . . In New York I only ever get to see the end result of all your hard work. And now here I am, among all the glass rods and the colors and the silver bath. It's just like old times—it's like a dream!"

Wanda was sitting by the window with Sylvie in her arms. She was amused to see Cousin Anna peer sullenly over at her aunt from

America—unlike her twin brother, Johannes, who was staring at their visitor in awe.

Johanna smiled. "The first thing that Peter and I did when we joined forces was to knock down the wall to Peter's house. That made this big room here. But we still don't have enough space; we've thought about moving production out of the house for years. But as it is . . ." She rolled her eyes. "There's so much work coming in that I haven't even had time to look for a suitable building."

"You can't seriously be thinking about leaving our parents' home?" There was an edge to Ruth's voice as she asked the question.

Well, look who's talking! Wanda looked over at Johanna, curious how she would respond, but her aunt simply shrugged. That could mean anything or nothing at all.

"Five lamps, five benches, and a separate storeroom for the raw glass and finished products . . . Really, it's quite different from Father's old workshop." Ruth looked from her sister to her brother-in-law, Peter. "I know that the way you make Christmas baubles now is quite different from the old days—I mean, of course you can't blow all those with just one lamp. But I had no idea you'd gone about it so professionally."

"Believe it or not, time hasn't stood still here," Peter said with a hint of irony. "But just to put your mind at rest—there are plenty of things that are just like the old days. Come along!" He pointed toward his own workbench where he made glass eyes for clients who had lost an eye in an accident or to some other misfortune. But Ruth hurried off in the other direction.

"Father's bench . . ." Carefully, almost reverently, she passed her hand over the black wooden surface. "You kept it! This brings back so many memories . . ." She smiled sadly at Johanna. "This is where our little Marie sat and blew her first baubles. In secret, so that nobody had any idea what she was doing, not even us! Do you remember that first Christmas when she surprised us with the ornaments on the tree? They were like nothing we'd ever seen! Silver and . . ." She stopped and frowned.

"Aunt Marie decorated her first globes with ice crystals," Wanda said. "And Aunt Johanna put them on the tree this past Christmas. They really are lovely."

"We hang those globes on our tree every year. It wouldn't be Christmas without them," Johanna added.

"How romantic," Ruth said. Then she hugged Johanna. "How lovely that you keep up with all the old traditions! Oh, it does me good to be back home! Even if it took a tragedy to bring me back here . . ." Her gaze drifted over to Wanda and Sylvie. She sighed deeply, then straightened up and smiled almost mischievously.

"Do you remember, Johanna, how I went into Sonneberg with Marie's baubles to show them to Mr. Woolworth?" She shook her head. "The great American businessman—everybody wanted to sign a contract with him. And then I came along with Christmas ornaments blown by a woman. My goodness, I was in such a state! It proved to be quite a challenge even to see the man. But I managed in the end." She looked from Johanna to Peter, triumphantly. "You never thought I could do it, did you? You never expected me to be the one who got us out of our fix."

Peter shrugged. "Johanna was still very distraught at the time; otherwise, I'm sure she would have found the courage to do what you did. Don't you remember what that terrible man did to her—?"

"Peter!" Johanna said. Her eyes were sparkling with fury. "You're quite right, Ruth," she said. "What you did was very brave. And it saved us! But I did pick up the reins soon enough after that, you'll have to admit."

Wanda looked from one to the other with concern. Did the two of them really have to go over old quarrels right away? Mother had only been here a few hours! It hardly mattered now who had done what all those years ago.

By now Ruth had moved on to the next workbench, where Johannes was blowing globes at a steady pace. Her fingers glided over the round shapes set out to cool on the rack.

"It's just like Marie always said. Every globe is a little world of its own. There's no up or down, no beginning and no end . . ." She fell quiet. Then she spoke again, hesitantly. "And now . . . Marie's life . . . is over, ended, so suddenly!" All of a sudden there were tears running down Ruth's face. She fumbled for Johanna's hand and looked intently at her sister.

"What a team we were back then! The whole village talked about the Steinmann sisters. Nothing and nobody could come between us, isn't that right?"

Johanna nodded silently.

"And then . . . at the end . . . there wasn't a thing we could do for Marie. She was all on her own!"

Wanda rocked Sylvie back and forth in her arms. She hoped the little one wouldn't start to cry just then.

"Oh, Ruth, Marie wasn't alone. Wanda was with her—thank God. If anything comforts me at all, it's that!" Johanna said in a choked voice, and took Ruth in her arms.

Wanda looked at the two women in the middle of the room and felt very alone.

Ever since her mother had arrived she had felt as though she were simply the spectator at a play in which Ruth was playing the lead role. She had been pushed aside, with nothing to do and nobody to take her seriously. So it was good to hear Johanna's words now.

The other roles seemed well cast too: There was Johanna, doing her best to conceal her own grief and be strong for Ruth. There was Cousin Anna, who had reacted ungraciously when Ruth praised her new designs for Christmas baubles and muttered, "We've had to get used to some changes around here . . ." while she threw venomous glances at Wanda. Then there was Johannes, who sat there wide-eyed and silent and later told all his friends that the "American girl"—which is what everybody in the village called Wanda—was nothing compared to her mother.

Peter was the only one who was behaving normally. He had greeted Ruth like a childhood friend, which was, after all, what she was, and he was quite sincere and straightforward about it.

As for Wanda . . . Of course her mother had hugged her and held her tight, as if she never meant to let her go. And she had admired little Sylvie—though she had also raised her carefully plucked eyebrows in dismay when she felt the coarse material of the baby's smock. "You're here at last, Mother!" Wanda had whispered in her ear. When they walked into the house arm in arm, Wanda was already looking around for a quiet corner where the two of them could sit. She had so much to tell her mother! About Marie, about Richard, about their plans to get married—and that she was living up at the top of the village now with her father . . . She wanted to tell her mother everything. That was why she had come, wasn't it?

But Ruth had surprised everybody by declaring that the first thing she wanted to do was visit the old workshop. So now here they were, while next door in the kitchen the cake that Johanna had baked waited to be eaten, and the coffee got cold.

Ruth and Johanna were still locked in each other's arms, sobbing. Peter looked over at the two of them helplessly. "If only your father, um, that's to say Steven, could have come," he whispered to Wanda. Then in a louder voice he said, "Perhaps a cup of coffee might do us all some good . . ." Sylvie began to wail.

Ruth abruptly tore herself free from Johanna's embrace. "The poor little scrap! Is the workshop any place for a baby?" The tone of reproach in her voice was unmistakable.

"Sylvie is a glassblower's daughter; of course this is the right place for her! You got her started with your crying. She's quite well

31

otherwise. Besides—didn't you tell me that I was in the workshop when I was a baby?"

"Times were different back then." Ruth waved away the objection.

"But since you mention it . . ." Wanda cleared her throat. "Have you thought about when you want to go and see the Heimer workshop? Things have changed up there as well." She found that she was holding her breath.

"The . . . Heimer workshop?" The corners of Ruth's mouth turned down. "What for? If I happen to run into Thomas on the street, well, there's nothing I can do about that. But I see no reason to actually go looking for him."

"But . . . Father works a great deal with Richard, so you would most likely find them both there. That way you could kill two birds with one stone," Wanda said, feeling Anna's eyes boring into her as she spoke. "Don't you want to see what a fine job Father did setting up a room for me and Sylvie? And then there's the wedding, the baby . . . There's a lot to talk about!"

"But not with Thomas Heimer," Ruth said decisively. "And as for this . . . Richard, I'm sure I'll meet him soon enough." She glared at Wanda and then turned to Peter, smiling girlishly. "Well then, whatever has become of the famous Lauscha hospitality? I'm half starved! But maybe I should have a relaxing bath first—my poor old bones ache from all the traveling. Anna, Wanda, could you be dear girls and put some water on to heat for me?" Ruth fixed her niece with a meaningful gaze, turned the same gaze on Wanda, and then hurried out the door.

CHAPTER SIX

Ruth's legs were trembling, which had nothing to do with the steep climb from Johanna's house to the top of the village, where Richard lived, and everything to do with the fact that she would shortly be meeting her daughter's fiancé for the first time. Fiancé! The very word made Ruth's knees tremble even more. And that infuriated her.

If only she had had more time to get used to all the changes in Wanda's life! But it had only been three weeks since that fateful telephone call from Munich. The connection was bad and there had been a dreadful whistle on the line, but she had heard enough to understand that her youngest sister had died in Genoa and that she had left a baby, and that Wanda was on her way back to Lauscha with the child. "Back home," Wanda had said. It seemed that she was seriously considering staying in this small town. As a glassblower's wife. Exactly the situation that Ruth had escaped once upon a time. What an irony!

Ruth snorted, which made Wanda glance over at her. Wanda was chattering away, without drawing any more response from Ruth than the occasional "Ah" and "Oh." Ruth decided her daughter was just as nervous as she was.

Ruth had begun to plan her trip to Thuringia the day Wanda called. She would be there to help her daughter—of course she would. But what exactly did that mean—to help her?

How should she react? Could she give Wanda her blessings for all those plans she had? Should she? Wouldn't it be better to persuade her daughter to come back to New York? Or simply to drag her back, if need be? It was just too soon for Wanda to even consider marrying Richard. And a glassblower? What was becoming of her daughter? She couldn't allow it. Even if Wanda couldn't yet see the match would never work, Ruth certainly did.

She had talked the matter over with Steven a thousand times. Although she trusted his judgment in almost all things, he had been of little help with this.

"You'll have to go and see for yourself—we can't make a decision like this from a distance," he had said. Ruth would have to meet Richard, he thought, and make up her mind only when she had seen what it would mean for Wanda to marry him.

Ruth snorted again just thinking of what he had said. She had a fairly clear idea of what a marriage like that would mean.

She wished that Steven were not so urgently needed at work just now. She would give anything to have him there by her side. And it would have done Steven good to see his daughter again.

His daughter . . . Ruth refused to think of Wanda any other way. Steven had raised Wanda. Had held her hand when she took her first steps. Had taught her to dance, long before she had first taken lessons.

When Marie had made an unguarded remark the previous summer and Wanda had found out that Steven was not her biological father, Wanda had turned away not just from Ruth but also from Steven. He had tried to hide his pain and disappointment, but Ruth had known her husband was suffering.

Wanda had asked over and over again why they had kept the truth from her for so long. Ruth had not been able to make her see that she and Steven had only ever wanted the best for their daughter. Thomas Heimer, her brief first marriage, her husband's brutality—for Ruth, these were all dark shadows from her past. And since you never see your shadow if you never look down, Ruth had simply never looked down. Of course she had missed her sisters! But that was the price she had paid. The price of freedom, of being with her great love, Steven, the price of life in New York with all its comforts and conveniences.

And now Wanda wanted to give all that up. And let history repeat itself. Her daughter, marrying a glassblower—Ruth could have wept!

"How are you feeling, Mother? Shall we stop somewhere to catch our breath?" Wanda asked.

"My shoes are killing me." Ruth held on to Wanda with one hand for balance as she massaged first her left ankle, then her right.

It had been eighteen years since she left Lauscha. Eighteen years! And the sidewalks were just as rough and pitted as they had ever been. She looked dubiously at Wanda, who was wearing sturdy, sensible shoes and seemed to take every obstacle in stride.

Her daughter . . .

Whatever had become of her elegant daughter who had left New York in the fall? Back then she had had fashionably short hair—scandalously short, Ruth had thought at the time—but now it had grown out to her shoulders and looked straggly and unkempt. Her clothes were just like Johanna's—practical, old-fashioned, and terribly dull. There was nothing left of the dazzling young lady who had drawn admiring glances at every fashionable society party in New York.

35

How can you be so fixated on superficial details at a time like this? she scolded herself. *God knows Wanda has had bigger problems in the last few weeks than finding a hairdresser.*

"Oh, my child," Ruth said sadly, as she put her feet back into her shoes, which were too narrow and too high in the ankle. "It'll take me a little while to get used to a few things back here . . ."

"No it won't!" Wanda said brightly, trying too hard. "Lauscha is your home!" She tugged Ruth's sleeve. "Look at the cherry tree in Karl Flein's garden with all its tiny fruit—isn't that a wonderful sight?"

Ruth made a face. *Wonderful?* When she thought of the hard work involved in harvesting the fruit, and then of the hours Karl's wife had to spend cooking it down for jams and jellies, she saw nothing wonderful about it.

She would have said as much, but she bit back her words. There was no need to bicker with Wanda right now. No, she would look at this Richard Stämme, his house, and his workshop. She would stay calm and ignore her prejudices. She would do just as Steven had suggested. And then she would decide about Wanda's future.

"Hallo? Hallo!" A loud voice interrupted Ruth's train of thought. A moment later, an old woman stood before her, holding a paintbrush in her left hand and a dishcloth in her right. Her cheeks sparkled with powdered glass—clearly she had just been painting glassware.

"I knew it! Ruth!"

Before Ruth could say a word, the woman wrapped her arms around her and she inhaled the musty smell of mothballs. She breathed a sigh of relief when the woman finally let go of her.

"How nice to see you," Ruth said, though she hadn't any idea who the woman was. She hastily declined her invitation to come inside and visit for a while.

"Ruth—well, whoever would have thought . . ."

Ruth smiled sourly. She knew that her visit to Lauscha was cause for local gossip. Ever since she had arrived, people had come knocking—neighbors, painters, and pieceworkers on the Steinmann-Maienbaum payroll. Nobody had breathed a word about the old scandal or her divorce. Instead they had wanted to know what Ruth's life in New York was like, why her husband wasn't with her, and so on. People had appeared genuinely interested rather than envious or disapproving. The general opinion had seemed to be that Ruth looked well after all those years abroad. The old woman in front of her said much the same thing now.

"Are you on your way to see Thomas? Or little Sylvie? Oh, what a dear child she is! And she looks just like her mother, the spitting image of Marie, didn't I say so, Wanda?"

Ruth snorted with impatience. Everybody in Lauscha knew everybody else's business. While Wanda was telling the woman that they were just on their way to see Richard, Ruth tried her best to put a name to the face. She still had no idea who this woman was or why she behaved as though they were old friends.

"We got married the same year, your mother and I," the woman said, turning to Wanda. "Though in my case I kept my husband . . . Nothing much has changed since then . . ."

Married the same year? Nothing much has changed? Ruth couldn't understand the look of satisfaction on the woman's face. Wouldn't it be rather dreadful for nothing to have changed since then?

The old chatterbox was already talking again.

"Wanda, did you know that your mother and I went to school together? We sat at the same desk, do you remember, Ruth?" The woman was looking at Ruth, her cheeks flushed and her eyes shining expectantly.

Karline Müller! Yes, they had shared a desk. And now Karline did painting piecework for Johanna.

She was called Karline Braun nowadays. Ruth was so relieved that her memory hadn't failed her that she even summoned up a smile. At the same moment she had an awful thought. Was she really the same age as this wrinkled old woman? Great Heavens above! Whatever had left such marks in Karline's face? She had been so pretty once upon a time.

"It was a long time ago . . ." she said in a small voice. And then she said good-bye hastily and dragged her daughter off up the hill before she was overcome by more depressing thoughts.

No, this was no longer Ruth's world, and she thanked God for it . . .

CHAPTER SEVEN

"So where's Richard?"

"I have no idea! Really . . . he knew that we would be coming today. I'm almost beginning to worry . . . Perhaps he thinks we're meeting at Father's house." Wanda ran her hands hurriedly through her hair and bit her lower lip.

Drat it all, why wasn't Richard there?

"Would you like to go out for another stroll?" Wanda asked hesitantly. "It's such nice weather, after all . . ."

"Anything but that! My poor feet . . ." Ruth waved the idea away. She folded her arms and paced through the room, making a great show of not bumping into the table, the sideboard, or the stove.

Wanda frowned. Yes, it was a small room, but—

"So this is where you'll live—you and Richard and the child." Ruth passed a hand over the various shelves and surfaces as if to test that everything was clean.

Wanda nodded eagerly. Thank Heavens she had polished everything to a high shine! She opened the back door that led into the little garden. The extra light that poured in made the room look a bit bigger.

Now Ruth was at Richard's workbench, which was cluttered with drawings, half-finished pieces, and rods of raw glass. There were all sorts of things stacked up on the floor around his bench as well.

Wanda cleared her throat. "I know that it all looks a little . . . plain at first glance, but . . . I don't demand much! Quite the opposite. I think this little room is quite cozy. And the fact that everything is old and used is rather idyllic, the way I see it." She made a gesture that took in the whole room. "Richard's furniture all came from his parents. Passing these things down from generation to generation—it makes me think of the English count who came to visit us last summer at Steven's, um, I mean my father's invitation. Do you remember? The man has three castles. Didn't he say that he would never give up his heirlooms for modern furniture?" Wanda was pleased to note that the smell of freshly mown grass was coming in from outside. Was there anyone who didn't like that smell?

Ruth rubbed her hands together and went to the doorway. She stood there in a wedge of sunlight as though to warm herself.

"Does this idyll of yours run to offering your mother a cup of coffee while we wait for your future husband?" she asked with more than a touch of irony.

Wanda hurried across to the stove. Why hadn't she thought to have coffee and cakes ready? Eva would certainly have baked a cake if she'd asked. She put her hand on the coffee tin and then stopped suddenly.

"Coffee—"

"Don't worry, I'll drink chicory coffee if I have to, I'm not that spoiled. As long as it's hot . . . It's cold in here, ten times as cold as out there!" Ruth was beginning to sound impatient.

Wanda looked at her mother piteously. "Coffee would be lovely . . . but to be quite honest . . . the stove's rather hard to get going. I . . . haven't quite got the hang of it yet . . ."

Ruth nodded as though she understood completely.

Wanda breathed out. But her relief didn't last long.

"And this baking tin—how charming!" Ruth pointed to the gleaming copper shape over the stove. "May I assume that you've learned how to bake by now?"

Wanda frowned.

"Well . . . no, actually. I haven't had much time for household tasks like that, not yet. But I'm sure Eva will be happy to show me—" She jumped, startled, as Ruth stamped her foot furiously.

"That's enough, Wanda!" Her mother spun round like a dervish. "You don't know how to heat the stove. You haven't even noticed that you'll never be able to bake here because you don't have an oven! As far as I can see, if you ever decide you do want to bake a cake, then you'll have to take your tin all the way through the village to the bakehouse!" As she spoke she counted off the various obstacles on the fingers of her right hand. She was at the middle finger now, and she went on: "It's cold in this house even in summer, cold as a cellar! I wouldn't like to think what it's like in winter—it must be freezing! And you really want to live here with Marie's daughter?" By now she was almost shouting. "This . . ." Ruth was so worked up that she had to stop just to catch her breath and swallow.

Wanda fumbled for words to soothe her fury. Ruth's visit was turning out nothing like how she had imagined it would be. It was . . . a catastrophe.

"Richard heats the stove every day in the winter. It gets very warm in here," she said quietly.

Ruth grabbed Wanda's hand and held it tight.

"Be quiet and just listen to me, my child!" Her face was only inches away from Wanda's, and the scent of her perfume—lilies and magnolias—hung in the air between them.

"You stand here and talk about an idyll—I almost want to laugh! Unlike you, I know how to fire up an old stove like this one.

And I know how much wood they use up. And what a mess they make with all the soot and ashes. There were times when I thought the cleaning rag had become part of my hand! And unlike you, I went to the village bakehouse almost every Saturday, but I wasn't taking cake to bake, oh no, I was taking four loaves of bread in a little handcart. Otherwise we would have had nothing to eat the next week! An idyll? Far from it! It was backbreaking labor." Ruth let go of Wanda's hand.

She gazed around the room as though looking for some means of escape, but then she sat down on one of the wooden chairs.

"A glassblower for a husband—right now it must seem a charming idea, but you have no idea how you'll come to hate this life one day! The way I hated it . . . Nothing else to talk about or think about but glass, day in and day out! Glass, glass, glass—I almost went mad!" Then her anger seemed to vanish suddenly like air from a bellows.

Wanda stared at her mother, feeling helpless and angry all at once. Nothing but recriminations—that was so typical of Ruth. Next she would burst into tears, just to make Wanda feel guilty! After that she'd get a migraine, or pretend to, so that she could hurry back to Johanna's house and lie down. Without even having seen Richard. Without even having talked about the wedding.

But Wanda wouldn't let it happen. Not this time!

Desperately she fumbled for the right words, but before she could think of anything to say, her mother had started up again.

"Have you even thought about what life would be like in this house, practically speaking? I mean, what you would do every day, from morning till night?"

To Wanda's surprise, Ruth's voice was quite level and there was no sign that she was going to feign a migraine. Wanda shrugged. *What's Mother getting at?* she wondered suspiciously.

"Well, basically I'd be a businesswoman, like Aunt Johanna is," she said cautiously. "Of course, I'll have to look after Sylvie and do the housework, but I would also help Richard with his work and—"

"Help Richard! How on earth do you imagine you could help? He'd set you to fetch and carry, nothing more. There's no comparison between what Richard makes at this little old bench and the mass production operation that Johanna manages. She's the head of a business. But you would be nothing but the cook and cleaning woman . . . You'd be a housewife, a mother, with a child clinging to your apron strings for the next few years." Ruth shook her head sadly. "Unless I'm much mistaken, haven't you always hated that idea? What happened to all your highfalutin plans about learning skills and having a career? Back in New York, you used to go to such lengths to find yourself a job! You always laughed at me and called me old-fashioned for wanting to see you married to Harold Stein. An ambitious young banker was too dull for you! What's become of all those plans?" Ruth heaved a deep sigh.

Wanda could hardly believe her ears. "You're not being fair, Mother. Nobody could have foreseen that I'd suddenly have a baby to take care of, from one day to the next! It was—fate! What wouldn't I give to have Marie alive and well—"

"Fate!" Ruth said. "Let me tell you: you make your own fate in this world, at least to some extent."

"I love Richard," Wanda answered softly. "And he loves me."

Ruth nodded. "Love—well, that's another matter entirely . . ."

Wanda swallowed and said nothing. She was tired. The conversation was so different from the one she had hoped for, and it had worn her out. If only Richard were here . . .

Richard's work! When Ruth saw what a talented glassblower he was, she would have to admit that not everything was as gloomy as it might have seemed at first glance.

"Let me show you some of Richard's glass!" she exclaimed, though her voice sounded forced. She fought against a queasy feeling in her belly. Richard didn't like it when anyone but him touched his work. But since he wasn't here . . .

Carefully Wanda reached for the most beautiful piece in the display cabinet, a goblet on a long stem that he had made using a complicated cameo glass technique.

At that very moment the front door opened.

Wanda was so startled that the glass promptly fell from her hand and shattered loudly on the ground.

CHAPTER EIGHT

Just like every evening, almost all the tables in the Black Eagle were full. The tavern buzzed with conversation and arguments, laughter and shouting, just as it always did. The air was full of tobacco smoke and other smells that Wanda knew well by now. The smell of potatoes fried in bacon—a dish that the landlord prepared every day for those of his customers who could afford to eat out. The smell of the beer that the glassblowers drank to wet their whistles after a long and thirsty day's work. The smell of sweat and tired bodies.

The Black Eagle was where all the glassblowers went to drink. Wanda had been there often enough with Richard before she set out for Genoa. Her father and her uncle Michel were frequent guests as well.

Wanda liked the atmosphere of the place, and she liked the fact that the glassblowers always seemed happy to see her. "It's the American girl!" they would call out, and they'd shake her hand. Lauscha was a little place and news traveled fast, so everybody knew that Thomas Heimer mostly had her to thank for all the new orders coming in. And many of them had heard how hard Wanda worked to persuade her father to make more modern pieces.

"So what plan is our American girl hatching now, eh?" they often asked her in jest. Some of them declared that she was welcome to drop in to their workshops any time and "modernize" them, if that meant they could turn the sort of profit Heimer was making. Wanda always laughed at the suggestion and enjoyed the way they made such a fuss about her.

This was her first visit to the tavern since Sylvie had come into her life, and she was only able to go because Eva had said she would be delighted to look after the baby.

"Go on, get out of the house! You young people need your fun!" she had said, practically shooing Wanda.

Fun! As if she could have any fun today!

How could her mother have been so mean?

Wanda took a swig of beer to get rid of the lump in her throat. It tasted bitter and the lump was still there, harder now.

She looked up from her tankard. Nobody else seemed to be having any trouble downing their beers tonight. Quite the opposite—weren't they emptying their glasses even faster than usual? The table where she and Richard had found seats was uncomfortably noisy too. She stared moodily into space, hearing only the occasional snatch of conversation.

"He always used to sit here just like he was one of us, Otto did! And now it turns out that he doesn't care a tinker's cuss for us. If he did, would he have had the nerve to sell the foundry to a Sonneberg wholesaler?"

A fist smashed down onto the table next to Wanda.

"He sold us out, the Judas!" the voice said loudly.

"Except that in Gründler's case he got more than just thirty pieces of silver," someone on the other side of the table said bitterly. "When I heard him talking earlier today, I thought he was joking . . ." The man looked around the table, a question in his eyes. "Says he wants to emigrate to America—well, when someone says that, you have to reckon he's joking, don't you?"

The others shrugged.

"I realized that Otto Gründler was dead serious when he told me that he's going to pay off his two brothers once the sale goes through," Martin Ehrenpreis grumbled, sitting next to Wanda. "America—he can go to the ends of the earth for all I care . . ."

"And he can take his brothers with him! They never cared about the rest of us, either! All they ever did was take their fee! One of them in that crate-maker's shop and the other one living over in Suhl, doing God knows what. Well, when the foundry's finally sold, that will be one last fat profit for all three of them!"

"Hasn't been sold yet, though. Weren't you saying earlier that all Otto Gründler told us was that he'd found a possible buyer?" another man asked. Wanda knew that he worked in another of the glass foundries.

She sighed. She should have guessed that the imminent sale of the Gründler foundry would be on everybody's lips in the Black Eagle.

At noon today it had only been a rumor—indeed, it had been the reason why Richard came home so late—but now it was an established fact: the Gründler foundry was up for sale.

Well, so what if it's sold? Wanda thought as the conversation rumbled on around her. Why were the men getting so upset? Surely it would be much worse if the foundry were closed and jobs were lost as a result.

Normally Wanda would have joined in the conversation, asking questions, trying to understand why it was so important to them. But this evening she just wasn't in the mood.

It had been Richard's idea to come to the Black Eagle. He had said that he wanted to hear the news about the foundry for himself.

Wanda didn't care what she did as long as she didn't have to spend the evening with her mother and the rest of the family, so in the end she had joined him.

But now she regretted her decision. She would much rather have gone out for a walk with Richard. What did the foundry have to do with her? Didn't she have enough worries of her own?

Richard's arm around her shoulders, his pace matching hers as they walked through the woods, only the chirruping of crickets and the slightly overcast summer sky above them—Wanda smiled sadly. Perhaps, surrounded by the healing power of nature, she would have been able to tell Richard that their marriage would have to wait for the time being. Her mother had flat out forbidden her to marry Richard, at least until they had been together for a year, which would be just around the new year. And even so, Steven wouldn't be able to come for a wedding until early spring. She couldn't imagine a wedding without Steven. But next spring? That was nine months from now!

Wanda bit her lip. No, she couldn't wait that long. They had to find some way to win Ruth over and get Steven here sooner! Perhaps Richard . . .

Wanda cast a longing glance at him. She felt a shiver, just as she did every time she looked at him.

He was so handsome! The way his eyes flashed under the dark locks of hair that hung down his forehead as he listened to the other men talk! As though nothing in the world could interest him more. No wonder he was so popular in the village.

Wanda sighed. They had not had any time to themselves since that night in Bozen, just before Richard set off for the art fair in Venice and she had gone on to see Marie. There was always someone in the way, and when they were finally alone and had time for sweet nothings, Sylvie inevitably began to whimper. But Wanda wanted him so much! Her man, her husband . . .

She felt a nudge in her side and sat up with a start.

"Would you like something to eat?" Richard nodded toward the blackboard on the wall, where Benno the tavern owner had chalked up in thick letters that today he was offering headcheese or sausage with sauerkraut as well as the usual potatoes.

Wanda shook her head. "I've lost my appetite."

Richard sighed. "If it's about the glass . . . forget about it!" He grinned. "Anyway, I think your mother liked the look of me, thank goodness. What did she say once the two of you were on your own again?"

Wanda swallowed. "She . . . she thinks that you're very dedicated to your work. And she says you have a lot of energy."

Richard's eyes widened and he beamed. "Well there you go!" He gave Wanda a peck on the cheek. "To tell you the truth you were beginning to scare me with all your talk of how much your mother values appearances and first impressions. You were so worried that she might find the house too small and plain. But I reckon I've managed to persuade her that we have all you'll ever need . . ."

Wanda forced a smile. Richard really had tried his very best. He had pulled out all the old order forms from Gotthilf Täuber, to show Ruth what he had been doing. He showed her his glassware and explained how he was combining Venetian techniques with old Lauscha handicrafts to create something quite unique. He even told Ruth of his dream of someday having his own gallery—one that catered only to the most discerning clients. He saw glassblowing as a fine art, and he was confident he could make it his future and earn enough for himself and his family.

Mother had listened attentively, her face quite motionless. Wanda had tried desperately to read her features—but in vain.

Why didn't he talk more about what life would be like with me and the child? Wanda thought. Glass, glass, glass—where Mother was concerned, that was like waving a red rag at a bull! Perhaps

Mother would have given her blessing for them to marry sooner if Richard had talked less about glass and more about practical matters such as putting a new room in the attic, replacing the windows, and getting a new stove fitted. The two of them had discussed those things often enough, after all.

"It hardly made a good first impression on Mother that we had to wait so long for you to turn up," she said snippily.

"Well yes, that was unfortunate," Richard admitted. "But I couldn't just leave Karl Flein standing there in the street when he wanted to tell me about the foundry being offered up for sale. The man's been working there for donkey's years. Of course the news upset him!"

"Upset is putting it mildly," said young Hansen, who had obviously been eavesdropping on Richard and Wanda. "It's a disaster!" He looked around the table. "It's always the same story. In the end, it's always us glassblowers who are left holding the short straw!"

Everybody around the table nodded. "A Sonneberg wholesaler owning the foundry! That's the beginning of the end," Martin Ehrenpreis muttered, his face pale.

"What would be so bad about it?" Wanda asked, though in truth she didn't feel the least desire to know. Why did these men always have to interfere with their conversation? Couldn't they leave Richard be for just a little while? "Surely it's a good thing that somebody is willing to invest in it!"

"That's not investment! All the wholesalers care about is grinding us deeper into the dirt! Pretty soon we glassblowers won't have a say in anything," Richard replied.

"It's a sign of the times," someone said darkly. "We poor beggars can't do anything to defend ourselves against the men with the money. They can do just as they like with us."

Richard nodded. "Am I ever glad I don't have to work for a wholesaler or in the foundry!" Then he turned to Wanda and said so softly that nobody else could hear, "I really feel sorry for the men in the Gründler foundry."

"To be quite honest, I couldn't care less at the moment," she hissed back just as softly. The mood of helpless rage hanging over their table like a dark cloud only made her feel more angry and disappointed.

Wanda took a sip of beer, then tried again.

"Mother says that we should—"

Richard looked at her rather vaguely, then stroked her hand. "I know, there's a lot to discuss. The wedding, choosing a date . . . Has she said whether she'll stay for it? I mean it would be nice, of course, to get married in the new church in September, but it looks like it might not be ready by then." He shrugged.

Wanda bit her lip. She had to tell him the whole truth before he got too caught up in his plans for the future.

"The church isn't the issue, Mother says that—" But she couldn't say another word because Richard interrupted her.

"And of course it has to happen just as I'm expecting a new order from Täuber. I'll have to work day and night for that one . . . Not that I mind work, of course, quite the opposite! I'm already itching to get to work on it, but—" He stopped as young Hansen leaned over toward him.

"You don't seem to care much about our troubles!" he snarled at Richard. "But of course you see yourself as an *artist*! And you've made a good match . . ."

"What's that supposed to mean?" Richard asked hotly. "Are you suggesting that—"

Wanda tugged hesitantly at his sleeve, but he brushed her hand away. "It's all right, Wanda. We'll talk about all that tomorrow, yes?"

Wanda had no choice but to sit there in silence as Richard dove back into the larger conversation.

CHAPTER NINE

Late June 1911

In late June Ruth got a big bowl of early cherries, pale red and juicy, from the tree in Karl Flein's garden, just as Wanda had hoped she would. Wanda fleetingly wondered her mother would call for a fruit knife and fork to cut out the stones, but she was happy to see Ruth pop cherry after cherry into her mouth, enjoying every bite and paying no attention to the red juice that ran down her lips and her fingers.

Another week or two and the raspberries would be ripe enough to fall from the bushes. But Ruth would have to forego that pleasure—she would be leaving in early July. And she did not plan to leave alone . . .

Summer had crept into every corner of the Thuringian Forest since Ruth had arrived. But Wanda hardly noticed. When her cousin Johannes told her that there would be a festival for the summer solstice up on a hill above Lauscha, she was startled. Would the days really be growing shorter from now on? Johannes made the whole affair sound very tempting, with music, dancing, and a huge bon-fire, but she doubted that she would take part. Though the festival was one of the high points of the year for the town's young people, she didn't feel especially youthful at the moment. And she was in no mood to go to a party. Her days were far too full of Sylvie, Richard, and conversations—albeit fruitless ones—with her mother.

Ruth had grown more restless over the last few days, constantly looking through her travel documents as though to be quite sure that the date of departure really was approaching. She pleaded with Wanda again and again to come back with her. She and Sylvie would have everything they could possibly need in New York; she would hire a nanny for the baby and Wanda could begin training for any job of her choosing. Or she could get a job right away, working in Steven's company. But Ruth eventually had to concede, albeit with a heavy heart, that Wanda was immune to all these temptations; she appeared to be set on staying in Lauscha. There was one point, however, on which Ruth would not concede—Wanda would not be permitted to marry Richard until more time had passed.

Although mother and daughter frequently squabbled and hurled recriminations at each other, they both tried to smooth over their troubles—the knowledge that Ruth would soon be leaving and that they would not see one another for some time stopped them from taking their arguments too far. Ruth was waiting for Richard to come and plead his case to her, but he was obviously smarter about these things than her daughter; he knew that when Ruth said "No," she meant it.

Of course, Ruth strongly disapproved of the fact that Wanda was living in Thomas Heimer's house and not with Johanna. That said, she had to admit that it was the best solution; Johanna simply didn't have room for Wanda and the baby, while Thomas Heimer had a whole floor that he had set up especially for Wanda. And then there was Eva, who was a great help.

A few days before she was due to leave, Ruth finally plucked up her courage and set out for the top of the village. She felt a little weak at the knees as she walked. This time, Wanda was not with her.

It was awful to see Thomas Heimer again. Of course, Ruth had not been expecting otherwise. She had been prepared for the fact that her ex-husband wouldn't have much in common with the strapping young fellow she had once known, the man she had left in the dead of night so many years ago. But it was quite another thing to see him, gray-haired and stooped from years bent over the lamp. The same was true of seeing her father-in-law, Wilhelm Heimer, who sat in a rocking chair in the kitchen and didn't even recognize her. Was this really the ogre who had frightened her so much back in the day? She had made sure that she knew exactly what she wanted to say before even setting out, but she was so taken aback by how much he'd changed that she almost lost the thread right at the start.

Ruth had to admit, however, that Wanda was right when she talked about how much better things were in the Heimer household nowadays. The kitchen, once so dark and gloomy, was bright and well scrubbed. A loaf of bread and some smoked sausages sat on the sideboard by the table, covered with a snow-white cloth. There were no dry trails of crusted mustard around the rim of the jar, and a stack of thick white china dishes had been set on the table. Doubtless they were getting ready for lunch. This was certainly an improvement for a family that had once upon a time eaten from one greasy dish! All the same, Ruth felt almost heartbroken at the thought that Wanda was satisfied with such a modest life, when she could instead have the very best of everything. Her only comfort was that at least her daughter was not living in Richard's cottage . . .

Of course, Thomas turned down Ruth's proposal that she should pay for Wanda's board and lodging. He was clearly affronted by the very idea and asked her whether she thought he couldn't afford to keep his own daughter. It was the most natural thing in the world, he said, that he should look after Wanda and Sylvie until Richard took over that responsibility. He didn't mention the fact that Ruth had not given her consent to the marriage, which made her wonder whether he too had his doubts about the wedding.

Or was it just that he didn't want his daughter to move out? Was he feeling the same old jealousy that every father feels when his daughter loses her heart to another man? Not wanting to dwell on such thoughts, Ruth focused instead on what she had really come for. And in the end, she handed over the money. Even if Thomas didn't want monthly contributions to Wanda's room and board, he could at least take the money and use it for her dowry. If Wanda and Richard were to marry the following year, then Ruth wanted to be able to buy the young couple a suitable house. Thomas said darkly that he had had the same idea, and that he insisted on paying for a portion of it. He even offered to keep an eye out for a suitable property over the next few months. Ruth agreed and suggested that if he found one, he should put her money down as a deposit. As she handed the handsome sum over to Thomas, she told him how much he should let Wanda have every month. Her daughter shouldn't have to go begging every time she needed a new pair of stockings, after all!

Her visit to the Heimer house had gone well enough. They hadn't revisited their old arguments, and they hadn't had any new clashes. All the same, her steps were slow and tired as she set off for Johanna's house. She had done all she could. The die was cast. She had lost Wanda to Lauscha, and now she had no choice but to wish her daughter luck.

* * *

Johanna gnawed her lip. "Perhaps I should pop back into the house and pin it to the wall?"

Anna laughed. "Mother! Aunt Ruth's telephone number is written down in at least five different places in the house—how often do you think we're going to call you in New York?"

"If you have any questions, you'll be glad to be able to reach us!" Johanna shot back. She looked restlessly from her daughter to the mountain of luggage that was being loaded up onto Hansen's wagon. Unlike Ruth's suitcases, Johanna and Peter's luggage consisted of a motley collection of bags and trunks, all of which had seen better days. And unlike Johanna, Ruth was still sitting in the house calmly drinking one last cup of coffee, happy in the knowledge that somebody else was looking after her things.

"Put the trunk with the coats on top of everything else!" Johanna called to Hansen. "It might be chilly on the train, and then we'll be glad to be able to reach our coats."

Anna rolled her eyes. "Yes, of course," she said. "You never know, it might snow today!"

Although it was still early, the day was already hot. The horse pulling the cart had dark bands of sweat under its harness. It shook its head again and again to rid itself of the flies that buzzed all around.

Wanda stood a little off to the side, watching as the others bustled about. She smiled quietly to herself. All they needed now was for Johanna to declare that she had to check the dozens of lists of instructions she had written out for emergencies. If she got started on that, the cart would never get under way . . .

She would have liked to ask her aunt, "Didn't you once tell me to stop flapping about like a startled hen?" But she bit back the remark. Johanna quite clearly felt as though the ground were giving way beneath her feet. Even Peter looked rather lost. They both gave the impression that they already bitterly regretted their decision to go to America with Ruth for a long-deserved vacation.

Ruth had set to work trying to convince them to return with her as soon as she had arrived. In all the years they had been married, Johanna and Peter had never taken a vacation—business had always come first. Now that the children were grown up and could take over from their parents for a few weeks, it was only right that Johanna and Peter should take the opportunity to relax. And what better place for a vacation than New York? Just imagine: the three of them sailing across the Atlantic together, and then Steven welcoming them with delight at the end of the crossing.

Peter had been the first to warm to the idea. The older he got, the faster the years seemed to be passing. He had wondered aloud if it might someday be too late to take such a journey. Johanna had retorted that she would feel no shame if she had to turn up at the pearly gates and tell the good Lord that she had never seen New York. If Peter wanted to take a vacation, then they could go to the Bavarian Forest for a few days. It was only when Peter remarked that a trip to New York might be a good opportunity to make new business contacts that she relented.

Ruth had wasted no time setting things in motion: Steven would order the tickets from Hamburg to New York, and all the documents would be waiting for them when they got to Hamburg. From that moment on they had talked of nothing else. Johanna and Peter's schedule grew ever busier, filled with trips to the theater, sightseeing, and client meetings. Wanda doubted that they would be able to manage even half of what they had planned. She remembered how tiring Marie had found the city . . .

Wanda found herself thinking of how she and Richard had set off for Bozen in the spring. He had checked his train ticket at least a dozen times to be sure that the number on the ticket matched his seat number in the compartment. When Wanda asked whether he wanted some of the sandwiches they had brought for the trip, he had hissed, "Put those away at once! Do you want everybody to think that we're a couple of hillbillies?" Wanda had just laughed and devoured her own sandwich with gusto. It had taken Richard quite a while to relax enough to enjoy the journey.

Is everybody from Lauscha like this? Wanda wondered, as Johanna fussed around the cart. Were they so attached to their hometown that the very thought of leaving Lauscha scared them?

"Now let me see . . . That's the trunk with the shoes, there are our coats, that one's got the clothes," Johanna muttered to herself. "Johannes! Where's the picnic basket? . . . What do you mean you don't know?" Johanna put her hands on her hips and glared at her son. "Good Lord, if the boy can't even be relied on to know where the luggage is, what on earth will happen when we're away? . . ."

Wanda and Anna grinned at each other. For once, they were both thinking the same thing. Wanda put Sylvie over her shoulder, then went over to her aunt and hugged her tight.

"Nothing will go wrong," she said. "The business is in good hands with Anna and Johannes. And everybody else will do their best as well. You have a well-trained team here! It's only three months, and you'll be back well before the Christmas orders start coming in."

Johanna looked at her niece, her lower lip trembling. "We'll be gone almost four months, not three!"

"Well then, four months—it's hard to say good-bye, of course . . ." Wanda forced herself to nod and smile.

Then suddenly Ruth took Wanda in her arms. "My child . . ." Wanda was enveloped in her mother's familiar scent of lilies and magnolias.

"Mother . . . I . . . I'll miss you so much," she murmured, her eyes growing moist.

"If anything goes wrong, then you must simply pack your bags and come home!" Ruth sobbed, and then she hugged her daughter so tightly that Wanda could hardly breathe.

CHAPTER TEN

Hansen's horse drank one last pail of water, and the cart finally got going.

Anna began bustling about as if to remove any lingering doubt about who was in charge of the household now. Without saying a word, she turned and hurried indoors; Johannes followed, his head bowed.

Wanda set out for the top of the village with Sylvie, who was asleep. Wanda sniffled noisily as she walked—she had been crying so much that her nose was quite blocked.

"If anything goes wrong, then you must simply pack your bags and come home!" Her mother's words echoed in her ears. Why hadn't she replied that she was already home? That Lauscha was her home? She hadn't been able to utter the words because of the lump in her throat, that was all. But if this was home, why did she feel so terribly lost?

Although everything was just as it always was and the village was bustling with activity as usual, she felt as though the sun had gone behind a cloud. Had it really only been a few weeks since she had had to bury her dream of marrying Richard this summer?

Richard . . . Wanda had feared that he would be offended by Ruth's refusal to consent to an early wedding, but that hadn't been the case. She had secretly expected—even hoped—that he would move Heaven and earth to win Ruth over. But he had taken the news in stride, which was just like him. "Who knows, it might even be good to wait a while."

Wanda had been about to object when he grinned and said, "Though I won't wait forever!" Then he explained that this way he would be able to concentrate on his next commission, which he expected to have in writing any day now. It would bring in a tidy sum, and they needed all the money they could get for their little family. The building work on the house would cost money and so would the wedding . . . Then he broke off and heaved a deep sigh, frowning in thought. Wanda laughed and told him that her mother was thinking of buying them a house as a wedding present, so he needed not worry quite so much about the future.

"Are you joking?" he had asked incredulously. Once Wanda had persuaded him that her mother was perfectly serious, his enthusiasm knew no bounds and they had spent some time imagining what their new house should look like. It would have to be on the sunny slopes of course—not all of Lauscha had sunshine, because of the surrounding mountains—and it would have to have piped water, and electricity. And a big front door leading to a spacious showroom for his works. It would be light and airy, with white walls! Then he would be one step closer to achieving his dream of having his own gallery, to which rich clients from near and far would come to buy his pieces. He had smiled, hugged Wanda, and declared that this was all the proof they needed that there were two sides to everything and that it all depended how you looked at it. Even Wanda could see that in a way it was good that her mother had refused to give her consent.

Richard, ever the optimist . . . She wiped away the last few tears and smiled. A glass showroom . . . She was full of admiration for the single-minded way he pursued his dream.

Wanda was so lost in thought that she didn't even notice the figure huddled beneath the cherry tree in Karl Flein's garden. She had almost walked past it when she was shaken from her thoughts by a stifled sob.

"Martha! Is everything all right? Can I help you?" Wanda left the baby carriage where it was and hurried over to the garden fence. Looking at the old woman, she was shaken by what she saw.

Martha Flein waved away the offer of help with one hand, keeping the other over her face. Her whole body was racked with sobs.

Wanda hesitated for a moment. Then she opened the latch on the garden gate and took a step toward Martha. Karl Flein's wife was usually such a calm, capable woman—what could have upset her so?

Martha looked up. Her eyes were red and there was an ugly swelling on her left cheek.

"That dreadful Otto Gründler! He'll be the ruin of us all, with that idiot idea he has of emigrating to America."

Wanda knelt down beside her. The ground was covered with cherry pits and bird droppings.

"It's not the end of the world if the foundry is sold," she said softly. She recalled that Karl Flein was the foreman at the Gründler foundry. It was his job to decide what all the other glassworkers would be doing and to supervise them as they worked. The owners hardly ever came by the foundry, so a lot rested on his shoulders.

"Karl has a lot of experience and everybody thinks well of him, so I'm sure the new owner will want to keep him on," Wanda said, trying to cheer her up. She glanced over at the carriage. Sylvie was still sound asleep, of course, just when a crying baby would have been the perfect excuse to get away! There was nothing she could do to help Martha.

"You try telling him that!" Martha spat. "Karl hates these wholesalers. They're a bunch of cutthroats! But you don't understand these things . . ." She waved a hand dismissively.

Wanda heaved a sigh. People were always telling her that. Although she was in no mood to engage in this conversation, she sat down next to Martha. It was uncomfortable—she seemed to be sitting right on some cherry pits.

"Perhaps it's time someone told me why the wholesalers are so *awful?*" she said, with a hint of irony on the last word.

Martha Flein looked up. "The Sonneberg wholesalers have always been a blessing and a curse for us in Lauscha. We'd never sell our wares without their business contacts. The buyers for all the big department stores in Germany and beyond would never bother to go door to door, ordering a couple of candlesticks here and a dozen bowls there. They'd rather go to a wholesaler and have a look at his samples book. And then the wholesaler passes on the orders to the glassblowers. When you look at it like that, you could almost call it a harmonious working relationship." She laughed harshly.

"But Johanna, I mean the Steinmann-Maienbaum business, gets by without a wholesaler," Wanda said, frowning.

"She's the exception, though. Johanna realized very early on that it's not good to have to depend on men like that. She built up her own contacts, and it worked out well for her, especially with Ruth being in America."

"Hmm." Wanda nodded, as though that explained everything.

Martha could tell that the American girl still didn't understand. "Don't you see? A wholesaler comes along and gives an order. Let's say he wants fifty dozen bowls on a stem, painted with a particular pattern, due in three weeks. He doesn't ask whether the glassblower can do it in time. He doesn't ask whether the price is right. He doesn't ask whether the glassblower has the money for the raw glass and all the paints he'll need. Why should he, after all? There are plenty of glassblowers who are ready to work night and day on starvation wages just to have any money coming in at all! The wholesalers rely on us being in competition with one another. They don't shoulder any of the risk; they don't have to invest in materials or even in storage costs. All they do is rake in the money! At least that's how I see it." She shook her head sadly.

"Before—a long time ago now—Karl used to be in business for himself as a glassblower. Back then it was sink or swim, I tell you. Oh, when I think of those days! How anxious we were when there were no orders coming in. And then when one did come, we were always in such a panic over whether we'd be able to finish on time. We worked day and night. Karl blew the glass and I painted the wares until my hands trembled!" She held her hands up as though to emphasize her words.

Wanda thought about what would happen if one of the wholesalers bought the Gründler glass foundry. Wouldn't that give him a little more responsibility? Wouldn't it mean that the whole exploitative system would change for the better, and benefit the villagers? She was about to ask about this when Martha started talking again.

"What a happy day it was when Karl got a job with the Gründler foundry! At last he had a job where we knew how much money we would have coming in from one month to the next. And now? Karl says he'd rather throw himself in front of a train than work for one of the wholesalers again. He . . . hasn't been himself ever since we got the news . . ." Marie fell silent and put her hand to her swollen cheek. "He doesn't come home in the evening, he just goes out and drinks half the night and then wakes up in a foul mood in the morning and takes it out on me. I hardly know who he is anymore . . . he was always such a good husband to me!"

Wanda nodded helplessly as she wondered how on earth she could get out of this situation. Could it be that Karl Flein was over-reacting? He could use a little of Richard's optimism!

"My brother paints porcelain wares for a living. He could pass on some work to Karl. But you should have heard the way Karl carried on when I suggested asking about it for him. 'Do you want me to spend my days painting gents' tobacco pipes and ladies' brooches?' he yelled. It was as though I'd suggested he go and empty all the outhouse pails in Lauscha. He said that porcelain is just a cheap stand-in for glass and that nobody who cared about his art would ever think of working with it." Martha Flein looked at Wanda imploringly. "I mean—he's right in a way, isn't he?"

"I don't know . . ." Wanda shrugged. The American proverb beggars can't be choosers came to mind, but she said nothing.

She cast a glance at Martha. How tired she looked! As though she ached all over . . .

Was she in pain? Had Karl hit her? Was that why her cheek was swollen that way?

The thought frightened Wanda. Was Karl so scared of what the future may bring that he would hit his wife? Marie had always spoken so highly of him, and Johanna and Ruth held him in high regard too.

"You don't understand these things," Martha had said when she walked over to her. Wanda hated hearing that, but it was true. Drat it all. She could be of no help here and she had no comfort to offer.

She tried one more time, nevertheless. She put a hand on Martha's arm.

"Don't let it get to you! It will all look better in the morning." She could have kicked herself as the cliché escaped her mouth, but she couldn't think of anything else to say. So she plowed ahead. "There must be one or two honest men among all the rogues and cutthroats, and I'm sure Otto Gründler will want to sell his foundry to one of the decent ones. Someone who wants to treat the glass-blowers well! You'll see, it will all turn out all right in the end . . ."

Martha Flein didn't look comforted, but she nodded.

"Let's hope you're right. Though I think it's much more likely that Lauscha will go to the dogs . . . You be glad that none of this affects you, my girl! And please forgive an old woman for telling you all her troubles."

Well, I certainly wasn't much help, Wanda scolded herself as she set off for home a little while later. Her mother or Johanna would have known what to say. They would have been able to offer real comfort and advice.

Halfway up the hill Wanda stopped and wiped the sweat from her brow. Could she be so sure? People had been talking about the sale of the Gründler foundry all over Lauscha, but Ruth hadn't shown the slightest interest in the news. And Johanna had been indifferent as well.

"If we don't get along with the new owner, we'll just have to find somebody else to supply us with raw glass." Johanna had said. "The Kühnert and the Seppen foundries both turn out first-rate material." She had added that it would be a little less practical, since the Gründler foundry was located near the Steinmann workshop and the other foundries were a good way off, but it wasn't much of a problem. Johanna also said that she didn't believe the new owner would raise the price on raw glass—the owners of the other found-ries would never raise their prices, and that would be the end of the Gründler business.

Wanda's father wasn't especially worried, either, nor was Richard. Neither of them cared where they got their raw material as long as it was of good quality. Certainly they felt sorry for the Gründler foundry workers and said as much whenever they were at the Black Eagle, though they didn't do anything to help them.

It seemed that everybody was looking out for themselves first . . . No wonder Martha thought it was likely Lauscha would go to the dogs.

CHAPTER ELEVEN

"What do you mean, you didn't get an order from Täuber?" Wanda asked, glaring at Richard.

It was a little after ten in the morning. Sylvie had been awake and crying half the night, and Wanda had passed her off to Eva that morning and set off to visit Richard, despite the rain that had just started pouring down. She had to get out of the house! She needed an hour to herself, a break from wondering whether the baby had colic or whether she was just hungry or over-tired.

She wanted nothing more than for Richard to take her in his arms and hold her! Instead she stood in the doorway, soaking wet, while Richard stared in shock at the letter the postman had brought just minutes before.

"Hello, Richard, you've got a visitor! It's me, Wanda!" she snapped. Her jacket was clinging uncomfortably to her skin. Wanda didn't take it off, though. If Richard didn't start paying attention to her right now, she'd turn around and leave on the spot.

"Wanda, I . . . I'm so sorry!" His face shone with excitement. He looked young, bold, ready for adventure. He leapt to his feet and took Wanda's hand, then led her to the table. He waved his other hand animatedly as she sat down. "You'll have to see this for yourself. Gotthilf Täuber . . . He says . . . Good Lord, I can hardly believe it! This is much better than an order!"

Wanda snorted. She snatched the letter from his hand and read it. It was only a few lines.

"You'll have your own exhibition?"

Richard nodded proudly. "This fall. And it will be in Meiningen, which is a real destination for art lovers!" Richard's chest rose and fell as though he had just run all the way through Lauscha.

"But that's wonderful . . ." Wanda was pleased, of course she was, but she was so tired she couldn't stifle a yawn. Richard looked a bit put out.

"Now's my chance to show what I can do—what happens when we combine Lauscha glasswork with the Venetian techniques." There was triumph in his voice. "Wait till I tell your father—won't he be surprised! Wanda, this is the beginning of something big!"

Wanda laughed as Richard took her hands and danced gleefully around the room.

She had wanted to ask him about looking for a house. She already had a couple of properties in mind—there was Widow Klöden's house, which was large but rather run-down, and she'd also spotted a spacious wood-shingled house that was clearly empty, though she didn't know who it belonged to. It would have been pointless to try to talk to Richard about houses just then, though. When he let her go and went to pour himself a glass of water, she picked up the letter.

"He doesn't go into much detail, your Mr. Täuber," she said at last. "He doesn't say what else will be going on during the exhibition, how long it will last, whether there will be other artists showing their work alongside yours . . ."

Richard frowned. "Of course there won't be! Do you see any mention of other glassblowers?" He took the letter from Wanda's hand.

"No, I don't." Wanda put her arms in the air and stretched like a cat. A bone in her neck popped softly and she yelped. If only she weren't so tired! She tried to suppress another yawn.

"An exhibition like this can really make an artist's name," she said, and enjoyed the eager look in Richard's eyes when he heard that. "You'll be famous! When Marie visited us in New York, we went to see a glass exhibition. Mind you, that was with two artists. If I remember rightly, they had come from Venice. The colors were just wonderful! There were bowls and glasses made of thousands of tiny flowers all stuck together. They were real works of art, you would have loved them!"

Richard snorted dismissively. "Millefiori—they sell that type of glass to every tourist who visits Italy and has a few coins to spare. It's got nothing to do with the real art of glassworking. But you're right . . ." He tugged at his ear with his left hand. Wanda knew the gesture well; he always did that when he was uncertain about something.

"Perhaps I should go see Täuber and find out a bit more about what he has in mind. He doesn't even say here how many pieces he'd like to include in the exhibition."

"And he doesn't mention whether there will be any costs for you to pay, either," Wanda added. "If you like . . . we could go together." A trip to town—that was just what she needed. Suddenly she was no longer tired. "I could buy a few things for Sylvie and—"

"Wanda, my darling!" Richard interrupted. "We're not going shopping! I'd rather go on my own today. Then I can get back home sooner and get to work."

"But surely we can mix business with pleasure," Wanda replied, frowning.

Richard was already putting on his jacket. He shook his head. "I'd love to, but it'll have to be some other time. If I walk to the station with you now, we'll have to stop and talk to a dozen people along the way. I'll lose precious time. And to be honest I don't want to hear any more of their complaints about the Gründler foundry!"

He kissed Wanda hastily on the cheek, and then he was gone.

Wanda set off back home, feeling depressed. The rain had stopped. The first birds were already down on the damp ground, hunting for worms. The sky was mottled like a pickled egg, and every needle on every tree on the surrounding slopes stood out sharp and clear as an etching.

Wanda saw windows and doors opening as she walked— Lauscha had paused temporarily while the rain fell, but now it was back to business as usual.

She had almost reached her father's house when she saw Jockel coming toward her. "Here comes trouble," she muttered to herself.

Jockel was a friend of Richard's and worked blowing glass in the Gründler foundry. His face was worn and lined from too little sleep and too much schnapps. As he greeted Wanda, she could smell the alcohol on his breath. He was only a few years older than Richard but he moved and talked like an old man. He was barely capable of having a civil conversation without cursing, and he especially liked complaining about women. Down at the Black Eagle he took every opportunity to declare that "Anyone who's dumb enough to marry deserves whatever he gets!" He had even said this to Richard, who just laughed. "Let him talk, he's just jealous, that's all!" he told Wanda, trying to soothe her ruffled feelings.

Jockel was single, of course, and would probably stay that way forever since Wanda could hardly imagine a woman desperate enough to marry such a sourpuss. Jockel always had something to complain about. He grumbled whether the weather was good or bad, whether there was lots of work at the foundry or not enough.

And she had to run into him here on the street!

What has any of this got to do with me? she wanted to scream when he stopped her and launched into a tirade about the "blasted foundry," peppering his speech with references to "cutthroats," "villains," and "bastards."

Instead of yelling at him, however, she tried to sound sympathetic as she shifted from one foot to the other. Couldn't Jockel see that her jacket was soaked? That she had to get home and change before she caught a cold? Her thoughts wandered as she tried to find a way to bring the conversation to a close.

"But why am I telling you all this? None of it matters to you!" Jockel said bitterly at last. "That just shows how unfair the world is. Some people are born with silver spoons in their mouths while the rest of us have to fight for every inch!" And with that, he hunched his shoulders and marched off without even saying good-bye.

"Fool," Wanda said as she watched him go.

CHAPTER TWELVE

"Father, do you know why Karl Flein dislikes the wholesalers so much?" Wanda asked as she settled down in a chair in the workshop, a cup of tea in her hand.

The house had been as quiet as the grave when she walked in. It was only when she went through the long hallway to the back that she found her father and Michel in the workshop, each of them working at their bench. She had greeted them quickly and then gone into the kitchen, where she hung up her jacket to dry by the stove and put a pot of tea on to brew.

Then she had gone upstairs to change. She could hear soft singing from the nursery next door; Sylvie was sleeping peacefully while Eva sang her a lullaby that Wanda didn't recognize. Wanda stood in the doorway smiling and fought back the impulse to pick up the baby. She wanted to inhale the scent of her skin, to forget all about Richard and how he had preferred to go to Sonneberg on his own . . .

As she stood there, she wondered why the baby always fell asleep straight away when Eva sang to her, while Wanda's singing seemed to have the opposite effect. Then she pulled herself together and tried to ignore the pang of jealousy she felt. Wasn't it a blessing that Eva was such a help to her?

"Karl?" Thomas Heimer said without looking up. "What about him?" He was surrounded by dozens of boxes filled with clear rods of raw glass. Thomas reached back without looking, lifted a rod from a box, then held it to the flame.

"Might as well ask us what we have against the wholesalers," Michel said. He pointed at the mountains of rods. "Three thousand napkin rings in six days—nobody can do that!"

It was only then that Wanda saw how pale Michel was, with dark rings under his eyes. Her father looked no better. He was unshaven and his skin looked almost gray. How late had the two of them worked last night? Wanda recalled that when she had gone down to the kitchen to warm some milk for Sylvie, she had been surprised to see a crack of light under the workshop door. That had been just before one o'clock in the morning.

She knew, of course, that they had another order, not from Karl-Heinz Brauninger but from one of the wholesalers her father used to work for in the old days. Wanda had been pleased at the news since it meant people knew the Heimer workshop was still in business. But she hadn't heard the full details of the order because she had been spending as much time as she could with her mother in the last few days of her visit. Now Michel filled her in.

"These napkin rings have to be on a ship that will sail from Hamburg to England in ten days. Which means we have to deliver them to Sonneberg at the beginning of next week. Our friend the wholesaler doesn't care how we manage to do that!" He spat the words out. "But what can we do? He knows perfectly well that we can't afford to let an order like this slip through our fingers, even if the pay is terrible."

Thomas Heimer looked critically at the glass ring that he had made. Seeing that it was a perfect circle, he put it down to cool on a grid alongside dozens of others just like it.

"The wholesalers know that there'll always be someone to take the orders. They take advantage of that, of course they do, they'd be daft not to!" He was already reaching for the next rod of raw glass. He bent low over the lamp to warm it in the flame, his shoulders hunched.

"Can I help?" Wanda asked. She was about to pick up one of the rings that had already cooled when Michel shook his head.

"Later maybe. We're still waiting for the box-maker. He'll bring us some more material so that we can pack them all." He sighed and stretched out his leg, then took another rod of glass and held it to the flame.

For a moment all three of them were quiet. Wanda felt a surge of affection as she looked at her uncle. After years of suffering and lying idle he had pulled himself together and taken his place at the workbench again to help his brother. And to make the Heimer workshop what it had been once upon a time: one of the best in the village.

"In the meantime, we have to forget about those sample pieces for Brauninger," Thomas Heimer said, casting a regretful eye over the heap of sketches they had made for the "cuckoo project."

Wanda took a sip of tea and started thinking. She'd been in Lauscha for a while now—she was always in and out of the glass-blowers' workshops—but only now did she truly grasp the terrible conditions they worked under. She knew, of course, that glassblowing was hard work, both physically and mentally, and that it took a great deal of concentration. If a glassblower was having a bad day, or if his hand shook, then by evening his table would be covered with faulty wares. But she had never really considered the fact that most orders had to be filled under such tight time constraints, nor that her father had to buy all his raw glass and even the packing materials himself—even though the wholesaler would only pay him once the wares were delivered.

I have a great deal still to learn, she thought as she left the workshop.

The men didn't even look up.

CHAPTER THIRTEEN

Eva showed no signs of wanting to give Sylvie up, her father and Michel were hard at work, and Richard wouldn't be back from Sonneberg until that evening—Wanda was the only one who wasn't busy. She was so bored that she spent the rest of the morning cleaning the front parlor. It was a large room, but rather bare and dreary, and only rarely used. In fact Wanda couldn't remember any occasion when the family had gathered there. A thick layer of dust covered all the furniture. Perhaps it was time to brighten the place up a bit and invite a few guests over, and they could use this room for their work meetings. After all, they could hardly ask Karl-Heinz Brauninger or other important guests and clients to sit down at the kitchen table. That is, if they ever came . . .

After an hour or so the wood gleamed, the mirror shone brightly in its golden frame, and the glass panes on the display cabinet were spotless. But instead of feeling pleased with her accomplishments, Wanda flopped down into one of the chairs. The upholstered backrest was hard and smelled musty.

Wanda remembered what her mother had said about being nothing more than a cleaning woman. Before she could stop the memory, she heard her mother's words about Richard in her ear.

"How on earth do you imagine you could help? He'd set you to fetch and carry, nothing more."

If her mother could see her now . . .

But what else did she have to do? There was no wedding to arrange. Her father had no time for her because he had so much work. And Richard thought of nothing but his exhibition.

She was the only one who had nothing to do. Wanda wasn't happy with that realization.

Ever since Mother had left, the days had dragged by. There was peace and quiet once more, but instead of enjoying it, Wanda felt more restless than she had since leaving New York.

She was bored.

Johanna would have said something like, *Find some work to do before the work finds you! There's always enough to be getting on with, and at the end of the day you'll find that you didn't have time for everything.*

Oh, what she wouldn't give at that moment for a cup of coffee with Johanna! She would surely have felt better after a heart-to-heart talk! But she would just have to do without for the next few months.

If only Anna were a little more open and friendly . . . But Wanda couldn't think of anything she would like less than to sit down for coffee with her stubborn, tight-lipped cousin.

She picked up one of the glasses that stood on a silver tray along with a carafe. She could only remember one occasion when they had even used these glasses. When the first order from Karl-Heinz Brauninger had come in, her father had sent Eva off to buy a bottle of wine. Everybody stood around awkwardly, their fingers clamped around the fine stems of the glasses, in which the wine had glittered ruby red.

They had all sipped at the wine without really tasting it, instead talking away nineteen to the dozen about the order and how they should approach it. They had all been brimming over with ideas, suggestions, and questions. It had been a wonderful day.

Wanda smiled as she turned the glass in her hand.

How thin it was! What had people drunk from before there was glass, she wondered. And when had people first started to use glass? She decided to ask Richard that evening.

Although Wanda couldn't have said why, her good spirits began to return. She got back to her feet and grinned. There was no time to be bored!

She would wash the windows next. Eva would be glad that somebody else had taken on the job. Wanda put the damp cloth to the windowpane and then stopped. She let her hand drop as she watched trickles of water run down the glass.

The wineglasses.

The window.

Wanda glanced around the room as though seeing it for the first time.

The glass shade on the gas lamp.

The magnifying glass that her grandfather used to read the newspaper.

The panes in the display cabinet.

The mirror in its golden frame.

There was glass everywhere.

It was lovely to look at but it was more than that. Without his magnifying glass, her grandfather wouldn't be able to read the newspaper at all. Without the glass shades for the gas lamp, they would still be using smelly oil lamps and the rooms would be much gloomier. Without glass panes in the windows, houses would either be dark and gloomy or the wind would gust through the rooms.

Wanda smiled as she carried the bucket through to the kitchen, her mind racing now.

Ships, cars, the shop windows of the great department stores—everywhere you looked, glass made people's lives better and simpler. Could you make windows from porcelain? Unthinkable. Could you make reading glasses from wood? Of course not.

The world was full of glass. And Lauscha was at the center of it all.

Which made it all the more upsetting that the glassblowers profited the least from their art.

But wasn't that the way it was everywhere? Wasn't it always the little people who were ground underfoot? Was there even any point getting upset about it?

"*You be glad that none of this affects you, my girl!*" Martha Flein had told her. And Jockel had said much the same thing. Wanda had only been half-listening at the time, but now the remark made her angry.

Why *didn't* it affect her? Wasn't she a glassblower's daughter? Wouldn't she soon be a glassblower's wife?

She had come to Lauscha because her roots were here. She had been born here, and it was home. She wanted to live here, and she wanted to play a bigger role in village life. Was she supposed to just stand back and watch while everything fell apart?

With a wholesaler about to buy one of the foundries, Lauscha was about to shatter like glass. While she dusted rooms and washed windows.

"*He'd set you to fetch and carry, nothing more.*"

She threw the washcloth into a corner in disgust.

How could she help the villagers? She knew next to nothing about how life worked here; she didn't know the rules. Even if she had a good idea, nobody would listen to her.

Wanda was even a bit relieved at the thought. No, there was nothing she could do to help the glassblowers. That was the mayor's job, wasn't it? And he seemed to have plenty of other problems to deal with at the moment, since the new railway line out to Ernsthal was turning into such a headache. Before the sale of the foundry became the only topic of conversation in the Black Eagle, there had been plenty of talk about the "railway war."

There was also a rumor of an arsonist at work ever since another of the village taverns had burned down. Three houses had gone up in flames along with it, and it supposedly hadn't been an accident. The mayor had promised a full and thorough investigation.

It was clear that the Gründler foundry workers couldn't expect the mayor to advocate on their behalf. Which meant that Karl Flein, Jockel, Karline's husband, and all the rest of them would have to handle the matter themselves.

Why didn't the villagers of Lauscha buy the foundry for themselves? As a group?

Ha, that would certainly teach the mysterious wholesaler a lesson! Then they could sell their raw glass directly to other glassblowers without having to let the wholesaler take a cut. Then the glassblowers would be their own bosses at last.

CHAPTER FOURTEEN

"Did you let the bacon fry for a bit before you put the beans in?" Eva asked Wanda as the family sat around the supper table. She was frowning.

Wanda, who was just picking a bit of bean out from between her teeth, shrugged.

"What do you mean? I put everything into the pot and then—"

"It's a fine thing that you want to help, my dear, but your skills in the kitchen do leave something to be desired!" Thomas Heimer said. He held out his fork to Eva and showed her a wobbly lump of white bacon lard. "If you didn't spend all your time playing nurse-maid, we would have a decent meal in the evening!"

"Well, I like it. It tastes a little different from the way it usually does, of course, but . . ." Richard said. He had come straight to the Heimers' house when he got back to Lauscha.

"Tell me, why don't the glassblowers buy the Gründler foundry themselves?" Wanda asked.

"What?" Richard looked at her, perplexed.

"Yes, just think about it! If a stranger can come in and do that, then so can the villagers of Lauscha. That would be the answer!"

Michel laughed. "And what an answer it would be! All they would need is the goose that lays the golden eggs, and then in the morning they could go to Otto, lay all that gold on the table before him, and then live happily ever after as their own masters for the rest of their days!"

He shook his head. "You can tell such fairy tales to Sylvie, but I'm afraid we're a bit too old for them!" He pushed his plate away and reached for a slice of bread. He bit into it and started chewing, with little sign of enjoyment.

"But—I'm serious," Wanda said. "They can borrow the money from the bank. I'm sure that this wholesaler doesn't have the full purchase price sitting around the house in cash, either. And if everybody gets together, they can spread the load. Just because nobody's ever done anything like it doesn't mean that it can't be done, does it now?"

By now the soup with its undercooked bacon and beans had been quite forgotten.

"I can give you a thousand reasons why something like that would never work," Richard said. "For one thing, the glassblowers all look out for themselves; they never really work together. Just look at the way we all protect our designs from each other so that nobody copies them! And you want us to join forces for something as big as this?"

Thomas Heimer nodded. "Richard's quite right, I'm afraid."

"You're impossible." Wanda said. "What a pack of pessimists you are! But seriously now, everybody's shuddering at the thought of having a Sonneberg wholesaler in charge of the foundry. So the obvious thing to do is look for another solution. Perhaps the other glassblowers just need somebody to take them in hand. Somebody with ambition and vision and the entrepreneurial touch, somebody young . . ." She looked directly at Richard.

"Forget it," he said, shaking his head. "I'm just glad all this has nothing to do with me. I'm independent, and I want to stay that way. A man makes his own luck in this world, as the saying goes." He cast a meaningful glance at the folder of documents on the bench next to him. He was obviously bored with the turn the conversation had taken and itching to break his own news to the group.

"I understand that you've got other things to think about at the moment," Wanda said. "But—" She broke off as she felt a hand on her shoulder.

"My daughter, the American! Just you wait, Richard, next thing she'll decide that she has to take on the task of saving the foundry herself!" Thomas laughed.

"Well why not?" Wanda retorted. Why did nobody take her seriously? It wasn't an entirely outlandish idea, was it?

"Oh, my girl, it's one thing that you helped your old father out of a tight spot, but you mustn't imagine you can save all Lauscha. What do you know about how a foundry works?" Thomas asked irritably.

"Have you ever even been inside a foundry? Well, there you go then!" Richard added when Wanda shook her head.

"I'd expect a crazy idea like that from your mother or your aunt!" said Michel, who had said nothing until now. "They were always wanting to change the world, overnight if possible. That's just the typical Steinmann way!"

"Well, why isn't it the Heimer way?" Wanda snapped back at him. "Why is it that the Steinmanns always do so well for themselves?" She searched desperately for an argument that the others wouldn't just squash straight away. "Don't you care at all about the people from the Gründler foundry? Isn't it time to defend yourselves against the wholesalers at last? And isn't the best way to do that by working together? Everybody else always earns a tidy profit on your glassware, while you . . . Father, you were telling me just this morning how the wholesalers put so much pressure on you. Surely you can see that it makes sense to change the system."

"Changing the system . . . Goodness gracious! Next thing you'll be telling me you want to join the Socialist party." Thomas stood up so abruptly that his chair scraped loudly on the floor. "If you'll excuse me, I'm going back to work. While Richard dreams of his exhibition and Wanda dreams of putting the world to rights, I need to keep earning money to put food on the table. And I hope the next meal tastes better than today's mess!" He nodded darkly at Eva, then left. Michel followed hot on his heels.

"Well, you made a fine mess of that!" Eva said. "First you spoil the soup and then you run on with your silly speeches. You know how hard those two are working at the moment, and then you go and upset them when they finally get to take a break!"

Wanda glared at Eva as she filled a bowl with soup to take to Wilhelm.

"I don't understand!" Wanda said, throwing her hands in the air. "All I want to do is have a reasonable conversation about an idea that I had, and they treat me like a criminal. Or a fool."

"Wanda, my love . . ." Richard took her hand in his. "You're . . . you're asking too much of your father right now. Eva's right. He's so busy with this latest order." Richard shrugged.

"And you?" Wanda replied reproachfully. "You're thinking of nothing but your exhibition. But seriously, think about it! If you glassblowers got together to buy the Gründler foundry, then you'd own it! You wouldn't have to spend your money on raw materials; you could credit what you buy against your share of the ownership. And it would open up new possibilities for your art as well. You could create much bigger bowls and vases by using the big firing ovens at the foundry. Pieces that you simply couldn't make at home, or even in Father's workshop, because they're too small. Wouldn't that be something?"

"But I'd always be dependent on other people. I would have to take them into account as well—it would be a nightmare!" Richard said, laughing. He kissed Wanda quickly, once on each cheek, then on her mouth and her forehead—little pecks that always made her laugh, whether she wanted to or not.

"Oh, Wanda, I know that you mean well, but sometimes you take it a bit too far. We have a saying here in Germany that a cobbler should stick to his last—I'm sure you have a similar expression in America, don't you?" He kissed her again, then got to his feet. "Work calls! I'll probably be at my lamp half the night. Come by later if you like."

Wanda thought his invitation was rather lacking in enthusiasm.

CHAPTER FIFTEEN

Wanda hurried down the steep street, in such a rush that she almost stumbled over the uneven paving stones. With some effort, she forced herself to walk more slowly.

Once she had reached the square in front of the foundry, she toyed for a moment with the idea of making a detour to the Steinmann-Maienbaum workshop. She hadn't seen her cousins at all since Johanna and Peter had left, and Wanda wanted to know how the two of them were getting on. But instead of turning down the street toward their house, she stayed her course. There would be time to visit her family later. Today she had something else in mind.

Although Sylvie had been awake half the night again and Wanda had had to feed her twice and change her diaper once, she felt as fresh as the morning dew. Silver drops glistened on the grass and flowers all around.

That Richard. Drat it all, he was right. She really didn't know anything. Or little more than that. But did he really have to say so in front of everybody? She wasn't going to give him another chance to say that she was ignorant.

Men were all the same. Whenever a woman had a good idea, their hackles rose. They would be happiest if everything stayed just how it was.

Wanda found herself thinking of Marie, and she snorted loudly. Ha, she could just imagine the uproar in the village when they had found out that a woman had dared to break the male monopoly on glassblowing. That had been more than twenty years ago! Had nothing changed since then?

There was still only a handful of women working as glassblowers, among them her cousin Anna. Women still usually worked on silvering, painting, and packing the wares. Other than Johanna, Wanda didn't know a single woman who was in charge of her own glassblowing workshop.

She thought of what Michel had said the night before. She had been surprised at the bitterness in his voice, but that sort of remark was typical of Michel. He'd never achieved anything notable in his life, and he must have been filled with envy when he looked at people who had. Especially when those people were women.

Steinmann women, at that.

Like Marie and Johanna. And Ruth.

And like Wanda as well.

A few minutes later she reached her destination. *It's certainly not much to look at.* She made her way around the big square building in search of the entrance. It looked like a huge wooden barn built on a stone foundation. The only signs that it was not used for storing hay were the many little windows and the clinking, clattering sounds that could be heard inside. And the chimney stack, as tall as a tower, at the back of the building.

Now that she had reached the entrance, Wanda hesitated. Could she really just stroll in and . . . ?

Before she could pluck up her courage, the door opened and a giant of a man walked out, colliding with Wanda and cursing loudly at the impact. Startled, she leapt back.

"It's the American girl—what are you doing here, miss?" Karl Flein asked, looking down at her and frowning.

Wanda cocked her head and smiled up at him.

He was just the man she had been looking for. And now here he stood before her, greeting her in the typical singsong Lauscha accent. Wasn't that an auspicious sign?

She took a deep breath, ignoring the sharp smell of sweat from him, and said, "I'd like to take a look at the foundry."

"Well, now you've seen everything," said Karl Flein, looking around the building like a nobleman surveying his estate. "I'm the foreman here, and it's my job to see that the whole shop runs smoothly. If it weren't for me telling them all what to do . . ." He stopped and shrugged. But his eyes gleamed and there was an unmistakable note of pride in his voice.

Wanda waved her hand in front of her face to cool down a little.

"I'm . . . I'm still overwhelmed," she gasped. "When I first walked in, I thought, *what a mess!* But now I can see that everything is organized right down to the last detail. It's incredible. Everything is in such perfect order, and they all work with such discipline!" She waved toward the huge furnace where the stokers were busy feeding the flames while the glassblowers worked in perfect unison and other men hurried off to place finished wares in a special oven to cool down. Everywhere she looked, glass shone in beautiful colors. No two pieces looked alike, for every single item was a special commission. The men mostly worked in silence, seemingly aware of exactly what was expected of them at any given moment. Their meticulous movements reminded Wanda of the many ballet performances her mother had taken her to in New York. Every worker appeared to be entirely devoted to his work. It was magical!

Yes, glass was a very special material . . .

Karl told her that she had chosen a good day for her surprise visit, since the master glassmakers were busy with their special commissions that day. Although it was entertaining to watch the foundry workers make the rods of raw glass, this was more interesting. Wanda nodded vigorously, overwhelmed by all she saw.

The air was full of scents that she could hardly begin to describe, smells that tickled her nose pleasantly but also made her want to cough, the heavy smells of work and sweat and effort. It was also boiling hot inside the foundry. Though the workers wore thin pants and sleeveless shirts, even these garments were dark with sweat. Wanda had initially been rather embarrassed by the sight of all these half-naked men and tried her best not to stare. But she was sweating as well and had to lift her arms out from her sides to cool off. She couldn't imagine how anybody could work in such oppressive heat. Karl had told her that in the past the Gründler foundry had only fired up its ovens for the year's second round of production in August. But a few years ago they had switched to a new schedule and now they only took four weeks off in the summer, which meant starting the second firing early. After all, the foundry didn't bring in money when the furnaces were cold.

"When I see how well the men here work together, I have to wonder what the owner actually does. He can't have much to do," Wanda said. Otto Gründler seemed to have picked just the right men for the jobs.

Flein laughed. "I can't speak to that, I'm sure you understand why. But I can tell you that this is one of the most important men in the place!" He nodded toward a table where young Gustav Müller was picking up glass pieces one by one and examining them critically. Flein told Wanda that Müller was the sorter. "What Gustav doesn't like goes for scrap. And that doesn't bring in any money for the glassmakers. Quite the contrary, it costs us!"

Wanda waved at Gustav. She knew him from the Black Eagle. Whenever voices rose around the table or an argument threatened to break out, he was always there to calm tempers. Sometimes he simply took out his harmonica and played a few tunes until the storm blew over. Oddly he didn't seem to be able to create the same aura of calm at home. Anybody who went past his house could hear his wife nagging away. Rumor had it that sometimes she even threw plates and cups at him, which Wanda could hardly imagine.

She smiled. "If I know Gustav, I dare say he sometimes turns a blind eye . . ."

"Too often, if you ask me," Karl said grimly. "If you don't keep an eye on these lads all the time, they start cutting corners. Jockel! What's going on there at the furnace? Can't you see that . . . Oh, look at that! I'll be right back!" he told Wanda, and ran off.

Wanda dodged around a cart full of firewood and went over to Gustav. "I was wondering what would change if the foundry were sold to someone outside the village. If the new owner's clever, he'll just leave everything as it is, won't he?"

Gustav put down the glass bowl that he had been holding up to the light.

"And when has a foundry owner ever been clever?" he said. "They haven't got a clue what the work's really about."

He picked up another bowl and examined it.

"The new owner probably won't change much when it comes to the actual work, but he can change how things are run . . ." Gustav snorted gently. "He can have us work longer hours, he can dock more pay for faults and errors, he can tighten up the regulations for sorting the wares. I'll probably be the first to be replaced! And he can also—" He suddenly stopped and stared over Wanda's shoulder, embarrassed.

"Who have we here? My word, it's . . . Thomas Heimer's daughter! The American girl! To what do we owe the honor of such a visit?" said a man standing just behind Wanda.

He took a step forward to stand next to her, and Wanda looked over at the unassuming man. He was of medium height, with unusually broad buttocks and a thin, frail torso. His thin arms hung down from narrow shoulders—it seemed as though everything about him was out of proportion.

She swallowed. So this was Otto Gründler. The man who had set all of Lauscha in an uproar. The man who wanted to fulfill his dream of emigrating to America. A man who looked as though he were made up of the wrong body on the wrong legs.

"I . . ." Wanda struggled for an explanation as to why she was there.

"I was sorry to hear about your Aunt Marie. I didn't know her personally, but I had heard a lot about her—who hadn't?" Gründler said. "And she worked with our glass rods, so she was a good customer as well!" He gave a small laugh.

"Mr. Gründler, you want to sell your foundry—I've come to inquire how much it would cost." The words tumbled out of Wanda's mouth before she could stop them. There was a tinkle of breaking glass at the sorting table behind her. Gustav inhaled audibly and cursed.

Wanda was so worked up that she could feel a vein pulsing at her neck. *Just don't lose your nerve now*, she told herself.

Gründler stood there, as startled as anyone.

"You want to—what?" He looked at her with the same searching gaze that Gustav used to check glass at the sorting table—as though he wanted to be quite sure that Wanda wasn't cracked. The thought was so funny that she giggled nervously. Let him look! As long as he named his price.

The foundry couldn't cost a king's ransom. In the end, it was just a big oven with a barn around it.

"Will you tell me how much you are asking?" she repeated, opening her eyes wide and giving him the look that had always gotten her a seat and prompt service in the bars of New York, however crowded. *Oh goodness, what am I doing here?* Richard would bite her head off when he heard about this, and her father would curse and say that she had lost her mind.

"That's got nothing to do with you," Gründler said brusquely. "I found a buyer a while back—a man from Sonneberg. We've already agreed on a price." He glared at the other men. "Do I pay you lot to stand around doing nothing?" Gründler's rigid mask slipped for a moment, and Wanda saw a hint of helplessness flit across his face, along with some other expression that she couldn't quite identify. But a moment later he was back in control. He shifted his feet a little farther apart to show his strength.

Some of the men hastily went back to work as though nothing interested them more; others, however, didn't even try to disguise their curiosity and stood listening, openmouthed. Some nudged their workmates, and a few even laughed.

Karl Flein joined them and glared angrily at Wanda. Gustav would probably have to mark a lot of pieces as rejects today—the conversation between the pretty young American and the man who wanted to go and become an American himself was just too captivating to ignore.

"But you haven't signed a contract yet, have you?" Wanda asked, more boldly than she felt.

Otto Gründler looked at her, irritated.

"I've already said that's nobody's business. To hear you talk, anybody might think you wanted to buy the foundry yourself!" Then he turned to Karl and hissed, "What's the girl doing here anyway?"

"Me, buy the foundry? Great Heavens above, I'm just a simple young woman!" Wanda answered before Karl could say anything. "But—what if there really were a second party interested in making such an investment?" she added thoughtfully. Since she had already made herself look ridiculous, she might as well go all the way. "Someone from Lauscha who knew what the business was about . . . Wouldn't you rather sell to someone like that?"

CHAPTER SIXTEEN

"And why should we have anything to do with such a madcap scheme? Especially when it's suggested by an outsider?"

Jockel's question provoked a flurry of excited murmurs from all sides, but then the room at the Black Eagle fell quiet again.

Everybody was waiting for an answer from Wanda, who had climbed up on a chair half an hour ago and been talking excitedly ever since. Benno's wife, Monika, was brushed away when she dared to try to come through with an armful of tankards. Benno was sitting on a stool behind the bar, smoking his pipe. Though the tavern was so full that there was hardly room for a mouse, the people in the Black Eagle had other things on their minds than beer and schnapps that night.

The news that the American woman had paid a visit to Otto Gründler had spread like wildfire, and the most far-fetched rumors had been circulating ever since: There was another investor, a mystery man from Lauscha! Wanda herself had bought the foundry. Wanda had been sent by Mr. Woolworth, the department-store magnate, who wanted to get into the foundry business.

Karl Flein, Gustav Müller, and others were doing their best to dispel the rumors, but to no avail. In the end, nobody could confirm anything. But they all knew that the Black Eagle was the place to find out more. If Wanda hadn't come of her own accord, somebody would have gone to the Heimer house and hammered on the door until she appeared.

"It's not a madcap scheme; it could save the lot of you!" Wanda declared in response to Jockel's taunt. She shot him a scornful look. "Otto Gründler said himself that there's no signed contract yet—all he has is a statement from the wholesaler that he's interested. He also said that he wouldn't have any problem selling to a Lauscha investor—he's no great friend of the wholesalers, either! He's willing to give you until the beginning of September to look into the possibility. He . . ." Whatever else she had to say was lost in a burst of excited chatter.

Thomas Heimer leaned back, his arms folded, while the babble buzzed around him on all sides. He didn't know whether to drag Wanda out of the tavern by her hair or to raise his fists to the men who were mocking her. So he simply sat there, staring ahead, and said nothing. His daughter—what a girl! The way she stood up there on the chair, flailing her arms until she almost tipped over, her hair loose and unruly. And the way her eyes flashed! Oh, that girl had fire in her belly, that much was sure! If he weren't so angry with her, he would almost have admired her. But why couldn't she just do the usual women's work? Why did she always have to stick her nose into other people's business? Hadn't he warned her against doing precisely that? "You mustn't imagine you can save all Lauscha"—he could remember saying those very words to her.

Was this the way people behaved in America? Over there they would probably all shout "Hooray!" and applaud what Wanda was saying. But Lauscha wasn't America. The clocks ran more slowly here in Lauscha. When they ran at all.

A half-amused, half-annoyed smile spread across Thomas's face.

After their supper of bread and cheese he had been so tired that he had wanted nothing more than to fall into bed, but he had pulled himself together and come down to the Black Eagle. Wanda had been talking so excitedly about her visit to the Gründler foundry that he knew she wouldn't drop the matter anytime soon. And so here he sat, though he hadn't the least idea what he should do about his daughter and her bold ideas.

"Tell me, did you know anything about this?" Richard hissed into his ear. He was trying furiously to get Wanda to look at him, but either she truly hadn't noticed him or she had simply decided to ignore her fiancé.

"I knew that Wanda had been down to the foundry today, of course—she told us all about her visit in detail. You'd have known too if you'd stopped in to see us today," Thomas replied calmly.

"No, I mean about all this!" Richard gestured around the room. "Did you know about this?"

Thomas shrugged. "What do we ever know, where women are involved?"

Richard turned away, shaking his head.

"It's about working together to get something done. Showing our true colors! And letting the wholesalers know that they can't walk all over us."

Seeing the frowning faces all around him, Thomas couldn't help but admire the way Wanda kept on talking, evidently unconcerned.

"There was a strike among the factory workers in New York recently. The women at the sewing machines in the garment factories got together to improve their terrible working conditions. And they did it! They changed things for the better!" Wanda beamed down at the crowd. "When everybody pulls together—oops!" She waved her arms to keep her balance on the rickety chair.

Gustav Müller was sitting closest to where Wanda stood. Thomas signaled him to hold the chair steady.

"But not all of us work in the Gründler foundry. And we've got our own worries!" somebody called from the floor before Wanda could finish her sentence.

"That's right!" shouted someone else. "We should each of us mind our own business!" He looked around for support. "I wonder why we're even listening to this nonsense! From a woman, at that! And an American to boot! She's probably never done a day's work in her life and she comes here and wants to tell us how to go about our . . ." He muttered the last few words into his beard, but Thomas could hear what he said.

"You watch out," he snapped. "You're talking about my daughter!"

"OK," the man said, raising his hands in apology.

Richard stared down at the last few drops of beer in the bottom of his tankard. "Why does she have to be so ridiculous?" he muttered in despair.

"You've found yourself a little revolutionary there, haven't you?" Jockel chuckled, and nudged Richard in the ribs. "Tell us then, does she have such ideas at home as well?" He cackled with laughter as though he had made a fine joke. "Oh, she'll lead you into a merry dance, that one!"

"One more word against Wanda and you'll have me to answer to!" Thomas clenched his fist and held it under Jockel's nose. "You old grumble-guts! When did you ever have an idea in your life?" He glared at the man contemptuously, then turned to Richard. "And you! What do you find so ridiculous? Is it ridiculous to have an opinion and voice it out loud? Maybe if I'd done that a few more times in my lifetime, things would be different now!" For a moment he thought that if he were in Richard's place he would do far worse than just grumble into his beer, but he chased the thought away as soon as it appeared. It felt much better to be open to new ideas!

"Wanda's one of those people who can dream by daylight. And she can see things that those who only dream in their beds at night never see! What's wrong with asking why the world has to be the way it is? Sometimes change is for the better!" Great Heavens, he was digging himself in deep here. Why couldn't he just say that he was at least as upset at Wanda's stubborn ideas as Richard was? Wasn't that true? Or was he more annoyed now at Richard, who sat there looking as though he wished the earth would swallow him up?

Richard looked at Thomas, astonished. "You . . . you're not telling me you approve of all this wild talk?"

I do indeed! Thomas was about to reply. Out of sheer obstinacy. But before he could open his mouth, a young voice spoke up.

"You're all behaving as though there had never been any solidarity in Lauscha! But back when we were setting up the museum, I found a document . . ."

Thomas saw Wanda turn her head so suddenly that the chair she stood on began to wobble again. Apparently she hadn't even noticed that her cousins Johannes and Anna were in the crowd.

"It said that in 1873 the craftsmen making glass eyes got together and agreed not to sell below certain fixed prices. And then the owners of the foundries undertook not to sell any raw glass to eye-makers who hadn't joined that agreement, for the space of six months. I'm sure that the arrangement was . . . very . . . very helpful to all concerned!" By the time he finished speaking, Johannes was bright red and stuttering. His shoulders slumped as though he already regretted having spoken.

Anna, who was sitting next to him, snorted. "You don't know much about local history, brother of mine. Otherwise you'd know that the agreement broke down not long afterward because the craftsmen couldn't agree on the prices. So much for solidarity!" She glared at her brother, and then at Wanda.

"Now calm down, you young folk!" Karl Flein said, speaking up for the first time. "Ten years ago we founded the Christmas ornament agreement—"

"Yes, and then not long after that the wholesalers moved in," the man next to him interrupted. "They didn't like the idea that Lauscha glassblowers had joined forces. And the bauble-blowers got cold feet, and how did the whole thing pan out? They gave in without a murmur and the agreement was dissolved!" He turned to Wanda accusingly. "You ask your Aunt Johanna how long she stuck to the deal! She saw soon enough that she could do better looking out for herself!"

Wanda looked around the crowd, upset. There were bright-red spots on her cheeks, and her lips trembled. For a moment Thomas was afraid she would burst into tears.

If only I'd told the girl a bit more! he thought irritably. *Then she wouldn't be standing here all surprised and disappointed.* Wanda was certainly interested in Lauscha's history; indeed she asked him so many questions he sometimes thought his head would burst. But he didn't like raking over the coals of the past that way.

"What about the Meiningen Glassblowers Association? You're all talking away here until you're blue in the face, but we've already got our system up and running!"

Everybody turned to look at a table by the door.

Thomas Heimer squinted through the tobacco smoke to see who had spoken.

"Joe Steiner! Now you're going to tell us that the way to save the foundry is to join the Social Democratic Party!" Jockel called across the room. Several of the men laughed.

Steiner waved away the suggestion. "I'm not even a party member myself, that's not a condition of membership for our association. But what this girl's saying"—he nodded toward Wanda—"doesn't sound so bad! You don't even all need to take part. All you need to found an association like ours is nine men who have some courage. But . . ." He grinned and shrugged, as if to say, Are there nine brave men in Lauscha?

Wanda drew a deep breath. "Exactly! I was thinking of something of the sort. But just as this gentleman says: it takes courage!"

"I'd say what it really takes is a pile of money!" Karl Flein shot back, laughing. "Tell the people the price that Gründler so generously named!"

"Sixty-five thousand marks," Wanda replied, and all of a sudden her voice was even shakier than her chair.

The hubbub that broke out at these words was louder than anything that had gone before.

"And that would only be the start of it!" Karl shouted out over the uproar. "Gründler has hardly invested a cent in the foundry these last few years. As foreman, I can tell you that there are some major repairs that need doing . . ."

"We could handle some of them ourselves!" Gustav Müller called out in reply. Wanda shot him a look of gratitude.

"Sixty-five thousand marks—we'll never be able to get a sum like that together! Who do you think we are? Do we look as though we're made of money? Why the hell are we even sitting here wasting our time like this?" Jockel waved his tankard toward the bar. "Can't a man get a drink in this place?"

"There are one or two wealthy people in Lauscha!" Gustav Müller called out. "Herrmann Greiner's son was just telling me yesterday that his family is paying for six windows in the new church! Old Kühnert was standing next to him and said he was donating money for the church clock! If we could just find a few people who would be so generous when it came to the foundry, it would be easy! So—who's going to volunteer?"

The only answer was a roar of laughter.

"There are banks. And loans," Thomas Heimer heard himself say. Sitting next to him, Richard inhaled sharply.

Everybody looked at Thomas. "Don't tell me that you . . ."

"Thomas! Are you saying that . . . ?"

Thomas Heimer raised his hands. "All I'm saying is that you should take Wanda a bit more seriously. Like I did. God knows it didn't do me any harm."

A moment later they heard a clatter. Wanda had fallen from the chair.

CHAPTER SEVENTEEN

It was just after midnight when Benno shut the door behind the last of his customers. Thomas Heimer and his daughter had left much earlier, but the debate over Wanda's ideas had raged on. Though the men had hardly touched their beers while she was there, once she was gone and it was their turn to talk, they more than made up for it. The atmosphere had been so charged that it would only have taken a single word out of place to start a fight. Benno had kept a close eye on the most argumentative drinkers, but it never got out of hand.

Once the guests had all left, the owner of the Black Eagle opened the windows to let out the smoke and fustiness that had built up throughout the evening. He drew himself one more beer and sat down to run the numbers for the evening. He was surprised at how much he had taken in that night. If it took a debate to bring in the money like this, well, that was fine by him.

* * *

Wanda asked herself afterward what she had wanted to get out of the evening. Had she hoped that the glassblowers would greet her idea with a round of applause? That they would get to their feet, one after another, and empty their purses out on the table to collect the starting capital that would be needed?

The next morning the idea seemed so absurd that she had to laugh.

She grew more and more relieved as the days passed and nobody mentioned the topic again. While she sensed that Richard had not been pleased by her public appearance, she was proud of herself. Whatever had come of it, she had had the confidence to stand up in front of the men and tell them her idea. She hadn't backed down! Not like all those times before, when she hadn't had the nerve to say anything. She recalled an occasion that she hadn't thought of for some time.

It had been back when Marie was visiting New York. Wanda had applied for a job as supervisor in a garment factory that made overcoats. But when she arrived at the factory gates, there had been a strike in full swing. Hundreds of women had blocked the way, agitated and not a little frightened. The strike leader had told her roughly that she should either join the strike or leave. Wanda had put her tail between her legs and crept off like a beaten dog.

Yes, times had changed. She had changed!

And besides, hadn't the evening given her something else that she would never have expected? It warmed her heart to think of the way her father had taken her side and defended her ideas in front of everyone.

A week later Wanda had almost entirely forgotten the matter. Richard told her that the whole village was still talking about her speech at the Black Eagle, but nobody brought it up directly with her.

She spent her days taking Sylvie for walks in her carriage, climbing up and down the steep streets of Lauscha for hours at a time. She often passed the site where the new church was being built. Wanda could hardly believe how quickly it was progressing. She thought sorrowfully of her original plan of marrying Richard in the new church in the fall. None of her plans seemed to be terribly well received at the moment, she thought in a fit of black humor. But it would happen eventually, she comforted herself as she walked on. She took a wide detour to avoid the Gründler foundry.

A few days later she found a new path that led away from their house toward a steep valley in the forest. That evening, when she described the path to her grandfather, she learned that a girl had been murdered while walking out that way a few years ago. Though he was upset and suggested that she walk up to Count Kasimir's Peak or any of the other beautiful spots nearby, Wanda reassured the old man that such a thing wouldn't ever happen twice.

Out in the forest, where it was cool and shady and the paths were covered with thick layers of old pine needles, Wanda reflected on her life. The turmoil within her slowly vanished like mist on a sunny morning. Perhaps it was the smell of resin in the air that calmed her, perhaps it was the many shades of deep green that soothed her eyes, perhaps it was the ever-changing play of light and shadow. She had everything she needed to be happy, she decided. A family. A beautiful child. Eva, who was such a huge help with Sylvie. Richard, who was so attentive—though less so than she would have liked at the moment. That was hardly any surprise, though, with his exhibition coming up.

Richard's exhibition . . .

Deep in thought, Wanda watched as a glittering green dragon-fly flew in circles over a puddle.

Here she was, worrying about anything and everything, but she had never thought to help Richard with the preparations for his exhibition in Meiningen. No wonder he hadn't been impressed by her speech down at the Black Eagle.

Wanda checked that Sylvie was peacefully asleep in her carriage and then sat down on the forest floor. The soil had soaked up the summer heat and felt soft and warm.

It was time she took some of the load off Richard's shoulders! She could write out cards with descriptions of the individual pieces. She could pack the glassware. Perhaps she could even look into advertising the event? She had heard that Lauscha would soon have its own print shop, so it would be no trouble to have a few flyers and brochures printed up.

Wanda squeezed her eyes shut as a bright beam of sunlight shot down through the high treetops.

She wasn't quite clear on where they could hand out the flyers. But weren't there plenty of other things she could attend to?

Richard hadn't mentioned a catalog for the exhibition. Was Gotthilf Täuber planning to do one? If so, who was going to write the captions?

All at once she stood up, brushed the moss and leaves from her skirt, and turned the carriage around.

Great Heavens, here she was taking strolls in the woods when there was work waiting for her at home. After all, Richard's success—or failure—would determine what her future would look like as well. It would be a great deal more pleasant to be the wife of a successful glassblower than of a starving artist. When she looked at it like that, she had no choice but to be by his side right away.

Late July 1911

"It's madness to come to the bakehouse in heat like this. No wonder we're the only names on the list." Eva sighed and swept a lock of hair off her forehead. Then she went to the long table along the bakehouse wall and lifted a cloth. She prodded the fourteen loaves of bread, testing each one with a practiced finger to see whether the dough had risen enough.

"These are fine," she said. "If the oven's hot enough by now, we can put them in!"

Wanda cast a yearning glance outside, where Sylvie was sitting in the shade of a linden tree and babbling contentedly to herself.

It was late July, and it seemed that the summer heat couldn't get any worse. It had already been warm when they loaded up their handcart with the bread dough early that morning. Now that it was almost noon, she found it hard to breathe. Perhaps she should have chosen another day to ask Eva to teach her how to bake bread.

It might have been a better idea to spend the day making rags for a new rug? Then she would have been sitting comfortably in the shade by the side of the house, tearing up old cloth into little strips.

Housework—Richard didn't seem to trust her to do anything else, Wanda thought irritably as she followed Eva to the huge oven. As soon as they opened the oven door, the bakehouse grew even hotter.

Richard had thanked Wanda for her offer of help with his exhibition, but he had turned her down. Since this was the biggest challenge of his life so far, he said, it was important that he face it alone. It was the only way he would really feel that he had done all that was necessary.

What could Wanda say to that? She had tried not to let her disappointment show. But it wasn't simply that she wasn't allowed to help him—Richard had no time for her at all! He always had his sketchbook in hand, and wherever he went, he drew sketches of extra pieces that he wanted to include in the exhibition. When he wasn't busy drawing, he sat at his workbench, either working in total silence or cursing so loudly that it made Wanda flinch. How could a man be so driven? At such moments, he didn't even notice that she was there. Once she had worked up the nerve to approach him from behind and put her arms around his shoulders. She had just wanted a cuddle, a few caresses—there was never any chance of anything more here in the village, where the walls seemed to have ears—but Richard had sat up with a start and then gently pushed her away. "That very nearly went wrong," he said, pointing to the glasswork that he was holding in the flame.

Glass, of course.

What chance did she have against glass?

Wanda had left. That evening, he had come by and asked her to bear with him. It was a difficult time for both of them right now, he said, but once the exhibition had opened he would have more time for her.

I'll believe that when I see it, Wanda had wanted to say. Why couldn't Richard just stop work by the evening? The way other glassblowers did? Why did he have to work through half the night?

And then Wanda answered her own question. It was because he didn't see the work as work. He enjoyed it.

She was so lost in her thoughts that she was startled when she felt a nudge in her ribs.

"Look there, don't they look like yellow fleas hopping all over the floor?"

Wanda looked skeptically at the orange sparks that were all that was left of the beechwood fire.

"It looks to me more as though the fire's about to go out."

"Nonsense, child! This is just how it should be. You need patience to bake bread. And then you have to choose just the right moment!" Eva hurried from the table to the oven door and back again, putting one loaf after another into the oven to bake.

Wanda stood and watched. She had given up trying to help Eva a while back: before she had even washed her hands, Eva had been up to her elbows in dough. When they had made the dough the night before, Wanda had wanted to knead as well, but she very soon found out what hard work it was. Not even five minutes had passed before her arms were trembling so badly that Eva simply took over. When it came time to shape the dough into loaves, Eva worked three times as fast as Wanda, who had trouble handling the sticky mass.

Baking bread was not only hard work, it was boring. And she wasn't cut out for it—Wanda was sure of that by now. She had imagined that baking bread must be a cheerful, friendly business, two women laughing and chatting as they worked the dough. She had also imagined that they might have time for a little treat while the dough was rising, that all the women might bring something to share—a jug of apple juice, a dish of berries . . . It would have been a good opportunity to meet the other young women in the village and perhaps make new friends.

But instead it was just the two of them in the heat, and Eva holding forth on what made good and bad bread. Naturally Eva's own bread was the best, while the other women in the village only made nasty stuff that was the texture of cotton wool.

"You know Martha, Karl Flein's wife, don't you?" Eva called over her shoulder as she wiped down the table with a damp cloth.

Wanda suppressed a yawn as she nodded.

"Well, Martha never kneads her dough; she just stirs it about . . ."

Wanda's eyelids were growing heavier.

"Her loaves have no shape, no shape to them at all . . ."

Would Eva be upset if she went out to join Sylvie under the tree for a while? She decided not even to ask, but simply to slip out of the bakehouse.

She had just put her hand on the door handle when she called out in surprise.

"Heavens above—Karl! We . . . we always seem to bump into each other in doorways!" Wanda said, forcing a laugh that came out too loud.

He looked so serious! Almost angry. She hoped Karl hadn't heard Eva speaking ill of his wife's baking.

"I'm not alone," Karl said, and pointed over his shoulder. Gustav Müller and Martin Ehrenpreis were standing in the shade of the tree.

"What is it? Have we done something wrong?" Eva snapped. Although she was putting on a brave front, Wanda could tell that she was unsettled. "We brought our own firewood, don't you worry; we're not baking at anybody else's expense!"

Karl Flein shook his head brusquely.

"We're here to speak to Wanda! Your father told us you'd be down here. It's like this . . ." He turned to his colleagues, looking for help, but they simply nodded at him to go on.

"It's about the foundry . . . We've thought about it . . ."

Wanda frowned. "Yes?"

"Well, we'd be willing to give your idea a try."

CHAPTER EIGHTEEN

"And then he put the money in my hand and said that he and Gustav Müller and Martin Ehrenpreis were ready to be the first to pay their share for the new venture."

Wanda's hands shook as she held out a wooden box to Richard. It was full of bundles of worn banknotes. Then she pointed to the little notebook that came with the box.

"Karl kept note of who gave exactly how much." Wanda felt a pang as she looked at the careful handwriting, the lines drawn neatly from each name to each amount. "They really gave everything that they had. All of their savings, and all of their available cash as well . . . It looks like some of them make good money from Christmas ornaments." She glanced over at the carriage. Sylvie was whimpering softly. The baby should have been in bed by now, but since Eva was visiting family in Steinach, Wanda had had no choice but to take her along when she went to see Richard.

She had expected him to come to the Heimer household for supper. When he didn't show up, she had put the baby into the carriage along with the box and the documents and gone to find him. He had to hear this wonderful news directly from her!

But Richard looked as though he still couldn't believe the news. Or rather, as though he didn't want to believe it.

"And then Karl and the others went through the village looking for other . . . investors?" he asked, frowning.

Wanda nodded. She lifted Sylvie out of the carriage and rocked her gently back and forth. The child calmed down right away.

"And he sent them all to me. He said that since the whole thing had been my idea, it was only right that I should be in charge of it all. He also said that since I'm a neutral party, people would feel better entrusting their money to me . . ." She laughed. Her gaze fell on the shabby rag rug on the floor, and she made a face. Unfortunately she wouldn't have much spare time in the next few weeks to look after Richard's cottage.

"Those three . . . they must have gone around the whole village, door-to-door!" Her voice was filled with excitement. "People were coming up the hill to see us all afternoon! Oh, Richard, I wish you could have seen it!" Wanda shut her eyes for a moment.

"I knew that people were still talking about your idea, but I had no idea that they were taking it so seriously . . . that they were planning anything like this."

Wanda nudged him playfully in the ribs. "Well, were they supposed to ask your permission first? Is that why you're making such a sour face? You never wanted to have anything to do with it, you said so yourself." She lifted Sylvie up and sniffed. She needed to be changed again. Wanda got to her feet with a sigh and looked in her bag for a fresh diaper.

"That's still true!" Richard said loudly. He leafed through the notebook. "Christoph Stanzer, Oskar Hille, Gustav Müller, Griseldis—there must be at least twenty names here . . ." He whistled softly. "Christoph Stanzer gave a lot!"

Wanda nodded. "He gave me all the money that he got from the government in compensation for his timber rights. He told me that when they lost the right to chop firewood for free, that was the beginning of the end for the old main foundry, but now that money should be the beginning of something new! Isn't that marvelous? Of course, he'll have to have an important post in the new foundry. If I understand it right, he had quite an important job when he worked for the old foundry. But we don't have to figure all that out yet. For now we've just decided that Karl will take care of the organizational side of things and I will look after the finances."

"You'll look after the finances!" Richard exclaimed. "What are you, a bank? A financial expert? What does your father say about all this?"

"Father? He was just as astonished as I was. But as more and more people came and gave their money, he said he'd look into whether he couldn't contribute a small sum as well. Just as a sign of his solidarity, he said." Wanda smiled as she put the baby on the table. "What a day! I'm still quite overwhelmed!" she said as she took Sylvie's dirty diaper off.

Richard waved his hand in front of his face, disgusted.

"Christoph Stanzer told me that in the old days the master glassmakers all used to own and run their own workshops inside the foundry. It turns out my idea isn't really new at all. In fact it's something that has worked very well in the past."

"In that case, I wonder why the men even bother you with it!" Richard grumbled, but Wanda ignored him. She was still far too excited about the day's amazing turn of events.

Every single person who had stopped by had had his or her own reasons for wanting to be part of buying the foundry, and every single one of them had wanted to tell Wanda about it in detail. Most of them currently worked in the foundry. But others weren't involved in it at all. Griseldis, who worked for Johanna, had explained that she wanted to take out a mortgage on her house and buy her son Magnus a share in the foundry. She could tell that Magnus and

Johanna were due for a falling out soon. Without a hint of resentment, Griseldis said she knew that Johanna had never liked her son and she had only ever put up with Magnus for Marie's sake. Shares in the Gründler foundry would give Magnus his independence, so Griseldis had asked Wanda to put her down for a considerable sum. She would bring the money as soon as the bank had granted the mortgage.

"And all the money's here in this box? And it all corresponds to the amounts noted down in this notebook?" Richard asked.

Wanda nodded. "What a silly question!" she said, concentrating on the safety pins for Sylvie's new diaper. "Do you really think I'd keep any for myself?"

"Give me the money!" Richard ordered. Before Wanda could say or do anything, he had grabbed the box and the notebook. His eyes were blazing, and the skin under his left eye pulsed nervously.

"What . . . You can't just . . . Richard! Where are you going?" Wanda tried to grab him by the sleeve, but he broke away.

He turned around and fixed her with a look that said, *Don't you dare try to stop me!*

Then the door swung closed.

Wanda wanted to run after him, but her feet were rooted to the spot. She wanted to call out, "You can't just take all that money! It doesn't belong to you!" but her throat was so tight she could not speak.

Sylvie began to whimper and complain. Stunned, Wanda glanced from the door to the crying baby and the dirty diaper next to her.

Richard had taken the money! And now he had run off who knew where. While she was stuck here with Sylvie . . .

What in Heaven's name did it all mean?

CHAPTER NINETEEN

Benno looked in astonishment at the door of the Black Eagle as it slammed shut for the second time in minutes.

"Can anybody tell me what that was all about?" he asked, directing his question to everyone in the tavern. "First Richard comes running in, slams the money on the table and tells us that Wanda has had second thoughts and wants nothing more to do with the whole thing." He pointed at the middle of the table, where the wooden box had stood just a few moments ago.

"Didn't he look pleased with himself—as though he thought Wanda had changed her mind just in time!" young Hansen said. "Perhaps he had something to do with changing her mind for her! Maybe our fine artist doesn't like that his fiancée wanted to help us out?"

Karl Flein shook his head. "And then not ten minutes later Wanda herself comes in talking about some sort of 'regrettable mis-understanding' and swearing up and down that nothing's changed and saying that of course she still wants to help. I don't understand it a bit . . ."

"Why does she have to be involved at all?" Hansen said. "Any one of us could look after the money just as well! It's not as though we're unreliable. I was against working with the American girl right from the start." He stared into his beer with a sour look on his face.

"Without the American girl there wouldn't even have been a start, don't forget that!" Karl Flein said.

"And she knows how to deal with banks. Thomas says that she's even studied business. That's more than any of us can say, isn't it?" Gustav Müller looked across the table at young Hansen, who ignored him. "It's not just that our money's safe with her, she might even help us get the loan. I suggest we ask Wanda to come with us to talk to the bank!"

*   *   *

"How could you?" Wanda hissed, her voice choked. Her heart was still pounding in her chest as she struggled for air. She had hurried home to drop off Sylvie—luckily Eva was back from her trip to Steinach—and then run to the Black Eagle. Then she went back to Richard's place. But it was more than just the effort of running all that way that made it hard to breathe. It was the tumult of her feel-ings—rage, hurt, confusion, fear.

"What must they think of me now? I look like a spoiled brat who doesn't know her own mind!" She closed her eyelids for a moment as though she didn't want to see her own shame.

Shame because Richard had made her look ridiculous.

Shame because for a moment she had thought he had run away with the money . . .

"And what must they think of me? Have you thought of that?" Richard shouted back at her. "You've completely disregarded my decision—they must be laughing themselves silly!" He slammed his hand against the wooden box that Wanda had brought back with her, as though he wanted to smash it to smithereens.

Wanda sank down into one of the chairs.

"We're getting nowhere like this." She glanced around Richard's cottage, trying to rest her gaze on one of the old familiar objects: the copper baking tin, the stove that was so hard to light, the frayed rag rug. But it all looked strange to her now, small and insignificant. Meaningless compared to Richard's betrayal.

"Can't you just tell me why you did it?" she asked sadly.

"Because I'm not stupid!" he shot back, with an arrogant note in his voice that implied, *unlike you.* "You have no idea what you're getting yourself into! As if such a thing could ever possibly succeed! They're just taking advantage of you. And then, when something goes wrong, they'll blame you for it!"

He pulled up a chair and sat down. For the first time, his proximity made Wanda feel uneasy. She would much rather that he carry on pacing the room like a lion.

"Wanda, please see reason! You don't need to get mixed up in this . . ." He tried to take her hand, but Wanda snatched it away.

"It's not about what I do or don't need," she snapped. "It's about something wonderful happening here in Lauscha, and all you can do is criticize. Aren't you pleased to see people finding their courage?"

"Courage or no courage—all I'm saying is that this has nothing to do with you!" Richard said heavily. "It will all come to nothing anyway," he muttered.

Wanda snorted contemptuously. "You talk like an old man! You're even worse than Father was when I first met him. There aren't many people who are ready to change the world for the better. I thought that you were one of them—after all, you're bold enough when it comes to shaping your own fate. But woe betide anyone else who dares to do the same! And you certainly don't want to see me take charge, oh no!" Her eyes glowed like coals. She felt the rage rising inside her again, felt her hackles rise.

He hadn't wanted her help! Her mother was right. If it were up to him, she would just cook and clean and take care of Sylvie. And he was jealous when other people thought that she was capable of more than that—why?

"Wanda, Wanda . . ." Richard shook his head. An almost imperceptible smile flitted across his lips. "I only want you to be happy! I know very well by now that you grab life like you're taking a bull by the horns. You don't need to prove anything to me, or to anybody else, either. Just look how well you're taking care of Sylvie. Look what a help you've been to your father."

This time Wanda let him take her hand. *What am I to you?* she wanted to ask. *What will you let me do for you?* But she said nothing.

"Why do you want to take on one more task?"

She looked at him and saw from his face that the question was honestly meant. She calmed down a little. He wasn't her enemy. He was Richard, the man she loved. The man who loved her. The man who wanted her to be happy. Despite everything . . .

"Because . . ." She shrugged. "Because . . ."

"*He'd set you to fetch and carry, nothing more!*" Wanda heard her mother's voice in her ear.

Before she could find the words to answer him, Richard waved his question away.

"Look, by this time next year, you'll be my wife and you'll be in charge of your own household. I'm sure Sylvie will have a little brother or sister soon. When the art lovers come flooding in to visit after the exhibition, somebody will have to tend to them, say a few kind words so that they'll open their wallets! Who can do that better than my beautiful American?" He laughed. "Somebody will have to keep them from bothering me! You'd best get used to the idea now and realize that you won't have time for all these other daydreams."

"Daydreams! Well really, I—"

"Now, now, let's not quarrel again," Richard said before Wanda could get worked up again. "As for this business with the Gründler foundry: if it's that important to you, then go ahead and keep the money for Karl and the others until they go to the bank. That, I hope, will be the end of the matter. And then perhaps we can spend our time on other things . . ." He smiled in a way that was probably supposed to be encouraging—but which Wanda found overbearing—and then he stood up and pulled her in his arms. Wanda had trouble enjoying his caresses—he was holding her too tight; he was trying too hard to be tender. *Like a father who wants to comfort a child but has more important things to do with his time*, she thought, then scolded herself for such an ungracious feeling.

* * *

Richard's wish was not to be fulfilled. Early in August, eight days after he and Wanda had quarreled, everybody who had contributed any amount of money, large or small, to the wooden box met at the Black Eagle. Karl Flein, Gustav Müller, Martin Ehrenpreis, and Christoph Stanzer were all there, along with some twenty-five others. Only Griseldis was missing, for after talking it over with her son and realizing that he wanted nothing to do with the foundry, she had taken her name off the list. The purpose of the evening was to draw up and sign the statutes defining the terms of the new venture.

Everybody who invested now would own a share of the foundry later. They raised their tankards again and again to drink to the success of their plan. Christoph Stanzer, who had once been the master glassmaker at one of the other foundries in the village, made a little speech saying that the Gründler foundry should be what the old foundry had been for three hundred years—the center of Lauscha, a gathering place for the whole village, a place where everybody belonged. Benno served a round of drinks on the house when he heard the speech.

Otto Gründler was there as well, sitting in his usual spot and basking in the approval of his fellow men. It was agreed that Karl

Flein, Martin Ehrenpreis, and Gustav Müller would go to Sonneberg to visit the bank and apply for a loan. Otto Gründler declared the three of them could have the day off from work for the purpose, and he beamed as though the whole thing had been his idea. He wanted to see a Lauscha foundry stay in Lauscha hands, so he would give the Lauscha investors the same chance as the Sonneberg wholesaler—whose name he had still refused to divulge. As long as the investors managed to find the money for the purchase by September 20, he'd seal the deal with them and the wholesaler could go hang. But if the villagers couldn't come up with the money . . .

The glassblowers waved away the suggestion. Of course they would get the money! Given the starting capital they had already gathered, the matter of a loan was a mere formality.

Everybody approved of Gustav Müller's suggestion that Wanda should go with them to the bank. An American who was trained in financial matters and knew important businessmen like Mr. Woolworth was exactly who they needed for this negotiation. Just look at the way the girl had gotten Thomas Heimer's old workshop back on its feet! That told them all they needed to know. Wanda tried again and again to explain that she hadn't had much training in finance, but nobody listened. Instead they declared that she was modest as well, and that that was another virtue.

In the end Wanda had no choice but to let them celebrate her as a gifted businesswoman.

Richard sat by and watched with a grim look on his face.

CHAPTER TWENTY

Wanda was so blinded by the sun as she climbed down the steps from the train that she stumbled and almost fell onto the platform. She bumped straight into the woman who had gotten out just before her. There was a jingle of glass. The woman was carrying a heavy pack of glassware on her back and more pieces in a bag besides. She cursed loudly, but stopped when she saw who had jostled her.

"Ah, it's the American girl! Well, I wish you luck! Today's the big day, isn't it . . . ?" She looked at Wanda and her three companions with something like awe.

"We could certainly use some luck," Wanda replied, shielding her eyes from the bright sunlight.

"Luck's what you make of it!" said Karl Flein.

It was still well before noon, but the sun was already high in the sky.

If only I'd brought a parasol, Wanda thought as they left the railway station. She had decided against it because she thought it might make too frivolous an impression. After all, she didn't want to appear to be a dainty little miss, but rather a woman of the world. A businesswoman.

Wanda snorted. As it was, this woman of the world would soon turn up at the bank dripping with sweat, which would hardly make a good impression, either . . .

"It's glorious weather, isn't it?" Karl Flein said, laughing, as he set off for the main square.

"Bright skies for a bright future," Gustav Müller added with a laugh.

"Let's look on the bright side, then," Martin Ehrenpreis chuckled.

Wanda took a deep breath. This could get awkward.

The men had undergone a transformation as the train traveled from Lauscha to Sonneberg. When they had set out, they were serious, sober men, hard workers and good neighbors, but as they got closer to town, they had turned into chuckling schoolboys. At first Wanda had laughed along with them, glad to see that the men were in good spirits on such an important day. But when she had tried to bring the conversation around to their meeting at the bank and to talk about how they might make their case, her words had fallen on deaf ears. The men had kept on with their jokes, so much so that other passengers in the compartment had cast irritated glances their way.

Wanda found herself thinking of her journey south with Richard. He had acted in much the same way. Not himself. Uncertain. Aggressive.

Wanda exhaled softly.

Richard. Thank goodness he wasn't here today. And that her father wasn't. She didn't need either of them! Though it would have been nice to have a supportive hand to hold, someone to lean on. Wanda sighed.

"I'm so glad the big day is finally here!" she had said to Richard that morning when he came by for breakfast. "All this waiting is practically driving me mad!"

Richard had looked at her—first with surprise and then beaming with pleasure—and said that he was excited as well, that he was looking forward to seeing the rooms that Täuber wanted to show him. They were making good progress . . . Then he had taken a hearty bite of bread with jam.

Richard hadn't even known what she had been talking about. Even though the whole village was talking about it! To him, his exhibition in Meiningen was more important. So much more important that he hadn't even wished her luck.

A shudder passed through Wanda. What on earth had she let herself in for? Why hadn't she simply said no when the others had asked her to come to Sonneberg? What did she know about the world of finance? Granted, she had grown up in a business household. And she had been engaged to a New York banker for a while. But did that really count as experience with banks and business? She had tried to explain all that to the men.

Then they had said at least she could come along as moral support. A pretty and articulate young woman from New York would certainly make a good impression. Perhaps she could even mention Steven Miles. Wanda's stepfather was hardly a stranger to Sonneberg, after all; he was a valued business partner for many of the wholesalers and craftsmen.

Karl would do all the talking. All Wanda had to do was keep her eyes and ears open, just in case, so to speak.

Moral support—that sounded harmless enough. Why did she feel so responsible then? None of these three had any experience with banks. Karl was the only one who even had a savings account with the local Lauscha bank. He had decided that it would be no good for a loan, though, declaring that it was a bank for "the little people." Clearly he thought that he and the others who had signed on for the venture were above all that now.

Karl had decided they would go to Grosse & Sons, the biggest and richest bank in all of Sonneberg. Grosse & Sons had financial experts who specialized in unusual business ventures, and they would certainly see the potential in the Gründler foundry. Wanda and the others had no objection. Quite the opposite, in fact, as the men all seemed to know somebody who had been turned down for a loan by one of the other banks. Times were hard and the banks were being careful with their money. But none of the people involved in the foundry had ever approached Grosse & Sons for a loan.

All the same, Wanda hadn't wanted to rely entirely on hearsay, so she had asked the only man she knew in Sonneberg, the bookseller Alois Sawatzky, when he was recently in Lauscha.

Sawatzky had been very pleased to see Wanda. Over tea he had scolded her gently for only coming to Sonneberg to see him once since she had returned to Lauscha. That had been when she had told him in a tearful voice about Marie's death. He had been a close friend of her Aunt Marie.

The bookseller had had good things to say about Grosse & Sons, which had an excellent reputation in Sonneberg and beyond. When they had said good-bye, Wanda had promised to visit Sawatzky more often in the future.

Sawatzky's words about the bank had confirmed the investors' decision, and it wasn't long before they made an appointment to talk to the bank.

At their last meeting in the Black Eagle, Wanda had suggested speaking to her stepfather, Steven Miles, about the venture. Perhaps he would be willing to put some money into it, as a silent partner? Then they wouldn't need to ask the bank for a loan at all and they could buy themselves some time as well. But the others wouldn't hear of it. An American investor? They might as well sell the foundry to a stranger! That would leave them dependent on someone else's goodwill, just like before. They didn't seem to realize that the bank would be a stranger as well—if it gave them a loan at all—and that they would be just as dependent on the bank in that case. They preferred a Sonneberg bank to a New York businessman, and that was that.

"Be careful!" Thomas Heimer had told his daughter that morning before she set out. "Whenever we Lauscha folk turn up in Sonneberg, they treat us like hillbillies. I'm sure those bank people will rob you blind if you let them!"

Wanda had laughed and told him not to always think the worst of people.

"Is it much farther? I thought that Grosse & Sons was right on the main square," Wanda said, more to have a chance to catch her breath than because she really wanted to ask the way. She stopped in the middle of the sidewalk and fanned her face with her hand.

"We're nearly there," Karl Flein said. "Grosse & Sons is behind the town hall, didn't you know?"

Wanda shrugged. "I've only ever been on the main square once. I was with Johanna, and she was in a hurry." *As always*, Wanda thought.

Gustav Müller shook his head. "I don't understand your aunt. If I had a visitor from America, I'd spend all my time showing her around! No effort would be too great. And my wife would do the same, I'm sure. It seems to me you hardly ever left the workshop!"

Wanda said nothing. The man was right; from the very start, her time in Lauscha had not been the usual sort of visit to relatives. Johanna had had no time for sightseeing: there was always far too much to do in the workshop. Her cousin Johannes had shown her around Lauscha, though, and that was how she had met Richard, after all.

But Sonneberg was a very pretty little town! The tall, narrow houses, each of which had a shop or a business on the ground floor. The picturesque streetlamps. The buckets full of fresh-cut flowers in front of the florist's shop. While Lauscha was a cozy little village where everyone knew everyone else, this larger town had something of the anonymity that she knew from New York. She was rather startled to find how much she enjoyed being able to walk down the street without being greeted by a familiar face every few yards. The streets were so lively that Wanda was tempted to skip the bank meeting altogether and go shopping instead. She could hardly remember what it felt like to browse through shops, to have assistants show her their lovely merchandise, to run fabric through her fingers, to hold a silk flower up to her lapel, to choose between two different styles of shawls! She resolved to do so again as soon as possible. Perhaps she could take Sylvie and Eva with her? She would buy Eva something nice for all her help, something fashionable. But who had time or interest for fashion in Lauscha?

She glanced at her companions. All three of them were wearing their Sunday best, which meant that even though it was the height of summer, Karl was wearing a pair of heavy leather boots polished to a high gleam. Martin Ehrenpreis's belly bulged beneath his embroidered waistcoat so that the gilded buttons were almost bursting out of their buttonholes. Gustav Müller's long-sleeved shirt was neatly ironed, but it was hanging out of his pants at the back.

Wanda had to smile. The men didn't really make a very businesslike impression. But did that really matter? Wasn't it more important that they had a sound business proposition?

"Do you think you're going to a state banquet?" Eva had asked mockingly when Wanda had fetched her dark-blue silk outfit from the wardrobe. She was wearing low shoes with it and a hat, and she carried a matching handbag.

The last time she had worn this outfit had been on the crossing from New York to Hamburg. It had made her feel grown up, self-assured. And the clothes had symbolized a new start for her. She did her best to ignore the fact that the new start had turned out entirely differently from what she had expected.

CHAPTER TWENTY-ONE

August fills the larder so that September can eat—where had he heard that saying before?

David Wagner stared out the window. It took him a moment to remember that his grandmother had always said that. As a child, he and his siblings had often helped her out in the field, and she always told them all kinds of old country sayings.

Grandmother's field—who harvested the oats there now? And did the new owner plant potatoes as well?

August was harvest time. Out in the fields and meadows the crops were ripening, getting ready to be gathered.

Only his own life was barren. As dry and parched as the ground around the chestnut tree he saw outside his window.

What old country saying would his grandmother—God rest her soul—have for him now? Cobbler, stick to your last, perhaps?

He only had two meetings scheduled in his appointment book for this morning. The second looked quite promising. But the first . . . David made a face. A look at the clock told him that the clients—glassblowers from Lauscha—were probably already waiting outside the door. *Well, let them wait*, he thought, though he felt a little ashamed as he did so.

Power spoke softly.

He would have liked to roll up his sleeves, undo the top buttons of his shirt, and open the windows wide to get some fresh air. He hated sweating—and suffocating—in this confined office.

Instead he stood up, went to the little mirror that he had hidden behind a filing cabinet, and checked his tie. Dark-gray silk, slightly worn at the place where he tied the knot day in and day out, but otherwise most presentable. The dark tone made his skin look pale. Did it make him look like a recluse? Like a man who was never invited anywhere? A man who spent his days in his office and his evenings sitting all alone in a rented room?

David frowned and stared at his shirt. He calmed down. His shirt was snowy white, the collar a little too stiff but almost free of wrinkles—yes, he was slowly getting the hang of using the iron.

He smiled as he remembered the face his landlady had made the first time he asked for hot coals for the iron. Apparently she had never heard of a man ironing his own clothes. *Well, who else is going to do it?* he had almost asked. He didn't earn enough to send his laundry out. And he couldn't let them do it at home—neither his mother nor his sisters knew how to deal with the fine clothes he wore now. They would probably have scorched the fabric on the first try! So he went up to his attic room in the evenings and ironed his clothes. Wasn't the first impression the most important? Would the businessmen of this world take him seriously if he turned up looking like a beggar? No, he was quite pleased with the way he looked: mature, experienced, and businesslike.

Power spoke softly.

And dressed well.

Which was why it was important to make a good impression even when there were just a few meager craftsmen sitting outside his door, waiting for their chance to tell him their tale of woe and ask for a loan.

Don't look, concentrate on your work, David told himself as he went back to his desk. But all the same his glance fell on the stack of newspapers that he had bought before he came in to work, and he was already reaching for the first in the pile to have a look at the headlines. He would have liked to read it from cover to cover, but that would have to wait.

Like so much else.

Why couldn't someone just march into his office, drop a fortune onto his desk, and say, "There you go, get to work!" Shares, loans, foreign exchange—oh, he already knew what he would do to make the money grow! He had his reasons for reading such a mountain of newspapers and journals—he even read the occasional women's magazine! He tried to keep them hidden among all the others. But he had already found out, for instance, that there were large companies in America that made a fortune producing nothing but lipstick, blush, and face cream. It was worth bearing that in mind—maybe one of those companies would list shares? You could make good money off women's vanity if you picked your moment. And so he invested a good portion of his salary in these newspapers and journals, which he collected every week from Alois Sawatzky's shop. When he had asked the bookseller whether he could also order specialty publications, they had fallen into conversation. As soon as Sawatzky discovered that David was reading the newspapers and journals to learn more about business—about companies and the world of finance and political developments and so forth—the bookseller had offered to sell him older back issues as well, half-price. David had gratefully taken him up on his offer.

Oh yes, he had his finger on the pulse of the times. He knew where money could be made in this world. He knew what was what. And the director of the bank would eventually recognize this. Of course, his current job—scrutinizing loan applications—was entirely respectable. It was an honor for a young man like him to have such a responsible position, as Gerhard Grosse never tired of reminding him. And David could hardly contradict him on that point. But for all the honor of his current role, he really wanted to be in the stocks and shares department three doors down.

David sighed and adjusted his chair behind the desk. Until the management here at Grosse & Sons recognized his true calling, he would have to spend his time listening to clients make their cases, feigning interest in what they had to say, responding with "Aha" and "I see" at the proper moments, and jotting down notes. He needed to appear both sympathetic and somewhat aloof. Then he would go to Gerhard Grosse and report on each case. But however forcefully he argued on the client's behalf, he knew in advance that his boss would in all likelihood refuse the loan. Or, if he agreed to it, that he would set a horrendous rate of interest.

"Times have changed, young man!" David heard over and over again. "None of us can afford to be softhearted now. Even a bank like ours has to watch its step!" Then he would add his favorite saying: "Better ten lost clients than one lost loan!" Then his boss would slap him on the shoulder and remark that of course, the right client with the right investment would be welcome any time. It was David Wagner's job to attract the right clients with the right investments. To land the big fish. After all, his older colleagues managed that well enough. Did he, David Wagner, want to look like a fool next to his more experienced colleagues? What would the management think of him then? Not that any of this was ever said out loud, of course.

Power spoke softly.

And blocked many a path.

David had learned a long time ago that the rules of the game were different—more nuanced—here at the Grosse & Sons Bank in Sonneberg.

Where he came from—the little village of Steinach, just a few miles away—the rules were simple. Whoever brought the money home from the slate quarry had power. Since this was mostly the men, that meant that they had the right to yell and shout and get their way, to threaten and bluster to no end. The men who came to him here, hats in hand, begging for loans, were the very same ones who boasted and bragged every evening in the tavern that David's father kept. That was how a man made his mark there.

In Steinach, power shouted at the top of its voice.

Why are you wasting time with such thoughts? David scolded himself. It wasn't like him to daydream like this, especially about Steinach and his family. He glanced at the clock. Nearly nine thirty—time to ask his next clients to come in. David adjusted his tie one last time and pressed the brass button that informed his receptionist that he was ready for business.

CHAPTER TWENTY-TWO

"We are here to represent the Gründler Foundry Company, which we are just in the process of setting up!" Wanda forced a smile. "We have nine founding members, as required by law, and have drawn up all the necessary paperwork." The bank official looked from her to his other three visitors and nodded. Wanda had no idea what that nod meant. Why didn't he say anything? He must have a thousand questions! And why weren't the others saying anything? Hadn't they agreed that she would only be there to lend moral support? That Karl would do all the talking? Instead the three men sat there, shifting around uncomfortably on their chairs.

So what choice did she have but to start talking once David Wagner finally agreed to see them? The long wait in the sparsely decorated reception room, the stern looks that the secretary gave them every time one of the visitors dared so much as cough, the absurdly fragile chairs that no normal man could sit on comfortably—none of that had soothed the glassblowers' nerves one bit. There was nothing left now of Karl's earlier bravado, when he had declared, "We'll show this bank fellow that he's dealing with real entrepreneurs!" and "He'll jump at the chance to give us a loan!" When they were finally called in to his office, it took almost forever for the four of them to sit down. Largely because the men insisted that Wanda should sit directly in front of Wagner's desk, while Wanda would rather have sat in the back, on the chair by the door. She had finally acquiesced just to put an end to it.

That had turned out to be a mistake—by taking that chair, she had automatically taken on the role of spokeswoman for the whole group.

She turned to Karl and nodded encouragingly at him, which was supposed to mean "Now say something!" but all he did was nod back at her in silence.

"Here to represent the new company, I understand . . ." David Wagner cleared his throat. Judging from the look on his face, though, Wanda could tell that he didn't understand much, especially why a young woman and three old glassblowers should be coming to see him on the same business.

Wanda leaned over his desk. She could smell her own perfume as she did so—perhaps she had put on a little too much? She sniffed the air cautiously and only then realized that it was David Wagner's aftershave—a much sharper scent that her own. She frowned. The man must be rather vain.

"It's really rather urgent, don't you see? Mr. Gründler has agreed to give us until mid-September to come up with the rest of the money. I am aware, of course, that approving a loan involves a certain number of formalities and that these can take time . . ." She fixed Wagner with a look that meant, *So get on with it! We are important people, and important people don't have time to waste.*

"You are quite right there, miss . . ."

"Miles," Wanda answered with a winning smile. "I am the step-daughter of Steven Miles, who owns a large trading company in New York, you may perhaps have heard of—" Wanda stopped when Gustav Müller leaned forward.

"David Wagner," he muttered to himself. He was staring at the bank official as though at a two-headed calf.

Wanda realized that David Wagner was trying to stare Gustav down. She cleared her throat to get Gustav to look her way. In the end, though, it was Wagner who looked away first, suddenly busying himself with the papers Wanda had given him. The pages outlined the company's existing capital and the number of investors, and contained Otto Gründler's signature declaring himself ready to accept the new company as a potential purchaser—Wanda had written everything down neatly and clearly. Why didn't he say anything? The documents had to make some sort of impression.

"I keep thinking I know him from somewhere," Gustav whispered into Wanda's ear.

"That's no reason to stare at him!" she answered just as quietly. "Mr. Wagner has to concentrate." She was, however, tempted to stare at David Wagner much the same way.

The man was so young! Given the reputation of the Grosse & Sons bank—and the way the glassblowers had spoken about it—Wanda had expected to find herself sitting across from a grizzled old man. But David Wagner couldn't have been older than his late twenties, if that, and not even his old-fashioned suit and formal manner could disguise his youth.

Now Wagner was busy copying some of the figures from Wanda's dossier onto a form of his own. That was a start! His eyes gleamed like two live coals as he worked, but that didn't mean he was any worse at his job, did it? And the fact that he had a certain amount of roguish good looks didn't mean that he had no head for figures.

All of a sudden Wanda found herself thinking of Harold, her former fiancé. Did he have to deal with the same sort of skepticism that she felt about Mr. Wagner right now? He had been even younger than Wagner when his bank appointed him manager of the New Mexico branch.

Wanda couldn't have said why, but she would have preferred to deal with an old man with pale eyes and an arrogant manner, than with this handsome young fellow with the gleaming eyes and the dark locks of hair that kept falling down over his forehead. As she watched, he stuck out his lower lip and tried once again to puff the hair away unobtrusively. Wanda had to suppress a giggle.

David Wagner looked up briefly from his papers. "The matter is somewhat complicated . . ." he said slowly. "As you know, there is a second interested party who wishes to purchase the foundry. The gentleman is . . . also a client of our bank, a valued client of many years' standing, if I may say so. We are negotiating with him on the same matter and have been doing so for some time." He looked meaningfully at Wanda.

"You are wondering whether this would be a conflict of interest?" she squeaked in a high voice. Drat it all! None of them had even realized that the bank might not even consider their application in the first place.

The bank official shrugged apologetically. "Loans are made for a specific purpose. This means that we can hardly issue two loans for the same prospect. In this case it's rather like buying property. When there are several interested parties, as a rule we must favor the purchaser with the best credit rating. That's simply the way banks operate these days. In this instance your . . . rival has applied for a significantly smaller loan and can also offer convincing collateral. Unlike you . . . You are asking for a loan of fifty-four thousand marks, which is quite a large sum even for our bank."

"The wholesaler! Convincing collateral, pah!" Karl spat out the words before Wanda could stop him. "Have you ever wondered how your wholesaler client got so rich?" he asked, leaning in toward Wagner. "On the backs of us glassblowers, that's how!"

"Karl . . ." Wanda murmured.

David Wagner didn't flinch. "I'll discuss your application with Mr. Grosse, of course, but I can't offer you much hope in this case." He opened a thick, rather shabby folder and began to leaf through it. When he had found the right page, he ran his finger down a column.

Wanda found that her eyes were following his every movement as though her life depended on it.

"Mr. Gründler would prefer to sell to our company if at all possible, as long as we have the money! If it would help, I could ask Mr. Gründler to confirm this with you personally . . ."

David Wagner nodded, lost in thought, then closed his folder.

"Come back tomorrow afternoon at three o'clock, by which time I will be able to respond in more detail to your application and—"

"The Devil take it! Now I remember!" Gustav burst out. "David Wagner! Son of Wagner the tavern keeper over at Steinach!"

"That's it!" Martin Ehrenpreis said loudly. "I knew I recognized the lad from somewhere! Oh, those were the days, when we always used to stop off for a drink at your dad's place in Steinach on our way home from Sonneberg!" He laughed until his belly shook. "Well look at that! The tavern keeper's son, sitting in Sonneberg's finest bank! Whoever would have thought . . ."

Wanda thought that she would drop dead of embarrassment.

"Martin, Gustav!" she hissed. "This really isn't the time." She smiled apologetically at David. The fire in his eyes had died away, leaving only a cold glimmer.

"He was such a tiny little thing!" Martin Ehrenpreis said to Wanda as though she hadn't spoken. "Tiny!" he repeated, holding out his hand at belly height. "Used to run around between the tables begging for the dregs of beer. And his father is notorious all up and down the valley for—"

Wanda had no desire to hear what David's father was famous—or notorious—for. She cleared her throat so forcefully that she burst into a fit of coughing. At least that made Martin fall quiet.

Wanda snatched up her handbag and got to her feet.

"It's very kind of you to say that you'll have an answer for us tomorrow. We will be here at three o'clock on the dot. Although perhaps I'll come on my own . . ." she added, looking venomously at the men.

CHAPTER TWENTY-THREE

The years had not been kind to Friedhelm Strobel. Anybody who saw him hurrying through the streets of Sonneberg saw a haggard, sour-faced old man who limped a little as he walked. His left leg had never recovered from a sound beating he had received many years ago. But the grimace on his face today had nothing to do with his leg.

He hated the heat. Whenever other people praised the summer sunshine, he felt like hitting them. What was so wonderful about days when the light was so bright that his poor, tired eyes watered? What was so wonderful about the sharp smell of sweat that followed him everywhere, whether he was on his own or with company? And what was so wonderful about swollen feet, sweat pooling at the nape of the neck, and a moist handshake?

The only thing to do on days like this was to stay indoors, in the dark.

Instead, he was in a hurry not to be late for his appointment at the bank! Here he was running through the streets like a fool, and why?

Because of that smug buyer from the Munich department store! He'd been perfectly happy to put threaded glassware on his order forms year in and year out, but now all of a sudden he had decided that the style was no longer à la mode. In fact he'd called it *old-fashioned*—but Strobel didn't believe that for a moment! From the start, the fellow had only been interested in driving the price down.

"Four marks and eighty pennies per dozen is a very good price for real Lauscha glasswork, but I suppose I might be able to make an exception . . . One moment please!" Strobel had said, pulling out his leather-covered notebook and pretending to look through the figures. As it was, the page was quite blank, apart from the reminder that he had an appointment at the bank that day. No social engagements, no invitations, nothing to dispel the monotony of the daily grind. Nothing that would have made it more tolerable to do business with small-minded men such as this Bavarian buyer. And now he wouldn't even be able to get to his bank appointment on time!

He stopped abruptly. Had he remembered to lock the shop door in his hurry? Yes, he could remember turning the key in the lock.

And even if he hadn't, it wouldn't kill him. The days when he had felt a warm glow of pleasure just looking at the fine wood paneling all around his place of business were long gone. These days, he felt bored by the stately solidity of the premises, which didn't even hint at the latest styles but instead embodied timeless good taste. Once upon a time he had taken pride in knowing exactly which wares were stored in each drawer and compartment. Handmade soaps in the baskets on the upper left. Porcelain dolls from Heubach in the middle of the large cabinet. Slate pencils from Steinach down at the bottom, wooden toys in the middle three drawers. And so on and so forth. But after some thirty years, this bored him too.

And besides, the boom days were over. Buyers were becoming ever more demanding, ever more difficult. The man from Munich was no exception in that regard.

Strobel snorted softly. There had been a time when he would have welcomed the challenge of working on a hesitant buyer until his order sheet was full. It had excited him to see how he could influence and manipulate his clients until they danced to his tune as though he were the Pied Piper of Hamelin.

Those times were past. Now it was all about money.

It was hard to explain to the craftsmen of Lauscha that prices for glassware were dropping all the time and that he couldn't stick to the deals they had made long ago. But it was downright impossible to tell them the real truth, which was that the prices were dropping because the wholesalers were engaged in a price war, each of them trying to undercut everyone else.

But those days would soon be over—thank Heaven! On the other hand, Heaven had very little to do with it. Rather, it had everything to do with today's bank appointment and Strobel's nose for a business deal.

With a sly grin, Friedhelm Strobel dabbed the sweat from his brow with a handkerchief. He stopped in front of one of the many shop windows to check his reflection.

No, the years had not been kind to him.

He had lost the chiseled good looks of his youth, which had appealed to men and women alike. Now his face was creased with deep lines. On days such as this one—when he was in a bad mood and burdened by irksome duties—they looked deeper than usual. These were not the shrewd lines of wisdom that came with age; they were the marks left by a lifetime of debauchery.

Strobel lifted his chin, hooded his eyelids, and attempted one of his famous arrogant glances. Once upon a time he had been able to make people squirm with that look.

Strobel swallowed. Carefully, as though he feared he might have fish bones in his throat.

His narrow nose, which had once looked like a falcon's beak, was now only a sharp bump. His nostrils had sunken in and an ugly liver spot spread across the left side of his nose.

And he had once prided himself on having a nose for business! Well, just look at it now.

He raised a hand in greeting to the shopkeeper whose window he was using as a mirror, then marched on. He would have liked to go into the shop and clip the fellow on the ear!

Strobel felt his aggression mounting. He felt that he had to bare his stinger, like a wasp that knows that the long, hot summer is drawing to a close and that it too will die soon.

The Munich buyer had called his wares cheap trash. That would have been unthinkable before. Of course, the buyers had always driven a hard bargain, but none of them would ever have dared to look at him, Friedhelm Strobel, with such overt rudeness as they—

Strobel swallowed again. His mouth was so dry that the corners of his lips were sticking together. The fish bones had gotten stuck in his throat now and were rubbing and tickling.

That buyer had said he wanted *art*—ha! That puffed-up popinjay. Demanded art but only wanted to pay for trash. They were all like that, the lot of them!

Strobel would have been ready to bet his own right hand on the outcome of the bargaining. Once he had lowered his prices one more time—painful though it was—the so-called trash had suddenly been good enough for the fine gentleman from Munich, who ordered in quantities that in earlier days would have put a smile on Strobel's face. But when he looked at the prices he had agreed to for these quantities, he hadn't been able to conjure so much as the ghost of a smile.

It couldn't go on like this.

And that meant that his appointment with the Grosse & Sons bank was perhaps more than just a tiresome duty.

Perhaps he shouldn't unleash his bad temper on that young bank official. What was the lad's name? He had forgotten again. Anyway, the boy could hardly help it if his boss was a self-important windbag who liked to pretend he was too busy to see people. Who told even important clients like Friedhelm Strobel to deal with his younger associates, though they had known one another for at least twenty years! They met every week at the tavern in the Swan Hotel along with the other important men in town, to talk about Sonneberg's fortunes and the state of trade in the town and beyond. Grosse was always open and friendly during the evenings at the Swan, but he was a changed man when he had hooked a client! He clearly thought he didn't need to attend to matters of business in person. When it came to that, he sent an underling.

Strobel took a deep breath and walked into the bank. It made no sense to waste valuable energy on fools like Grosse. One day he'd show the fellow what he really thought of him.

But perhaps there was no need to indulge in such petty dreams. When the realization of a much greater dream awaited him.

Once he owned the Gründler glass foundry, he would be bargaining from quite another position.

How many pieces do you need?

Really, and so soon?

That won't be any problem. I will simply tell my men to work until they have them ready.

Oh, you don't want to pay for that? Or you want to pay less?

No worries, I'll just pay my men less.

You ask whether they'll grumble about that?

Rest assured, they will not. There are plenty of unemployed foundrymen in this world.

Strobel was so lost in his thoughts—thoughts that smoothed the lines of his face and lit the fire of arrogance in his eyes once more—that he didn't notice the young woman who was coming down the hallway toward him.

She was talking over her shoulder to somebody, and she didn't notice the man hurrying toward her.

The collision was more unexpected than painful. The woman gasped aloud in surprise and rubbed her upper arm.

Strobel was just about to snarl, "Don't you have eyes in your head?" when he felt a tingling course through his body. Like goose bumps, but more intense. The tingling settled between his legs and he felt himself stiffen. Slowly, like a dog that catches a hint of an interesting scent, he raised his head. He flared his nostrils. His old nose would serve him one more time . . .

She was young. The rosy skin, the dark eyes, the heart-shaped face . . .

The sight of her troubled Strobel. It was like trying to remember the tune of a long-forgotten song. Who did she remind him of?

She was tall. Almost as tall as he was. And slender. She moved like a young racehorse—a high-spirited, warm-blooded filly. Just as restless, just as . . .

That look in her eyes! So haughty!

The memory broke over him like a wave. The first few bars of the song that was buried so deep inside came back to him now. Oh, how well he knew that look; he had never forgotten it! Back in the day, he had seen that same look in the eyes of a young woman who used it to carefully mask her insecurities. She had seemed proud and arrogant too.

No, nobody could outdo him in that respect. Not then, and not now.

Her name had been Johanna, Johanna Steinmann. Enough, though! He didn't want to think of her. He didn't want to revisit that time in his life.

While he murmured an apology and stepped aside to let three men pass by as well, he shifted his weight from one foot to the other, enjoying the surge of life in his loins. Energy that he had not felt for some time now flooded through him. Bringing back memories that he thought were long lost.

Who was this woman?

What was she doing here?

And how had she gotten here?

Before he could do or say anything to draw her into conversation, she glanced at him one last time and hurried on.

CHAPTER TWENTY-FOUR

"You must see a great deal of the world in your position . . ." Strobel said, nodding meaningfully toward the door. As he grinned at the other man, he racked his brains to think of how he could get this underling to loosen his tongue. A little flattery had done the trick often enough. A little flattery, and most people were putty in his hands. Even if just a moment earlier they had argued in favor of A, when Strobel made a case for B, they would change their minds and agree with him. But if this approach was to work, then at the very least he needed to remember this bank official's name . . . Walter? Wanner? Wagner?

"I do indeed," the young man said, and leaned back in his chair. He folded his hands together behind his head and stretched until his bones cracked.

Strobel bit his tongue, but a moment later he couldn't remain patient.

"The young lady I met out in the hallway just now . . . She looked familiar to me for some reason."

The man stretched his arms again, across the desk toward Strobel this time. "That may well be. Her name's Wanda Miles. She's from Lauscha."

Strobel nodded as though that explained everything. Wanda Miles—he knew the name from somewhere. But before he could put his finger on it, his thoughts scattered.

The way she had lifted her shoulders.

The way she had looked at him. Askance. She hadn't fixed her gaze on him directly, but she hadn't lowered her eyes, either.

"She's very young—it's hard to believe that she could have any business with a bank." Strobel shook his head. "On the other hand," he went on, "you are also very young, and, judging from what I've heard from your superior, you are excellent at your job."

A dubious look flitted over Wagner's face, before he composed himself and assumed a businesslike expression.

"The papers approving your loan are ready. All you need to do is sign here, here, and—"

Strobel waved a hand. "Good, good, thank you, my young friend." He began to chew absentmindedly at a hangnail on his right index finger. How could he bring the conversation back around to that young woman?

He cleared his throat. "Is the young lady a client of the bank?" His voice was just a shade too high, too eager.

The other man shrugged. "I wouldn't go so far as to say that. She came in with three glassblowers and—" Hesitantly, David Wagner began to tell him about the previous meeting.

Strobel listened carefully. Wagner was clearly much more concerned with preserving the bank's confidentiality than with letting Strobel know what had really gone on. But he didn't want to antagonize Strobel by keeping completely silent. It was a tricky situation, and Strobel had to concede that the young man handled it well. He used vague turns of phrase, left sentences unfinished and their significance unspoken. All with great reluctance, as though picking his words with great care. A less attentive listener might have made nothing at all of his explanation, but Strobel understood one thing with certainty: another party was interested in buying the Gründler foundry.

How dare Otto Gründler open negotiations with somebody else? How dare he not tell Strobel about this? Why did he have to hear the news from a low-ranking bank employee?

Somebody was trying to block his purchase.

Normally such a development would have infuriated him. He didn't want any complications. Not now, not with this deal, the investment that would change his whole life and guarantee the future of his business. But the thought that this astonishing young woman shared his interest in the Gründler foundry amused him more than it angered him. It even excited him. And it was all the more entertaining because he knew that Gerhard Grosse would never approve the villagers' request for a loan. He was familiar enough with the other local banks to know that they wouldn't dare grant a loan, either. Glassblowers getting together to launch a venture! A young woman as their spokesperson? Just what a troubled bank needed . . . No, the topic would be off the table almost as soon as it was raised. And Otto Gründler would nearly kiss his feet with sheer gratitude that he had found someone to buy the place.

There was no reason to get upset.

But perhaps it gave him a reason to drive down the price that Gründler was asking. The man had to be taught a lesson.

Her back, ramrod straight . . . Her strong spine and—

What brazen cheek! The girl really thought that she could compete with him.

But how had she become involved with the Gründler foundry? The young man hadn't said a word about how or why she had been with the glassblowers, though that was the part that interested Strobel most of all.

"To be honest I'm not sure whether I'm allowed to tell you all this," Wagner said now, obviously expecting some reaction.

"You have told me no more than I already knew," Strobel said casually. "Otto Gründler mentioned that there was a second potential buyer. I simply never would have thought that a young woman of that age might be involved." These words, and a smile, were enough to make Wagner relax.

"Yes, I rather thought that you would already know about it, being a businessman, after all! To know things in good time is the alpha and omega of business, isn't it?" He looked at Strobel for approval.

Strobel nodded. The girl—that proud glance of hers . . . Was it just the memory of Johanna that disturbed him so, or . . . ?

Strobel struggled to suppress such thoughts. Didn't he have more important matters to attend to?

The bank clerk was chattering away. "I admire your composure! I wonder whether I would be able to remain so indifferent, if I were in your position. After all, now that Mr. Gründler has suddenly found a second potential buyer . . ." He shrugged.

Strobel waved his hand. Did this underling really believe that he would let them steal the foundry out from under his nose? Did he really believe that Strobel sought his approval? The idea infuriated him. All the same he said mildly, "Competition is the lifeblood of business—isn't that so?" *And not just business*, he thought, and crossed his legs to conceal his growing excitement. A new thought occurred to him: Why not combine business with pleasure here? Just as he had before. He would get the foundry and have a little fun along the way.

The bank clerk laughed softly, and Strobel thought that he even heard a touch of pity in it. "I would hardly call this group from Lauscha competitors, my dear Mr. Strobel. After all, Mr. Grosse has already approved your loan. All that is required now is your signature, and then . . ." He made a face that was meant to suggest,

And then you'll have the world at your feet! He began to look busily through the stack of folders on his desk.

Strobel folded his hands in his lap and watched. He would have liked to beat this lad until he dropped those airs and graces of his! Acting as though he had God knows how many loans to approve, when in fact Strobel had already seen that his name was on the very top dossier. But he held his temper.

He would need this underling. The lad was still young. Young people were vain. And malleable.

Though he still felt pangs of lust, he himself was too old a fox by now. He would have the lad hunt on his behalf. Then he would take over once the quarry was down.

But what trap could he use to catch this quarry? How could he hunt Wanda Miles? He thought feverishly, looking for a way to lure her.

He had to proceed cleverly, not be too obvious about it. Whatever he did, whatever he made this young bank clerk do—the most important thing was that it all look plausible.

Wanda Miles . . . Miles . . . Miles . . .

The daughter of Steven Miles! *The* Steven Miles. Why hadn't he realized that straightaway?

Wanda Miles was "the American girl." Her mother was . . . Yes, that was it! Ruth. Ruth Miles. Johanna Steinmann's younger sister.

Which meant that Wanda Miles was also a Steinmann!

The sudden realization struck Strobel like a blow.

CHAPTER TWENTY-FIVE

"The young lady deserves a chance! As indeed do you! As do all industrious, ambitious young people!"

David Wagner couldn't get Strobel's words out of his head.

Young people and their ambitions! Who would have thought that someone like Friedhelm Strobel would be interested in them? Who would have thought that Strobel would go so far as to take sides with his young competitor, to the extent that he was willing to step back from the deal?

In the interest of fairness?

David shook his head, perplexed. He would never have thought that such a thing was possible.

His gaze fell on the piles of newspapers, and for the first time he found that he wasn't looking forward to reading them. It was almost embarrassing to look at them. Did he really believe that there was anything to be learned from them? That they could teach him about the world, and about people?

He hoped that Strobel hadn't seen the newspapers.

Strobel was truly a man of the world. A man with character and insight.

David hadn't felt quite right telling Strobel about Wanda Miles's application; however, he hadn't told the man anything he didn't already know. And he hadn't breached the bank's rules on confidentiality—thank goodness! After all, Wanda Miles and her associates were not clients of the bank and probably never would be—meaning that he was not bound to strict silence about their application.

All the same the question remained: Why had he been so talkative? That wasn't like him . . . But it was precisely because he had been talkative that Friedhelm Strobel had noticed him. The way he had always wished to be noticed. Strobel had even shaken his hand when they said good-bye.

If David managed to move matters forward in the way Strobel wanted—however that might be—then perhaps the next time Strobel sat down in the tavern with his good friend Grosse, he would utter some words of praise on David's behalf.

That's a clever young man you have sitting there in the loans department, Gerhard! You should keep an eye on him; this David Wagner has great things ahead of him, don't you think?

Grosse would nod and think things over on his way home, and perhaps he would look at David with new eyes after that.

Just as David had always hoped.

David stretched his arms out above his head and took a deep breath. Why then did he feel a slight sense of foreboding?

What if he gave Grosse a report that cast the villagers and their application in a bad light? So that Grosse would then be bound to turn them down for a loan? Then he could hint to Strobel about what he'd done, suggesting, *If it hadn't been for me, who knows what would have happened?*

David let his arms drop and heaved a deep sigh. No, that wasn't the way he did things. If he wanted to impress Strobel, then he had to do it honestly and fairly.

Impress Strobel, ha!

When David had made a point of saying that he knew Steven Miles's name from the newspapers, Strobel had mentioned that he had first met the American twenty years ago when Miles had been an assistant to Mr. Woolworth—whom Strobel knew as well, of course.

When David had grown indignant about the unfair way Otto Gründler had behaved, Strobel had simply said, "He must do as he sees fit." Then he had added, "Of course I would like to buy the foundry, but that doesn't mean that I want to play an unfair game. And it would be unfair not to give this young woman and her associates a chance. Let them try to raise the necessary sum in time!" At that point Strobel had leaned forward over the desk and looked at him quite severely. As though he, David, had suggested using unfair methods.

Perhaps he really had said too much? Maybe Strobel thought that he would be just as talkative about Strobel's own affairs?

David began to massage his temples vigorously.

His mind was still spinning with everything that Strobel had told him about the first woman to blow glass, about the invention of Christmas tree ornaments, about a workshop that was run by women and belonged to Wanda Miles's aunt. Johanna Steinmann— David had heard the name before. He hadn't quite grasped every detail, but one thing was clear enough: Wanda Miles didn't just act as though she were important—she really was. And she didn't need to get her hands dirty with work. Or by taking on other people's problems. David didn't understand why she was doing it, then. Why didn't she just sit back and enjoy life?

What a woman! So self-assured! And pretty as well . . .

What a woman . . . She was far beyond someone like him, that much was certain. He didn't even need to waste time thinking about that.

You're not paid to sit here and daydream! he scolded himself.

He got up abruptly and poured himself a glass of water from the carafe. Then he held the glass against his forehead. All that frantic rubbing had simply made his headache worse. What he wouldn't give to be able to go home! Or even simply to take a walk.

Out to the pleasant streets of Sonneberg. The streets shaded by wide canopies of trees. The streets lined with fine new houses. Streets where you never saw furniture wagons loading and unloading by the houses. The people who lived in those houses moved in once and then never moved out again. Unlike him. David knew that he would have to look for new lodgings in the next few months, since he wouldn't last another winter in that unheated attic room.

Back at his desk, he pushed back his chair and put his feet up. As he did so he listened carefully for any sound at the door—he didn't want his receptionist coming in and finding him like this.

Wanda Miles. Before David could stop himself, his thoughts wandered back to the American girl. He judged her to be a few years younger than he was. He found himself picturing her dark-blue outfit and recalling the businesslike way she talked. Had she been trying to make herself seem older?

And her perfume . . . he could still smell it: a flowery scent with a subtle astringent note, rather like the smell of quince. Quite wonderful . . . he had had to make an effort not to lean forward over the desk and sniff her neck.

Strobel had murmured her name over and over again. Yes, Strobel was a man who would enjoy the company of a woman like that. A man like Friedhelm Strobel wouldn't waste time wondering what Wanda Miles thought of him or whether she liked him.

Wanda Miles. The very name sounded soft, feminine. Not a bit like Katharina Krotzmann, his landlady's daughter, who made eyes at him every morning.

Wanda Miles.

Although David still wasn't quite sure why Strobel had taken her side, he had also insisted that he should be kept informed about the status of the new venture. Was that really fair play? Who was keeping Wanda Miles and the glassblowers apprised of Strobel's affairs?

No, in the future he would not talk quite so much when Strobel was there. If indeed there was even anything to talk about. Most likely he would never see Wanda Miles again after the meeting the next day.

He picked up his jacket, looked one last time through the documents that Wanda had left him, and then set off to see Gerhard Grosse.

Perhaps he would be able to persuade his boss to approve a loan for the glassblowers.

CHAPTER TWENTY-SIX

"What do you mean, the bank won't give us the loan?" Gustav Müller looked at David Wagner uncomprehendingly.

"There's no doubt that the Gründler foundry could be a rewarding investment. But that's not the issue here, as I tried to explain to you yesterday." David Wagner raised both hands apologetically. "If your rival did not happen to be a client of this bank . . . and if he were not applying for a significantly smaller loan than you are asking for. And if he did not have such good collateral . . ."

Gustav Müller bit his lip like a schoolboy who'd been scolded.

It was Karl Flein who said out loud what all four of them were thinking. "And now? What happens next?"

The only answer was baffled silence. Was this the end of their venture?

It couldn't be. It mustn't be! Wanda thought feverishly while David Wagner shuffled papers from one pile to the next and tried to look terribly busy. *Not so fast*, Wanda thought. *You can't get rid of us that quickly.*

Drat it all!

Even on their way into Sonneberg on the train that morning, Wanda had had the queasy feeling that it wouldn't all go as smoothly as the men assumed. Although Wanda had drunk along with them when they had raised their glasses around the table at the Black Eagle the night before to celebrate their "successful" visit to the bank, she had not shared their optimistic belief that the visit to the bank the next day was a mere formality. Quite the opposite: David Wagner had already hinted that there could be problems. Wasn't it bad luck to celebrate something before it was certain? Wasn't that just inviting disaster?

Look where that got us, she thought now as the silence stretched on.

Karl was staring out the window as though he expected to find an answer among the leaves of the chestnut tree. Gustav Müller tugged nervously at the button on his waistcoat until it came off in his hand. The bank official looked at the clock meaningfully, as though to say, *I have other appointments! Appointments that will bring me better business.*

It was that look that pushed Wanda to do something more.

He couldn't get rid of her that easily! Had she spent all those hours with Harold in the Brooklyn Bar in vain? Hours when she had had nothing to do but listen to the stockbrokers telling of their triumphs? Perhaps this was the moment when all the lessons she had learned in the Brooklyn Bar would pay off.

She took a deep breath and pulled the thick bundle of banknotes out of her bag. It was all of their starting capital, and she put it on the desk. She stared at David, her eyes flashing.

"There are other ways you could help us get our money . . ."

* * *

"What do you mean, the villagers wouldn't be put off?" Gerhard Grosse frowned. "Since when do the clients decide whether or not we will do business with them? Why didn't you just send them to another bank? Let someone else consider their application for a loan, we certainly shan't."

David Wagner struggled to conceal his excitement.

"That's exactly what I told the men. By the way, they're still sitting in my office downstairs," he answered as calmly as he could. "Although—now it's no longer a loan application." He paused, and his boss frowned again. He went on hastily, without taking the time to phrase it as carefully as he might have wished.

"It rather seems that the investors from Lauscha have the utmost confidence in our bank." He hopped from one foot to the other like a nervous bridegroom.

It had happened!

He had dreamed about it for so long, and now it had happened. Somebody really had come into his office and dropped a bundle of banknotes onto his desk and said, "Make something of that!" Whoever would have thought that somebody would be Wanda Miles?

The way she had looked at him as she spoke! With a challenge in her eyes, as if to ask, *Do you think you can do this?* David had struggled not to shout, *Yes! Yes! Yes!*

Two floors down, there were 11,000 marks in cash sitting on his desk. Great Heavens above—the possibilities! He already knew exactly what he wanted to do first. He would go through the stock market news from the last four weeks again, looking for every opportunity, however small. He would divide the money carefully and put a little into this pot, a little into the next . . . What was it his grandmother had always said? "Don't put all your eggs in one basket."

However . . .

The money wasn't his to invest. Nobody had asked him to take charge of it. Nobody thought he was capable of such a thing.

Instead he would have to entrust it to his colleague Siegbert Breuer, who was in charge of stocks and shares for the bank.

When David had explained in broad strokes what the villagers from Lauscha wanted, Gerhard Grosse shook his head.

"Tell them they should go to one of the casinos in Berlin and sit down at a roulette table. Or they can wait for the fair to come to town and give their money to a conjurer." He waved a hand, obviously already bored by his own joke. David dared to speak up again.

"Six weeks—I know that it's not very long. But with a little imagination and—"

"And what?" Grosse snapped. "Recklessness? Is that the word you're looking for?"

"The villagers know very well that there's no surefire way to increase their money, that there are always risks involved. All the same they're ready to entrust their money to us. Shouldn't we reward their trust by accepting it? Of course, I'm not so foolish as to think that we could raise the full purchase price of the foundry on the stock market in such a short time." He shrugged. Privately he was convinced that he could do just that—but Grosse didn't need to know that. He went on. "Even if we only increase their investment by a small amount, these people will have more than they did when they came to us. It certainly won't be less. The markets are looking up at the moment and—" Recalling that Grosse had no reason to suspect that his loans clerk knew anything at all about stock markets, he hurried on to safer ground. "We can't lose. Quite the opposite, in fact. The bank will make a tidy profit off the commission and fees."

Ha, if Wanda could hear him now! Or even Mr. Strobel! David sat up a little straighter.

Gerhard Grosse looked at him as though he had never seen him before in his life and was wondering whether he was in his right mind. His gaze wandered from David's carefully polished shoes to the sharp creases in his pants to his hands, which he clenched and unclenched with excitement. He looked David in the eye.

David struggled to stay calm as he went on. "By the way, Friedhelm Strobel has no objection to giving the villagers a chance. He even said that he would welcome a fair competition for the foundry."

David wasn't quite sure whether Strobel would welcome having this information disclosed. It was only once he had spoken that he realized that he had just indirectly admitted to having said too much in front of Strobel. But the admonishment he was expecting never came. Instead his boss gazed levelly at him for a few more moments, then took a deep breath. He shook his head, then smiled almost imperceptibly.

"Ah, well then. Send them to Breuer. Let him show them what he can do. We'll give these fellows from Lauscha their chance. Friedhelm Strobel, pfff!" Then he laughed.

David's sense of triumph was mixed with defeat. Siegbert Breuer was a competent man. He handled a small fortune in investments every year and he took good care of the money his clients entrusted to him. It was a triumph for David's powers of persuasion that Gerhard Grosse had accepted the villagers' request—it showed that David was on the right path—but he would have to say goodbye to that pile of money downstairs on his desk. Clearly nobody trusted *him* to invest it. Although David was acutely aware of his defeat, he didn't want Grosse to know that was how he felt.

CHAPTER TWENTY-SEVEN

"I don't know." Karl shook his head. "Playing the stock market . . ."

"With our hard-earned money," Gustav Müller added, sounding just as worried.

"Can we trust them?" Martin Ehrenpreis said. He looked at the stack of folders on Wagner's desk as though he feared they might bite.

Wanda shook her head, laughing. "You're not serious, are you?" But then she looked from one face to the next and saw the worry etched on each one. The men were quite serious, she realized.

"What other choice do we have?" she whispered, watching the door. "We simply must invest the money properly! And you were so impressed by the Grosse bank! You were the ones to tell me what splendid people they have working here. Now you have to trust them."

"It's not our money alone," Karl said. "You know how hard the others had to work to get this money together. And now you want us to tell them we're putting it into the stock market?"

Wanda made a face. "To hear you talk, anybody would think we're handing it over to fraudsters. But the stock market is a perfectly honest business. There's a whole army of stockbrokers in New

York who spend all day, every day doing nothing else! Men who make their living that way to support themselves and their families. And they make good money."

"How do they make a living, eh?" Gustav asked. "They don't produce anything. They don't buy or sell anything. All they do is shuffle numbers around on bits of paper. Or swap bits of paper with other bits. And you're telling me that's honest work?"

Wanda waved away his objections. She didn't have time just then to explain the way it all worked. She fixed her gaze on each of the men in turn.

"We have just two choices: either we go back home and forget the whole thing . . ." She paused for a moment to let that sink in. "Which would mean no venture, no company, no foundry. The end of all our plans. Or—"

Before she could continue, David Wagner flung the door open.

He took his time explaining to the men, patiently and in simple terms, what kind of investments they would be making. They would be putting their money into futures contracts, because they didn't have the time for anything else. Of course, Grosse & Sons would keep a careful eye open for other opportunities.

When Karl asked whether there was any chance they could actually make a big enough return on their investment to purchase the foundry, Wagner shrugged. It was possible, he said, but he couldn't promise anything.

"We'll trust you with our money!"

Karl had taken over as spokesman.

Wanda was glad that he had. She folded her hands over her handbag and leaned back in her chair as though she listened to conversations like this every day.

Dear Lord, please let this be the right decision, she prayed silently. *And please let Grosse & Sons be as good as its reputation. Because if something goes wrong, I'll be to blame!* She was quite sure that she was responsible for Karl's decision.

Richard will be furious, she thought suddenly. But then again, he didn't even know she was there. When she had tried to tell him about this second visit to the bank the night before, all he had said was, "Ah, the bank." The tone in his voice had suggested that he meant, *Not this again,* and so she had dropped the topic.

"We'll give you the money with the understanding that you're going to put it to the very best possible use for us." Karl was emphasizing every word now, speaking in almost exaggerated tones. "You know that we will need all our money back by the second week of September. Our money, and"—he turned to face his companions—"the money that you have earned on our behalf. That will be the only way we can buy the foundry. The only way to ensure a future for a great many glassblowers and their families."

Gustav and Martin nodded.

Wanda nodded also. She was so proud of Karl! Just a few weeks ago he had been so eaten up by worry that he was making his wife's life a misery, and now he was talking about "a better future" for the glassblowers' families!

"Grosse & Sons will do its best on your behalf," David Wagner assured them. It seemed to Wanda that his voice was trembling a little. Was he touched by the obvious sincerity of Karl's words? Did he sense what an extraordinary act of faith this was? Did he even feel honored to be a part of it?

Wanda liked the thought. She smiled. David Wagner may be somewhat pompous, but he was now part of this wonderful venture as well.

I trust him! she thought suddenly.

David Wagner looked at the pile of money on the desk in front of him. There was a look of longing, almost reverence, in his eyes, as though he were looking at a valuable work of art rather than just a bundle of paper. Then he sighed, looked up at Karl, and cleared his throat.

"My esteemed colleague Siegbert Breuer is a very capable man with a great deal of experience on the stock exchange. He will—"

"Siegbert who?" Karl asked. "We don't want anything to do with any Siegbert! You're the son of Wagner the tavern keeper. We've known your father for decades! And trust is the most important thing in this business, isn't it?" He turned to his companions, and both men nodded.

What's Karl getting at? Wanda wondered. What did he have against this Siegbert? He didn't even know the man! And why in Heaven's name was he going on now about how Wagner the tavern keeper always matched his guests drink for drink?

Karl Flein took a deep breath. "Your father's a good fellow. Which is why—"

"Yes?" croaked David Wagner.

"Which is why we want you to look after our money!"

* * *

"You really let those men . . . ? You didn't try to stop them?"

Wanda didn't bother to answer.

She had told Richard, her father, and Eva every detail of her visit to the bank. She had seen the skepticism in their faces as she relayed the entire conversation.

How they were now investing in the stock exchange.

How Karl and the others trusted young David Wagner.

How the men had been so excited that they had to stop for a beer at Wagner's Tavern on the way home.

That explained why she was so late getting home and why she was hungry. Not that Richard had been especially interested in what she had to say up to that point. He was much too busy with some drawings that he had been showing her father.

Wanda's voice had trembled as she told her story. The only time she spoke without stumbling was when she mentioned David Wagner's name. In fact, she may have mentioned his name rather too often . . . She felt a slight thrill every time she said it, but she attributed this to the general excitement of the whole venture.

By now Michel and her father had gone down to the Black Eagle, and Eva was upstairs with Sylvie, who had been crying all day. She was alone with Richard.

As she heard Sylvie wailing upstairs, Wanda felt a cloud of guilt come over her. She had spent too little time caring for the child recently. What would Marie think if she could see her now? But Marie would surely have understood how important this venture was. She would even have encouraged Wanda to get involved.

Unlike Richard. God knows Wanda would have welcomed a little support from him. Instead he sat there looking at her as though . . . Wanda was so annoyed that she couldn't think of a suitable comparison. In any case, he certainly didn't look pleased at the news. It seemed that a bank official was more willing to lend his support than her future husband!

Wanda bit angrily into a thick slice of bread and butter and then looked at the pattern her teeth had made in it. At least she still had her appetite . . .

"You're sitting there eating as though there was nothing wrong! You . . . you've gone mad."

CHAPTER TWENTY-EIGHT

If Benno had thought that the Black Eagle had turned into a debating club, he had been wrong.

It had become a madhouse!

He was quite convinced that he was surrounded by madmen this evening. Madmen who shouted for beer and schnapps as though there were no tomorrow. Madmen who leapt up from their tables, then sat down again, then jumped back up again—madmen who were red in the face, with wild staring eyes and harsh shrill voices.

A little bit of fresh air might cool the tempers in here, Benno thought, as he opened the front and back doors. The smell of fresh-mown grass drifted in, reminding Benno of the simple pleasures in life. If it weren't for the madmen banging their fists on the tables!

The madness had broken out when Karl had announced that the foundry capital would be invested on the stock exchange for six weeks starting today. Benno could understand the men's response. He was outraged by the very idea that someone might decide to use his hard-earned money in such a way.

So young Hansen's reaction was perfectly understandable. Granted, he shouldn't have raised his fist to Karl like that, but then young Hansen was such a reedy little fellow that the gesture was more laughable than threatening.

Benno had less patience with Jockel, who had marked the American girl as the target of his attacks. He hadn't used force, of course, but a few well-chosen and hurtful words instead.

"This is what happens when we welcome a total stranger into our village!" he had yelled, staring so pointedly at Wanda that nobody could possibly have had any doubt about what he meant. "And someone who was born with a silver spoon in her mouth, at that. She thinks our money is nothing more than a toy! A toy that she can throw away when she's bored with it."

Wanda wanted to defend herself from the charge, but nobody would listen to her. Of course not—for nobody liked to hear their money being compared to a toy.

It grew louder and louder.

Thomas Heimer declared at the top of his voice that he didn't like hearing his daughter called a total stranger.

Benno had enough experience with tavern arguments to know when words threatened to come to blows. It was time to step in. He warned that anyone who got up from their chair would be thrown out the door and wouldn't be allowed back in. This didn't stop the verbal attacks—indeed it unleashed a torrent of harsh words—but at least it spared his furniture from damage.

It was Thomas Heimer who finally managed to soothe tempers a little.

"The fact is that the banks are to blame for everything," he said. As soon as he spoke the words one or two others in the room nodded. "They don't have the courage to support fellows who come along with a good idea, so they just leave us out in the cold! If we'd been given a bank loan, nobody would even have dreamed of putting their money in stocks! A fair loan was all we needed, isn't that right?" Karl, Gustav, and Martin nodded vigorously.

Benno was relieved when all the hotheads in the room joined in to denounce the banks as the real enemy.

Thomas Heimer spoke up again. "That's life, though. Nobody gets anything handed to them on a silver platter. Everything has a price, and nobody knows that better than I do!"

"Do you think we don't know that?" Jockel snapped at him. "Do we look as though we were ever given anything for free?"

"That's just what I'm saying!" Heimer said heartily, much to Jockel's bafflement. "But that's also why it's worth taking this chance! Take a risk once in a while!"

Benno didn't quite understand why Heimer glared at Richard as he spoke, or why his future son-in-law didn't lift his eyes from his tankard. Was Heimer hoping that Richard would support him? If so, then why didn't it happen? After all, Richard was devoted to his glassblowing. Of all the villagers he was best known for his stubborn courage and for taking chances. Besides, he should have come to his fiancée's defense. Instead he sat there, looking grumpy, almost disengaged, his shoulders hunched and his arms crossed before him. *That's young people for you,* Benno thought. *When push comes to shove they don't stand up for anything. Or they only look out for themselves.* And look at that! Richard took that blasted notebook out of his pocket and started scribbling away like a mad thing. As though none of this had anything to do with him!

Thomas Heimer was still speaking. He was telling the whole tavern that his daughter had taught him that life could hold pleasant surprises. Given what Karl Flein had told them about the conversation with the bank, as well as the general economic situation, the stock exchange was the only thing that could help them buy the foundry. They just had to hope it would all work out. Heimer stopped talking and shrugged.

"The best thing we can do is forget the whole crazy idea!" Jockel shouted.

"I propose that we drop the whole debate," Karl Flein put in. "Let's just have a vote to see who's in favor of investing on the stock exchange, and who's against!" The crowd agreed.

Otto Gründler hadn't said a word all evening. He looked as though he were about to die just then. His whole posture said, *What have I started?*

They took the vote, and a small majority of paying members were in favor of the new stock investment.

Otto Gründler relaxed and, to general acclaim, declared that they could have an extra week to raise the money.

CHAPTER TWENTY-NINE

"Tell me, Wanda, I didn't want to ask yesterday . . . I was worried it might be a silly question . . . and I wasn't even sure whether Karl would be able to answer. But—" Martha Flein peered up and down the street as though to be quite sure that nobody was close enough to eavesdrop.

"Yes?" Wanda said, a bit impatiently. The sky had begun clouding over when she had left the house with Sylvie to go to the store to buy some smoked fish for lunch; it wouldn't be long before the rain started to fall. Wanda was in no mood to stop and chat with Martha Flein just then.

"How does the stock exchange work?" Martha burst out, seemingly unconcerned by the looming clouds. "I mean—how does anybody make money from it?" she added when Wanda didn't answer at once.

Wanda accepted defeat. The more people knew, the better they would feel. She steered Sylvie's carriage under Martha's cherry tree, where it would be at least partly out of the rain, and began to explain about stocks, dividends, share prices, and bull and bear markets.

But the more Wanda explained, the more confused Martha looked.

So much for that theory, Wanda thought. She took a deep breath. Time to try again!

"Let's assume there's a company that makes . . . um . . . umbrellas," she said, glancing up at the darkening sky. "Handmade, high-quality umbrellas, first-class work—"

"How can an umbrella be first-class?" Martha asked. "The main thing is that it doesn't let the water through, surely?"

Wanda waved the objection away. "It's just an example! So anyway, this company makes the most wonderful umbrellas, and they sell well. Then one day a large American client comes along and he's impressed by these handmade umbrellas. He offers to buy a certain number every year. Let's say five thousand."

"He would have to be a very big client," Martha said skeptically.

"Exactly! Like Mr. Woolworth for example," Wanda said. Then she took a deep breath and went on. "In any case—after this order, the shares in the umbrella company are worth a lot more, do you understand? So the trick of it is to buy their shares while nobody's interested in umbrellas and then to sell them when everybody is crying out for shares in umbrellas. So if Grosse & Sons puts our money into a company like that, we've got it made!"

Martha chewed her lower lip thoughtfully.

Great Heavens above, what's so hard to understand about this? Wanda thought. She could hardly put it any more simply than that!

"But why . . ." Martha stopped as though she were having trouble framing her question. "Why did the umbrella manufacturer ever issue shares in his company in the first place? Why didn't he just keep it all for himself? Then he'd be a rich man once that big order came in. But as it is, don't the shareholders keep the profit?"

Wanda nodded vigorously. "That's it! The shareholders keep the profit."

"But why—"

"Oh come along now, Martha, don't keep asking questions all the time," Wanda said. She laughed, but couldn't keep a note of irritation from creeping into her voice. "Maybe the manufacturer didn't have enough warehouse space. So he needed to buy a new warehouse, and, of course, that costs money. Or perhaps he wanted to build a whole new factory and needed the money for that. There are plenty of reasons why a manufacturer might issue shares in his company. When I think about it . . . this little company we're setting up for the foundry may turn into something like that someday."

Martha nodded thoughtfully. Then she grinned mischievously and nudged Wanda gently in the ribs. "I bet you never would have imagined us villagers could be so forward-thinking, did you, my girl?"

The umbrellas were just the beginning. Next time—when Wanda happened to run into Magnus in the street—she talked about gas lamps, and another time about a soap manufacturer. She found it helped to tailor the examples to whoever was asking the questions.

Not a day went by when at least one person didn't want her to explain the ins and outs of the stock market. *Harold, if you could hear me now, you'd be proud!* she found herself thinking more than once.

Her efforts bore fruit. A couple of days later when she went into a shop to buy some sugar, Martha was explaining to Karline how to make money by trading shares, using the umbrella factory as an example. When Karline asked why the American wanted to buy umbrellas and not walking sticks or cuckoo clocks, Martha almost snorted out loud. "It's just an example!" she declared, with a tone that implied, *What kind of silly question is that?*

It was hard for Wanda not to burst out laughing.

CHAPTER THIRTY

The air was heavy with perfume, cigarette smoke, and the sour smell of cheap champagne.

Friedhelm Strobel sat down at one of the little round tables by the stage. The smoke stung his eyes and he had trouble seeing anything in the half-light of the bar. He was hardly in his seat before one of the hostesses was already trying to sit in his lap. "Welcome to the Blue Owl," she purred, then cried, "Ow!" as Strobel slapped her forcefully on the bottom to get rid of her.

Later perhaps.

Once he had ordered his drink, he leaned back in his chair. His eyes were watering, and he momentarily regretted not going straight back to his hotel after dinner.

The trip to Berlin had worn him out. Was it because even in a first-class carriage, a train journey was almost intolerable in this heat? Was it because he was getting old? Was he too old for such pleasures? He refused to believe that.

The waitress came and put a glass of absinthe in front of him, along with a cut-glass water decanter, a saucer of sugar cubes, and a spoon with several holes.

Strobel smiled indulgently and gave the girl a banknote. Would the gentleman require anything else, she asked, rubbing her nose significantly.

Strobel declined. He had been known to indulge in a pinch of cocaine every now and again when he came to Berlin, but this evening he wanted to keep a clear head.

"Tell Santiago that Friedhelm is here," he said. The young woman nodded.

Strobel carefully placed two lumps of sugar onto the spoon and held it over the absinthe. The water in the carafe was ice-cold, just the way he liked it. He poured it in a slow trickle over the sugar and watched the lumps dissolve. As he watched, he felt the strain that had gripped him over the last few days dissolve as well.

He had done what he had set out to do. His trip to Berlin had not been in vain, and his old contacts had once again proved to be very useful. The first steps of his plan were now underway.

Strobel grinned as he picked up his glass and admired the cloudy note in the green absinthe.

He spoke a silent toast before taking the first sip.

To his plan!

As it happened, it had been a Lauscha glassblower who had brought Friedhelm Strobel the good news. He was one of Strobel's suppliers, a pieceworker who specialized in vases, and when he had made his most recent delivery, he had talked about his visit to the village tavern the evening before. He had been so caught up in the debate that he had repeated every detail to Strobel, unaware there was any reason he shouldn't.

They were playing the stock market? In the hopes of being able to buy the foundry after all? Friedhelm Strobel could hardly believe his ears. But when the man explained that Wanda Miles was behind the whole thing, his doubts vanished straightaway. The villagers would never have come up with an idea like that themselves! But with that Steinmann girl by their sides . . .

The stock market—that was all Strobel needed to hear. His mind immediately started churning. He needed a plan. A counter-plan, so to speak.

But soon he had to admit that he didn't have enough infor-mation to come up with a viable plan. He needed something that would guarantee him the purchase of the foundry and at the same time teach certain people a lesson.

So he had gritted his teeth and brought up the subject of the Lauscha villagers to Gerhard Grosse the next time they met at the tavern.

"So you've heard about that as well, have you? And to think we used to call them hillbillies! They're canny businessmen, that lot! Ah, yes, we townsfolk will have to get used to that . . ." Grosse had laughed. And then he had said that Strobel clearly had serious competition for the foundry.

Grosse! *He'll be laughing on the other side of his face soon enough*, Strobel thought. Grosse had put on a false smile and regret-fully announced that he could say no more at that point because of banker-client confidentiality. He was quite sure that Strobel understood . . .

Yes, Grosse would learn his lesson too.

Friedhelm Strobel took another sip from his glass, enjoying the bitter taste and the burning in his throat. The Blue Owl was well known for offering all kinds of pleasures, one of which was the qual-ity of its absinthe. But the evening was still young—perhaps there was more fun to be had?

By now the curtain had gone up. A dancer wearing nothing but a cloth around her waist began to move in time with the piano music. Her skin was pale, almost transparent, and her veins were clearly visible in several places. Strobel licked his lips. The dance was erotic, hypnotic, but he could not switch off the part of his brain that was busy thinking about why he had come to Berlin in the first place.

Was it coincidence that his bank in Hamburg had suggested a very profitable shares deal just then? Or was it the hand of fate?

Strobel stared at the stage, lost in thought, without really seeing what was going on. If the investment really was as good as his bank manager in Hamburg claimed, then he wouldn't even need Grosse's loan. He would take it all the same, as it was best not to attract too much attention.

The information from Hamburg was worth more than just money, however. It had also given him the idea for an ingenious plan—

Strobel sat up with a start as he felt a hand on his shoulder.

Santiago. He hadn't heard him coming.

"Is everything all right, *mon ami*?" The owner of the Blue Owl sat down on one of the little chairs. "Did your meeting with our mutual friend work out to your satisfaction?"

Strobel nodded. "I gave him his task, everything's in order."

"Tell me then, do you need a new passport? Are you thinking of fleeing Germany? Perhaps you have gotten yourself into the kind of trouble where that is the only answer?" Santiago laughed.

Strobel laughed also, but he waved the idea away.

"All I need are some . . . documents. Nothing important! But nevertheless, thank you again for your help. This printer certainly seems to know his business."

Strobel had been planning to ask the man for another favor as well, but he decided against it. There was no need to let Santiago know too much about what he was up to. He would find other accomplices elsewhere.

He raised his glass and drank, then nodded toward the stage. "She's a wildcat, that one."

"And she's not afraid to use her claws! Shall I send her over to you later?" Santiago grinned.

"Why not?" said Strobel. "But first I shall have another glass of absinthe."

"Indulge yourself, my old friend!" said Santiago. He laughed and clapped his hand onto Strobel's shoulder once more, then he stood up and went over to the bar.

Friedhelm Strobel watched him go. A pleasant shiver ran down his back as he recalled the old days, when Santiago had been known only as "the Spaniard" and owned a quite different establishment. Certainly the Blue Owl had much to offer. But it did not cater to the wishes of those—men and women both—who had unusual tastes. Unfortunately . . .

However—when he looked at this dancer . . . her wide-open eyes, her vacant gaze, the way she danced as though in a trance . . .

"Bravo! Encore!"

The applause from the other guests interrupted his memories.

The dancer jumped down from the stage and hurried over to his table. "Santiago told me that you are a very special guest this evening." She took the chair that Santiago had been sitting on and pulled it closer to Strobel before she sat down. Then she smiled and licked her top lip, where the sweat was beading on her face. Her lips were full and sensual.

Strobel licked his own lips. It excited him to have the woman so close. He shifted restlessly in his chair.

"A very fine dance," he said. "But I am sure that you can do more than just that." He could feel the envious glances of the other guests on his back.

"I can indeed," the woman whispered, leaning so close that her naked nipples brushed his jacket. Her hand was on his knee. He felt her fingers wandering up his thigh, feeling through the heavy fabric, seeking, finding . . .

Friedhelm Strobel wanted to lean back and close his eyes and—

A moment later he reached down and grabbed the woman's wrist. She cried out softly.

"Thief! What kind of a whore's trick is this?" He snatched his wallet from her hand and put it back into his pocket.

By now the other guests were staring openly, unsure whether the spectacle unfolding was part of the show.

"I didn't mean to . . . I beg you, don't tell Santiago! Please, I . . ." The words tumbled from her mouth. "I'm sure that we can . . . clear up this misunderstanding!"

Strobel snarled softly at her, "Let's get out of here, you little minx." He held the dancer firmly by the wrist as he steered her toward the exit. Santiago looked at him quizzically from behind the bar, and Strobel smiled at him, saying, "I'm sure you will have no objection."

Santiago shrugged.

When they pushed through the heavy velvet curtain, the cloak-room attendant rushed up to them.

"Klara! Claire, my darling! What's happening . . . ?"

"My husband," the dancer murmured, her shoulders slumping.

"Did she . . . ? Oh, no! I beg you, kind sir, please don't—"

Strobel raised a hand. He didn't want to listen to the man's pleading. He needed a moment's peace.

He had to think. He had to understand the stroke of luck that had so suddenly presented itself.

The cloakroom attendant took Strobel's arm.

"Please, sir! I don't know what went on in there. But I'm sure we can come to some arrangement."

Strobel nodded thoughtfully. He looked again at the woman, then back at the man.

"Yes . . ." he said slowly. "I'm sure that we can."

CHAPTER THIRTY-ONE

While Strobel was in Berlin and Wanda was explaining the stock exchange to the villagers of Lauscha with the help of umbrellas and gas lamps, David Wagner was looking for a company just like the ones from Wanda's stories. He found nothing. Not for lack of trying. He looked very nearly everywhere, including at umbrella manufacturers and even soap factories!

He began every day by going to Alois Sawatzky's shop to purchase an armful of newspapers, which he read in his office—he no longer had to wait until the workday was over to read them at home. He was on official bank business now, and the newspapers covered his desk. There were newspapers from Berlin and Frankfurt; he had even started to read the *Illustrated London News*, which was not easy since he knew very little English. However, Sawatzky threw it in for free along with all the others, so David did his best. He read the serious papers and the gossip sheets, the so-called yellow press, even the Social Democratic newspaper, though its coverage was not to his taste. Still, news was news, no matter who wrote it.

Ever since Gerhard Grosse had allowed him to take on the villagers' commission, he spent an hour a day reading the newspapers before turning to his regular duties with a heavy heart.

An hour a day in which to work miracles. An hour a day when he could feel important. Or sometimes the opposite.

Because no matter how many hours he spent reading, he had not found a single company with such glowing prospects as the ones Wanda described in her examples.

David began to pace back and forth between his desk and the filing cabinet like a caged animal.

What was he missing?

Why couldn't he spot that one big investment?

Was it a mistake to hope to find one in such a short time? As far as David knew, Siegbert Breuer had never made a spectacular return, not in all his years at the bank. His older colleague invested the clients' money in a careful, cautious manner—a few dividend payouts here, a profitable shares trade there—and the money grew, slowly but steadily. But that wasn't going to work for the Lauscha villagers. He had to make them more than 50,000 marks in a few weeks' time.

When David read that Berlin's leading producer of laundry detergent had competition from a new company that had opened nearby and was making cheaper goods, he played the Berlin stock exchange, betting that the market leader's share price would soon fall. He sold shares in a lightbulb manufacturer on the Hamburg exchange, selling them *in blanco*—meaning that he did not even own those shares at the time—and then buying them at a better price three days later. The first deal made him almost 300 marks; the second was worth 480 marks. These early successes were most gratifying, of course, and proved that he knew how to play the game. But would gains like these be enough to reach the villagers' ambitious goal? David Wagner became increasingly skeptical.

Of course, Gerhard Grosse had been far from enthusiastic about letting David dabble in the futures market. There was no doubt that the bank would have to deal in these highly speculative investments—there simply wasn't enough time for anything else. Nor was there any doubt that Karl Flein was principally motivated by friendship between the Fleins and the Wagners when he insisted that David should be in charge of the investment. Since Gerhard Grosse was always encouraging his employees to use personal contacts in business, he could hardly object when David did just that.

Instead he had said, "I insist that you keep Siegbert Breuer informed about every step you take, no matter how small, and that you get his approval for everything you do. And don't think that this will lead to other such responsibilities in future. If you are not happy with the work we have given you to date, then . . ." He left the rest of the sentence as an unspoken threat.

David Wagner had hastened to assure him that while he would do his best in this case, he was very happy with his current job. And he said that he was not planning on taking any more work from Siegbert Breuer. But even as he spoke, he thought to himself, *Just wait till you see how well I do, then you'll be begging me to carry on!*

Arrogant fool!

Self-important idiot!

On this morning in mid-August, David was running out of names to call himself.

A whole week had gone by since Wanda Miles had put the money on his desk, and he had made a grand total of 780 marks. Siegbert Breuer, who had approved both deals in advance, called the profit a "respectable result." David Wagner could think of other words.

Failure, right down the line.

If only he had more time, two or three years perhaps . . .

Then he would put a sizeable sum of money into New Zealand, into orchards. David wasn't quite sure whether such an investment was even possible, but there were ways to find out. He was quite convinced that kiwi fruit was going to be the next big thing in the fruit market in the coming years, as popular as bananas and pine-apples were now, perhaps more so. They gave a good crop, had a long shelf life, and were tasty—what more could a fruit-grower ask for? David didn't know quite what the fruit looked like—the first seeds had only been brought to New Zealand from China five years earlier, which was why they were sometimes called Chinese goose-berries—and he would probably never taste one in his life, but he would have loved to invest in them.

He also thought that Little Texas might be an interesting investment. This region around Wietze in the sandy flatlands of North Germany produced eighty percent of Germany's oil. The two thousand drilling rigs working away must be a wonderful sight! And production was bound to grow in the coming years—after all, more and more machines used petroleum these days.

It was ripe for investment. For long-term returns, of course.

No, he could forget Wietze. Just as he could forget the jute factory in Bremen. Though it would be worth keeping an eye on that factory in the months to come, if he ever dealt in stocks and shares again. David had read a lengthy article about the company in which he'd learned that the founder had spent an enormous sum on workers' amenities, including homes for the workforce and daycare facilities for their children. A company that could afford such luxuries must be extremely profitable.

Deep in thought, David reached into the stack of newspapers and found the article again. The company was based in the free-trade zone by the port of Bremen. The jute was cheap, imported directly from India. The workers were happy with their jobs and there was no danger of strikes, as there was elsewhere.

How ironic! The workers in this Bremen jute factory mostly came from Thuringia, from the Eichsfeld region, which had once been famous for the flax that was grown and spun there. When the industry became mechanized along English lines, many of the people had left their homes and ended up in Bremen.

Today Eichsfeld was a byword for poverty, while Bremen was a boomtown.

David closed his eyes. Wouldn't there be a certain justice if Karl Flein and other Thuringian investors could profit from Bremen's good fortune?

Justice? Great Heavens above, his thoughts really were wandering!

David took a deep breath in an attempt to clear his mind of such thoughts. No more daydreaming about German oil fields and Indian jute and New Zealand orchards.

But inspiration failed to strike. It wouldn't have taken much for David to get up from his desk and go down the hallway to ask Siegbert Breuer's advice. He was practically desperate. He had the chance of a lifetime here, and he was letting it slip through his fingers. And it wasn't only his chance! After all, it was the glassblowers' money, and he was dealing with the futures of their families—he simply couldn't afford to fail.

And he mustn't even think of the American girl. Of the hope—and the trust—that shone in her eyes when she looked at him. He didn't want to disappoint a woman like that.

Yes, that was part of it too, David admitted, grinding his teeth. It wasn't just about his career. It was about Wanda Miles as well. About what she thought of him.

If only there were a war on the way . . .

Horrified to find himself thinking such a thing, he tried to justify the thought to himself. Last year the Zeppelin company's LZ 5 airship had made a successful flight from Lake Constance to Munich and then onward to Northern Germany. Everybody had expected the company's shares to soar, but as it happened, investors were wary of the many unsuccessful flights and launches that had come before. David was convinced all that would quickly be forgotten if the War Ministry bought some airships for scouting and surveillance operations.

A large order from the War Ministry sometime in the next few weeks. That was what he needed.

That, and a little bird to whisper in his ear when it happened.

That would be the miracle he needed!

He looked at his watch. It was already past one o'clock. Lunchtime—no wonder it was so quiet in the hallways. Half the day was over and he hadn't done a stroke of useful work.

He grabbed his jacket. It was time to get out of his office.

CHAPTER THIRTY-TWO

Strobel shifted about restlessly on his chair in an effort to let in some air between the fabric of his pants leg and his thigh.

It was so sticky in here!

He took a silk handkerchief from his pocket and dabbed at the sweat on his brow. He tried not to think of his cool dining room, where the shutters would be closed and not a single ray of sunshine could intrude. He tried not to think of a glass of chilled white wine. Or of the slices of cold roast meat, served with white bread and a little salad, that his maid would have prepared for his lunch if he were home.

You are not here for the pleasures of the table, he scolded himself. The waitress had just brought him a plate of potato gratin, but he pushed it aside in disgust. He pulled his table toward the wall to get out of the sunshine, as far as that was possible; the sunbeams were flooding in through the dirty window. There were no curtains to protect customers from either the sunshine or the passersby on the street. It was disgraceful, perfectly disgraceful!

All the tables were taken except for one by the kitchen, and Strobel seemed to be the only guest who had any objection to the food. Two old people sitting on his right were shoveling the food into their mouths without even looking up. To his left were three young men who acted like snobs but who had ordered only one dish of the day, with three forks—the waitress grumbled, but brought their order. Even as he came in, Strobel had noticed them and deliberately taken a table nearby. But none of them was the man he was looking for.

The waitress hurried over to Strobel. Would he like to order anything else? Something sweet? He forced a smile and ordered an extra-strong coffee. Anything but more food.

Potato gratin today, roast potatoes yesterday, potato soup the day before that. Strobel had been coming here at twelve o'clock sharp every day for the past three days, and as far as he could tell, the cook couldn't afford anything but potatoes. The dining room smelled so strongly of bacon fat, grease, and potatoes that it had seeped into every fiber of his clothing. Strobel had to stop at home to change his shirt and jacket before he went back to the shop.

What a difference from the fine restaurants he had visited in Berlin! The dishes there were delightful. The service was perfect, but unobtrusive. There were beautiful people wherever he looked. Whereas here . . .

He sighed and opened the newspaper he had brought with him. He tried to simultaneously keep an eye on the door.

Despite the unappetizing potato dishes and the overeager service, the restaurant had two distinct advantages: it was directly opposite the Grosse bank, and it was so cheap that even the lowly bank clerks could afford to have lunch there.

Or at least so Friedhelm Strobel had thought when he had begun his daily potato pilgrimage upon his return from Berlin. But he had now subjected himself to this torture for three days running and David Wagner hadn't shown up once. Could it be that he worked straight through lunch? Or did Wagner make sandwiches and bring them with him to the office?

Strobel took a mouthful of beer. It had gone flat. The impulse to spit it straight out again was so strong that he gagged.

Enough was enough! He dried the corners of his mouth and straightened his tie. Oh yes, he was ready to make a few sacrifices for the sake of his plan—he was even willing to eat bad food—but if Wagner didn't show up today, then he would simply have to go and visit the clerk in his office. That wasn't what Strobel wanted. No, a "chance" encounter, a lunchtime conversation, man to man, would be far preferable. But time was of the essence. And time was running out. He had been back from Berlin for several days and he was no closer to his goal.

Strobel took a deep breath and forced himself to stay calm. Weren't his plans all running entirely to his satisfaction otherwise? All the wheels were turning together . . .

As far as he was concerned, it was a stroke of good luck that David Wagner was in charge of making money for the villagers.

"The lad's ambitious," Grosse had told him. "More ambitious than I had realized. The villagers are insisting that he look after their investment. As I see it, this is his chance to prove what he can do! Then he'll learn that you never get something for nothing in this world." Grosse had laughed at that, and Strobel had joined in.

Now he made a face as though he had toothache. So much for "his chance to prove what he can do!" Young Wagner deserved to be taught a lesson as well. What fun it would be to watch his youthful self-assurance collapse once he saw how insignificant he really was. Once he saw that it was men like Strobel who really ruled the world.

David Wagner—the way that young man sought to ingratiate himself, when all the while he was on the glassblowers' side . . .

The glassblowers. His future employees, ha! Well, they deserved a lesson anyway.

And Wanda Miles. Her above all. Oh, how wonderful that would be!

Wanda Miles . . . niece of Johanna Steinmann. Who had once been his assistant.

The same family. The same features. The same hot blood, he was sure of that. He was older now, but he had not forgotten the pleasure he had taken with Johanna, his diamond in the rough. Oh, how fine it had been to polish her! To bring her to a high shine, to work on the facets that nobody else had seen in her. Even today she should thank him on her knees for what he had done for her!

But how had she repaid him? She had run away, and then sent her man to beat him. The worm who was now her husband. The worm who had seen to it that Strobel limped to this day, and that his leg ached with every change in the weather.

Oh, he knew all about her. About her, and her whole clan. He had not lost sight of them over the years. And he hated the lot of them.

When he looked back on his life, which he did more and more often these days, he saw Johanna's departure from his shop as a turning point—no, *the* turning point—in his life.

He took a deep breath. If he had not reacted quickly at the time and covered his tracks, the whole story might have ended very badly. He would never have thought that Johanna would react so prudishly. He had only escaped without damage to his reputation because he had moved quickly. But life had never been the same again after Johanna had left.

And now fate had shown him a way to change all that. Oh, revenge would be sweet!

But first his plan would have to work. He had laid the groundwork in Berlin. But he could forget the whole plan if he did not run into that young man from the bank soon. Strobel glanced up and down the street one more time.

He knew that there were dozens of points at which his scheme could go wrong. This was true even if he managed to see the clerk.

What if, for instance, Wagner didn't react the way Friedhelm Strobel expected?

He was also worried about the man he had taken on as accomplice. He was better than nothing, of course, and Strobel was confident that he would cooperate and say nothing. To that extent, it was a gift of fate that he had met the fellow in the first place. But there was still the danger that someone like him might not be convincing . . .

If he had had more time—oh, he knew quite well where he would have smoothed the rough edges to make the whole thing more plausible! He could have made it into a first-class show, he was sure. But as things were, he should be grateful for the chance that fate had given him. He would teach them all their lessons and he would have the foundry as well.

Friedhelm Strobel grinned in satisfaction.

And it would work! Wasn't his plan built on the firmest footing in existence? Human greed. Greed makes people careless; Strobel knew that. And the most wonderful part of it was that everybody was greedy in their own way. Strobel prided himself on being a connoisseur of greed. He knew what David Wagner yearned to have. He believed he knew what Wanda Miles wanted too.

And he knew exactly what he wanted himself. He wanted to see Wanda Miles before him. On her knees. Pleading. Her back bent, her shoulders hunched, her eyes humbly downcast. Broken, forever. He wanted her to give him what he had not been allowed to have from Johanna Steinmann.

His plan included all of these things. All the parts fit together. It was like exquisitely precise clockwork. He had gone to Berlin to find a printer who was willing to take on his task. The man wasn't cheap, of course, but he produced first-class goods. All he needed to get started was a sample, and that was already on its way from

Hamburg to Sonneberg. As soon as Strobel had it in hand, he would send it on to Berlin.

The anticipation made Strobel impatient. It was hard to sit here and wait—if only the lad would come!

Just then, he spotted the tall figure of David Wagner in the doorway.

CHAPTER THIRTY-THREE

"And how is the stock market treating you, my young friend?"

"The stock . . . um, I don't know what you mean, exactly . . ." *How the Devil does Friedhelm Strobel know about that?* David Wagner wondered, taken aback.

Strobel smiled. "Don't be so secretive, now! A little bird told me that you're setting your imagination to work for the villagers! I had expected to hear the news from you, but as it happens Gerhard Grosse told me. Don't we both have the same goal, after all? That the villagers should have their fair chance?"

David shrugged. *Setting your imagination to work?* Was he joking? Friedhelm Strobel was acting as though David's investments were the talk of the town. But surely it was just a matter of Grosse saying more than he should one evening at the tavern. It was odd, since David believed that Grosse couldn't stand Strobel. Or was that perhaps precisely why he had told him so much?

"I don't know what I can tell you—sadly I haven't made my fortune yet . . ." David Wagner raised his hands apologetically. Though he was burning to tell someone about his troubles and badly wanted someone else's advice, Strobel wouldn't get any more out of him than that.

As Strobel took a sip of coffee, their eyes met over the rim of the cup.

"You are an industrious young man . . . I'm quite sure that the villagers can rely on you."

David smiled, embarrassed. It wasn't easy with his mouth full.

When he had walked into the restaurant, he had spotted three colleagues and was just on his way over to join them when he saw a movement out of the corner of his eye. Friedhelm Strobel was sitting at a table by the window with his newspaper and waving. David had had no choice but to head toward him. His colleagues had looked a little surprised when he had gone to join the well-dressed gentleman as though it were the most natural thing in the world. He had given them a friendly nod as he passed, though he wondered a moment later whether that might have seemed a bit condescending. Well, if he wanted the same self-assurance Strobel had, then he had to get used to appearing haughty from time to time.

Strobel had insisted on ordering for him and then they had fallen into small talk. David was trying desperately to think of something that he had read in the newspapers that he might talk to a man like Strobel about—he didn't want to seem dull—when Strobel had turned the conversation to Wanda Miles and the stock market.

"Making a fortune on the stock market—many people spend their wholes lives trying to do just that," Strobel said with a sigh. "However, I hardly think that Otto Gründler would be ready to wait quite that long to sell his foundry. Let's hope that you make your fortune quickly . . ."

David laughed awkwardly. What was the man trying to do? Cross-examine him? No, he would have asked more probing questions in that case. On the other hand, he was clearly interested in the investment. He obviously wanted to know all he could about the competition, which was understandable.

"Making a fortune," Strobel repeated, tearing David away from his thoughts. "If I may say so, my young friend—"

David squirmed inwardly at being called "my young friend" but nodded politely all the same. Why did people have to put on such airs when they spoke?

"Perhaps you are going about things the wrong way?" Strobel looked at him significantly, the coffee cup raised halfway to his lips. "Perhaps all you need is a little luck!" He leaned forward.

David flinched and leaned backward a little, involuntarily. He couldn't have said quite why he felt so uncomfortable whenever this man came too near.

"I hardly think that the villagers of Lauscha would be happy if I relied solely on luck." *What a silly conversation*, he thought. He looked longingly over at his three colleagues, who had produced a deck of cards and were just dealing out a game.

Strobel smiled softly. "Oh, I wouldn't say that. Just look at me: by sheer chance I have happened upon some information that will probably make me quite a bit richer in the coming weeks. Of course, one could debate whether this was just luck or the result of my excellent contacts. Be that as it may, however—have you ever heard of the Schlüter shipping line, of Bremen?"

David shook his head.

"There's no reason why you should have. Granted, the Schlüter company owns an impressive fleet, among the largest in the industry. But if you look more closely, you realize that the ships are mostly sitting at anchor in the North Sea rather than working to bring in money for their owners. Which is why shares have been so cheap— any investor would worry that the company might go bankrupt at any moment!" Strobel laughed again.

"But that's changed now?" David asked, and his voice was just a little too high. Why had he never heard of this company? If it was trading on the stock market, he must have seen the name somewhere! Most likely the share price hardly ever moved. Or had he simply failed to notice some important information? If that was the case, then what else might he have missed?

Strobel grinned broadly, which gave him a roguish look. The elegant man of the world had vanished. David listened to him, fascinated.

Strobel evidently still had excellent connections to the world of high finance in Hamburg, where his family had been major players at one time. Hamburg, Bremen, and contacts in the shipping world. At this point Strobel winked slyly. That was how he happened to have come by some information that really ought to go no further. Secret information. *Top* secret.

Isn't Strobel from Berlin? David thought briefly, but he had no time to ask the question or to think about it anymore.

According to Strobel, rumor had it that the shipping company was about to sign a contract with a cotton plantation in the American South. Up until now, the shipping line had barely been able to make ends meet and its share price was down. The contract itself was secret. Not the sort of thing one reads about in the newspapers. But almost all of the Schlüter line's ships were now on their way to the Mississippi to load up on cargo and bring it back to Bremen. If this first crossing went well and none of the ships were lost—at this point Strobel clapped his hands—then the contract would be approved, Schlüter's future would be assured for years to come, and the share price . . . Strobel's hand fluttered upward like a bird taking wing.

"I have liquidated some of my assets and invested myself," he said. A moment later, his eyes widened, then narrowed, and he looked intently at David. David had a queasy feeling, as though he sat eye to eye with a beast of prey.

"I would be grateful if you could keep this information to yourself. Gerhard Grosse is a dear friend of mine, of course, but he would be upset to learn that I give some of my business to other banks."

David nodded slowly. It hurt to move. His neck felt stiff.

"Why are you telling me all this?" he burst out. "I mean—how could it possibly work to your advantage? You must be well aware, of course, that as soon as I leave here"—he nodded in the direction of the Grosse bank—"I will gather what information I can about this shipping line on my own behalf . . ." But the burning question was whether his sources were good enough to have heard the same rumors.

Bremen! He had been thinking about the jute factory in Bremen for days now, and now it seemed that there was a fortune to be made in cotton. How much of what Strobel was telling him could he believe? Was the man trying to lead him up the garden path? But what would that get him? And what would it mean if Strobel's information turned out to be true?

Strobel leaned back in his chair, and David admired the easy way he did so. The chair didn't wobble and the joints didn't creak—it was a simple gesture, but it revealed a great deal about a man who felt at ease in the world.

"First of all, I tell you all this because I want to show you that luck may favor you too, just as it has smiled upon me. And secondly . . ."—he paused significantly—"you may certainly find out all you wish about the shipping line. I rely on your discretion here, and you will find that everything I have told you is true. But . . ." Here Strobel paused again, then continued quietly. "Even if you decide that this is the way for you to make real money, you will not be able to invest since, officially, there are no more shares on the market. There's only one place you could get them . . ."

David asked the same question, over and over again.

"Have you heard anything about the Schlüter shipping lines recently?" He gave no explanation, no additional details, no background information.

One question, and one question only.

Some of his contacts could be reached by telephone, and he spoke to them directly. Others he contacted by telegram. He couldn't care less what Grosse or Siegbert Breuer had to say about the costs he ran up. They could say whatever they liked, later.

Right now, he didn't have time to worry about that.

He still had some contacts from a three-month stint he had done at the Berlin stock exchange. He had kept close by the brokers' sides, eager to learn all that he could. While some of them had regarded David as little more than a nuisance, others had been amused by the overenthusiastic young volunteer, tolerating him and even teaching him more than they had to.

He couldn't expect a response to all of his telegrams. Why would anybody bother to send an answer if he didn't know anything? Indeed, why would anybody bother to send an answer if he *did* know something? It was different when he made a telephone call—once he actually had someone on the other end of the line, he had to say something.

"Schlüter lines? I've heard nothing." David heard that, or some variation of that, over and over again.

He had talked to Siegbert Breuer, of course, but it was quite obvious that the man knew nothing. David found it easy enough to understand his silence. He also realized that Breuer didn't like it when David put him on the spot with questions like this. He would likely complain to Grosse about it later.

Well, let him!

Later.

David had no time for any of that at the moment. The last call that he made confirmed everything that Strobel had told him.

"Have you heard anything recently about the Schlüter shipping lines?" he asked Hans-Dietrich Klamm, his mentor from his time in Berlin, a sly old fox if ever there was one.

"How in the world does a landlubber like you hear about that?" Klamm asked in response.

David didn't need to hear any more than that. His mouth watered at the thought of getting a slice of this pie—for himself, for Wanda Miles, and for the glassblowers.

CHAPTER THIRTY-FOUR

"This is the best deal I can offer you. If it works"—David Wagner looked from Wanda to her companions—"you'll have more money than you need within four or five weeks." He laughed. "Then you can renovate that old barn from top to bottom!"

Karl Flein frowned. He regarded the Gründler foundry almost as his own property, and he didn't like it being called an old barn. But he liked the rest of what Wagner was telling them.

"This deal seems even more promising than that umbrella factory I've been hearing so much about lately." He scratched his head.

Wanda hadn't said a word. She groaned softly and put a hand to her stomach, as though she hoped to stop it from grumbling. She looked around Wagner's office. Everything looked just as it always did—the cluttered desk; the shelves full of folders, the dust dancing in the sunlight. And yet something was different. She felt a new and massive energy. Wanda took a deep breath.

David Wagner watched her. "You're wondering where I got my information."

That's not all I'm wondering, Wanda wanted to say, but she kept quiet.

Could it be true? Could it really be true? There was no umbrella factory; she knew that much.

There couldn't be a shipping line with the same sort of good luck, could there?

That's what the nervous grumbling in her stomach told her.

On the other hand, this was exactly the sort of deal she had been describing to others the whole time. She had been hoping for this very thing. Hadn't she persuaded the men that this could be their big chance? Now it looked as though they really might get just such a chance—and she was tucking in her tail like a dog that barks and barks but doesn't dare take a step forward! Wanda was deeply unsettled by it all.

To distract herself, she tried to recall what she knew about Bremen; it was in northern Germany and had a big harbor. There were regular crossings from Bremen to New York. Indeed, when Wanda had been getting ready to come to Germany, her family had considered a ship from New York to Bremen. At the time, Steven had told her that Bremen was called Europe's gateway to America, but he had also said that he preferred Hamburg because the connections to other cities were so much better.

Wanda frowned. Had Steven ever said anything about cotton shipments from the southern states of America to Bremen? If he had, she couldn't remember anything.

David Wagner put both hands on his desk, as if to say, *I'm playing all my cards out in the open, I haven't got anything up my sleeve!*

"I was skeptical myself the first time I heard about this opportunity. In part because it was none other than your competitor who told me about the Schlüter lines."

"Who? What? What's that supposed to mean?" Karl burst out.

"The wholesaler? Now why on earth would he give us a hot tip like that?" Martin laughed.

"He's telling you fairy tales, and you believe him!" Gustav snorted like an angry bull.

Wanda said nothing. She was too angry to speak. Just how naive was Wagner anyway? How could he sit here and tell them about a deal that their rival had pointed him to? No wonder her stomach was rumbling!

Martin Ehrenpreis was already halfway to the door, and the other two were showering curses upon the young bank official while he wrung his hands and asked them to be quiet.

Wanda worried that the sour-faced receptionist would march in at any moment and throw them all out.

She straightened the straps on her velvet handbag, smoothed the folds in her skirt, put her feet together, and—

David Wagner jumped to his feet, fetched a stack of papers from his shelves, and waved them at Martin.

"I've looked into it and the story checks out. The company exists, and the contract is apparently about to be signed. Your rival and I . . . we're friends, in a way. Everything that he told me has been confirmed by someone else. A source I take very seriously, who had direct contacts in the company itself. Your competitor is not lying! He even said that he would welcome the outcome if a Lauscha foundry were to end up in Lauscha hands." Wagner's gaze darted frantically from one face to the next, stopping on Wanda for an extra beat before moving on to Karl.

"He says that he only made his initial offer because Otto Gründler couldn't find any other interested party. As a wholesaler he has an interest in keeping Lauscha glass production alive; after all, he makes his living from glassware."

"And quite a good living, too, I would imagine!" Martin snapped.

"Keeping production alive—what kind of talk is that?" Karl said defensively.

"I never knew the wholesalers could be so kindhearted!" Martin said mockingly.

All three of them laughed.

Wanda relaxed a little. It was good to see that Karl and the others weren't taken in. David Wagner was genuinely excited by the whole idea—she found it almost charming to see him so eager—but the three glassblowers could see what he was too naive to notice. Nothing in this world was free. Which was why they had good reason not to trust an offer like this. Especially when it came from a wholesaler.

Wanda sat up straight in her chair and settled her handbag back in her lap, ready to watch the show for a little while longer.

"What does our American friend say to all this?" Karl asked so abruptly that Wanda almost jumped.

She shrugged. "There's one question I can't get past . . ." She looked at each of them. "If our competitor"—she put a touch of irony into the word—"is so determined to have the glassblowers take over the foundry, then why didn't he withdraw his own loan application and his interest in the purchase? I mean, if he'd done that, then we would have gotten a loan from your bank, wouldn't we? And all this"—she pointed to the stacks of papers—"wouldn't be necessary."

Karl and the others frowned.

David Wagner cleared his throat. "To be honest I've wondered the same thing. I don't have an answer. I'm assuming that he will withdraw his offer when you've got the money, if not before."

"But—" Wanda began, but Wagner interrupted her.

"As for myself, I swear to you that I will do everything in my power to see to it that you can buy the foundry. However, there is one small obstacle . . ."

"An obstacle, indeed!" Karl scoffed.

David Wagner explained that the shares in the shipping line were currently listed at a very low price, but were unavailable on any of the German stock markets. However, a Berlin stockbroker who happened to be staying in Sonneberg just then—a private sales agent—had a number of these desirable shares to sell. They had been intended for a rich family of the local aristocracy, but the family had suddenly run into a cash-flow problem and now had to step back from the deal. Wagner told them that his informant, the wholesaler, had bought his shares from the same broker, and had used his services in the past for some profitable deals.

The information that the wholesaler himself was investing lifted their spirits. The rumbling in Wanda's belly stopped for a moment.

Perhaps . . .

"The papers are all in order. I met the gentleman from Berlin yesterday, I looked at the share certificates myself, and I examined them carefully. Everything's just as it should be." David Wagner laughed. "It's hard to believe—but this could be the goose that lays our golden eggs . . ." His laugh died away in the silence.

"Do you think we're being too cautious, Gustav?" Karl asked at last.

Gustav shrugged. "It doesn't sound bad."

"What's the obstacle you mentioned?" Wanda asked. The Berlin stockbroker sounded more like a stroke of good luck to her.

Wagner explained that under the circumstances the Grosse bank was not prepared to act as their intermediary. Gerhard Grosse had refused to have any part of the deal. It would be one thing if the shares were freely available on the exchanges . . .

As it was, if the Lauscha investors bought the shares at their own risk and wanted to entrust them to the bank at a later date, then Grosse would be ready to sell them on the exchange for them. For the usual commission, of course.

"Naturally," Karl muttered.

"Goes without saying," Gustav grumbled.

"Hmm," Martin said.

Wanda said nothing. She listened to her stomach. She heard nothing. She didn't know whether this was a good or a bad sign. She searched Wagner's face, looking for an answer.

"I can't make the decision for you, nor would I want to," he said, his cheeks flushed with hectic red spots. "But . . . the bank has no better deal to offer you. This is our one chance. And if we don't grab it with both hands . . ."

CHAPTER THIRTY-FIVE

Anna knew that when a day started out the way this one had, it didn't get better. The trouble had started that morning when she got word that two of the women from the packing department were down with a summer flu and couldn't come in to work. Then the cart arrived to collect a shipment of Christmas ornaments for a large client in France. Anna was still busy assigning the day's tasks, so she had sent Johannes out to supervise the loading. It was only once the cart was long gone that she noticed that her brother had overlooked three crates of goods. Three crates! So now they would have to send them by rail. At their own expense.

But despite the morning's troubles, Anna was beaming.

Johannes kept looking over at her from his workbench. Whenever their eyes met, she looked away hastily. Johannes knew why she was in such fine spirits, and that annoyed her.

Richard had stopped by. Just as he used to do. When everything had still been all right.

Anna found it difficult to concentrate on her work, despite how much there was to do. Hundreds of rods of raw glass were waiting to be blown into globes, and that evening they would have to take the globes over to Karline Braun so that she could paint them the next day.

A sigh escaped Anna's lips. She would never have believed that it could be such hard work to run the workshop while Mother was away. There were countless little decisions to be made, and everybody—including Johannes—assumed that she would be the one to make them. Anna had to admit that she was flattered, but she also felt a weight on her shoulders that her brother didn't. Johannes had his own work at the bench, nothing more.

She cast an irritated glance at him, but he simply grinned back knowingly.

Anna took a new rod of glass from the bundle next to her and began to warm it in the middle, turning it evenly in the flame.

Why was there never any privacy in this house? Why did everybody always know everybody else's business?

An orange glow in the middle of the rod startled her from her thoughts. The glass was beginning to melt!

She hastily took the rod from the flame and then pulled it apart, so that each half had a long, straight tail on the end. She set one half aside and then pulled the other into little pieces. Then she did the same with the second half.

When she thought of making hundreds more pieces just like these, she felt a little dizzy. *Why didn't I give Magnus this job?* she wondered. *Then I could have moved straight on to blowing.* However, this job was monotonous enough to give her a chance to think in peace. And luckily, Johannes wasn't the sort to butt in with unwanted advice.

Don't get your hopes up! Richard only came to see you because he needed your advice as a glassblower. Don't read anything more into his visit.

Anna's smile died away. Was that her inner voice, warning her?

It had felt so good to sit side by side with Richard at the bench! The way their thighs had met—*accidentally*, of course . . . She hadn't been that close to him for a long time. Oh, if only she could tell him how much she loved him—he must know it!—and that she would be a much better wife to him than the American, who could never understand a man like Richard. A glassblower.

If only they could spend more time together! Have a few more chances to see each other, just the two of them. Without the others always getting in the way . . .

"Hello? Where is everybody? In the workshop, of course, how silly of me to ask!"

The door opened and let in a draft that blew all the flames sideways for a moment.

Anna looked up, irritated.

Wanda.

Anna's lips clamped tight together. *What's she doing here? How does she know that—*

"Busy as always, eh?" Wanda strolled across the room, making herself quite at home in the workshop. She stopped at the large sideboard where the cardboard boxes were waiting to be folded, and opened a drawer. She took out a handkerchief that Anna had only just washed and ironed and put away that morning, and sneezed into it mightily. *Doesn't Madam have her own handkerchief with her? Why does she have to help herself to one of ours?*

"Wanda, how nice to see you!" Johannes said, smiling broadly. "It's good that an important investor like you has time for simple folk like us . . ."

"Investor—stop, please!" Wanda laughed. "Sometimes I wonder how I ever got mixed up in all that." She shook her head and walked on, chatted with Magnus for a moment and talked to Griseldis by the silver bath. Johannes watched her longingly, as if he were hoping that Wanda would come back and pay attention to him again.

Anna stared stubbornly at her work.

Mixed up in all that—ha! Wanda had made sure that she was in the middle of the whole thing!

Anna still didn't know how Johannes could be so taken in by their American cousin. Why couldn't he recognize Wanda for who she really was? Was it because he was a man, blinded by her charm?

Anna had to admit that her cousin could be charming—and that she was wildly envious of her ability to walk into a room and make the air spark and tingle!

"Can you believe it?" Wanda said, sneezing again. "I was quite all right this morning, but then my nose began to itch on the train back from Sonneberg to Lauscha. I hope I don't get ill; that really would be a nuisance."

"Two of the women who pack for us are out sick," Johannes replied.

"What do you want here?" Anna asked coolly when Wanda passed by her bench. "If you're looking for Richard, he's no longer here!" So he'd told her that he was going to see Anna—he really was under her thumb! Anna felt a lump of disappointment in her throat and swallowed it down.

"Richard?" Wanda frowned. "What was he doing here?" She sneezed again and wiped her nose with the handkerchief. "Oh goodness—this always happens. I can hardly walk into the workshop before I get glitter absolutely everywhere!" She laughed and pointed to her hand, which gleamed gold in the sunlight.

Anna didn't say a word but just took another rod and held it into the flame.

Richard didn't tell her . . . Wanda didn't know that he'd been here . . . Anna trembled with happiness, only sorry she'd said anything.

Johannes turned back to his lamp with a disgruntled expression. It was obvious that he would far rather have been chatting with his cousin than attending to his work.

Wanda cleared her throat. "I don't want to disturb you, but may I use your telephone quickly? I'd like to call my parents."

"Mother called just a couple of days ago," Anna said without looking up from her lamp. "Everything's fine. I don't think she'd be very pleased if you called for no good reason." Somebody like Wanda never stopped to think how much things cost!

"I don't want to call about your parents—I'm sure they're having a lovely time!" Wanda said. "When I think of the sightseeing tours that Mother had planned for them . . . No, I want some advice from Steven. It's rather important. And somewhat . . . confidential. I wouldn't like to make this kind of call from the post office."

"Of course you can use the telephone!" Johannes said hastily. "You know where it is." He nodded toward the hallway.

Although Anna did her best not to pay attention, she couldn't help but overhear scraps of Wanda's side of the conversation.

"Oh, Mother . . . I miss you so much! Nobody to talk to . . . a cup of coffee with you . . ."

Coffee! Wanda never thought of anything but her own fun. No wonder Richard wasn't happy with her.

That said, Anna had to acknowledge that Richard hadn't complained about Wanda's frivolous habits. Quite the opposite. "Wanda thinks of nothing but this company of hers and the investments," he had grumbled. "She doesn't seem to realize that this exhibition is make-or-break for me!" Oddly enough, he had also declared in the very same breath that he didn't want Wanda *interfering* with his business. Anna couldn't see how that all fit together. After all, Richard had never been bothered before by women having their own jobs! He had always had great respect for Johanna and her work, and for Anna and hers as well. And why was he coming to Anna for advice if he didn't want anyone to interfere? Why didn't he go to Thomas Heimer? They shared the Heimer workshop, after all! So many questions . . .

Wanda had finished talking to her mother. Her voice sounded different now, almost uncertain, which was quite uncharacteristic of Wanda. She probably had her stepfather on the other end of the line.

"A shipping company, based in Bremen—do you understand? Shares for sale, but—oh, it's all too complicated to explain," she said, her voice shaking. "Drat it all, what a dreadful connection!"

As Anna sat there, pulling rods into little pieces and listening to Wanda talk, she couldn't untangle all the questions in her head.

"Information . . . A cotton plantation in Mississippi called . . . Really? You know it? And what do you—Father! Daddy! Hello, Steven, hello?"

Anna smiled spitefully. What a bit of bad luck for Wanda that just when she needed to have a highly confidential conversation, the line should be so bad . . .

"You own some shares in the plantation? And they really are just about to . . . Yes, that's right—the contract! Thank Heavens, that means that our information really is sound. Oh, Father, you can't imagine what a relief this is!"

Wanda gave a loud, near-hysterical laugh, and it was such an odd sound that even Johannes glanced at the hallway with a flicker of doubt in his eyes. Anna looked from him to all the others, annoyed—not one of them was concentrating on their work. Wonderful. So Wanda had managed to turn everybody's life topsy-turvy again!

When Wanda came back into the workshop a little while later, her cheeks were flushed and her eyes were sparkling.

"Oh, we had such a dreadful connection!" she groaned. Anna didn't respond. What was she supposed to say? Couldn't Wanda just leave? But instead she came closer and looked over Anna's shoulder.

"You really are a wonderful glassblower," she said. "The things you can do!" She nodded toward the box full of prepared pieces. "If only Marie could see you now . . ."

Marie—she had only ever thought about her own work, just like Wanda, Anna thought. How often she had gone to her aunt with a new design or even a ready-made sample piece, only to have Marie say that she had no time for her. She was too wrapped up in her own fine ideas. Ideas that Anna couldn't possibly have—because there was only one Marie, after all. And there could only be one great glassblower.

All at once it was too much for Anna. The irritations of the morning, the worry that perhaps she wasn't yet ready to run the workshop on her own, all the questions swirling around in her head . . . and on top of all that, the fact that she had no idea where she stood with Richard.

She pushed her stool back so abruptly that it scraped loudly on the floor. Then she turned on Wanda.

"What do you know about work? You, who've never done a day's work in your life?" she snapped. "You come waltzing in here and stop other people from getting on with their work, you use our telephone at our expense, you cause chaos wherever you go—and you don't even notice!" Anna heard how shrill her voice was, but there was nothing she could do about it. "You can spare me your compliments. They won't get you anywhere!" Anna crossed her arms in front of her so that nobody would see she was trembling. "Ever since you arrived in Lauscha you've done nothing but cause trouble! If you hadn't turned up, Richard and I would still be a couple! But no, you had to steal my man, and then you took Marie's child—" She heard Wanda inhale sharply. She could see Johannes out of the corner of her eye as he almost fell off his stool in shock. But she didn't care. Somebody had to tell the American what they thought of her. "And now you take other people's money and fritter it away on shady stock-market deals! I've never heard anything like it! You never worked for anything that you have. You're a thief—you live at everybody else's expense, and you don't care what it costs as long as you have your fun. You're . . ." Anna waved her hands frantically as though she could grab the right word from thin air—"you're . . . a freeloader. You're . . . just awful!"

* * *

Karl, Gustav, and Martin were waiting for Wanda down on the old foundry square.

"So? Did you reach your father?"

"What did he say?"

"Has Steven Miles ever heard of this cotton plantation? Does it have a good reputation?"

"Have the ships reached America yet?"

"Does he know anything about—"

Wanda looked at the three men as though she had never seen them before in her life. She had quite forgotten that she had arranged to meet them here.

She had fled the workshop as fast as she could and run up the steep hillside without worrying about her shoes or her red swollen nose or the odd looks that people gave her as she passed. But she could not run from what Anna had said. With every step, her cousin's accusations rang louder in Wanda's ears.

"*You live at everybody else's expense.*"

"*You're a thief.*"

"*You've done nothing but cause trouble.*"

The words raced through Wanda's head like cockroaches, and she felt so disgusted that she could barely breathe.

"Wanda! Come on, girl, say something!"

Karl took her arm, jolting her from her thoughts. She cleared her throat.

What did these men want from her?

The crackling in her ear . . . the telephone line and the bad connection . . . Mother asking her to come home. Steven . . . cotton . . . the ships . . . Richard . . .

Why had he gone to see Anna?

The thoughts swirled in Wanda's mind and her head pounded. She passed her hand over her forehead to drive the cockroaches away. To get rid of the pounding. *Don't take it to heart so!* she scolded herself. *Anna's just a silly girl! She doesn't know how hurtful her words can be. She's just jealous. She always has been. Because of Richard.*

Wanda took a deep breath. "Everything's . . . all right." This wasn't the time to think about Richard. Or Anna. She took another breath and tried to put on an encouraging smile. "Steven has a lot of shares in that plantation himself. He confirmed everything that David Wagner told us . . ."

"But that's . . . that's wonderful news! My child, why on earth do you look so upset?" Karl laughed. They looked at one another and then threw their arms around each other's shoulders. Wanda blinked. She didn't laugh with them. She couldn't.

"You don't care what it costs as long as you have your fun. You're a freeloader."

CHAPTER THIRTY-SIX

The next day Wanda found herself back in David Wagner's office at the bank. She told him that the villagers were ready to buy into the deal and that he should arrange a meeting with the Berlin broker.

When David Wagner heard that Wanda had checked up on his information, he was pleased rather than offended. He admired Wanda for calling her stepfather, and he told her so. He almost felt like getting up from behind his desk and kissing her. Just like that. Because everything was all right. Instead he sat where he was, grinning broadly. He noticed, however, that Wanda didn't look equally pleased. He was baffled that she could remain so unmoved. Was she ill, perhaps? Or was she losing her nerve? Making money was men's work, after all . . . For a moment he toyed with the idea of inviting her for a beer in a nearby pub, but he didn't dare.

It was their money, Karl and the others had argued, and they were the clients. So the Berlin broker had to go to them, rather than the other way around. Since Gerhard Grosse had forbidden David to be there when the deal was made, he didn't really care where the share certificates were handed over. He told Strobel's private broker to go to Lauscha.

Strobel had warned David about the broker: "The gentleman may behave rather oddly and speak crudely, but he has unique connections in the world of high finance," Strobel had said, shrugging dismissively. It was as though he were saying, *Only a narrow-minded fool would bother about external appearances in such a case.* David had nodded wisely. In turn, he warned the villagers that the broker may seem rough around the edges.

* * *

Two days later the Berlin broker was in the Black Eagle to meet Karl Flein, Martin Ehrenpreis, and Gustav Müller.

Knowing that this was an important occasion, Benno hung a sign on the door announcing that the tavern was closed for a private function—he had to take care of his guests, after all.

Wanda sat at the table with them, sweating and shivering. Her sniffles had developed into a full-blown summer cold.

The broker sniffled the whole time as well, but otherwise he seemed entirely focused on the transaction. He counted the money three times, neatly stacking the notes and coins on the table. Finally he took delivery of 11,000 marks.

In exchange he handed over a folder containing the richly engraved and illustrated share certificates. The glassblowers looked at them in awe.

A large sailboat dominated the design, and the words Bremen Schlüter Lines curled elegantly around it, partly covering the sails and a red-and-gold border. The broker told them that each share had a value of 500 marks, and pointed to the number on the certificates. Karl and the others nodded, impressed.

"To think that a piece of paper can be worth so much," Karl murmured, while he held up a certificate against the light in his calloused hands. "Don't they look lovely . . . ?"

The broker laughed. "You can say that again!"

They drank a round of schnapps to seal the deal. Then the broker left in a hurry, explaining that he had to be in Schweinfurt that same evening.

"Here's to the goose that lays the golden eggs!" Karl shouted as soon as the door closed behind the man. He reached for the bottle, and his hands trembled as he poured more schnapps and passed the glasses round the table. He put the folder with the certificates into a thick leather case—they had all agreed that he should look after them. Wanda would rather have taken the certificates to the bank for David Wagner to keep, but Karl dismissed the idea. He said that the certificates were safe with him until the day they would bring them to the bank to sell.

"To the goose that lays the golden eggs!" the men shouted. Wanda nodded. She felt rather dizzy. The glasses clinked and the schnapps burned their throats as it went down.

"It's very odd, but I get the feeling that I've seen that fellow somewhere before . . ." Benno muttered as he held up the bottle to offer another refill. "I'm trying to think where that might have been . . ."

"Oh, yes, you're always doing deals with stocks and shares, you are!" Martin said, holding out his empty glass.

"He must be a regular visitor, dropping by all the time with his certificates!" Karl laughed.

"I'm serious!" Benno said. "You don't forget a man like that in a hurry. But I can't for the life of me think where I've seen him! It wasn't in Lauscha, at any rate."

CHAPTER THIRTY-SEVEN

Mid-September 1911

The new church was packed, the men in their heavy black Sunday suits and the women in their fine white Sunday dresses. They sat in the pews, jammed in elbow to elbow. Even people like Thomas Heimer, Richard, and Wanda, who didn't normally attend church, had made their way there today, on September 17—partly because they were curious about what the new church looked like and partly because they simply wanted to be part of the event for which they had already played a role. Without the generous donations from the villagers, the church would not have been half as lovely: Herrmann Greiner had donated money for six of the windows. The large window over the main door was a gift from the Steiner family. Ernst Müller had paid for the organ. Another family had paid for two lamps on the altar, and the crucifix was from the widow whose house Wanda had thought about buying back when Richard had still seemed interested in sharing a home with her and Sylvie.

The village newsletter had published a list of the donations the week before. *No wonder people had next to nothing left to give when we were raising subscriptions for the company*, Wanda thought when she saw the sums published—some people had given a great deal of money.

She looked around the church in amazement. She could hardly believe that the first stone had been laid only the summer before. How on earth had they built something like this in only thirteen months? "The good Lord held his hand out to protect the work," Eva had said on the way to the church. "He sent nothing but good weather for the workers, and he protected them from accidents." Eva had embroidered an elaborate altar cloth, and she pointed it out to Wanda as soon as they entered.

What a lovely building, Wanda thought. It was built of heavy blocks of dressed stone, and up in the belfry were the three great bells that had arrived by train just a few days before. There had been quite a celebration at Lauscha station when they were delivered, though Wanda hadn't been there to see it, for she had been looking after Sylvie that day.

The cross above the simple altar was a fine piece of wood carving. Everybody in the church had a clear view of the suffering on Jesus's face. This was the altar where she and Richard planned to stand. Where they would become man and wife. For richer, for poorer, for better, for worse . . . But they weren't even talking about that at the moment. Nor were they talking about the house that they wanted to buy. There was no time for any of that—because of the exhibition.

No time—to talk about their future together?

Wanda slid her hand unobtrusively into Richard's. She opened her mouth to tell him what she was thinking, but he was staring so fixedly ahead that she lost the will to speak. Today was a special day, not a day for brooding on dark thoughts.

The stained-glass windows provided a rich display of color. The sun was shining, and the windows glowed as though lit from within. The members of the congregation nudged one another in the ribs and pointed up at the pictures in the glass, smiling. Some had tears in their eyes.

Wanda found herself blinking back tears as well. Not because of the Christian message of the Bible scenes in the windows, but because they made her think of Marie. How she would have loved them! She had made glass pictures just like these in her workshop in Genoa. Trees, flowers, landscapes—Marie had taken cold glass and brought it to life with her artist's hand. She had breathed life into her work, but then she herself had died . . .

Wanda sniffed loudly and her father looked over at her. She forced a smile and then shut her eyes. The priest announced the next hymn, but she couldn't sing along. She didn't know the tune and the words were old-fashioned and hard for her to pronounce. But the sound of many voices in song wrapped round her like an embrace. Wanda sighed.

Anna and Johannes were sitting on the opposite side of the aisle. Wanda had seen them as she came in. She had nodded briefly to Johannes but ignored Anna. Her cousin's words still stung. "Don't pay any attention to that sort of talk!" her father had said when Wanda came to him in tears after her visit to the Steinmann workshop. "Anna's jealous because of Richard, that's all! People like to get into fights. Men use their fists and women use words. But it boils down to the same thing in the end—people like to hurt others, but they hurt themselves at the same time." Wanda knew that he was right. All the same it had hurt her terribly when Anna flung those accusations at her.

Richard had said nothing more about the episode. Yes, he'd been to see Anna, he admitted when she'd asked; it was about his work. When Wanda had asked why he hadn't gone to her father, he just shrugged. "You lot only ever talk about one thing in that household these days! Nobody can get any real work done there," he answered. And Wanda hadn't asked any more questions.

"You had to steal my man, and then you took Marie's child—"

Forget Anna, Wanda scolded herself as the congregation raised their voices together in song. Tomorrow was the big day—that was all that mattered.

Dear Lord, please let everything be all right.

Tomorrow she would go to Sonneberg to give David the shares so that he could sell them. Although it had seemed that these weeks would never end, the time had come at last.

Wanda sighed. She would never have thought that doing nothing could be such torment. Given the choice, she would rather have worked breaking stones in a quarry until her fingers bled! Anything would have been better than the endless waiting of these last few weeks. Days when the minutes seemed to last for hours, when the hours seemed to last for days. Night after night when she could not sleep.

And thinking all the time of the ships on their way back to Bremen from the American South, hoping that they were safe. There were so many things that could go wrong! There might be a storm at sea, a shipwreck; in the worst case, several ships could be lost to storms. Pirates looking for a fat prize. Wars breaking out.

Wanda scolded herself for such thoughts. *Be optimistic!* she told herself. Her father smiled at her fears, and Richard said, "Don't fret so much—even if something happens, there's nothing you can do about it!" Neither of them exactly helped her to get over the waiting.

Waiting, waiting for the big day. David had said that it would be September 18.

Wanda looked up again at the wooden cross over the altar and pleaded for help.

The only relief from the endless waiting had been a few trips into Sonneberg. Sometimes Wanda had taken Sylvie with her, but she had occasionally left the baby with Eva. Wanda could feel the summer heat gradually giving way to something else. Summer was over but fall had not yet arrived. Something new was on the way. She could feel it in the crystal-clear air. She could see it in the leaves falling from the trees. Something was coming to an end—and something new was starting.

In Sonneberg she always went to see David Wagner. She was the spokeswoman for the investors, so it was only right that she should find out how their investment was performing, wasn't it? That at least was how she justified her frequent visits. She would have been shocked at the suggestion that she was taking up his precious time. Not that David Wagner had ever made her feel that way!

He did not share her worries about the ships, but he took her fears seriously and explained that the captains of the Schlüter line were well trained, that pirates tended to prefer ships carrying spices or precious metals, and that there was no prospect of a war. Wanda nodded. All the same . . .

"Read these!" David said, pointing to the thick pile of newspapers that he always had in his office. "It's important to keep up with what's happening in the world," he told her. "The more you know, the better you can assess a situation and the less you have to rely on speculation."

When Wanda had learned that he got the newspapers from Alois Sawatzky, she told David that Sawatzky was a friend of hers as well.

At first Wanda had been less than keen on sitting and reading with him like this. She would rather just have talked. About this and that, about life. But she soon realized that when she was reading, her worries diminished and her nerves were steadied. There were no reports of tropical storms in the Atlantic. Nothing about piracy. And nothing about ships from America to Bremen sinking.

"You just wait until the ships arrive in Bremen in good order! My contact in Berlin says that as soon as they've docked, the Schlüter company will officially announce the contract with the Americans. Then, of course, the information will reach the finance pages of the newspapers. And that's the only news we're interested in, because that means that the share price will soar!" David always waved his hand in the air when he said that as though he were urging the share price upward all by himself. He often ended by saying, "We'll show them all!" and then he and Wanda would laugh.

Wanda fell into the habit of going to the bank in the afternoon, when most of the employees were finishing up for the day and she and David could sit and read together undisturbed. Sometimes they were so absorbed in their reading that Wanda barely caught the last train back to Lauscha. When that happened, she would arrive in the village in the dark and see the lights of the glassblowers' lamps flickering in the windows. Wanda always came back from Sonneberg in a good mood. Why did she always feel so at peace when she was with David?

Because she trusted him and enjoyed their time together?

But the feeling vanished almost as soon as she got home. Then her thoughts began going round and round again as before. What if . . .

Unlike her, the investors from the village didn't fret so much. Wanda didn't know why exactly they were so optimistic—was it religious faith, or simply a lack of imagination? The glassblowers took it for granted that their investment would be wildly successful.

They met at the Black Eagle almost every night. If they were to form a registered company, there were still some formalities to attend to and some letters to write. They also had to assign jobs and responsibilities within the future company. Everybody quickly agreed that Karl Flein would stay on as foreman. It wasn't immediately clear what Gustav Müller would do. Some of the investors thought that he was too strict about the sorting of the wares—though this came from glassblowers who sometimes delivered second-rate goods themselves—while others claimed that he was not strict enough. In the end, they decided that Gustav should stay in his post. People who had never worked in the Gründler foundry but had invested in the company asked what role they would play in the new business. Arguments inevitably ensued; everybody had his own ideas and was offended when the others didn't take these up enthusiastically. But overall, the evenings were filled with constructive discussion. Little by little they drew up a plan for the future organization of the foundry that most people could live with. Otto Gründler often joined them. The prospect of being able to sell to the villagers had made a new man of him. His cool manner was quite changed now; he laughed along with the others, argued, and gave away trade secrets that he would never have dreamed of revealing in the old days. "When I'm on my way to America in January, it will be with the happy knowledge that my life's work is in the best of hands back here!" he said one evening, and the glassblowers were touched by his words. They quickly ordered another round of beer and drank a toast to Otto's new life in America.

Wanda attended most of these meetings as well. She couldn't stay at home in the evenings—it drove her mad to be there. *"You take other people's money and fritter it away!"* After Anna had let fly at her, she mostly held her tongue and only spoke if she was asked a direct question. That happened often enough, though.

"You are such a stroke of good luck for Lauscha!" Martha Flein had told her just a few days ago. "I've never seen my Karl in such a good mood!" And she had hugged Wanda so hard that she had hardly been able to breathe.

Now that she was no longer the center of attention, she enjoyed watching the group grow more unified without even being aware of it. Even Richard, who was still very skeptical about the whole business, had to admit that he had seldom seen the villagers so enthused. "Each and every one of them can get excited about an idea, of course," he said. "We've always been that way, and no wonder, given the competition in our trade. But to see everybody working together like this . . ." He shook his head in amazement. And Wanda beamed with delight.

The trust that the villagers had placed in her and the warm welcome she received everywhere she went made it easier to cope with Richard's indifference.

Oh, when the world was watching, he was still her loving fiancé. Sometimes he pushed Sylvie's carriage when the three of them took a walk through Lauscha—though that happened only rarely these days. It was as though he wanted to say, *Look at this, people, I don't mind my future wife wheeling and dealing.* But when they were alone Wanda always felt that deep down he really did mind her getting mixed up in the world of business.

Richard . . .

The thought of her fiancé's strange behavior made Wanda sigh.

"What's wrong?" her father asked. She glanced at him, uncertain what to say.

She occasionally found herself wondering if perhaps her mother was right. Perhaps she really wasn't suited to be a glassblower's wife? She tried not to worry about Richard and to follow the church service. But instead she started thinking about the company again. As the deacon intoned a prayer she realized they needed a new name for the foundry. She decided to raise the question at the next meeting.

The next meeting . . .

By then the glassblowers really would own the foundry. After she presented the share certificates at the bank tomorrow, everything else would be a formality. The Bremen company's ships had gotten back to harbor safe and sound two full weeks ago. The share price rose and rose and rose. In just a few days it had tripled, then quadrupled.

Wanda, Karl, Gustav, and Martin had been to see David Wagner three times.

And three times he had given them the same answer. "Just wait! The price will keep going up!"

On Friday, when Wanda had been in Sonneberg on her own, he had finally said, "The time has come!"

Wanda hadn't even noticed that she had closed her eyes. Now she opened them again. She blinked and looked up at the altar. Red and blue beams of sunlight fell through the colored glass above the altar and into the church.

Into the paradise of glass.

CHAPTER THIRTY-EIGHT

Wanda walked toward the railway station, her back straight, her face expressionless. As always at this time of day the station was busy. Glassblowers from nearby Lauscha who had delivered their wares to a wholesaler in Sonneberg mingled with housewives from Steinach and the surrounding villages who had finished their shopping in town and were hurrying home. Solemn businessmen stood around, important-looking briefcases in hand. Many of them tilted their faces upward to catch the last warm rays of sunshine.

But Wanda didn't feel the sunshine, even though it was unusually warm for mid-September. Nor did she notice the tempting scent of grilled sausages wafting through the air from a nearby stall.

When she finally reached the platform, the tension drained from her face. Over. Finished. She didn't have to put on a brave face any longer. Nobody would care if she howled or screamed, if she sobbed and sniffled and her nose ran like a child's.

But she didn't howl. And she didn't scream.

She didn't even feel her own sorrow.

Because she'd lost everything.

She had let down her nearest and dearest. She was a failure, utterly and completely.

Hadn't she always known that?

"*You're a freeloader.*"

"*You live at everybody else's expense.*"

"*You don't care what it costs as long as you have your fun.*"

She gazed down at the railway track. Oh, how well she knew the train ride from Sonneberg to Lauscha! She knew its every curve, the corners where the motion of the train pressed her against the side of the hard bench, the spot where the engine began to huff and puff and slowed down. She knew where the shadows lay on the steep mountainsides, when the compartments would be invaded by sudden gloom.

She'd always considered it such a romantic ride! And she'd always thought that Lauscha, where she got off the train, was romantic too. The little town nestled into its high valley, the very heart of the paradise of glass . . .

Wanda groaned. The thought of all those people waiting for her at the station made her stomach cramp. There must be a welcoming committee there already, probably ready to greet her with wine and song—why else had they all insisted on staying behind in Lauscha, today of all days, instead of coming along with her to Sonneberg? And now she had to face these dear, sweet souls—the people who had trusted her with everything and who wanted to celebrate her return—and she would have to look them in the eye and tell them that they had lost everything.

Her gaze fell on the stack of worthless paper that she had stuffed carelessly into her bag at the bank.

"*What do you know about work?*"

Nothing, Anna, nothing. .

The end of a long summer.

The end.

She'd never take that train again; she'd never ride the railway to Lauscha.

She had reached the end of her journey.

Her visit to Friedhelm Strobel had shown her as much. She had been so desperate that she could think of nothing better to do than go and talk to him. The wholesaler who had tipped them off about the shares in the first place. David Wagner had let his name slip when she was in his office.

Wanda shuddered again. *Don't think about it, don't think about it*, she said to herself again and again.

The way his hands had reached out to grab her, his sour breath in her face, his eyes, so—arrogant.

At first she had not understood what was about to happen, within the neat wooden walls of his shop—the very thought was simply ludicrous. By the time she had grasped the truth, it was almost too late. If she hadn't run to the door that very instant—if she hadn't been quick enough—he would have gotten a hold of her and . . . *No, don't think about it!*

She heard the train pulling in behind her. There was already a hint of coal in the air. The closer the train came, the stronger the smell of soot would become. Right now the people on the platform were gazing up into the sunshine, enjoying the warmth, but soon they would begin to cough and wrinkle their noses.

Only last winter a young woman had thrown herself in front of a train as it came into the station. Her appalling death had been headline news in all the papers. At the time Wanda could not imagine the depths of despair that could drive a person to do such a thing. She had said that it was cowardly to end your life that way. She could still remember talking to Eva about it right after it had happened—they had ended up arguing about it. Eva said that she understood why the woman had committed suicide, she understood her despair, and that she would never say that a person who did such a thing was a coward. After all, it wasn't an easy death to be torn to pieces on the rails, to have your limbs ripped apart by several tons of metal, your whole body crushed . . . Wanda hadn't wanted to listen.

You and your self-satisfied arrogance! You always thought you could take care of everything on your own. Imagined that you were better than the rest of them. That you were smarter, cleverer, braver.

"Ever since you arrived in Lauscha you've done nothing but cause trouble!"

Yes, Anna.

But that's all over now.

The shrill sound of the braking train grew louder and louder. Wanda turned around, saw the black colossus approaching, belching out smoke.

Over. Finished. She'd lost it all.

She took a step forward.

Just then, somebody behind her grabbed her shoulder hard.

CHAPTER THIRTY-NINE

The man's hands come closer, closer. Strong, damp hands, reaching for her, just a hair's breadth away. His breath reaches her now, smelling of rot and decay. She presses her lips together; her nostrils quiver as she tries to hold her breath. She wants to scream, but to do that she would have to open her mouth and breathe. All she can do is groan softly, too softly to be of any use. Who would hear her? The walls are thick and solid, the door made of heavy wood. The door is closed; the man blocked it when she came in.

His voice. "We don't want anybody to disturb us . . ."

Another groan, louder, more fearful. Nobody to hear her.

She has to get away from here, get away . . .

She tries to tear herself away with all her strength, but her feet are stuck to the floor. The floor is as damp as his hands and as rotten as his breath. Don't breathe, don't breathe. In a panic, she stares up at the wooden ceiling, whose pattern begins to blur before her eyes. Everything is dark; there is no sunlight, no lamp. It is as dark as a crypt. And the man at the center of it all. Don't look at the man; perhaps he will melt away into thin air. Shut your eyes . . .

There is a cackling laugh that makes Wanda think of a bird of prey in the forest.

Before Wanda can even think, fingers sink into her arm, tearing at her jacket, and the fabric digs painfully into her flesh—

Wanda screamed. She thrashed, twisted and turned, and screamed some more.

"My child! For Heaven's sake, Wanda!"

No, don't open your eyes!

Hands shook her by the arm, but these hands were warm and dry, not cold and damp.

"Wanda!" The voice—the voice was different.

Something tickled at her nose. The smell was different too. This place smelled of paper, dust, leather. It smelled—of books.

She wasn't in that dreadful shop any more.

"Wanda! Wake up!"

Wanda took a cautious breath. Her eyelids fluttered slowly, opening uncertainly, and she found herself looking into a pair of kind eyes.

"Mr. Sawatzky . . ." Her voice was hoarse and sounded strange to her.

"It's all right. You're with me, and you're safe. Everything's all right . . ." He reached behind her and tried to help her sit up. Wanda struggled upright, albeit unwillingly.

Alois Sawatzky looked at her sadly. "My child, you gave me such a shock! It was lucky that I happened to be at the station! I don't even want to think what would have happened if—" He jumped to his feet and was at the door in an instant. "I've made tea. I'll be right back. Chamomile tea, it will do you good."

Chamomile tea. Wanda nodded.

The station. Leaves dancing lazily across the platform. The tracks, the dreadful whistling in her ears. All a dream, nothing but a dreadful dream. Wasn't it?

She wanted to shut her eyes—not to think, not to feel—but instead she looked around the room, which was full of books, lined up in rows on the shelves, stacked up on chairs, lying on the floor. Oddly, there was also furniture among the books: a washstand with a shaving kit; a coatrack with a coat, hat, and scarf; the chaise longue that she sat on and a small table next to it; and, on the other side of the room, a narrow alcove with a bed covered by a brown blanket.

It took Wanda a moment to understand that she was in Alois Sawatzky's private apartment rather than in his shop. There wasn't much difference, in fact, apart from the few pieces of furniture.

She could no longer escape her thoughts. This was no nightmare; this was all too real.

Wanda groaned. She drew up her legs, wrapped her arms around them, and rested her head on her knees. She rocked back and forth, waiting for tears that did not come.

She replayed the whole scene in her mind.

David and herself, in his office. David sitting there looking like a whipped dog. David saying over and over again, "How could such a thing have happened?" and "I checked the certificates! There was nothing wrong with them!"

Her own confusion. "What is it? What's the matter?"

"The shares are forgeries! They're worthless!"

She had frowned and then laughed. "Don't make silly jokes!"

"I'm not joking, I'm deadly serious! Strobel—" David was talking so fast that he burst into a fit of coughing before he could go on. "I must go and see the wholesaler who gave me the tip! He bought shares from that broker as well. Perhaps he has some explanation as to how . . ." David stopped again and stared into empty space for a moment before he said again, softly, "Forgeries . . ."

"But it can't be! I don't believe it!"

David had tried to show her what was wrong with the certificates, but Wanda had simply covered her eyes with her hands. Who cared about the details now?

It was all over. They had been taken in by a swindler. They were ruined. The villagers' money was gone—which for many of them meant their life savings! The foundry would soon belong to somebody else. And all because she, Wanda, had persuaded them to invest in this deal. She had never felt so miserable in her life.

Every bone and muscle in her body had ached. She had stood up in a daze and left David's office. He had called after her to stay a little longer and calm down, but in vain.

Outside, in front of the bank, she had felt her resolve return. She hardly recognized her own voice as she asked the way to Friedhelm Strobel's shop. Every step was torture.

She had wanted to talk to the man. He had been taken in as well, after all. He was another victim—wasn't that what David had said?

What had she been hoping for? That he would say everything was all right, there was no cause for alarm? That it was all just a bad joke?

But he wasn't another victim. He was repulsive. Horrible. The greed in his eyes had frightened her. The way he had licked his lips! And those hands! If she hadn't managed to wrench open the bar on the door and run, run, run—

"Wanda, here, I've brought the tea. Drink some. Everything will be all right."

The smell of chamomile reached Wanda's nostrils. She lifted her head from her knees and took the cup that Sawatzky held out to her. Her hand trembled. The cup was hot.

She put her lips to the rim and drank. The tea didn't taste as strong as the smell had led her to expect. Wanda's eyes stung, though no tears came.

The bookseller watched her drink. His quiet friendship was more than Wanda could bear.

"Why didn't you just leave me be earlier, at the station?" she murmured as she placed her teacup on the table. "Why? It would all be over for me by now."

Sawatzky frowned and the friendly concern in his eyes died away. "Don't commit yet another sin, Wanda! You have family, you're engaged to be married, you have a child, Marie's child! She entrusted her baby to you! And you want to sneak away from those responsibilities like a thief in the night?"

Wanda began to cry. Hot tears that spilled down her cheeks.

A thief. That was exactly what she was.

"Anna was right," she sobbed. "She was right about everything."

Burying her head in her arms, she cried so hard that she could barely breathe.

Alois Sawatzky shook his head helplessly. "Whatever am I to do with you . . . I could talk to your fiancé! Perhaps he'll know what—"

Anything but that! Wanda raised her head abruptly. The thought of having to see Richard was so appalling that she could barely stand it. At the same time she longed for him so much that it hurt.

"I'm a failure!" she shouted at the bookseller. "Richard doesn't need me! Nobody does. When I think of all the people who trusted me! I should never have opened my mouth! But I always have to blurt out my silly ideas. Make myself important. And all I do is bring people bad luck!" The thought that there were people in Lauscha awaiting her return was more than she could bear. Her sobs grew louder. So loud that she could hardly hear Alois Sawatzky's words.

"You fell victim to a confidence trickster! That's dreadful. Most upsetting, of course. But these things happen. That's the bitter truth about life. It's no reason to kill yourself!"

"How do you know—"

"How do I know?" Sawatzky replied impatiently. "Do you think that you were the only one who could barely wait for this day to come? Our mutual friend David Wagner has been talking about nothing else for weeks now; he mentioned this investment of yours every time he came to visit! He was even here yesterday, on a Sunday, disturbing my day of rest. And today you throw yourself in front of a train—my God, child, all I had to do was put two and two together."

"David . . ." Wanda murmured.

"Yes, David Wagner! A fine young man. You didn't even give him a thought when you were trying to end it all! If you had died, you would have left him too—left him with all his rage, his despair, his anger. He would have felt guilty for the rest of his life. But you didn't even consider that! It would all be over for you, but . . ." Sawatzky knew his tone was harsh, which wasn't like him at all.

"How can you be so cruel? What's left for me now in this life? Everything that I've ever tried to do has gone wrong! It's always been like that. How can you just say what's happened is the bitter truth about life? I don't want any more of it. I can't go on . . ." She lay back down on the chaise longue, drew up her knees again, and curled into a ball.

"Don't think so much of yourself, Wanda!" Sawatzky snapped. "Those glassblowers are grown men. Hardheaded fellows who are well accustomed to making decisions. Well, this time they made the wrong one. But it certainly wasn't because the American girl led them astray! You never had that much influence on them . . ."

"That's what you think," Wanda said bitterly. What did he know about the countless meetings it had taken even to set up the company? What did he know about Karl's indecisiveness or Martin's worries or Gustav's doubts? About all the tedious discussions in the Black Eagle? No, Alois Sawatzky knew nothing.

Neither of them said a word for some time. Eventually, Sawatzky cleared his throat and started again. "I don't know whether you're even interested . . . I was at the station to meet a fellow bookseller from Coburg, a friend of mine. While you were asleep earlier, I sent my friend to see David at the bank. I wanted to be sure that my assumption about the investment was correct. David insisted on coming straight here." Sawatzky shook his head. "He turned white as chalk when he saw you lying here. He was utterly distraught, the poor fellow!"

Wanda lifted her head slowly. "Really?"

The bookseller sighed. "In any case . . . David Wagner believes that the best thing would be for you to stay here until you have recovered from the shock. He's already on his way to Lauscha. He'll try to explain what happened to the glassblowers."

"David's what?" Wanda sat up straight. The thought of what David would find in Lauscha horrified her. But she was also flooded with relief. Relief that she was not the one who had to bring the villagers the bad news.

Her eyes filled with tears again. "He would do that for me . . . ?"

"Oh, my child," Sawatzky said. "Calm down. I'm sure it won't be that bad. After all, we're not in ancient Rome. We no longer kill the messenger who brings us bad news . . ."

"I wouldn't be so sure about that," Wanda said quietly, and burst into tears again.

CHAPTER FORTY

David stared ahead, his face void of emotion. He didn't notice the stillness of the air in early fall; he didn't feel the passing of time as the seasons turned. His first big stock market investment—his big gamble! Ha! Swindled. How could such a thing have happened?

David clenched his fists involuntarily, digging his neatly trimmed fingernails into the balls of his hands until they left marks.

How could it have happened?

If only this train journey could last all day! He didn't want to think of what awaited him in Lauscha. If it weren't for Wanda . . . But he had to be strong for her. He had to face this trial, for her sake.

The morning had begun so well. Despite the secretary's protests that it was too expensive, he had insisted that she arrange a telephone connection to the Berlin stock exchange so that he could sell the shares when he judged the moment was right. She had pursed her lips, looked down her nose at him, and declared that she would have to inform Mr. Grosse about it. David had merely shrugged.

He had been elated when he heard over the phone line that the Schlüter shares had climbed again! The Lauscha investors' shares were now worth more than 60,000 marks—and they had cost barely 11,000. Even David thought that making so much money in such a short time was very nearly a miracle. He planned to sell the shares at noon and had already gotten it all lined up.

He had hardly been able to wait for Wanda and the glassblowers to arrive. He had considered over and over again how he would tell them. He couldn't announce a profit like this in plain and simple words, could he? It needed a touch of drama to increase the tension and then the rejoicing. Oh, he had so looked forward to the moment when the villagers' luck would change! And all thanks to him!

When there was a knock on his door at eleven o'clock, he had straightened his tie one last time. He found it hard to conceal his disappointment when he saw that Wanda had come alone. This was his big moment—he would have liked a bigger audience for it.

But all thoughts of his big moment had vanished seconds later when he stared in horror at the stack of certificates that Wanda took from her bag and placed on the desk in front of him.

He leafed through the papers several times. This . . . this just couldn't be! It was impossible! He ran his fingers along the edges, felt the paper, and held the sheets up against the light to check for watermarks—but it was all in vain. The guilloches—the complicated geometric lines around the edges of the paper—were simply printed on! They should have been embossed into the sheets with a special machine. A machine that only a very few printing houses owned, namely those that were authorized to print share certificates. And these printing houses were obliged to state their name at the bottom of each certificate, so that everybody could see which printer had issued which shares. But the sheets of paper David held in his hands had nothing but a smudged diamond pattern.

They were forgeries! Well-made forgeries.

Of course he had felt Wanda's questioning eyes upon him. She may even have spoken aloud.

How in the world . . . ?

He was so astonished that it practically knocked the wind out of him.

He had checked the Berlin broker's certificates with his own eyes! Everything had been in order—from the paper to the watermarks to the serial numbers and the guilloches. They were originals! There had been no doubt about that. He would have recognized forgeries straightaway. Just as he recognized the ones in his hands.

David swallowed and fought against a rising wave of dizziness. The shares must have been switched at some point. But when? Who had done it? And where?

It was Strobel's Berlin broker! David hadn't liked the sound of the man from the start, but Strobel had said that he should not be put off by his rough manners and that the man was an experienced private broker.

Strobel! What about him? Had he fallen victim to the same trick? He had known this man from Berlin for a while, had done several deals with him. At least that's what Strobel had said. And now this . . .

"What is it? David . . . Mr. Wagner!" Wanda had fixed her gaze on him, a look of confusion in her eyes.

A thousand thoughts shot through David's head as he had stared at Wanda and struggled for a way to explain the inexplicable.

"We have a small problem . . ."

Wanda laughed nervously—at least it sounded nervous to David—and said, "Just a small one, though, I hope?" That look in her eyes! Oh, God . . .

Tell me that everything's all right, it said. *Tell me that we can celebrate soon! That we can be proud of ourselves, our youth, our courage—and our cleverness!*

And what did he do? He shook his head and mumbled something about the security features that indicated whether a share certificate was genuine and wondered aloud about Strobel's broker.

Damn it all, why hadn't he been there when the shares were handed over? Why hadn't he once looked at the certificates in all these weeks? Why hadn't he kept them here at the bank?

Why, why, why . . .

Wanda had stood up and left. She didn't scream and shout. She didn't complain. All she did was murmur very quietly, "This can't be true."

He had wanted to stop her, had called her name, wishing that she would turn on him in a rage. Anything would have been better than to see her walk away like that, her back stiff and straight. He couldn't bring himself to run after her; the fear and panic and shock kept him glued to his chair. Afterward he didn't know how long it had taken him to recover his wits. A quarter of an hour? Half an hour?

He eventually got to his feet, gathered up the papers that Wanda had left on his desk like so much rubbish, and went to see Gerhard Grosse.

At first, his employer didn't believe him, either, and asked whether it was just a bad joke. David shook his head and thought, *This is the end then! No more banking for me, I'll have to go back to my father's tavern.* With a trembling hand, he pointed to the printed guilloche lines and once again began to deliver the same explanations that Wanda hadn't wanted to hear. When he was done he added that the certificates he had seen had been genuine. And that he feared that Friedhelm Strobel may have fallen victim to the same fraud.

Gerhard Grosse had laughed at that point. How he had laughed! "Don't make that face!" he had said once he recovered. "The bank hasn't lost any money on the deal, that's the important thing. So you see how wise it was to insist that this transaction not go through us. Ha, that will teach some people to come to us for advice in the future, rather than trusting themselves to shady stock jobbers . . . Well done, young man!"

David had fled from that laughter. From Grosse's coldhearted indifference. He hadn't uttered a word about the villagers and their loss. Not a word about the tragedy behind their story. If the shares had been genuine—they would have become rich overnight! For David, it made the fraud even worse.

He had grabbed his jacket and run from the bank.

He had never been in Strobel's shop before.

"Well, well, my second visitor this morning who hasn't come to spend money," Strobel had said when he came in. Then he had gone to a sideboard and poured himself a cup of coffee from a silver pot. He didn't offer David any. Not that David was in the mood for it.

"The shares—"

"Are forgeries, I know," Strobel said, finishing his sentence before David had a chance to speak. He calmly stirred several spoonfuls of sugar into his coffee. Then he went to the large table in the middle of the room and sat down.

"I sent the certificates to Hamburg last week so that my bank could sell them for me, and that's when the fraud was discovered." He waved a hand casually. "*C'est la vie!*"

"You've known for a week? Why didn't you come to me straight-away?" David shouted. "You're sitting here calmly drinking coffee while . . ." He was so worked up that he burst into a fit of coughing.

Strobel looked at him, frowning. "Believe me—I have not been idle during that time! I called on all my contacts to help me. I sought that Berlin broker high and low, but all in vain. The bird has flown! Vanished without a trace! Then I tried to trace those forged certifi-cates—they had to come from somewhere, after all—but I had no luck there, either." Strobel spoke as though the swindle hardly mattered. His voice did not sound like that of a man who had suffered a heavy loss.

"But you said that you had done business with the man before . . . You must know his address, his . . ." David stopped speaking, like a schoolboy who had forgotten the lesson he was to memorize.

"Yes, once. But once a man has made up his mind to commit fraud, he will go to great lengths to stay out of sight." Friedhelm Strobel laughed. "I daresay the fellow feathered himself a new nest with our money long ago! Somebody who is able to forge share certificates will easily be able to forge new documents for himself—we should be under no illusions about that."

"But . . ." *But we have to arrest a fraudster like that! Seek legal redress, call in the police!* Forgery was a serious crime, after all.

"I am sorry," Strobel said, and his voice was so cool that David shivered. "I only meant the best for the Lauscha glassblowers— I have been doing business with them for decades, and I do well enough out of it. If it reassures you, my young friend, I won't let them down now, either. I will be as good as my word and I will buy the foundry. I will arrange to meet Otto Gründler for the purpose today. Nobody will lose his job once the foundry belongs to me. Not everything will carry on as before, of course. There will have to be a few changes . . ."

His grin made David shudder. How could he ever have felt even a spark of admiration for this man?

David had his hand on the door handle when Strobel spoke again. "Wanda Miles . . . the American girl . . . I would be ready to negotiate with her as spokeswoman for the glassblowers. Clearly that has been her role up to this point."

"Negotiate? Spokeswoman? What do you mean?" David frowned. What was this about?

"My employees will not like many of the changes that I plan to introduce. It may be beneficial for the young lady to visit me so that we can discuss the glassblowers' future."

The way he licked his lips when he spoke Wanda's name . . . It was repulsive! David groaned aloud at the memory of it, and his fellow train passengers looked at him dubiously. By now they had passed Steinach. It wouldn't be long before they came upon the first houses of Lauscha.

He was afraid to face the glassblowers. Of course he was. He could understand why Wanda had felt so uneasy at the prospect of delivering the news. But was that any reason to throw oneself in front of a train?

How desperate the poor girl must have been . . .

He thought of how she looked when he saw her at Sawatzky's—her face, pale as death. David felt his own fears dwindle by comparison.

Why hadn't he noticed her desperation? Why had he just let her walk away like that? He had been a fool. Why hadn't he run after her, taken her in his arms and comforted her? The train slowed and crept up the last steep curves. When David looked out of the window, he could see red and white ribbons decorating the platform even from a distance. There were about twenty men and women standing up toward the front—they were probably getting ready to burst into song in greeting.

They'll have to keep their song for some other occasion, David thought grimly. Dozens more people were pushing their way past the choir, headed toward the train.

What a crowd! All of them ready to celebrate . . .

Why hadn't Strobel come to him last week with the bitter truth? Then at least he would have been spared this scene today.

David's pulse was racing with fear. If only he had something positive to tell them! But as it was—he wouldn't be surprised if the villagers of Lauscha tried to lynch him. He couldn't let that happen, though. He still had a score to settle. With the damned villain who had taken their money and given them only worthless paper in return. He would hunt the fellow down like a rat, even if it took years to find him!

And he had a score to settle with Strobel, who talked about the whole affair as though the baker had shortchanged him for a loaf of bread. *C'est la vie!* He had a score to settle with Gerhard Grosse as well, who found the entire scandal so funny.

He owed all that to Wanda.

CHAPTER FORTY-ONE

The news that the investors had fallen victim to a fraud and lost 11,000 marks—for many of them, these contributions were their life savings—struck Lauscha like an earthquake. The town shook with rage, anger, despair, fear—of course, those who were directly affected were hit harder than the helpless onlookers. But just as in a real earthquake, everybody was touched by the disaster in one way or another. The villagers were all either related or friends or neighbors, and that day at Lauscha station, everybody had lost something.

Their vision of a better future—one that would allow them to take control of their own fate at long last—dissolved in an instant. All was lost. All because of a fraud who was long gone. Who was doubtless laughing at the gullible hillbillies, as he lived high on the hog with their money!

Christoph Stanzer, who had given the lion's share of the money, went home speechless, unable to believe what he had heard, but most of the others stayed where they were, in need of human company. They didn't feel the cold east wind blowing over the station platform, didn't feel the damp mist that crept in with the darkness.

A few of them vented their rage right there and then, and David Wagner already had a few bruises by the time Thomas Heimer and Richard Stämme talked some sense into the angry men. They found it difficult to grasp that this banker, in his neat city suit, wasn't to blame. If he wasn't, then who was?

The wholesaler who had given them the stock tip! He was to blame! How could they ever have been so naive as to trust him? Jockel, young Hansen, and a handful of others were all ready to get on the next train to Sonneberg to track him down and confront him. Although David also would have liked to see Friedhelm Strobel beaten soundly, if only for his arrogance, he used all his powers of persuasion to talk them out of the idea. There was no proof that the wholesaler had anything to do with the fraud; indeed he had lost money as well. And soon he would be the new owner of the foundry. Did they want to ruin their relationship with him right from the start?

So where was the American girl? That was the next question. Where was she now that all her highfalutin plans had gone so far awry?

David hastened to tell the men just how upset Wanda had been. He went on to explain that she had fainted from the shock and was recovering in a friend's house in Sonneberg.

Women . . . as soon as things got serious, they fainted! Jockel spat at the ground in front of David's feet in disgust.

In the midst of all this, Otto Gründler hurried home as fast as his stumpy legs would carry him, hastily packed what he needed, locked up his house, and fled to stay with his brother in Suhl before the crowd could turn against him.

* * *

Nobody found it easy to go back to work the next day, but they had no choice. The glassblowers who had orders to fill at their workbenches at home had to make sure they fulfilled their contracts—it wouldn't help anyone if they lost money as well. And the foundry workers walked to the Gründler foundry at the usual time the next morning for the start of their shift—what else were they to do?

They found a hastily scribbled note on the foundry door from Otto Gründler, telling them to carry on as usual. The new owner would arrive soon enough. There was not a word of remorse. Not a word of other possible arrangements. The cowardly way in which Gründler had simply left his workers in the lurch was like an aftershock, striking the men while they were still reeling.

* * *

Friedhelm Strobel showed up in Lauscha exactly three days later. He strode through the door like a general early one morning when work at the foundry had just begun. He was flanked by two grave, burly men, and the workers felt a certain grim satisfaction at the thought that their new boss turned up with bodyguards. But if they believed that Friedhelm Strobel would be ill at ease, they were wrong.

He took a quick tour of the foundry, waving his hand airily to indicate that the men were not to stop work, then disappeared into Gründler's office as if he did it every day. During the course of the day, he called in the foundry workers one by one and asked each of them a series of questions. What was the man's job? How long had he been working in the foundry? Did he have anything to do with the failed investment venture? The men answered Strobel's questions in single syllables and watched him take notes before he sent them back to work without another word.

Nobody knew anything more when they left Strobel's office than they had when they went in, but most of them had a bad feeling about what was to come.

Shortly before six o'clock, just at the end of the workday, Strobel emerged from his office. While he looked for a place to speak, his two bodyguards herded the workers together. Strobel finally decided to take up his position in front of the big furnace. And then he began to talk.

"Please believe me when I tell you how upset I am by the course that events have taken! I would have liked nothing better than to see the Gründler foundry in Lauscha hands. But sadly, fate had other plans . . ."

"Fate," Martin Ehrenpreis muttered.

"Now that we're all in the same boat . . ." Strobel looked around at the assembled faces, as pious as a priest. "It is my task as the captain of the ship to chart a new course. Going forward, there will be a few fundamental changes . . ."

The men looked at one another in silence, and each could read the same thought in the others' faces. *Well, whatever comes, it can't be worse than . . .*

But what they heard over the next hour was worse than anything they could have imagined.

Up until now, the foundry had made rods of raw glass that were then sold to the glassworkers of the village. From now on, the rods would be used in-house and made into all sorts of glassware. Strobel divided his workers into teams, each of which had its own supervisor. Strobel made sure that the supervisors were chosen only from among the men who had had nothing to do with the failed company. The teams were named for their area of specialty—Christmas Ornaments, Tableware, and Sundries. Long benches would be set up in the front half of the foundry and every workplace would have its own gas lamp. The wares would then be sent out to pieceworkers in the village for finishing—Strobel had already selected the families who would do the silvering, painting, and packing, all of whom had worked for him in the past.

Making Christmas ornaments right here in the foundry? Upon hearing that, the men could no longer listen in silence. "You'll have us sitting here like hens in a henhouse!" one of them shouted out. Another wanted to know what would become of the families who used to buy their raw glass from the Gründler foundry for their own workshops. Strobel answered that from now on, no raw glass would be sold. Glassblowers in the Christmas ornament trade—like the Steinmann-Maienbaum workshop and others as well—would have to find new raw glass suppliers. And he would no longer act as wholesaler for any wares other than those made here in his own foundry. This new approach would guarantee that he would be able to respond more nimbly to changing market demands, to produce the wares more cheaply, and—

The rest of his speech was drowned out in the resulting outcry. Were they going to kick the glassblowers off their own home workbenches? Take their work away from them? Change the system that ensured that every glassblower and every worker had a place? It was a catastrophe that would be felt throughout Lauscha!

Strobel's bodyguards had to call for quiet several times before the new owner could speak again.

Of course, the position of sorter would be more important from now on, Strobel said, and he looked long and hard at Gustav Müller. Gustav nodded vigorously but a moment later heard Jockel would be taking over his position. Jockel? A man who was notorious for cutting corners in his own work? Jockel puffed out his chest but slumped back down a moment later when somebody thumped him from behind.

Karl Flein was no longer to be foreman, either. Strobel had chosen a man for that job who would be arriving in the next few days from the Unterneubrunn foundry. Karl and Gustav would both be working on the Christmas ornaments team from now on.

Karl was to spend his days making decorative angels and stars? The men could hardly imagine anyone better suited to be foreman, and now he was to be replaced like an old workhorse? Replaced, no less, by a man from the Unterneubrunn foundry, which was notorious for its poor working conditions.

Amid the muttering, Friedhelm Strobel took some papers from his pocket. The new regulations.

Strobel read them aloud while one of his men pinned a copy on the wall where everyone could see it. With the fire behind him in the big main furnace, Strobel looked more devilish than ever.

The first few rules were unchanged: children under fourteen years of age would not be employed, wages would be paid every fortnight on a Saturday, working hours remained the same. As before, the foreman was responsible for the foundry's work as a whole, while the newly appointed supervisors would ensure that the individual teams did their work properly. The men breathed a small sigh of relief, but a moment later they could hardly believe their ears. If the foreman or one of the supervisors deemed that a worker was not fulfilling his duties, he would be docked up to ten percent of his daily pay. Ten percent, instead of five! For coming into work a few minutes late when his wife or one of his children was sick at home. For speaking a word out of turn when tempers were running high and the heat was getting to him.

Strobel ignored the unrest among the men and declared that they would need to work hard and obey orders while they switched over from the old way of working to the new. In the first few weeks they would have to reckon with a few small mistakes or errors— which was why the reserve fund would also go up from five to ten percent. This was the money set aside to cover damage to tools and loss of material. If there were no losses, the workers were paid out their share of the reserve at the end of each quarter.

"This should be an incentive for you to work together! Remember: you're all in the same boat!" Nobody failed to notice that he now referred to "you" rather than "we" . . .

CHAPTER FORTY-TWO

"Your father's taking a nap—which is precisely what I'd like to do, but Ruth never gets tired! She wants to take me off to the hairdresser next, though we were only there last week. It's such a waste of money, as if anybody ever looks at my hair! Apart from Ruth, of course. She has all sorts of plans for us during our last days in New York . . ."

"Why don't you just tell Aunt Ruth that you'd rather have a quiet few days?" Anna asked as she looked at the block of notepaper next to the telephone. Dozens of little hearts had appeared on the paper, as if by magic, while she had been talking. She smiled. She had been smiling a lot lately. Tired? She didn't know what that word meant anymore! Bad mood? She'd forgotten what that was like. Anna wrote the letters *A* and *R* inside one of the larger hearts.

"Oh, you don't know my sister!" Johanna laughed through the phone. "Ruth would be morally offended if I suggested any such thing! New York is her city—Heaven forbid that we fail to do it justice!" Johanna sighed. "At any rate, it's all getting to be rather too much for me and . . . Oh, here come Ruth and Steven! Hello, you two, I have Germany on the line." All at once the mild tone of complaint vanished from Johanna's voice. "Ruth sends her love to everyone!" she trilled.

"Say hello to her from us," Anna said. She'd had enough of the conversation by now.

She had been busy drawing up a new order when the telephone rang. Twenty dozen Santa Claus figures with blue caps rather than red—well, if that's what the customer wanted. The customer was one of several who had not ordered much during the summer but who had suddenly decided that the Christmas trade would be better than expected, and come back for more. Everything had to be delivered double-quickly, of course.

Anna sighed. She was always worried that she wouldn't manage and that she would fail in front of her parents. She did all she could to disguise her fears. Johannes thought she was as calm as could be, as did the other workers, who saw her taking charge of everything with a steady hand, just the way Johanna did. Although Anna was proud that they placed so much trust in her, the responsibility was occasionally too much.

"Oh, Mother, I'm so looking forward to your getting home!" she said now. As she uttered the words, she felt just how much she missed her parents. She had so much to tell her mother! She toyed for a moment with the thought of telling her that Richard had invited her to the opening of his exhibition in three weeks. He had asked whether she would be kind enough to look after the guests' coats, and then serve them champagne. Anna had wanted to shout, *Yes! Yes! Yes!* Anything as long as it meant that he wanted to have her nearby on his big day.

It was odd, though, that he hadn't asked Wanda to help him. No, Richard had explained when Anna asked, Wanda wouldn't be coming to Meiningen. She didn't feel up to it at the moment.

Richard . . . she drew more hearts around the ones already on the notepad. Then she added a wreath of flowers around the letter *R*.

When Mother heard that there was still a chance for her and Richard . . .

"We're looking forward to being home as well!" said her mother in a heartfelt tone. "We'll see you in nine days! Well, dear, say hello to . . . Hold on, Steven has a question. Which plantation? Wanda said what? A shipping line based in Bremen? Oh, I understand!"

Anna rolled her eyes. Who was Mother actually talking to?

"Are you still there, Anna? Steven wants to know what happened with that shares deal that the glassblowers invested in. Do they own the foundry yet?"

Anna bit her lip.

"The shares deal, well . . ." She had been hoping not to have to talk about that on the telephone. How could she possibly sum up the whole catastrophe in just a few sentences? She did her best to keep her voice neutral as she explained the events of the past few days.

"We're so busy here at the workshop that I wasn't at the railway station two days ago. So I can only tell you about it secondhand," Anna said. She didn't mention that she hadn't wanted to see Wanda greeted with cheers and adulation. Wanda . . . Anna certainly wouldn't want to be in her shoes at the moment! In fact, she almost felt sorry for her cousin.

"The glassblowers have lost all their money? How awful . . ."

Anna nodded grimly, then remembered that her mother couldn't see her. Johannes put his head around the workshop door and beckoned to her. "I'm coming!" she called, then turned her back on him. Perhaps it would be better to prepare her parents for the Lauscha villagers' low spirits? And to let Aunt Ruth know about Wanda's humiliating part in the whole drama? Anna took another deep breath.

"They were talking of nothing else in the Black Eagle last night. Of course, some people say that Wanda is to blame for everything, which I find a bit unfair. I mean, they're grown men, aren't they? It was their decision as well to buy in on that deal! Wanda hasn't shown her face once since she got back from Sonneberg. Which means that it's easy for people to blame her for everything."

There was a loud crack, rattle, and hum in her ear, and she heard only a few scraps of words. Her mother's voice sounded rather shrill. Oh, how Anna hated these telephone calls!

"Poor Wanda," she sighed, hoping that her mother had said something similar at the other end of the line. "Hello? Can you hear me? At any rate . . . it seems that the new owner of the foundry is making quite a few changes. Even on the very first day, this man Friedhelm Strobel—"

"Strobel? Friedhelm Strobel? The . . . wholesaler?"

Anna frowned and held the receiver a little farther from her ear. Did Mother have to shout at her like that?

"Yes, that's the man. The one wholesaler you would never deal with now owns the Gründler foundry. Otto Gründler left Lauscha like a thief in the night and—"

"Strobel . . . No!" Even from thousands of miles away, Johanna's scream made Anna's hairs stand on end.

CHAPTER FORTY-THREE

Thomas Heimer stood helplessly in front of the door to his daughter's room. He had already knocked three times, tentatively at first, then louder, then the third time hammering with his fist. He didn't hear a sound. Was Wanda asleep? Or was she playing dead, just as she had done ever since he fetched her home from Sonneberg?

Sonneberg . . . he still felt queasy when he thought of what the bookseller had told him. His beautiful, proud daughter! His child! Trying to throw herself in front of a train! The thought was more than Thomas could bear. It was so dreadful that he was determined that nobody else should know. "Wanda fainted," he had told Eva and Michel. Richard didn't know what had really happened, either. They had been just about to set out for Sonneberg when Gotthilf Täuber had come by with some "important" documents. Before Thomas could say anything, Täuber had dragged Richard into his carriage and set off for Meiningen. So Thomas had gone to Sonneberg with David Wagner to bring his daughter home. It was only when they were sitting in the train that the bank clerk had explained what the bookseller had told him.

Now Thomas stared at the glass of water in his hand. He very much wanted to drink it himself. His head was pounding, and his tongue felt thick and furry. Damn it all, why had he drunk so much at the Black Eagle last night?

Eva had told him that Wanda hadn't been down to the kitchen all morning. The glass of water was his excuse to look in on her.

"For all I care she can starve herself, but she'll never recover from that fainting fit if she goes on like this!" Eva had hissed at him. "She needn't think that I'll be waiting on her hand and foot. As if I didn't have enough to do with Wilhelm and keeping the whole house running! And she obviously doesn't care a bit what happens to Sylvie! The poor baby . . ."

Thomas wished he could tell her to hold her tongue. But instead he had massaged his temples and fumbled for the words to explain to Eva that his daughter simply needed some peace and quiet so that she could come to terms with the catastrophe. But in truth, even he didn't fully understand what she was going through.

The pounding in his skull reminded Thomas that drinking never made anything better. All the same he didn't regret his visit to the Black Eagle.

It had been a strange evening. Of course, the disaster was the only topic of conversation, and the usual smell of beer had been mixed with the stink of fear. There was anger in the air as well. Anger at Wanda . . . Again and again Thomas had reminded the others that his daughter was not to blame for the whole sorry story, that they should blame the fraudulent broker, wherever he was now, living off their money. Skinny little Johannes had jumped up from his chair and shouted at the top of his voice, "The next man who says anything against Wanda will have me to deal with! She's a Steinmann too, after all!"

Thomas had nodded his thanks at the lad—he was the only one who had dared take Wanda's side.

Richard hadn't turned up all evening. Thomas was fast getting fed up with that lad's exhibition! He never seemed to have time to stop by the workshop or to ask Thomas for advice anymore.

Thomas thrust open the door. It was pitch dark in Wanda's room. The curtains were drawn, and there was a sour smell in the air. It wasn't the sort of smell that he associated with Wanda; it was more like the smell in his father's room.

"Wanda? Are you asleep?"

Not a sound came from the bed. Should he just leave? The girl clearly wanted to be left alone.

He headed over to open the curtains. As he was making his way uncertainly through the dark room, he stumbled and water spilled over his hand.

"Ah, damn it all—" He fought to regain his balance and caught hold of the windowsill. "What are you doing there?"

She was sitting in the rocking chair that he had placed in her room when she came back from Genoa. At the time he had thought that rocking would calm the baby.

"Father." Her voice was hoarse, as though she were no longer used to speaking.

"Eva said that you didn't have any breakfast. I imagine you must be thirsty." He held the glass out to her. Good gracious, she was sitting here in the pitch dark like a ghost! Damn it, why couldn't Eva take care of her? Or Richard, of all people! Thomas felt his anger at his daughter's fiancé rise. Didn't he care at all how Wanda was feeling?

She was pale, and the sparkle was quite gone from her eyes. Thomas felt his heart clench—a sensation he had never experienced before, and that he didn't like one bit.

She took the glass. Her hand trembled as she lifted it to her mouth and drank a little. Then she held it up to the sunlight that streamed into the room.

"It's cracked. You've . . . brought me a broken glass . . ." she said, forcing the words between trembling lips. Tears ran down her cheeks.

"Well, what . . . For God's sake, child! I never even saw that," he said. "I'll fetch you another glass. That's no reason to cry!" He held out his hand for the glass.

"Leave it," she whispered. "It's all right. This is . . . the right glass for me. It's worthless, just like I am . . ."

Thomas frowned. Had Wanda lost her mind?

"Why are you talking such nonsense?" he replied, more harshly than he had intended. "It has a crack, yes, but that's just a small flaw. The glass isn't worthless, not at all. No more than you are! Where did you get such a foolish idea?"

She looked at him uncomprehendingly. "Do you need to ask? It's my fault that the glassblowers lost everything. If I'd only kept my mouth shut! I wanted to show everybody what I was worth. That I really am a glassblower's daughter, that my roots are here in Lauscha, that I'm part of this place. Father—I wanted you to be proud of me, do you understand? Proud of your American daughter. And Mother to be proud of me as well. Of her daughter from Lauscha. I wanted Richard to be proud of me! Of his future wife. And instead he won't even show his face . . ." Wanda let out such a big sob that the chair rocked back and forth. "I'm like this stupid glass—worthless!"

Thomas stretched out his hand again. He wanted to stroke her hair, or put his fingers to her cheek, but he felt awkward. Instead he took the glass from her hand.

"If this were a wooden cup, you wouldn't even notice a flaw like that! Or if it were made of tin," he muttered, while Wanda cried softly. "But glass is different. It's a very special material. It's delicate and transparent and very pure. In its way, glass is—brutally honest."

What nonsense I'm talking, he thought. *As if any of this could help!* Suddenly he smashed the glass against the edge of the windowsill.

Wanda abruptly stopped crying. "Father . . ."

"Now it really is broken!" Thomas said, surprised by the satisfaction in his voice. "And I'll repair it for you," he said, and looked hard at Wanda. "It won't look the same as before, though. It will have cracks for everyone to see! But then again, it will have a story to tell, it will have a memory . . ."

He began to collect the shards of broken glass. He was just about to pick up the last of them when he saw Wanda's hand out of the corner of his eye. Hesitantly, she picked up the piece and put it into the palm of his hand with the others.

"Ever since Marie first told me about Lauscha, I've always thought of it as the paradise of glass." She gave a sad laugh. "And now all that's left of it is a shattered dream," she murmured.

For a moment neither of them said a word.

Thomas heaved a sigh. "Oh, my child," he said. "We all get a few nicks and bumps over the course of a lifetime. But most people don't shatter from them. Believe me, I know what I'm talking about."

CHAPTER FORTY-FOUR

Thomas knew what he was talking about—but Wanda didn't. All she knew was that it was her fault that the paradise of glass had shattered, and it was only right that she kept away. Though Thomas kept on cajoling her to come out, she stayed in her room day after day.

She only awoke briefly from her lethargy whenever there was a knock at the front door. Thinking that Richard would be coming up the stairs any minute, she would brush her tangled, unwashed hair back from her face and blow into the palm of her hand to check how her breath smelled—sour and horrible, but it didn't matter. She imagined his hands on her, warm and hardened by work. The rough wool of his jumper on her cheek as she lay her head on his chest. Soon, soon, the fog that cut her off from the world would lift.

But Richard did not come. And after a while, Wanda no longer even got up when there was a knock at the door. So she didn't know that Widow Grün had come by with a plate of cookies for her. Or that Johannes had stopped by to take her out for a walk. Wanda didn't want to talk to anybody. She couldn't. What would they talk about? She couldn't simply pretend that nothing had happened.

She didn't want to see Martha Flein, either, who knocked on the door, her eyes brimming with tears. How could she ever look that woman in the face again, knowing that she was to blame? How could she ever apologize to her? There was no way to make amends for what she had done to the villagers.

So, amid much sobbing, Martha told her story to Eva instead. "Karl's quit his job. He says that he can't work another day in the foundry now that Strobel is the boss there. Making Christmas tree decorations! It's as though they'd asked him to run naked through the village! It's a lucky thing that my brother kept his word and Karl can work for him, painting the designs onto porcelain pipes. It hardly pays anything, but it's better than nothing." Martha sighed, and then added that instead of being glad to have a new chance, her husband had become sullen and silent, speaking only when spoken to.

Eva nodded sympathetically, which made Martha feel a little better. She stroked Eva's hand as though to comfort her in turn, and then said, "Tell Wanda that I'm grateful for everything she did for us! At least she tried to help. And it . . . it could have worked." As she turned to go, the tears began pouring down her face again. Eva watched her leave, her lips pressed tight.

"Martha Flein sends news that Karl's quit his job and is now painting tobacco pipes for his brother-in-law. He doesn't utter a word to anyone," Eva said when she ran into Wanda in the hallway. Wanda was just on her way to the kitchen to heat some water, but at that she turned around and returned to her room. The fog around her thickened.

The fog saved her from hearing the news that Gustav Müller had lost more than just his job as sorter at the foundry. He had lost the good cheer that had made him so popular. Where he once had been loved by all for his even temper and the way he could dissolve a fight before it began, he was now brooding and morose. His neighbors once again heard his wife nagging at him every evening.

Since Wanda never left her room, she couldn't know that the mood at the Black Eagle was as changeable as April skies.

Sometimes dark and stormy and angry, other times gray and subdued and depressed. Of course, the changes at the foundry were the main topic of conversation, but Wanda's name still came up as well. When a few of the men plucked up the courage to complain to Strobel about the new working arrangements, he had laughed and said, "Send me your spokeswoman! Unless I am much mistaken, you have Miss Miles to thank for all this!"

As the days went by, Thomas tried less often to shake Wanda out of her isolation. Despite Eva's protests, he brought the baby to Wanda every day after lunch—surely the child's happy laughter could not fail to warm Wanda's heart! But when he saw how listlessly his daughter played with Sylvie, he felt sorry for the child, and returned her to Eva only a little while later.

Wanda took no interest in the glassblowing business, either. She clearly didn't care that he and Michel could have used an extra pair of hands to help pack the wares. And so Thomas decided to leave her in peace. He told Eva not to announce any more visitors. Wanda would come to her senses sooner or later.

Which is why Wanda never heard that David Wagner dropped by every couple of days, in the evenings, and that Eva sent him away again and again.

But Wanda often thought of him. Of the mountain of newspapers on his desk. And how they had competed to find the most important snippets of news. Those had been happy times . . .

Had she been wrong about David? Had she thought that there was more to their relationship than was really the case? Had they ever truly been close?

He could at least come and ask how she was! Perhaps she could have told him how she really felt. How she was desperately trying to pull herself together, but she couldn't seem to manage it. She couldn't just spring to her feet, leave her room, and resume normal life.

* * *

Although some at the Black Eagle still blamed Wanda, many did not. Christoph Stanzer, for instance, said the same thing that Martha Flein had: "It could have worked."

But even as the days went by, nobody was any less angry at the fraudster.

"Didn't you say once that you thought you knew the man?" Monika asked her husband Benno one evening, when they were behind the bar.

Benno jumped as though he'd just stepped on a pin.

"I must have been mistaken," he muttered, though nobody but Monika heard him. He busied himself with the beer pump and made a face. Monika looked quizzically at her husband, but soon there were so many customers calling for beer that she had no time to ask him anything more. Besides, Benno quite often made faces. It would really have been very odd if he had known a rogue like that. As far as Monika was concerned, the topic was closed.

Richard hardly ever came to the Black Eagle. On one of the few evenings when he made an appearance, he told Thomas that he was so busy that he hardly knew which way was up. Thomas coughed dismissively in reply.

But whenever Richard did turn up at the tavern, Anna would hurry to take a seat near him, smiling blissfully.

CHAPTER FORTY-FIVE

Richard waved the bouquet of flowers awkwardly. Little orange petals floated down to the floor.

"Wanda . . ." He put the flowers on the washstand and shifted his weight from foot to foot.

The way he stood there! Like someone who felt obligated to pay a visit to a sick friend. She could tell that he kept wanting to check his watch to see whether he could decently say good-bye yet.

She wanted to say, "Sit down, darling. Or better yet, let's go down into the kitchen to have some coffee and a bite of bread and honey just like we used to."

But instead she said, "Richard . . ." and her heart seemed to shrivel inside her.

Wanda had known that it was him as soon as she heard his steps thumping up the stairs. *Oh, God, Eva! Stop him in the kitchen for a moment, at least until I've combed my hair and washed my face!* She jumped out of bed and looked in the mirror—goodness, she was as white as a dead fish! Bloodless. Lifeless. A fresh nightgown! Where could she find a fresh nightgown? She couldn't even remember the last time she had changed this one. She tore open all the drawers but couldn't find one anywhere. Had Eva been too busy to do any laundry?

At least a little bit of perfume, then! Her hands trembled as she reached into the top drawer and poured half a bottle of lavender water over her neck. As she rubbed it in she thought, *What am I even doing? It's too late. It's all too late.*

His heavy steps were already nearing the top of the stairs—she could hear the distinctive creak of the second-to-last step as she jumped back into bed. She smoothed the covers and put her hands, reeking of lavender, under it.

"How are you?" Richard took the chair by the window, moved it over to the bed, and sat down.

Try to sound happy! Sit up straight! Smile at him!

"How do you think I am?" she replied bitterly.

Where've you been all this time? I haven't seen you for two weeks!

As though he could read her mind, Richard ran his hand through his hair. "I'm sorry I haven't come earlier, but you won't believe how busy I've been. This exhibition is taking up all of my time. I can't think of anything else, not even at night. I can't remember the last time I slept straight through until morning." He forced a smile. "Gotthilf Täuber says that everything will be fine, that there's no reason to get worked up. When I tell him that it's getting to be too much for me, he just laughs."

Wanda nodded. "Your exhibition—"

"Is on Sunday!" Richard broke in. "Just imagine, almost everyone we invited has agreed to come! Täuber is delighted. The guests are all very rich people with an eye for art. He says they'll really make my name."

"How lovely for you," Wanda said. The exhibition was this Sunday? That meant it was October already . . . Had Richard come to invite her? He hadn't kissed her yet, hadn't even taken her in his arms.

Oh, Richard, what happened to us?

He cleared his throat. "Wanda, I . . . What I'm about to say . . . Please don't think this is easy for me, but I really feel that I have to do it now, before the exhibition. I have to get it off my chest."

"Yes?" A heavy lump formed in her throat.

He took a deep breath. "I don't think this is working, the two of us, I mean. Our engagement . . . When I said I would marry you—perhaps it was too soon. Perhaps your mother is right and it did all happen too quickly. I was love-struck! You're a wonderful girl and you turned my head. I was flattered, of course. To think that Thomas Heimer's American daughter was interested in me, of all people. But . . . look at us, you and me—we don't work together. We don't want the same things!"

What do you mean? she wanted to ask, but the lump in her throat stopped her from saying anything.

Richard seems like a man rowing, who dips his blade deep in the water and pulls strongly at the oar, his eyes fixed on land, knowing exactly where he is headed—why did those words come to mind now? Then she realized they were her own words. She had written them in a letter to Marie in Genoa. In another life.

We don't want the same things? Didn't he even notice that she was out of her depth? Didn't he know that she had no strength left? All she needed was a hand to hold her up!

Wanda closed her eyes so that he would not see her tears.

His voice came from far off. "Dear Lord, say something! Don't make this so hard for me, I . . . Please don't cry!" He took Wanda's hand, still sticky with lavender water. "Look, it's just that . . . these last few weeks . . . my exhibition . . . I couldn't really think straight. And you? You were busy with all sorts of things, but you never asked what I needed!" His voice. So gentle. So reproachful.

Wanda took her hand away, and he let it go much too easily. So now it had come to this. He blamed her!

Another wave washed over Wanda, carrying her farther from shore. She did her best to pull herself together—*Keep your head up, breathe deeply, don't drown. Not here, not now, not in front of him.*

"I would have helped you!" she said. "I offered several times. I wanted to take care of the advertising, to write the labels for the pieces, all sorts of things. I'm sure I would have found something to do. But you insisted on doing everything yourself."

"Well, yes . . ."

"Then you can't blame me for that now!"

"I'm not blaming you, but . . ." He shrugged. "Damn it all, just look at what you've done!" he burst out.

He told her how foolish she had been. How self-important. He told her that he had tried again and again to protect her from her own folly.

Wanda could hear his voice but tuned out his words.

"And then when you went to the bank. Didn't I tell you to stay out of it? But no, you had to take charge of everything! And now? It's turned out exactly as I predicted."

"Then you can be pleased about that!" She said. Every word was painful.

He flinched. "Don't talk rubbish, I don't care about that! But you always make the same mistake, over and over again, that's what I don't understand. You never want to take advice from anyone!" He was leaning toward her now, his breath a hot gust in her face. She turned away.

"Ah, so you don't want to hear it!" Richard said. He laughed harshly.

Why can't I answer? she thought. Something like, *I've changed! I've learned from my mistakes. I know that there are some things I can never put right, but please give me a chance! Give us a chance . . .* She could form the words in her head, but she couldn't say them out loud.

His eyes were on her now, gazing steadily, desperately. "Wanda, please understand me: I just can't bear it. When I imagine what it would be like if we were married. You and your endless escapades . . . I can't cope with it! Never knowing what the next day may bring. I no longer even feel like going to the Black Eagle because all they ever talk about is this dreadful mess you made! How can I relax when I don't know what they will say about you next? I need my strength; I need to concentrate on my work. Can't you understand that? I'm an artist! Not that anybody here seems to care. Täuber is the only one to have recognized my talent. He supports me; he wants me to get ahead in life. This may be my only chance, and I can't let anybody spoil it!" He was raving now. The last sentence was angry and tormented too.

Wanda nodded slowly. "Yes, I understand." And she truly did: Richard only had one true love, and that was glass.

"You understand?" He looked at her incredulously.

She managed to smile. She was proud of that. "Perhaps it's better this way . . ."

After that it all happened very fast. He hugged her and said how glad he was that she understood, and that he hoped they could still be friends. He promised to tell her all about his exhibition—down to the last detail. He would come and visit her again in two weeks, three at the latest.

Wanda nodded.

"Are you happy that your aunt's coming home tomorrow?" he asked as he was leaving.

Wanda sat up with a start.

Johanna—she had quite forgotten about her. *And she'll blame me too . . .*

"Tomorrow?"

He laughed and put a hand to her cheek. "You haven't really been keeping up with the news lately, have you?"

"How do you know when Johanna's coming back?"

"Anna told me," he said. "Who else?"

CHAPTER FORTY-SIX

Alois Sawatzky cast a yearning glance at the ten crates of books that had been delivered that morning. He'd had the good fortune to buy up the complete library of a large villa in Suhl. The heirs to the property weren't interested in the treasures that their dead relative had collected over the course of his lifetime. Sawatzky had already spotted some wonderful volumes, including a few valuable first editions—some of which even contained personal inscriptions from the author. He'd spotted the works of several American authors—his gaze fell on Mark Twain in particular—and British writers such as Charles Dickens and Oscar Wilde, but the old gentleman had also owned many German books by the likes of Schiller, Fontane, and Goethe. One of the crates contained the complete works of Gotthold Ephraim Lessing—it was superb!

For a moment the old bookseller felt sorry he had never known the dead man in life—judging by his books, the owner had been a cultivated man with varied interests. Sawatzky saw it as his duty to ensure that the dead man's library was treated with respect, and that the books ended up with new owners who would love them just as much as the dead man had.

He wanted to sort through the crates just then, picking out which volumes could go on sale right away and which ones needed repair work first. Or perhaps he should clear a section of his shop and offer the library as a whole? Although that would mean—

"That Friedhelm Strobel is a dreadful man! I'm so ashamed that I ever wanted to get in his good graces. We just crossed paths out on the street. The way he struts along! Like a general on parade! As though the whole city belongs to him! He nodded at me without troubling himself to say a word, and I suppose I'm to be grateful that he didn't ignore me entirely. Ha!" David Wagner spat the last few words out. He took a deep breath, then began again. "As though that would make any difference to me! I don't want to have anything to do with a man like that! He hasn't said a word about the fraudster he brought here. The villagers in Lauscha went to the police station the very next day and lodged a complaint against 'parties unknown.' I was there as witness. The police told us at the time that they weren't holding out much hope, that villains like this one always take care to cover their tracks. I had assumed that Strobel would want to be listed as another injured party, but he did no such thing! When I asked him about it, he said that he didn't plan to waste his time on it and that he had much better things to do—ha!"

Sawatzky had no choice but to listen in silence to the litany of complaint. His young friend had been here for an hour already. An hour that Sawatzky could have used in far better ways.

"What I can't understand is how Strobel can be so indifferent! I can't shake off the thought that somehow he's not entirely innocent. I look at him and I think if he were guilty then surely it would show? But then I tell myself not to be so naive! It's not as though we can always see wickedness in people's faces. And then I find myself wondering how he could have arranged it! Then I tell myself that it's becoming an obsession, that I just want to believe it because then at least I would have someone to blame!"

Sawatzky smiled. David Wagner was a young man, but he had a good understanding of how his own mind worked. However, it didn't seem that his gift was proving the least bit useful just then . . .

"If I were honest with myself, I would admit that I didn't like the man from the start! Not from the very start! Why on earth did I trust him? Ha!"

Sawatzky flinched. The young man's voice was beginning to grate on his nerves, not to mention the constant pacing back and forth.

"Please, sit down and—"

"I'll tell you why I trusted him!" David wouldn't be stopped. He pointed his index finger at his own chest and said, "Because I'm an arrogant fool! Because I felt flattered that such a big businessman was ready to share his confidences with me!"

"You're judging yourself too harshly," Sawatzky said. He ran his fingers over the cover of a book bound in light-blue linen. *Tact and Decorum When Life Requires*—published in Leipzig, eleven years ago. He wondered whether this book would have told him how to deal tactfully with someone like David.

"What are all these books?" David asked all of a sudden. He glanced into one of the crates. "There are hundreds of them!"

Sawatzky smiled. "My latest acquisition. A real treasure trove!"

"But where in Heaven's name are you going to put them all? This place is full as it is!" David swept his hand around the shop. "I don't know how you ever find anything in here . . ."

"I will have to make room," Sawatzky said drily. "Making room for something new can be a good thing. It means bidding farewell to what weighs us down and is no longer really useful. Yes . . ." he said slowly. "That's what I'll do. Make room."

David nodded, not really listening. Then he began pacing again.

"And now I've disappointed everybody!" He slammed his hand down onto a pile of books. "The glassblowers, Wanda . . . Damn it all, why did there have to be a swindler mixed up in this deal, of all deals? It was the investment of the year—what am I saying?—of the decade! Shares in the Schlüter lines are still rising, can you believe it?"

Sawatzky sighed.

"Anybody who managed to buy shares has already made a fortune . . ." David collapsed into the nearest chair like a bellows suddenly emptied of air. "No wonder Wanda doesn't want to see me . . . I keep trying! But every time I go to her house, some old biddy sends me away. She says that Wanda doesn't want to see anybody, and she won't even let me in the house." David looked at Sawatzky. "You don't think that she's done something to herself after all?"

The bookseller frowned. "I haven't heard anything about Wanda since her father came to get her . . ."

David groaned. "It's driving me mad not to know how she's doing. No wonder I can't concentrate on my new job. Quite apart from the fact that—"

Was Sawatzky mistaken, or did David talk about Wanda a lot? Before Sawatzky could say a word, David had launched into a new tale of woe about a colleague of his who had apparently gotten into some accident and wasn't able to work.

"Now, of all times, I get the promotion I've dreamed of all my life! Gerhard Grosse reckons I've earned my spurs—ha! As if I had even a moment to enjoy the benefits of my new position! I would far rather Siegbert Breuer were still healthy and sitting at his comfortable desk! Then I could be in my old office with my—"

Sawatzky picked up a book, opened it, and then slammed it shut so loudly that David broke off in midsentence.

The bookseller fixed his gaze on David.

"You feel that you trusted the wrong people. You also feel that you have failed. You believe that you do not deserve your new position. You are worried about Wanda, and you are always thinking about her."

David nodded silently at every point.

"So what are you going to do?"

"How . . . what . . . ?"

"You've been pacing up and down here like a caged tiger, telling me what a mess my place is! Perhaps it's time you began to clear up some of your own mess! Just as I will pick up one book and then another, you should start to look at all the things that are weighing you down. If I may remind you—that's exactly what you originally set out to do! Or does my memory deceive me? I seem to recall that shortly after this whole terrible story broke you came in here and declared that you had some scores to settle?"

"But—"

"You've talked enough, my young friend, it's my turn now!" the bookseller interrupted. David raised his eyebrows in surprise, but he didn't say anything.

"You can't simply declare that you suspect Strobel of being mixed up in the fraud and then do nothing to investigate it!"

"But I—"

"Quiet! Do you still have the forged shares?"

David nodded.

"Excellent. That already gives us our first lead. Who printed them? Not every printing house will have either the necessary specialized machinery or the criminal tendencies to use it. Then there's the paper—where did it come from? There are dozens of kinds of paper—believe me, I know what I'm talking about here—but only a few particular kinds are used for share certificates, isn't that right? And you said yourself that they're good forgeries."

"The paper itself is fine, but—"

"Quiet, you young fool! Go and find out which paper mill supplied the paper. And follow the trail from there. Who knows?

Perhaps that will lead you to your swindler. Or even to our dear friend Strobel, if he really is mixed up in all this."

David suddenly looked a little less gloomy. Sawatzky went on. "You can't do anything about the fact that your colleague met with an accident. Look at me—I am always profiting from others' misfortunes! Real bibliophiles rarely sell their treasured possessions while they are alive; most of the time somebody has to die for me to get a new delivery of books. Does that mean I must regard my life as a chronicle of misfortune? No, rather I try to deal decently with what the departed have left behind. As should you! Get to know your new area of responsibility. Your colleague has left work for you to do, and you must treat it with respect! Then you will truly have earned that post."

"I never looked at it that way . . ."

Sawatzky nodded grimly. "And now to the next point. If you really are worried about Wanda, then don't just let that woman brush you off next time you are in Lauscha. You're not a peddler. She has no business slamming the door in your face! You—"

He didn't get the chance to say anything more. David grabbed his hat and snatched his jacket from the back of the chair so suddenly that the chair's legs danced across the floor.

"You're right! My God, I can at least deal with an old biddy!" He clapped his hand to his head. "And everything else that you said—damn it all, why couldn't I see it myself? What a tedious fool I've been! I've been taking up your time and I could have been doing a thousand other things all the while!"

Before Sawatzky could even voice his agreement, David was out the door.

The bookseller watched him go. Then he sighed, smiled, and reached into one of the crates of books.

CHAPTER FORTY-SEVEN

"What's this?" Johanna frowned as she picked up a glass that seemed to be made of a thousand splintered pieces. "Are you so short of money that you have to drink from patched-up glassware?"

"No, no!" Wanda cried out when she saw that Johanna was about to throw the glass into the rubbish bin. "It's mine! Father repaired it for me." She snatched the glass from her aunt.

Johanna looked at her, baffled.

"How was New York?" Wanda asked.

"New York?" Johanna repeated absentmindedly. She blew so hard into her cup that coffee splashed out and over the table. She wiped it away with her elbow.

While she reported halfheartedly on her travels, she looked around the kitchen. Everything was so clean!

She could hear Eva upstairs, trying to coax Sylvie to go to sleep, and the baby refusing at the top of her lungs.

"A Steinmann comes to visit at last!" Eva had said when Johanna showed up at the door. Then she had taken the tin of coffee that Johanna held out to her and gone into the kitchen to put the water on to boil. Johanna had followed without a word.

Eva had nodded over to the staircase. "If you manage to get the young lady out of her room—I'll make some coffee! Perhaps you'll have more luck there than the rest of us . . ."

Johanna had looked at her in shock. If Eva was ready to concede defeat like this, then Wanda must really be in a bad state.

"It's good to be home," Johanna said now, finishing her story. "I missed the children. And work!" She laughed.

For a moment, neither woman spoke. They took a sip of their coffee.

It didn't have its usual effect, though, and Johanna yawned.

All of a sudden Wanda asked, "What do you want from me? You're worn out from the journey, and you should be in bed! But instead you come running over here on the very same day you get back and drag me from my room. If you're going to scold me, go ahead and do it! Then you can go home."

Johanna sat up with a start and rubbed her eyes.

"Oh, child, that's not why I'm here . . ." She was indeed worn out, her arms and legs felt heavy as lead and she could barely think. She fumbled around in her handbag until she found an envelope, which she passed over to Wanda. The corners were worn and tattered.

"It's from your mother. Go on, open it!"

"Money?" Wanda looked up, baffled. "No letter, not even a note? What's this about?"

"Your mother says she promised to buy you and Richard a house as a wedding present. The money's a down payment, so to speak . . . But Ruth also said you might have other uses for it. You could spend the first few years living in Richard's old house if you must."

Wanda glanced up from the money and looked at Johanna.

"I won't be living with Richard at all," she said in a flat voice. "He . . . We broke off the engagement. It's over."

Johanna went pale. All of a sudden she understood why Anna was in such good spirits.

Wanda looked as though she would burst into tears any moment.

"Did Mother really say I can do what I like with the money?"

Johanna nodded but didn't add a word. Wanda didn't need to know that they—she and Ruth, Peter and Steven—had spent many hours discussing what should be done. Ruth thought that the whole thing was Wanda's fault.

"Then it's clear what I have to do . . ." Wanda began counting the notes as she spoke. "It looks like this is just enough to pay people back the money they lost because of me."

"What are you talking about?" Johanna asked rather brusquely. "You never stole anybody's money." Wanda said nothing and her aunt went on. "It's odd . . . Your mother was almost certain that's what you would want to do. So that nobody could any longer make you the scapegoat, she said. It's true that we Steinmanns have always paid our debts. We have our pride, after all, and we should keep it that way. At least that's what Ruth says." Johanna, however, didn't fully agree with her sister on that point. Wanda and the glassblowers had been the victims of fraud—what did that have to do with pride or honor?

"Is that what Mother thinks . . . ?"

"Well, you know her! She has an odd way of looking at things sometimes!" Johanna waved a hand as though to dismiss the idea. She was angry at herself for letting Wanda know what Ruth had said.

All at once it all became too much for Johanna. She had been putting up a good front, pretending that she didn't really care so that she didn't give way to weeping. But now she felt as though a string had broken somewhere inside her. Her feelings were too strong to be contained any longer.

"Oh, my child, whatever did he do to you?" Johanna covered her face with her hands and burst into tears. "That bastard! That . . . damn bastard!" Her voice was suddenly hoarse.

"Aunt Johanna . . ." Wanda was shaking her by the arm. "Don't cry! Richard didn't want to hurt me, and believe it or not—I'm not angry at him. He—"

"Richard?" Johanna looked up, her eyes wet with tears. "I'm not talking about Richard. I'm talking about—" But she broke off as somebody tapped at the kitchen window.

"I'm going to tell the two of you something that I've kept to myself for years. Something I never wanted to think about . . ." Johanna looked from Wanda to Anna. They both nodded, albeit hesitantly.

Anna had come by to say that a major French client of theirs had turned up unexpectedly at the workshop. He was an important customer and he liked to deal with Johanna directly. He always placed big orders, so Anna had set out in search of her mother.

Quite uncharacteristically, however, Johanna had said, "I don't have time for the Frenchman today; he'll just have to talk to Peter!" Her first instinct had been to tell Anna to look after the customer herself, but then she had changed her mind. Perhaps it was time that her daughter heard what had happened all those years ago.

Anna had pursed her lips and accepted a lukewarm cup of coffee. She sat down at the table, but kept casting hostile glances at Wanda.

Johanna sighed. It seemed that these two still couldn't stand one another—nothing had changed there while she had been gone.

"I should probably begin at the beginning. Anna, I was about as old as you are now when I went to Sonneberg to work as an assistant for a wholesaler. Father was dead, and Ruth and Marie were working here for the Heimers. But I didn't want to waste my days in their workshop. I wanted more from life. And I got it too!" She laughed harshly. "The wholesaler was none other than Friedhelm Strobel."

"Heavens above!" Wanda put a hand to her mouth.

Anna frowned. "The same Strobel who's just bought the foundry? The man that you and Father never wanted to have anything to do with? And now you tell me that you used to work for him?"

Johanna nodded. "I was young and naive when I went to work for him, and I was so eager to learn! Strobel was a good teacher, I'll have to give him that much. I learned a few tricks from him that I still use in business today. He's a master manipulator and he knows exactly what people want to hear. He can get anyone to dance to his tune!" She fell quiet. She had noticed the look in Wanda's eyes, which grew ever more troubled with each word Johanna spoke. Wanda was looking down now and fiddling with the worn old tablecloth. She was clearly fighting to hold back tears.

"Wanda?" Johanna said. When her niece looked up, she said, "You know the story, don't you? Marie . . . Marie must have been the one who told you." Her sister had given away the secret that she had kept to herself all these years. The realization pierced her like a knife.

Wanda nodded. "I had to promise her not to tell a soul. But she never mentioned his name! If only she had, it would have saved me a lot of suffering . . . It was Strobel who—"

Anna looked from her cousin to her mother. "Would anybody like to tell me what this is all about?"

Johanna began to talk. She told them how Strobel had brutally raped her one day. How she had walked back to Lauscha from Sonneberg with the last of her strength. She couldn't take the train, looking the way she did. She told them how she had collapsed on the way. How she had lain by the side of the road like a dying beast.

They heard steps in the hallway. Eva put her head around the door and raised her eyebrows when she saw that Anna was sitting at the kitchen table along with Wanda and Johanna.

She opened her mouth as though to say something but then changed her mind and shut the door. They could hear her murmuring to herself through the closed door. "Who needs hot soup anyway? We'll have a bread-and-cheese supper tonight." Then a little louder, "Be sure to put wood on the stove so that it doesn't go out!"

Johanna got up and went to the stove. She stirred the dying embers and put another log on. Her movements were slow and heavy as she walked back to the table and sat down again.

"That's when Magnus found me. I didn't recognize him straight-away. He had been gone for years and just happened to be on his way home from his travels that very day. He carried me all the way home and never asked a single question." Johanna's voice softened. She still felt a debt of gratitude to the silent neighbor who had done so much to help her in her hour of need. He had loved Marie with all his heart. It wasn't so easy to send him on his way now that Marie was dead, even if he was a bad glassblower.

Anna's eyes had grown wider and wider as Johanna told her tale. "But . . . why . . . why did you never tell us? That's just awful!" In a rare tender gesture, she reached out and stroked Johanna's arm.

Johanna bit her lip and tried to smile but couldn't.

"I was so ashamed! I thought that it was all my fault. I crept into my room and shut myself away for days on end. The others didn't know what to do with me." She glanced at Wanda. "I thought that my life was over! My dreams, my hopes—Strobel had trampled everything underfoot. I was just a whimpering ball of misery. I could see the look in his eyes night and day. The greed! The way he reveled in my suffering!" She shrugged helplessly. "I made Griseldis and Magnus promise never to tell anyone about my shame, and they kept their word. Ruth and Marie were the only others who ever knew. I didn't even want Peter to find out; it would have been too painful for me. Back then we were neighbors and good friends but no more than that. But one day, when Marie was feeling quite desperate, she told him everything. And then . . ." An almost imperceptible smile flitted across Johanna's face.

"Father beat the bastard black and blue, didn't he?" Anna asked grimly.

Johanna looked at her daughter. "How do you know that? Yes, Peter went to Sonneberg and thrashed Strobel. I only heard about it later. When Peter challenged Strobel, he didn't even deny what he had done, he just said that it was his word against mine." She shook her head. "It was so dreadful! And as if that wasn't enough, Strobel told everybody in Sonneberg that I had been stealing from him and that's why he had thrown me out! So I had more than just village gossip to put up with, the man ruined my reputation in Sonneberg as well! It took years before that story finally died down."

Anna looked intently at her mother. "How can a man simply get away with doing something like that? Couldn't you have taken him to court?"

Johanna laughed. "I would never have dared to go to the police. The shame of it! And where would it have gotten me? It really was my word against his. And even if the court had believed me—most men think that rape is hardly a crime at all. They would probably have said that it was my fault. But to this day I regret I was such a coward!"

"He tried it with me as well," Wanda said in a flat voice.

"What?" her cousin and aunt both screamed at once.

"I went to see him right after leaving the bank! I wanted to ask him for help with the shares. After all—he and the glassblowers were all in the same boat! I mean, he was swindled by that Berlin broker, just as we were! But Strobel just laughed. And then . . ."

Wanda shuddered. She squeezed her eyes shut as though to ward off some dreadful vision.

"What did he do to you? Tell me!" Johanna grabbed hold of Wanda's arm so hard that she cried out.

"Nothing! Nothing happened, I ran away as fast as I could. Ouch, that hurts." She pulled her arm away.

Johanna had turned deathly pale. "That bastard! He's as wicked today as he was back then. I can't believe it—he's done it again, he's hurt one of us!"

For a long moment none of them spoke. Anna was the first to break the silence.

"But why? I mean—why would a man do something like that?"

Johanna snorted. "Because he hates strong women. Because he likes to humiliate women. Because we are the Steinmann family. Pick a reason!" Her face was so tense she could barely speak. "Friedhelm Strobel has never forgiven me for making a success of my life. He wants nothing more than to see me suffer forever. But I wasn't going to give him the satisfaction! And what he couldn't get from me, Wanda, he tried to get from you. If Strobel knew how miserable you are just now, he would jump for joy!"

"But what do you think I should do?" Wanda said. "Take him to court? Nothing happened—thank God!"

Johanna nodded thoughtfully. "Somebody should take him to court, though. Because something did happen . . . Do you know what I think? That Berlin broker was just a cat's-paw for Friedhelm Strobel! The two of them were in on it together to swindle you—to sell you those forged shares and then pocket the glassblowers' hard-earned money. I think that Strobel planned it that way from the start. He wanted the glassblowers to lose everything! Or perhaps he didn't get that idea until he met you. Because as soon as he knew who you were, he wanted to hurt you and hurt me indirectly. Well, he managed that. He must be laughing up his sleeve now!"

"Oh," Anna said softly. Johanna glanced at her, puzzled.

"You think that Strobel . . ." Wanda began. Her voice was hoarse.

Johanna nodded. "Ever since Anna mentioned Strobel's name on the telephone I've thought of nothing else. Every feeling that I managed to suppress all these years has come back to haunt me. No matter how I look at it, the facts all lead me to the same conclusion—Strobel is the one who swindled you!"

"But David Wagner . . ." Wanda shook her head. "That would mean . . ." She looked distraught. "I can't believe it. He would never take advantage of the glassblowers that way."

Johanna took a deep breath. "Either this man Wagner was in on the plot with Strobel, or he was duped as well!"

Anna slammed her hand down onto the table. "Well, that's just what we'll find out!"

Johanna looked at her daughter in amazement.

"And how are we going to do that?" Wanda asked.

Anna's face was grim. It was almost funny to see someone so young look so fearsome.

"We'll get to the bottom of all these lies!" She put her hand on Wanda's arm. "I'll help you! We Steinmann girls have to stick together, don't we? But—why are you both crying?" she asked, astonished.

CHAPTER FORTY-EIGHT

It wasn't yet light when Wanda woke up the next morning. She should have been tired—her mind had been spinning all night—but Wanda felt fresher than she had in a long time. And there was something else. A new feeling: she was no longer afraid.

The darkest hours of her life were behind her now, and she had survived them. There had been nights when she thought that the morning would never come. But life went on, whether she liked it or not. The clocks kept ticking. And that was as it should have been.

Wanda swung her legs over the side of the bed.

It was time to get going! Johanna's visit had made that clear. And while Sylvie slept, she could make some preparations.

Wearing only a dressing gown, she hurried around the room and gathered several items. Then she crept downstairs. The tread on the second stair creaked, just as it always did. Wanda held her breath. She didn't want to wake anyone. She had to be on her own for a little while longer.

When she went into the kitchen she was pleased to see that a fire had already been made up in the stove. Eva had probably seen to that when she went to the bathroom in the early hours.

While the water heated up, Wanda sat down at the table. She took her notebook from the pocket of her dressing gown. Even the sight of it brought back painful memories. The villagers had trusted her so! She had written down every amount that each of them had handed to her.

A little while later Wanda finished sorting her mother's money into several piles of banknotes. She put the money into envelopes and wrote a name on each one.

She made a quick pot of coffee and then went back upstairs. She got dressed and looked in the mirror. She didn't like what she saw. She stuck out her tongue.

You look dreadful!

She tried to put her hair up with a couple of hairpins, but despite her best efforts, a strand or two always escaped. She would have to go to the hairdresser as soon as possible! For now, she tucked the loose pieces of hair under a hat with green feathers.

Wanda wore a wool skirt and a jacket over her white blouse and carried a wicker basket over her arm. She went back down to the kitchen.

"Well, what . . . ?" Eva put her hand to her mouth as though she had seen a ghost.

"Good morning, Eva, the coffee's made, did you notice?" Wanda nodded toward the pot. "Hmm—it smells delicious! I wish Johanna would bring us a tin of coffee every week."

"Why are you dressed and ready to go out so early on a Sunday?" her father asked. He was sitting at the kitchen table with a glass of water, unshaven and tousle-headed. "I wouldn't have thought that an exhibition would open before church."

Wanda frowned. *Church? Exhibition? Sunday?* She snorted.

"Oh, that . . . You can't seriously think that I want to go and see Richard's exhibition? That's not what I have in mind at all . . ." she said as she poured herself a cup of coffee.

It was odd—she hadn't even remembered that today was Richard's big day. Wanda stopped and thought for a moment, wondering how she felt about that. It didn't hurt, or perhaps only a tiny bit.

"Well I'd like to know what persuaded our young lady to get out of bed at last," Eva said, her hands on her hips. "We've worn ourselves out talking to you for weeks on end, then all of a sudden your aunt turns up and you're a new person. Would you care to explain that?"

"That doesn't matter now," Thomas said gruffly. "The main thing is that Wanda is feeling better. Although I would like to know . . ." He frowned and looked at Wanda. "Tell us then—where are you off to?"

Wanda stuck out her chin, pointed to the wicker basket that held the envelopes with the money, and took a deep breath.

"Johanna opened my eyes. This is no time to feel sorry for myself. Today I'm going to do what I can to repair the damage." The feathers in her hair swished as she spoke.

CHAPTER FORTY-NINE

"Wanda!"

This couldn't be happening! David stood up quickly. The other customers in the tavern looked up briefly, planning to go straight back to their food and conversation, but when they saw who stood in the doorway they stopped and stared.

"It's the American girl . . ." "The American—who would have thought it . . . ?" "Wanda!" "She's got some nerve . . ."

Wanda looked like a startled deer, and for a moment David feared that she would turn tail and flee. He held his breath as she walked over to his table. His hand was cold and damp from holding the beer stein, and he hastily wiped it dry on his pants.

"David! What are you doing here?" Wanda's hand was warm and dry, and David held it for just a moment too long. Then he cleared his throat and let go.

"Wouldn't you like to sit with me?"

Wanda looked at him hesitantly. "I wasn't expecting to find you here . . ."

They gazed into one another's eyes, then Wanda looked away. David blinked.

"Please, Wanda, I have something important to tell you! Something that . . . I—" He had to swallow hard. He could hardly speak. She must be angry with him. She probably didn't want to talk to him!

But Wanda smiled. "In a few minutes. I want to talk with you too. But I have some things I must do here first." She nodded and smiled again, then walked over to the table where the glassblowers sat.

David watched her go, crestfallen.

He had been sitting in the Black Eagle for an hour. When he had come in, most of the tables were free, but now almost every one was taken. It took him a while to realize just how nervous he was—he felt that he was walking into enemy territory—but it had all remained peaceful. Some of the guests had nodded in greeting, and Gustav Müller and Christoph Stanzer had even stopped by his table for a moment to say hello before going to their regular table. Gradually David was able to relax and enjoy his soup and beer. But he wasn't completely at ease—quite the opposite, in fact. The longer he sat here, the more nervous he was. He had come to Lauscha because he had a great deal of news to share! But instead of telling anyone, he was just sitting there . . .

And now Wanda had turned up, here of all places! He had been planning to go and look for her at her house after finishing his meal.

"She isn't here," the old woman had told him when he had gone by the Heimer family home that morning. She didn't say a word about where Wanda was or when she would be back. Let alone ask him to come into the house while he waited. *Whatever did I do to that old woman that she dislikes me so?* David wondered. He had no choice but to say that he would be back later.

David had gone for a walk after that. The leaves crumbled under his steps as he strolled. It was a clear blue day, and the first frost had come the night before. That wasn't unusual for mid-October. There wasn't a trace of the mist that sometimes draped itself across the steep mountainsides. When he had walked all the way down the village's steep main street to the railway station, he turned around and climbed back up the hill.

Even if he had to wait until nightfall for Wanda to return— he wasn't going back to Sonneberg without telling her his news! But there was no sense in freezing his backside off while he waited, David decided. So he set off for the Black Eagle for a bowl of hot soup and a beer—then he'd go and face the old woman again.

Now David pushed the empty soup bowl aside. He was nervous. Why didn't the tavern keeper come and clear his table? And what was Wanda doing over there at the other table? She had been talking to the men for at least ten minutes. Had she just given Gustav Müller a letter? What might be in it that she couldn't simply tell him? Judging by Gustav's expression, David sensed that the old glassblower didn't quite understand what was going on. And look at that! Christoph Stanzer had taken hold of Wanda and hugged her—wasn't that going a bit far? That was no way to behave!

If only she would come back to his table. He hadn't seen her for so long, and now that she was so near, he could barely stand waiting anymore. David chewed his lip until it hurt.

She looked lovely. A little thin and pale, perhaps. But she held her head high. She didn't look at all like someone who had been ready to end it all just a few weeks ago.

Finally she made her way back over to him. David stood up quickly to offer her a chair, almost tipping it over backward in his haste.

"Well, that's done!" Wanda smiled as she put her basket on the table and sat down. "That was the last one!"

The last what? David wanted to ask, but he kept quiet.

"May I invite you to eat?" His voice sounded hollow. He cleared his throat. "The potato soup's very good." He had hardly finished speaking when Benno appeared.

"Wanda! What a pleasure to see you again! We were beginning to think you'd died!" He laughed at his own joke. Nobody else did.

"Hello, Benno," Wanda replied. "I'll have the soup, please, and—"

"And a beer, as usual, am I right? I'll bring it right over! And this one's on the house, don't worry!" Benno said, glancing at David as he spoke. Then he slapped Wanda cheerfully on the shoulder. "And I have to say . . . What you did today—it was marvelous! The whole village is talking about it!"

David had no idea what was going on.

"Could you perhaps tell me what all that was about?" he said as soon as Benno left.

Wanda smiled. "It's simple enough. I've given back the money that people lost to the swindler."

David listened, speechless with surprise, as Wanda told him how she had gone from house to house with her basket. Who she had spoken to. How astonished they had been. How touched and moved. How grateful. But she also told him about the undercurrent of aggression she had felt.

"I went to see Karl Flein last of all. He was harder hit than anyone else, as I'm sure you know."

"He's not working in the foundry anymore, is he? He works for his brother-in-law now."

"Yes, that's right. And just imagine: in spite of everything, his wife, Martha, pulled me into the house and told me over and over again that nobody is angry with me. Well, if you can believe that . . ." She shook her head. "It was strange . . . When I saw Karl I had quite a shock! Somehow I had still been expecting to see him sitting at his workbench with the flame burning in front of him." She looked up.

"Did you know that almost everybody who does piecework has to work on Sundays now?"

David nodded. He could have told her it was no different in Steinach, where families worked seven days a week making slate pencils. But he didn't want to interrupt Wanda.

"But Karl's lamp wasn't burning, even though he's a glassblower through and through! He was sitting at the table with tiny little pots of paint all lined up in front of him and a tray full of porcelain tobacco pipes . . . He did his best to pretend it wasn't all that bad. 'What's the difference between sitting in Strobel's workshop blowing Christmas globes and painting porcelain for my brother-in-law?' he asked. He even laughed." Wanda sniffed noisily.

David shook his head and felt the prickle of goose bumps. The villagers of Lauscha were proud people!

Benno brought Wanda's soup and told her that he'd put in an extra wurst. He patted her on the shoulder again and told her to enjoy her meal. Then Benno's wife called him back behind the bar, and Wanda and David were alone again.

"I wonder whether Benno wanted something from me?" Wanda said, frowning. She dipped her spoon into the soup, lifted it halfway to her mouth, and then stopped.

"At any rate . . . I did what I could today. Or rather, this is the first day in a long time that I've done anything at all! And it felt good!"

"Where did you get the money?" David really wanted to ask her why she felt that she had to pay the villagers their money back at all, but he held his tongue. The whole mess was hardly her fault! After all, 11,000 marks was a lot of money . . .

"My mother sent it to me. It was supposed to be so that we could buy a house. Richard and I, that is. But that's not going to happen anyway."

"So you're giving up on that? Good Lord, you really have lost everything thanks to this whole dreadful story," David said. "And I—" How could he tell her that he'd been promoted? That his greatest dreams had come true? "But what about your fiancé? I mean, doesn't he have a say in how the money's used?"

While she ate, Wanda told him that they'd broken off the engagement. She seemed surprised herself at how easy it was to say the words aloud. "Anyway, tell me—didn't you say you had some news as well?"

"Yes, yes." David cleared his throat. He suddenly didn't know where to start. He took a deep breath. "Do you know what? Why don't we go for a walk after you've eaten? Then I can tell you everything I've found out!"

* * *

"Tell me, are you going to do that song and dance every time the American girl comes in?" Monika asked her husband as soon as Wanda and David had left the tavern.

"Eh? What do you mean?" Benno was staring out of the window, stroking his beard absentmindedly.

Should he have told her? Should he . . . But what would she think of him? And—never mind! It was too late anyway! Wanda and the bank clerk had gone. Perhaps it was best to not to bring it up.

"Am I not going to get an answer?" Monika folded her arms and looked at her husband. "Really, if I didn't know better I would say that you had fallen in love with the girl! Everybody knows that she has a way of winning men's hearts."

Benno stared at his wife. What on earth was she talking about?

"You treat me like I'm just the maid around here," Monika said, pursing her lips. "Good enough to do the dirty work and—"

"Stop talking nonsense!" Benno snapped. As though he would go running after other women at a time like this!

CHAPTER FIFTY

Wanda led the way. David said that he knew the footpaths around Steinach and Sonneberg, but he'd never walked these parts before. Since Wanda didn't want to walk through the village with David, she chose a path that led out to the woods.

Just a few minutes into their stroll, her calves began aching, she was short of breath, and she even felt a little dizzy. She stopped suddenly in the middle of the stony path.

"Sorry—but could we go a little more slowly?"

David answered in surprise, "More slowly than this? Maybe we should find a bench and stop for a rest?"

"No, no, it's all right, but . . ." She pointed to her shoes. "I think I should have worn better boots . . ." Goodness, she was at the end of her strength! But she could hardly tell him that. Just imagine, he wanted to find a bench, as though she were an old woman.

"Then may I at least offer you my arm?" David bowed in a somewhat exaggerated manner and grinned.

Wanda nodded graciously and took David's arm. Was she mistaken, or did he blush a little? She smiled.

Wanda didn't ask what David's important news was. And David didn't say anything. Instead they walked on together, in silence, at a snail's pace. The leaves rustled under their feet and birds sang here and there. Spring's passionate courting rituals were long over, the chicks had been born and flown the nest, and, now that it was autumn, Wanda thought that their songs sounded slow and lazy, as though everything important had already been said.

She still didn't know what the various birds were called. She still didn't know the names of the plants whose scent filled the air. She didn't even know the names of the deep-blue berries that grew on the thorny hedges, and she didn't know which mushrooms were safe to eat and which were poisonous. But despite all that, Wanda felt more at home here in the forest than anywhere else.

All of a sudden she was so happy that she laughed. She felt David look at her with a question in his eyes, but she didn't feel like talking. She just squeezed his arm gently, which seemed to be enough for him.

She felt freer and stronger with every breath she took of the sparkling clean air, and her head began to clear. The gloomy fog that had been holding her prisoner finally lifted, making way for this glorious fall day.

Oh yes, there were plenty of important matters to discuss. But they had time. Right here and now nothing mattered but the forest, the sun, and her hand on David's arm. The shattered wreckage of the paradise of glass was far behind her now.

The two of them stopped walking at the same moment, as though at some secret signal. From where they were standing, they could see straight down the valley to Steinach. The village's shingle-clad houses looked darker than ever in the golden fall sunshine. David's home . . .

David whistled softly. "What a view!" He snapped off a branch from an elder bush and began to strip the bark.

Wanda squinted and pointed to a small dark dot that was just visible in the distance.

"What's that over there? A church?"

"For once, I have the answer," David replied, smiling. "Unless I'm much mistaken, that's the Basilica of the Fourteen Holy Helpers over in Staffelstein. The little shadow there just beyond it"—he stepped even closer to Wanda and pointed—"could be Coburg castle. The view is quite splendid today!"

Wanda beamed. They enjoyed the view in silence for a long moment. Then a twig snapped, and Wanda gave a start. David stared down at the broken elder twig in his hand, and flung it away. A bird that had been pecking for worms took flight, startled.

"It was Strobel who swindled us!"

"I know," Wanda said. "My aunt Johanna Steinmann-Maienbaum came to visit me yesterday." She told him some of what had been said, keeping quiet about the rape. "Johanna thinks that Strobel saw me as a way to take revenge on her. He wanted to see the Steinmann family suffer some more." She shrugged. "And he got what he wanted . . ."

She took a few steps and sat down on a fallen tree. The bark was swarming with little beetles, and Wanda brushed one away as it tried to climb onto her skirt. David followed her. He clenched his fists and stood before her.

"That bastard . . ." He took a deep breath. "I'd like to hunt him down and thrash him within an inch of his life!"

Wanda gave a sad laugh. "What good would that do? Johanna says that we have to be able to prove in court that Strobel was behind the swindle, then we can take the foundry from him. That would really hit him where it hurts!"

David unclenched his fists, stretched out his arms, and took another deep breath. "I may be able to help there . . ."

Wanda listened breathlessly as David described how he had spent the last week calling dozens of Hamburg banks. He had introduced himself as Friedhelm Strobel's banker, and said that his client wanted him to transfer some money from Hamburg to Sonneberg.

"Hamburg? I don't quite understand . . ."

"Strobel mentioned to me early on that he had been tipped off about the shipping company by his Hamburg bank. When I went to see him on September 18, he claimed that he had sent the shares from the Berlin broker to the same bank the week before, and that they had told him that the certificates were forgeries. Back then, in Strobel's shop, I believed the story. But I've begun to have my doubts since then. The way he talks about it . . ." He shook his head. "Anyway I thought I'd try to find out whether he was telling the truth about that. To do that, I had to talk to the Hamburg bank that supposedly received Strobel's forged shares. Unfortunately I wasn't able to find any hint anywhere in our records at Grosse of any other banks where Strobel was a client. Hamburg is an important financial hub, with a big stock exchange. All the most important banks are there."

"It sounds like looking for a needle in a haystack," Wanda said, shaking her head.

David nodded. "In the end I only happened upon Strobel's bank by sheer chance." He grinned. "I had called a good dozen other banks by then. The fellows I talked to must think I'm a muddle-headed fool not to know how much money his client has or where he keeps it!"

"All those telephone calls! And what you did wasn't strictly legal, was it? What if your boss found out?" Wanda didn't know what to think. David had done all this of his own accord? While she lay in bed feeling sorry for herself? She felt herself turning red.

David looked at her with a sly grin. "I might just tell Mr. Grosse the truth. He can't stand Friedhelm Strobel anyway, and he'd certainly be pleased to know what I found out . . ."

"Well out with it then! What did you learn?" Wanda was so excited that she tugged at David's sleeve until he sat down next to her.

"Strobel's Hamburg bank never received any forged shares. The man I spoke to on the telephone had no idea what I was talking about! Strobel had used the bank to do a straightforward shares deal, and he made a pile of money! He has a fortune in his account up there in Hamburg. So his story of being swindled just like we were is an outright lie!"

"That's incredible! So Johanna was right when she suspected that Strobel was somehow mixed up in the whole thing. He might even be behind it all!" She looked at David. "And now?"

Would this be enough to convict Strobel of fraud?

David snorted. "If I only knew! Of course we could go to Strobel and tell him what we know. But where would that get us? He would just lie to us again and claim that he was involved in two transactions, one that went smoothly and one that lost money for all of us. He'd say that he'd never claimed otherwise."

Wanda nodded. "Yes, that's just what he would do."

"We can't go to the police with what we know so far. If we're going to prove it was Strobel, we have to show that he and the fake broker were in on it together. And that means we have to find the man! If we do, perhaps we'll even find some of the money that was stolen from the villagers." David kicked the toe of his shoe into the earth, raising a cloud of dust.

"Johanna says that she will happily help. Cousin Anna said as much too. Do you think we should hire a detective?"

"Hmm." David bit his lip. "I'm not sure . . . Perhaps there's something we can do ourselves first. Without anyone else's help." David told her about Alois Sawatzky's idea of visiting printing houses to find out more about the paper that the forged certificates were printed on. Perhaps they would turn up a clue as to where the forgeries were made.

"What a good idea! Once we know where the paper was made, we might be able to track down the bogus broker. Then all we have to do is prove he was working with Strobel!" Wanda laughed grimly. "Even if it takes me years, I'll track that scoundrel down; I owe that much to Johanna! And to the glassblowers," she added hastily. She didn't want David to think that this was a personal vendetta.

"But you have to promise me one thing!" David gripped Wanda's arm so hard that she flinched.

"What?"

"That I will be there when you take the foundry away from the bastard!"

"It's a deal!" Beaming with joy, Wanda held out her hand to David.

As they shook hands on the deal, they burst out laughing.

CHAPTER FIFTY-ONE

Sawatzky strode up and down in his bookshop, a cup of tea in his hand. Every five paces he stopped and turned and paused, so that Wanda could rotate her pencil so the point bore down evenly on the page without thickening or fading. Which was a waste of effort, really, since she still hadn't filled more than half a page in her notebook . . .

"Säubel Print Works, Goethestrasse fourteen—have you got that?"

Wanda nodded. Sawatzky hadn't been able to give them very many addresses so far; in fact she had just three written down. For each one she had marked down details, such as the name of the owner or the most skilled worker—the man she should speak to if the owner wasn't there.

Sawatzky had told her, Anna, and David that not every printing house could produce such good forgeries. He only knew a handful of businesses capable of working to such high standards. Two of these were far too honest to be worth even including in their inquiries. They would never get mixed up in such a shady business—forging share certificates was a serious crime, he said, one that carried heavy penalties.

So she had only three addresses, all near Sonneberg. Wanda didn't know whether to be disappointed or relieved. Fewer addresses meant less work for them to do, that much was certain. But didn't it also narrow their chances of success?

Lost in thought, she picked up one of the forged certificates from where it lay on a pile of books. It was the first time she had held one in her hands since that day in David's office. Her fingers trembled a little, as though the paper stung. Or as though it were cursed. How beautifully the colors shone! How elegantly the shapes and the design intertwined. She put the paper aside, feeling disgusted.

David cleared his throat. "I'd like to go with you. To be there when you find something out. But if I don't show my face at the bank sometime soon, I'll get into trouble." He shrugged apologetically and nodded at Sawatzky's clock.

"Is it already after ten? Gracious, we should be on our way!" Wanda said. She turned to David. "You get going, we'll manage well enough."

David cast one last glance at the share certificates. He stopped in the doorway and said, "Remember what you promised me yesterday? That I'll be there when—"

"Yes, yes, yes!" Wanda laughed and waved him on his way. "Now go!" David seemed convinced that they would learn something of vital importance on their very first day. She would have liked to have him there to help her instead of Anna . . . Perhaps she would feel more confident and her knees wouldn't be trembling so. Her air of self-assurance was as thin as the ice on the puddles after a frosty night. And it could melt away just as easily . . .

"I could shut the shop and come with you . . ." Sawatzky said, but even as he spoke his gaze was fixed longingly on the shelves of books, as though he might never see them again. Before he could start pacing again, Wanda took him by the sleeve.

"Thank you a thousand times over—for everything!" she said, her voice hoarse. He nodded silently.

Anna had said nothing up to that point, but now she sprang to her feet and said, "Wanda and I will manage on our own. There's a coach outside. My mother hired the driver for the entire day, and she gave us some lunch money as well. We have everything we could possibly need!"

Wanda nodded. Anna's cheeks glowed with excitement, but she had dark shadows under her eyes. Had she stayed late at Richard's exhibition yesterday? The thought popped into Wanda's head before she could stop it. Well, so what if she had?

She looked at her reflection in a window and settled her hat on her head. It was the same hat that she had worn the day before as she went from door to door in Lauscha. She felt ready for anything in this hat.

Sawatzky came outside with them and gave the coach driver instructions.

"Here, I've written down one more address for you," he said, handing Wanda a rumpled piece of paper. "Jean Blumeau. He restores old books, and his workshop is just a couple of streets from here. He's done some work for me in the past. He's a master craftsman. He knows all there is to know about paper, printing, and binding. Perhaps you should visit him first?"

A restorer? Wanda frowned as she put the sheet in her bag. She didn't think a book restorer would be of much help.

"Off we go!" she cried out as she climbed into the coach. The feathers on her hat nodded vigorously.

Nothing could stop them now! It wouldn't be easy, of course, since a printer would hardly say, *Ah yes, the forgery, that's one of mine, no doubt about that.* They would have to be subtle about it and watch the men's reactions closely as they asked their questions. They would have to note down every detail. What kind of detail? Well, they would find out soon enough.

Wanda took the blanket that the coachman had passed down and began to tuck it around her knees. She felt a tug from the other side of the blanket. She looked up and saw that Anna was doing the same thing. They both laughed.

"So how was Richard's exhibition yesterday?" Wanda asked, careful to keep her voice light. *Silly cow!* she scolded herself straight away. *Why can't you just keep quiet?*

"Very nice," Anna replied casually. Then she made a face. "To be honest, it was dreadful. So boring! It was just a crowd of old people all speaking in whispers, as though they were admiring stained-glass windows in a cathedral instead of some perfectly ordinary vases and bowls and plates!" She shook her head.

"Perfectly ordinary vases and bowls and plates—you'd better not let Richard hear you calling them that," Wanda replied, laughing.

"Oh, Richard!" Anna waved a hand dismissively. "He was in his element. That Täuber led him around the room from one knot of people to another. He was bowing and shaking hands and making little speeches—I never knew he had it in him."

"Richard has hidden talents," Wanda said, earning a swift sideways glance from Anna. She raised her hands to show she meant no offense. "No, really. I don't mean anything bad by that!" *And that's the truth*, she realized. She no longer cared about Richard. It didn't hurt to think of him anymore.

"All right then," Anna grumbled. After a moment's silence she added, "Richard was thinking of nothing but his art. I don't think he even noticed I was there . . ." All of a sudden she sounded young and vulnerable, like a sixteen-year-old girl who was in love for the first time.

Wanda fought against the impulse to take her hand and stroke it. They weren't such close friends as all that! And a moment later, she was glad she had resisted, for Anna's face hardened and she said, "But it was his big day, so we have to make allowances. I won't let him treat me like that all the time, though! Richard has to learn that much!" She smiled and all at once looked very determined.

"Absolutely!" Wanda said, and one of the horses neighed as though it had been listening the whole time.

Both women laughed.

* * *

Jean Blumeau took the share certificates between his finger and thumb and rubbed them. He laid his palm flat and ran it over the surface of one. He sniffed at the paper. He picked up a sheet and held it up to the window. He lit a candle and held the sheet to the candlelight too. As he studied the pages, he made soft sounds, sighing, grumbling, whispering to himself.

Wanda felt embarrassed as she observed all this. It was as though she were intruding on some intimate activity. Anna seemed uncomfortable also. She shifted from foot to foot like a schoolgirl.

At last the man looked up. "If these share certificates were issued by a legitimate printing house, they would have put their trademark here, but all we have is a blurred diamond shape. All I can tell you is that these were printed in a well-equipped workshop that prints books as well, but I can't see enough details to tell you which one. I know all the various distinguishing characteristics of the local printing houses, and I can tell you for certain that none of them made these certificates. That's the only thing I can tell you for sure . . ." Jean Blumeau said as he handed the certificates back to Wanda. "These were not printed anywhere around here."

"Oh," Wanda said.

"If you had come to me first, I could have saved you some time."

Wanda felt herself go weak at the knees. If only she had listened to Sawatzky's advice! She hastily put out a hand and steadied herself on the windowsill. She looked at Anna, who looked pale and dejected. Now what? Would this visit—their last of the day—also be in vain?

They had visited all three of the printing houses that Sawatzky had told them about—but without success. The first two businesses had been more or less polite, but the owner of the third had chased them off the premises, shouting that he would sue them for professional defamation. What did they think they were doing, he shouted as their coach left, making accusations like that? Wanda didn't have time to tell him that nobody was accusing him of anything, that they just wanted some information. Nor had they had time to stop for lunch anywhere, as they had planned.

Now it was five o'clock, and everybody was tired and hungry—including the two horses that pulled their coach. "Another stop? Must we?" the coachman had grumbled when Wanda gave him Jean Blumeau's address. He wanted to get home while it was still light and was reluctant to drive back into Sonneberg proper one more time.

Wanda almost had given in—she was very tempted to drive straight home—and she didn't need to see another unfriendly face today. She missed Sylvie and wanted to soak her feet in warm water and have a bite to eat, and—

Anna nudged Wanda in the ribs. "Say something!"

Wanda nodded. Her cousin was right. The restorer might be able to tell them something important.

"Well, it's like this . . ." she began, without knowing how she was going to finish the sentence. She lowered her eyelids and glanced around the room.

Paper, paper everywhere! Piled up on every surface, on every shelf, in boxes on the floor, in faded cardboard folders. And there were paints in every color imaginable, paintbrushes, pencils long and short, thick and thin, spilling out of jars, and glass bottles filled with some gray-black powder. A device that looked like an overgrown flower press sat on a stump of wood, and a clothes iron rested on another. What on earth did he need an iron for? Next to it old rags floated in a bucket full of thick white liquid.

When she thought about it, this was exactly what Wanda had imagined a forger's workshop might look like! How did they know that Blumeau wasn't the culprit?

The restorer leaned on the edge of one of his cluttered tables and looked down at the two young women.

"I suspect that your shares were printed somewhere near Berlin."

"Berlin?" It was all that Wanda could manage to say.

"The paper suggests as much," Blumeau said, reaching for one of the certificates. "Do you see the watermark here?" He held the paper up to the light so that Wanda and Anna could both see the mark.

"Yes. So?" Wanda said, her mouth suddenly dry with excitement. She badly needed a glass of water.

"It's been a couple of years since paper like this passed through my hands, which is why it took me a little while to remember which manufacturer uses this watermark. It's the Obergurig paper mill on the river Spree, not far from Berlin. That's where the paper was made, which is why I suspect that the printing work was done in or around Berlin as well."

Wanda and Anna looked at one another, speechless. "And you can tell all this from the paper?"

Jean Blumeau nodded. "It's not so hard, really. Paper like this is a rarity—it's exquisitely well made. The mill that makes it used to sell it as far as Brazil." He stroked the sheet tenderly. "Paper of this quality is only used to print share certificates and other high-value documents. It's far too expensive for any other use."

Wanda bit her lip. Berlin . . . What did Strobel have to do with Berlin? She didn't quite know whether to be happy about the news.

"I don't know what to say . . ."

"Nor do I," Blumeau said. "There's a problem, you see, that will not make your inquiries any easier . . . The mill burned down two years ago. It was completely destroyed."

"Burned down? But—" Wanda gasped for air like a fish.

"It was something of a scandal at the time. There was talk of arson, and some people said that the owner wanted to use the insurance money to modernize the factory. I don't know what became of all that." He shrugged. "But I do know that no paper has been made in Obergurig for the last two years."

"That means somebody must have saved a crate of paper from the fire," Anna said, her cheeks glowing with excitement.

"Or more than one," the restorer added. "And now he can do what he likes with the sheets, since nobody knows he has them. If you happen to turn up any extra supplies of this paper during your inquiries, let me know. I'll pay you a good price for them. And I promise I have nothing illegal in mind."

Anna nodded eagerly.

Wanda blew out a long breath. "What next? We know where the paper's from, and we know that the certificates were probably printed in or near Berlin. But what good does that do us?"

CHAPTER FIFTY-TWO

"You really didn't need to come and fetch me. I can find my own way to my aunt's house," Wanda said, pretending to scold him, but her heart had leapt at the sight of him. David had come all the way up here from the railway station—for her—when he could easily have gone straight to Johanna's house.

Out of the corner of her eye she saw the curtain at the kitchen window twitch. Eva! Or was it her father spying on her?

Naturally, they had all asked what the fuss was about this time, and who she was going to see. But all Wanda had said was that she was going to Johanna's house. Now she made a great show of taking David's arm. Let them watch!

"Do you think I don't know that?" David said cheerfully. "I think you could do anything you choose to do . . . But can't you understand that I'd like to spend a few minutes with you on my own before we join the others?" He stopped for a moment and looked at Wanda with an impish grin on his face. Her heart seemed to skip a beat.

"Ah, well . . ." Wanda swallowed. "Oh look, here comes my cousin Johannes!" She pointed down the street, almost relieved.

What could she have said to David just then? That she too wanted to spend the evening with him, alone? That there was so much they still had to tell one another? That his hand felt good on her arm, and that he mustn't take it away? That she had spent many hours over the last few days looking for a reason to visit him in Sonneberg, but failed to find one?

In the end Johanna had supplied the reason for them to see each other. She wanted everybody to gather that Saturday—David and Wanda, Anna and herself, and Peter as well, who had been brought up to date on the matter at hand—to decide what to do next. Wanda had been all too willing to send word to David. She wanted to go to Sonneberg to tell him in person, but then she decided that was a little too forward. David Wagner was a business colleague, no more than that. In fact, strictly speaking he wasn't even that, but that didn't change the fact that they got on very well together. Business colleagues . . . So why did she get butterflies in her stomach when she thought of him?

Now that Johannes had shown up, she didn't have to wonder about such things. Perhaps later.

But instead of stopping to chat, Johannes tried to walk past them, his head bowed.

"Hey there, aren't you talking to me anymore?" Wanda said, blocking his path.

Johannes looked at her coldly. "What would be the point? Nobody tells me anything anyway!"

"What . . . ?"

"Oh, don't pretend!" Johannes spat. "I know perfectly well that you're going to see my parents. Who don't need me to be there, unlike certain other people . . ." He shot a look at David. "I'd just like to know what you lot are plotting. And what Mother has to do with it. She told me to go to the workshop and help Magnus pack because she wanted to use the kitchen for a discussion. When

I asked why Anna was allowed to sit at the kitchen table and listen, she didn't even answer." As he spoke, his lower lip trembled.

"I don't care if the silly Christmas globes do need packing, I won't do it! I'm going down to Benno's place for a drink!"

"Oh, Johannes . . ." Wanda said, giving her cousin a hug. "I'm sure your mother didn't want to upset you. She just wants to keep you out of the whole unhappy business."

"Which unhappy business? I don't understand what's going on . . ."

"Well, what happened with the foundry, you know . . ." As she spoke, Wanda realized that Johannes knew nothing about the latest developments. She turned and looked at David questioningly, but he simply folded his arms and shrugged as though to say, *It's up to you.*

"The foundry?" Johannes looked down the valley. Although the Gründler foundry itself was dark, the glassblowers' lamps were flickering through the windows of the houses all around.

Wanda smiled a bittersweet smile at the sight. She could still recall how romantic she had considered the view when she first arrived in Lauscha. Now she knew what all those little lights meant; in each and every one of those houses, families were working right through the evening, toiling until they were overcome with exhaustion.

"Well?" Johannes said impatiently, pulling Wanda out of her memories. Why shouldn't he know what was going on? She took a deep breath.

"We have reason to believe that Friedhelm Strobel was somehow mixed up in that failed shares deal, and that he deliberately swindled the glassblowers." In a few words, she told him everything they had found out so far. "But we haven't been able to prove anything yet!"

"Please keep it to yourself!" David said to Johannes. "It wouldn't do anyone any good to have half the village go after Strobel if we have no proof against him. The fellow seems to have covered his tracks very carefully . . . We have a greater chance of finding something out if Strobel doesn't know what we're up to."

Johannes looked from one to another, his eyes wide. "Revenge, then! Well, I'll help you—"

"For Heaven's sake, no!" Wanda interrupted. "To be quite honest I don't even know what we'll be talking about tonight—so far our inquiries have led us nowhere. You go off to Benno's place; you won't miss anything!" Now she was annoyed that she had told him in the first place. She didn't quite know why Johanna hadn't let her son in on the secret, but surely her aunt had her reasons. Which she, Wanda, had ignored. Oh dear, why had she gone and acted of her own accord, again? And why hadn't David stopped her? A quick look at him confirmed that he wasn't particularly pleased she had said so much.

"If you say so . . ." Johannes already appeared offended again.

"Yes, that's just what I say!" Wanda said firmly, and then hurried off after David who had started down the hill before Johannes could protest again.

*　*　*

"I'm sorry I can't make it any more comfortable for you all," Johanna said, nodding at all the crates and boxes piled up around the kitchen. "The weeks before Advent are always like this. There's no room for anything, no time . . . I haven't even put on a pot of tea!" She hastily gathered some paint pots off the kitchen table and put them onto a tray. She gave the tray to Peter, who placed it on the draining board.

"Well then, let's have a beer!" Peter said, nodding to Anna. His daughter reached behind the bench and fetched out a few bottles. David took a pile of cardboard boxes from Wanda and passed them to Peter, who added them to the heap on the draining board. David had to suppress a smile—it really was a mess in here! Santa Claus figures with red caps peeped out from some of the boxes, while others held gleaming silver angels with glitter powder on their wings. Globes large and small, pinecones, bells . . . *Lauscha glassware really is a marvel*, he thought. He opened his mouth to say as much, then thought better of it—he didn't want these people to think he was flattering them. He glanced at Wanda's aunt out of the corner of his eye.

Johanna Steinmann—the great businesswoman. Despite her words of apology, she didn't really give the impression that she minded the mess. Rather she seemed absolutely at home in the seeming chaos, and completely in command of her business. Which made it all the more surprising that she had taken the time for this meeting.

Wanda seemed to be thinking the same thing, for she said as much.

"Oh, you know, I just want to be sure that our inquiries are getting us somewhere," Johanna said once everybody had taken their place at the kitchen table. "I don't want to give up so easily! What do you think, Mr. Wagner?" She was playing absentmindedly with a couple of paintbrushes, and the air smelled of paint and solvents.

David sat up straight. He was a little awed to be in the presence of this local celebrity, the first woman to run her own workshop. But he didn't want to let it show. "I think that what Wanda and Anna discovered about the burned-down mill and the stolen paper is just one more piece in the puzzle that points to Strobel as the guilty party."

Wanda cleared her throat. "What's next then? Should we perhaps hire a private detective after all? Someone like that would be able to do things that we would never even think of—" She broke off abruptly as a figure appeared in the doorway. David heard her swallow her words, and begin to cough.

"Richard . . ." Anna and Wanda said at the same time.

David looked toward the door.

"Good evening, everybody." Confused, Richard looked around at each of them. His smile died away and he dropped his hands. He was holding a sheaf of papers, which he had been waving in the air as he came in.

David raised his eyebrows, folded his arms, and leaned back in his chair. He felt as though he had been upstaged just as he was getting ready for his big speech. He didn't much like the feeling.

"Ah, well . . . Actually I wanted to talk to Anna. I managed to save a few copies of the exhibition catalog, although the others all went like hotcakes. The exhibition itself was sold out too. Who knows, the catalog may become a collector's item!" He smiled.

Conceited fool, David thought.

Richard looked at Anna. "I wanted to give you one as thanks for all your help on Sunday." He nodded encouragingly and held out a catalog toward her.

"Richard," Anna said. "How thoughtful of you. However, this really isn't the best time." She waved her hand around the table. "As you can see, at the moment we're talking business."

David looked at Wanda's young cousin with curiosity. There was a sharp tone to Anna's voice that not even Richard could have missed. He frowned, rolled up the catalog, and fidgeted awkwardly.

"Well, in that case . . ." He tugged at his left ear.

"Just put the catalog down there. I'll look at it later, how about that? I'll try to stop by to see you tomorrow, if I have time . . ." Anna said, nodding cheerfully, but she was clearly telling him to leave.

Wanda stared at her cousin in astonishment.

"So much for that!" Johanna said as soon as Richard was out the door. "At least you had the good sense not to tell him anything," she said to Anna. "Until we know more than we do right now—"

There was another knock on the door and a taller shadow appeared in the doorway.

"Yes, what is it? This can't be happening!" Johanna said.

"Benno?" Several of them said at once. "What are you doing here?"

The owner of the Black Eagle twisted his hat in his hands.

"Has something happened to Johannes?" Wanda jumped up so abruptly that David had no time to move aside. There was a loud tearing sound as Wanda's skirt ripped; they had been crowded so closely together that he had been sitting on the fabric.

"Johannes? No, he's all right," Benno said. "Well, that's to say, he's actually the reason I'm here. He's just been telling me that you're making certain inquiries."

"Inquiries—and how does my son know about those?" Johanna's eyes sparkled dangerously.

"We ran into Johannes on the street earlier," Wanda said softly. "And . . ."

Johanna shook her head in disapproval.

Benno cleared his throat. "It's like this . . . I might have some information that would help you."

"What?" they all said at once.

Benno nodded eagerly. "Right from the start I had the feeling that I'd met that broker somewhere before. But I couldn't for the life of me think where. I kept on thinking about it. Monika just laughed and told me I was imagining things. I almost began to believe that myself."

"Yes, and?" Wanda put both hands to her chest as though she were afraid her heart would leap right out. David tugged at her sleeve to get her to sit down, studiously ignoring her torn skirt.

Benno worked his lower jaw from side to side, looking around at the faces.

"I've finally remembered where I saw the man before. The way he kept sniffing and snuffling. It was in Berlin, but—"

"Berlin!" "The paper mill at Obergurig!" "David, did you hear that?" "So that means—" "Come on, Benno, tell us!"

For a moment the room was in a tumult, with everyone exclaiming at once.

Benno cleared his throat. "The whole story's a bit disreputable . . . I'd rather speak to Peter and Johanna alone." His cheeks reddened as he spoke.

"Disreputable—goodness gracious, who cares?" Johanna called out. She sounded slightly hysterical. "Just tell us!"

CHAPTER FIFTY-THREE

It was a strange group that gathered a few days later at the Lauscha railway station: Wanda and Anna, Karl Flein, Christoph Stanzer, and Benno. Not that a stranger would have realized that they were traveling as a group at all. Which was just how they wanted it.

The two women were standing on their own, each holding a small suitcase. Anna had pleaded with her mother until she agreed to let her go. Although Johanna would have liked to go to Berlin herself—she was all on edge at the prospect of some information that would help prove Strobel's guilt—there was no way she could take the time away from work. So she decided that Anna should go instead. It would be an exciting change for her daughter, and she could accompany Wanda. Johanna was reassured to think that Wanda would not be traveling on her own with the men—especially since she had noticed her niece casting glances at the young bank clerk whenever she thought nobody was looking. And David Wagner, who would join the group on the train in Sonneberg, seemed more than taken with Wanda.

Anna had some idea why Johanna had agreed to let her go along, and she had to smile. If Wanda really was making eyes at David Wagner, Anna would be the last one to stand in her way. As long as Wanda left Richard alone, Anna didn't care what she did. For her, the trip to Berlin was a great adventure. She didn't much care about the rest.

Wanda was surprised to discover that her cousin had a taste for adventure. It was a side of Anna that she hadn't seen before. But ever since Benno's visit, Anna had talked of nothing but the upcoming trip to Berlin. Would there be enough time to visit one of Berlin's many museums? Should she go visit Alois Sawatzky to buy a Berlin city map? Or did Wanda want to do that herself? What clothes should she pack? And how much money would they need? Would there be a chance to buy Christmas presents?

Wanda had laughed and answered that she had never set foot in Berlin in her life, so she had no answers to all these questions. A city map would certainly be useful, though Benno knew his way around Berlin, and so did David, who had spent three months working there during his apprenticeship.

Karl Flein and Christoph Stanzer stood a few yards away from the women. They nodded briefly at them, then behaved as though they had nothing to do with them. The men had decided that there was no need to stir up gossip in Lauscha.

* * *

The train had already pulled in, with much puffing and groaning, when Benno and Monika had arrived. Monika couldn't understand why Benno was accompanying Christoph Stanzer and Karl Flein on their business trip to Berlin, and she had a sour look on her face. What "advice" could he possibly give them? What use was he as a tour guide? As if Benno, of all people, could advise anybody on anything! He had been to Berlin only once, for his great-aunt's funeral, which hardly made him an expert—and he hadn't even been left anything in her will! That had been three years ago, and it had led to nothing but unnecessary expenses. And she had been worked off her feet while Benno was away. Not that the customers noticed! They just complained that their beer didn't come quickly enough. Nobody seemed to care that she had to both cook *and* serve the food when Benno was gone. One day before Benno finally came back, she had dropped a keg of beer on her foot. Her little toe still twinged when the weather was turning, and it was all Benno's fault! He might as well have stayed home—he had hardly known the old lady, after all. And now he wanted to go off on another jaunt? She had nagged and scolded and threatened. But Benno had insisted. Karl and Christoph were regular guests at the Black Eagle, he said; their business trip was an important one and if they asked him to come with them, he could hardly refuse.

Important business trip indeed! Was he trying to pull the wool over her eyes? Maybe there was even another woman?

Monika looked mistrustfully at each of the men in turn. At least Benno had been telling the truth about who he was going with. But it didn't look much like a business trip—quite the opposite; the two other men were carrying shabby old checkered haversacks that looked more like something they would take on a picnic.

Monika realized with a twinge of guilt that she hadn't thought to pack a lunch for her husband. Well, he would just have to look after himself! After all, nobody was offering to look after her!

She nodded sourly to the American girl, who hurried ahead of the men to climb into the train with her cousin. Those Steinmann girls! They always had to be ahead of everyone else! Well, at least Benno wasn't traveling with them!

* * *

Benno's trip to Berlin three years ago had involved more than just visiting the graveside of his penny-pinching great-aunt; he had also sampled some of Berlin's famous nightlife while he was there. After the meeting with the lawyer was over, his cousin Gottfried from Schwerin had suggested that the two of them go out and spend their inheritance of fifty marks each on a bit of fun.

So while the other relatives gathered in a café for coffee and cakes, they had set off for Friedrichstrasse in search of an establishment called the Blue Owl. Their expectations were running high, as the stories of Berlin's nightlife were legendary, especially out in the provinces. There were tales of naked dancers who would pick up coins with their breasts if guests threw money onto the stage. Benno suggested that they should change their fifty marks into five-mark coins, just to be ready. He hadn't counted on having to pay the first of these just to get through the door of the Blue Owl, where the doorman wouldn't let them in without a hefty tip. The two of them were so outraged by this that they paid hardly any attention to the cloakroom attendant who took their coats, although Benno did notice that he sniffled oddly. They gave him their coats, put their coins into their pants pockets, then took a deep breath, and finally thrust aside the heavy, dark-blue velvet curtain behind which lay the new world they had come to see.

In the darkness behind the curtain the men had trouble finding two unoccupied seats. So they had squeezed in at a table by the left side of the stage, joining another guest. They had hardly sat down when each found himself with a young woman sitting on his lap, skirts pushed up high, neckline low, grinning broadly. Benno was rather put off by the young lady's sniffling. Just like the cloakroom attendant . . . He whispered to his cousin, "Does everybody here have the flu?" Gottfried laughed and replied that it was "because of the white powder."

Benno was none the wiser for this answer. Only much later did he understand what his cousin had meant.

The night passed in a blur, its most lasting legacy that they spent another hundred marks on top of the money that Aunt Else had left them.

As he nursed his hangover on the way home, he had wondered how on earth he was going to explain to Monika that he had spent so much money. In the end he decided that silence was golden and said nothing.

It was no wonder that it had taken Benno a while to figure out that the cloakroom attendant at the Blue Owl was the same man who had sold the forged share certificates to the glassblowers at the Black Eagle. But in the end he had made the connection because the supposed broker had the same curious sniffle. Benno had smiled to himself and wondered whether he was going to spend some of his commission on a pinch of cocaine. But it was only much later that he realized the truth. Was it possible that this broker was nothing but a nightclub attendant? It was unthinkable!

It had taken Benno some time to get over the shock.

By the time he finally went to tell Johanna Steinmann, he had been certain of it for some time. He had been feeling so guilty that he could hardly sleep at night. But who could he have told? Who would it help?

When Johannes told him that his mother and several others were making certain inquiries, Benno had been downright relieved. At last he had someone to talk to! Ignoring Monika's grumbling, he had taken off his apron and immediately set out for the Steinmann house.

When he got there and heard that they suspected Friedhelm Strobel of being behind the swindle, Benno almost had a fit. If that was really true, then his information would be a bombshell!

Of course he would go to Berlin with the others, he told them. He would help however he could.

They knew that their chances of finding the cloakroom attendant were slim. The first question was whether the Blue Owl was even still in business. Establishments like that came and went with the times. Guests went to one bar one day and then a new one the next.

Karl and Christoph had nodded as Benno explained the difficulties. Fashion—they knew all about that. Hadn't they always had to follow the latest trends themselves, as glassblowers?

But all the same they knew that quality always triumphs in the end, despite the whims of fashion. If the Blue Owl offered good acts and the right ambience, then there was a good chance that it was still in business.

Acts and ambience—Benno felt his heart sink. Obviously the other men still didn't quite realize what kind of establishment it was, despite his best efforts to tell them without saying so outright. It was all very embarrassing, but Benno told himself it couldn't be helped.

The second big question was whether the cloakroom attendant would still be there. If Benno's memory was not playing tricks on him, and if this was indeed the swindler who had come to Lauscha, then it could well be that he had taken the money and was off living the high life somewhere. And even if they were lucky enough to find him, was there really any connection between the man and Friedhelm Strobel? And if so, would he be willing to implicate Strobel?

There was such a thing as honor among thieves, after all . . .

Everybody agreed with Benno on these points. But despite all the obstacles, neither Christoph Stanzer nor Karl Flein had hesitated for a moment when Wanda and David came to talk to them. They had been the spokesmen for all the investors—of course they would go to Berlin! This was their one chance to find proof against Strobel, and they would take it.

*   *   *

There were no delays on the journey. Once David Wagner had joined the group in Sonneberg, they trundled along in the slow train to Stockheim, where they transferred to the express train that would take them to Berlin.

More and more people got on at every stop. Soon there were no more free seats, and even the corridors were full. Since it had begun to rain, little puddles formed on the floor and those whose shoe soles were made of cardboard found them beginning to wrinkle up. The air was heavy with the scents of wet clothing and human bodies. The passengers treated these inconveniences quite stoically, eating the sandwiches they had brought along, chatting with one another or nodding off to sleep—even while standing up. Wanda was amazed. It seemed that everybody was going to Berlin. David told her that this wasn't especially surprising. Berlin was more than just the political capital of the German Empire; it was also a flourishing economic center with all kinds of industry, from furniture-making and porcelain factories to electrotechnology and engineering. Of course the city attracted lots of people! Siemens, Borsig—the company names that he mentioned meant nothing to Wanda, but the others nodded respectfully. If only the Thuringian Forest could get even a slice of that pie, Karl Flein muttered sadly. Then they wouldn't be so entirely dependent on glassblowing.

It was early evening when the train pulled into Berlin. They took the metro straight to Friedrichstrasse. By now it was raining even harder. David was the only one who had brought an umbrella, which he gallantly gave to Wanda and Anna, making do himself with a newspaper held over his head. He reassured the two women that it was only a few hundred yards to the hotel, but the disappointment on their faces was clear to see. Here they were in the big city, and it was raining cats and dogs!

Worried that he might not be able to find the Blue Owl again, Benno wanted to set out in search of it straight away. He didn't know the nightclub's address—all he knew was that it was somewhere near Friedrichstrasse station.

Christoph Stanzer, however, had been suffering from a migraine for hours, and wanted to get to the hotel as soon as possible. So Karl and Benno set out to find the Blue Owl, while David led the women and Christoph to the hotel with all of the luggage.

Wanda smiled as they passed the Hotel Adlon. She didn't need to look it up in Anna's guidebook to know that it was the best hotel in town. This must be where her mother had once stayed!

Oh, Mother, what would you say if you could see me now? Wanda thought as they followed David to a much smaller and less imposing hotel.

CHAPTER FIFTY-FOUR

It only took a little while for Benno and Karl to track down the Blue Owl. The others were relieved to hear that the bar was still in business. As for the cloakroom attendant, the two men could only shrug and plead for patience. They would have to wait until the next day to find out whether he was still there, because the Blue Owl was closed the day they arrived. But a brass plaque on the door announced that the establishment opened its doors at nine in the evening every other day of the week.

So they had a whole day in Berlin to do with as they wished. Though they were all impatient for answers, they had no objections to the extra time.

Wanda shrugged when David asked her what she wanted to do. Maybe they could go shopping? However, she didn't much feel like walking around in the rain, which was still pouring down. She had stuffed her shoes with newspaper as soon as they got to the hotel, but they were still damp.

Benno, Karl, and Gustav wanted to ride the city metro and then explore the neighborhood around the hotel.

Anna wanted to visit one of the famous museums, declaring that the works of art might inspire her own creativity. In addition, they could be indoors and they could stay dry. David suggested the National Gallery and offered to go along. So he, Wanda, and Anna set off the next morning after a light breakfast.

Anna went into raptures as soon as she laid eyes on the building, but Wanda felt ill at ease as they approached. Could she spend the entire day looking at paintings? Focus on the works of the great artists when her mind was swirling so?

"Look at the way the light falls into the room!" Anna pointed at a painting titled *The Balcony Room*. "This Adolph Menzel seems to have been a master of light and shade! Painted in 1845, a-hah . . ."

"I wonder what's behind the curtain," Wanda said, pointing to the right side of the painting, where a curtain blew in a breeze. "And I wonder what the landscape is like outside the room?" She sighed deeply.

David had been standing behind the women as they spoke, his arms folded. Now he took a step toward Wanda.

"Your cousin seems to be in seventh Heaven here!" he said, pointing to Anna, who had moved on to the next painting. "I think she can manage quite well on her own. If you aren't so keen on looking at art, I have another idea . . ."

"I almost feel I could be on Ladies' Mile in New York! This store is nearly as big as Macy's!" Wanda clapped her hands like a child. "Oh, David, thank you, this was a wonderful idea! I think that a shopping trip was just what my nerves needed." She put her hand on David's arm and they hurried over to the large building on the corner. David said the department store had everything from haberdashery to cookware, leather boots to evening wear.

David laughed, relieved. On their way from the museum downtown to the department store in Charlottenburg, Wanda had appeared a little put out, pointing at all the smaller shops they passed and asking why they couldn't start their shopping expedition there rather than going all the way to another part of town.

"This store is something special!" he had told her.

Several hours later, they sat down, exhausted, in a nearby café, laden with packages large and small. It was a pretty little place with pink curtains, paintings of flowers on the wall, and a marvelously elegant clientele that made Wanda and David feel like country bumpkins by comparison.

Why didn't I buy myself a new dress, at least? Wanda wondered irritably as she looked around at the fashionably dressed ladies. She certainly wouldn't get another chance again anytime soon.

"What kind of cakes is Berlin famous for?" Carefully, Wanda tried to stretch her legs among all the bags and parcels.

"To be honest, I don't know," David replied. "When I lived here as an apprentice I didn't have the money to try very many cakes."

When the waitress came over, they both ordered coffee and a slice of hazelnut tart.

"Oh, this is all wonderful!" Wanda sighed. "Can you believe that I haven't been shopping since I left New York? I got so many lovely things today!" She pointed at all the packages. She could hardly wait to spread them out on the bed back at the hotel. A silk lilac flower with matching buttons for Eva. A pocketknife with a carved horn handle for Michel. Violet-scented soap for Johanna. And, and, and—she would bring presents home for everybody! Farewell presents . . .

"Thank you again for the tie," David said, pointing to the thin cardboard box beside him on the table. "I still don't like that you insisted on paying for it. I—"

"Nonsense! It's just a small way of saying thank you for everything you've done for me—for us!"

He shrugged. "It's not worth mentioning. But I can tell you one thing. My old teacher, Mr. Graupner, would be very pleased with our choice. A hand-sewn silk tie in just one color—he'd say that it is timeless. He may have only been the village schoolteacher, but he always insisted on looking his best. He was at least as well-dressed as the mayor! Some people laughed at him, but I admired his style. He always used to say that it wasn't a matter of how much money you had to spend, but whether you looked like a gentleman or a ragamuffin. *Take good care of your clothes and shoes and always be sure they are of good quality . . .*" David shook his head. "When I think of it—anybody would have thought that we were at a young gentlemen's academy rather than the village school in Steinach, where most of the lads would only have a couple of years' schooling before getting a job at the quarry. Or the tavern." He laughed harshly. "As if even one of us turned out to be a gentleman . . ."

"But that's exactly what you are!" Wanda cried out. "I'm sure that your teacher would be proud of you if he knew . . ." She fell quiet. Yes, David had managed what she had only ever dreamed of. He had found his place in life. While she . . .

"Wanda, what is it?"

She looked at him. She didn't want to spoil the mood. But the words burst out of her before she could stop them. "Oh, if only there was something that I could be proud of! I've tried everything. But nothing has ever worked out for me, ever. I don't know whether I'm any good at anything at all. Or even who I am. Am I the daughter of Steven Miles, the successful businessman? Or of the glassblower Thomas Heimer? In America I feel I'm a Lauscha girl. And in Lauscha they call me the American girl. Who am I, then? What am I good for? Nothing at all, perhaps?"

David grabbed Wanda's hand so suddenly that he almost knocked over a coffeepot.

"Darling Wanda—as far as I'm concerned, you're the most wonderful woman in the world! I've never met anyone like you. So . . . full of life! Full of grace and energy and—" He stopped.

His cheeks had reddened. He hastily brushed a lock of hair off his forehead, and then he went on, a little less forcefully. "Of course you're your stepfather's daughter. He's given you his sense for business and his get-up-and-go! But you're Thomas Heimer's daughter too, and that's why you love Lauscha and glassblowing. But above all—" He put his right hand gently to her chin and looked into her eyes. "Above all, you're Wanda!"

The way he looked at her! For a moment she felt gripped by fear. Not that! Not now! She couldn't handle any more confusing feelings, any more excitement. David was a friend. No more and no less. She turned away from his hand and lowered her eyes, but the warm feeling in her belly remained. So he thought she was wonderful . . .

More loudly than she had intended, she said, "Wanda, the bird of ill omen! How wonderful! Believe me, if anybody has suffered at the hands of fate, it's me. The best you can do is keep well away. I only ever bring people bad luck!"

David laughed. "Ah well, now I'm shaking in my boots!" He made a face.

She tried to kick him under the table but only hit a package. "I can make fun of myself, thank you very much," she muttered.

"No, but seriously now," he said. "My grandmother, God rest her soul, had a simpler way of saying all that. She'd just say that you can't make an omelet without breaking eggs. The fact is that you have more ideas and initiative and courage than other people— and things are bound to go wrong from time to time! Perhaps you should just get used to that idea rather than trying to persuade yourself that bad luck follows you around."

"Hmm, I never looked at it that way . . ."

"Besides, nobody could ever say your life is boring! There's always something happening, you're always trying something new. How many other people can claim to lead such an exciting life? It's wonderful that you have such courage, that you're always ready to give something a try!"

If only Richard could hear this! Wanda thought. "There are plenty of people who think I try too hard! Don't you know that women are expected to lead a quiet life?"

"Nonsense. Just think of Marie—and all that you've told me about her. Or think of your aunt, who runs her own business!"

While the waitress cleared away their dishes, Wanda glanced up at David. He wasn't just talking for the sake of it; he meant every word he said. He reminded her of her stepfather just then.

David Wagner was so different from all the other young men she had known in her life. He wasn't as full of himself as Richard, and he was far more interesting than Harold, her ex-fiancé. And he was more sensitive to her feelings than all the others. She hadn't said a word, but he noticed all the same how unhappy she had been in the museum. And, instinctively, he had found just the right distraction for her.

Yes, David was someone who took care of other people. Only somebody who had found his own place in life could be so kind and generous to others. The son of Wagner the tavern keeper . . .

She took a deep breath.

"David, I . . . I wanted to tell you yesterday, on the train. I'm planning to leave Lauscha, at least for a while."

"What . . . ?"

"Please hear me out," she said. "You can't imagine how grateful I am to you for everything. You've been a good friend to me over the past few months—which makes my decision all the harder. But—" Oh, why did everything in life have to be so complicated? Why couldn't she just sneak away without a word?

"I've learned a great deal recently," she said. "About the villagers, and how they don't give up. How they stick together when it really counts." She looked at him. "I've learned that there's no shame in losing. That failure is part of life, just like success. Even if success is much more fun . . ." She laughed softly. "I've learned something about myself as well. From you. For instance I've learned that I'm not the bundle of bad luck I always thought I was. But now . . ." She looked out the window and thought of the painting in the National Gallery. Did the painter even know what the landscape looked like behind that curtain?

She looked back at David, who was staring stubbornly straight ahead.

"There's a time for everything—I understand that now, better than ever. Once we've put that bastard in jail, I'll no longer be needed in Lauscha." She thought of the letter from her New York friend Pandora; it had been lying on her bedside table for weeks now. Pandora had written that she had opened a dance school on the shore of Lake Maggiore, and that Wanda must come visit her there. Perhaps it was time to accept the invitation . . . maybe it would be good for Sylvie too.

"A-hah . . ." David said slowly, and nodded. "A-hah . . ." he repeated. "So that's how you see it! You win the fight, and then you just up and leave! You don't care a fig for what happens to your brothers-in-arms! You don't care about me!"

"That's not true!"

"Wanda, dearest, I . . . I hadn't been planning to talk to you like this. I wanted to wait until we had done what we came to do, and we were back home with our heads clear. But now . . ." He took a deep breath. "You can't just leave! You have to give me—give us—a chance! Ever since we met, it's been about making deals and making money. Apart from one walk in the woods together, we've hardly had a chance to talk about ourselves. But I have so much to tell you!" He stopped and looked at her expectantly.

"That's all well and good. But—"

"Wanda! I'm in love with you, hopelessly in love! Surely you must have noticed that!"

There was a roaring in Wanda's ears, so loud that she suddenly felt dizzy. That was exactly what she didn't want to hear. It was exactly what she was afraid of! It was why she had been honest with him about her plans.

She had been in love twice. And each time it had turned out to be nothing more than a fleeting passion.

Yes, she liked David. More than that! But she didn't want to fall in love again! What if this fizzled just as quickly as the other times? Would she ever be able to trust her feelings again?

"Wanda, my dearest, please don't sit there looking as though you consider it bad news that I love you! It's quite the opposite: we belong together! You and I—together, we're unbeatable. What a future we have ahead of us! The two of us—or rather the three of us! For if you choose me, then I will love Sylvie just as if she were my own child."

He stopped and took a deep breath.

"The very first time I saw you . . . When you came into my office, it was like a dream! I couldn't even breathe for a moment."

"And I thought at the time what an old-fashioned suit you were wearing! Well, you wanted to look older than your years . . ." She grinned.

"Which you would never do, of course, in that outfit you were wearing, with that hat!" David replied mockingly. Then he grew serious again.

"Wanda, I'm serious. I love you. If you don't feel the same way—" He paused for a moment as though hoping she would contradict him, but when she didn't, he carried on. "Love can grow. We just have to nurture it—like a tender plant."

"Don't tell me that's what your grandmother always said!"

David, Sylvie, and herself? A future together? In Sonneberg? On the edge of the paradise of glass . . .

David smiled. "Believe it or not . . ." He jumped up and knelt in front of her, ignoring the startled glances from the other tables. "Wanda, I swear to you here and now. I'll never give up hoping that you will love me back one day. Even if you don't change your mind until I'm old and gray—I'll wait!"

Wanda felt that time stood still for a moment, as though there were nothing in the world but herself and the man kneeling in front of her.

Then suddenly a voice spoke up next to her. "Say something, child! Don't keep the whole shop waiting!"

Wanda blinked at the waitress, and then at David.

"I wonder whether your grandmother would have some useful words of advice just now?" And then she laughed.

A bank clerk, of all things! What would her mother say to that?

CHAPTER FIFTY-FIVE

The clock behind the hotel reception desk began to strike.

Nine o'clock.

Anna, who was sitting next to Wanda, giggled nervously. The tension in the little hotel lobby was almost unbearable. Even the old lady at the reception desk, who after much persuasion had finally agreed to make a pot of tea for Anna and Wanda, seemed to feel that there was something in the air—she kept looking up from her ledgers and over at the little group. David Wagner, standing there in his hat and coat, smiled at her and then at Wanda.

"Don't worry, we have everything under control. You two sit here and enjoy your tea, and we'll take care of it all, won't we?" He put his arms around Karl's and Benno's shoulders.

The two men nodded grimly. Christoph couldn't go with them, unfortunately, because he was still suffering from his migraine.

"You won't forget to post someone at the back door?" Anna asked.

Wanda looked at her, astonished. The way she spoke, anyone would have thought that Anna went out hunting criminals every week.

David Wagner rolled his eyes. They had already talked over every detail of their plan over supper. He and the other men would go to the Blue Owl while Wanda and Anna waited at the hotel—it wasn't proper for women to visit such an establishment, after all, and it might even be dangerous.

He took a deep breath. "Karl will be at the back door if the fellow tries to make a break for it. Benno and I will go in at the front, just like normal customers. All we need now is to cross our fingers and hope we find the right man!"

"Well then . . ." Wanda raised her teacup as though drinking a toast. "Here's to your success!"

The three men were hardly out the door before Anna leapt to her feet. Wanda put her cup down so quickly that it tinkled in the saucer.

"To just sit here drinking tea—the very idea! If they think they can get rid of us so easily . . ." Wanda quickly put on her coat, which she had hidden behind the chair earlier.

"Men! Always thinking they know better!" Anna grumbled, as she wound her scarf around her head so that only her eyes showed. As they left, Wanda grabbed hold of David's umbrella, and they hurried out after the men.

The receptionist shook her head, baffled.

Benno had said that the nightclub was in a nondescript side street not far from the hotel. Even the front door was inconspicuous, more closely resembling the door to a cellar than the entrance to a club.

After they had turned left and right countless times, staying far enough back that the men wouldn't spot them, Wanda realized that Benno's definition of "not far away" was different from hers. The streets became narrower and darker, but there were plenty of people around. Newspaper sellers shouted out the latest headlines, little knots of people stood around grilled-sausage stalls, shadowy figures lurked in doorways calling, "Cigars! Cigarettes!" Wanda couldn't imagine why anybody would choose to buy their tobacco here rather than in one of the chic little tobacconists located on the more elegant streets. Although it was cold, there was a pervasive smell of decay in the air. Heaps of garbage lay around, and at one point a rat almost ran over Wanda's and Anna's feet.

After that the women tried to keep to the middle of the sidewalk, where the lighting was better and they were clear of the garbage and the doorways. Though they kept their eyes fixed straight ahead, they were constantly accosted by men offering to buy them a drink and women calling them terrible names.

"Right, left, right again—this place is a maze! We'll never find our way back to the hotel on our own," Wanda muttered, holding the umbrella up higher so that she didn't knock it into any of the passersby. She felt unsafe and was sorry she had ever decided to follow the men. What if she was putting Anna in danger? What if she was even jeopardizing their whole plan?

What have I done this time? If only we had stayed in the hotel like David told us to . . .

A moment later, Wanda almost stumbled. Anna, whose arm was linked with hers, had stopped abruptly.

"There!" Anna's hand shot out.

A little ways ahead, the men had also stopped. Benno was pointing toward a building, then back down the street. Wanda hastily lowered the umbrella to shield them from view.

"Not exactly inconspicuous, eh?" Anna chuckled.

Wanda wasn't sure whether she was referring to the two of them or Benno, who was standing up ahead waving his arms. She peered out from under the umbrella to get a better look.

A moment later, Benno and David went into the building and Karl began marching rather hesitantly up and down in front of it. Occasionally, he disappeared around the next corner.

"Now what?" Anna looked at Wanda expectantly.

Wanda took a couple of tentative steps forward until she could see the doorway better. It bore a brass plaque that was badly in need of a good polish, with the words "Blue Owl." She was so excited she felt dizzy.

"I would never have thought that Benno would go to a place like this," Anna muttered.

"Hmm," Wanda said. "We certainly can't go in. If the men see us, they'll be terribly angry. I think we'd better hide and—"

She never got the chance to finish her sentence. The front door suddenly flew open and a woman came running out, screaming, followed by a man who was yelling after her. Benno and David then emerged and ran after the man.

Anna put her hand to her mouth. "Good gracious!" She was trembling all over.

Wanda's heart was hammering so hard that it hurt. The broker! It was him, there was no doubt about it! And no doubt, either, that he was making his escape. As was the woman who had run out ahead of him.

What now?

The woman had on a white mask that revealed only her eyes and her mouth, the lips made up crimson red. Though she wore high-heeled shoes, she ran as though the Devil himself was after her.

Within seconds, the strange little group was practically upon Wanda and Anna. It was only then that Wanda realized that the woman wasn't wearing much apart from the mask and the shoes— the thin cloth tied around her hips could hardly be considered clothing. Her piercing shrieks chilled Wanda to the bone. This woman must be mad!

"Claire! Wait, my darling, wait! Claire!" the bogus broker cried out as he tried to catch up with the madwoman.

"Stop!" David shouted again.

"Wait, damn it!" Karl shouted.

Anna and Wanda looked at one another. Then they nodded decisively, took a step backward and cleared the path. Wanda had closed the umbrella by now and held it firmly in both hands.

"Watch out!" Anna whispered.

As the woman named Claire got closer, she looked as though she was capable of just about anything. A second later, she was past them.

"Claire! Wait!" The bogus broker came nearer and nearer—

Whoosh! Wanda swung the umbrella out to block his path.

The man cried out, stumbled, and fell to the ground. He shouted in pain, then began cursing violently.

The woman turned and hesitated for a moment as though wondering whether to turn back, but then she kept running.

David and Benno arrived a second later. Breathless from running, Benno knelt on the man's back while David grabbed hold of his legs.

"Damn it, what are you two doing here?" Benno gasped.

Anna and Wanda grinned at one another.

"Oh, we just didn't feel like drinking tea anymore . . ." Wanda said guilelessly.

CHAPTER FIFTY-SIX

Now that they had him, the man put up no more resistance, nor did he try to deny that he was who they said he was. Yes, damn it, he'd been in Lauscha. Yes, he'd sold them the fake shares. And yes, he knew Friedhelm Strobel—the man had hired him for the job, after all . . .

Benno puffed up his chest like a rooster. Thanks to him and his good memory, they had their prize!

Karl and Benno took hold of the man and pulled him up. He had torn his pants when he fell, there was blood running down his knee, and he was limping. David marched on ahead and the two women brought up the tail end of the procession. Back at the hotel, they all gathered in the lobby, where the receptionist looked on mistrustfully. They were going to call the police later, of course, but first they wanted to know how a cloakroom attendant from a Berlin nightclub came to be dealing in forged share certificates.

"I can explain everything, but please, please . . ." The man fell on his knees in front of David, the tears streaming down his face. "I have to find Claire first! She'll be lost without me . . ." he sobbed.

"Out of the question!" David told him. "First you talk!"

"That's right!" Karl shouted, and gave him a kick.

"Karl . . ." Wanda shook her head disapprovingly.

The man climbed heavily to his feet and wiped his face with his hand. "But—"

"Sit down!" David pointed to the chairs where Anna and Wanda had sat earlier with their tea. The pot and the half-empty cups hadn't been removed from the side table yet.

As was so often the case in life, the story began with a woman. Her name was Klara Borowsky—though she also went by the stage name of Claire. She performed as a dancer in the nightclub, and she was, of course, the one who had run out of the Blue Owl like a madwoman.

That evening one of the guests must have made some disparaging remark about her that Claire happened to hear. She leapt from the stage and almost scratched the man's eyes out, then ran off, shouting that she would never dance again in the two-bit dump where she wasn't appreciated as an artist. When Bernhard Borowsky, Klara's husband and the cloakroom attendant at the club, heard her raving, he went into the hall to calm her down. But she ran past him and out into the street before he could get to her. That was when Benno and David turned up.

Klara was addicted to cocaine. So was Bernhard, though he thought he could control his addiction better than his wife. She snorted cocaine every day and her nose was constantly inflamed, sometimes to the point that it bled.

Benno looked around at the little group meaningfully. Hadn't he always said that it was the sniffling that finally helped him remember?

Bernhard could see that his wife's health was suffering, and he tried to persuade her to indulge less often—but all in vain. Her addiction was stronger than she was, and it cost a fortune, particularly since cocaine had gotten more expensive in recent years. Klara could raise most of the money she needed by working as a dancer and by performing certain other services for guests at the nightclub—Bernhard himself earned much less in the cloakroom. Often a guest would invite her to share some cocaine, which Bernhard didn't like since he had no way to control how much Klara snorted or to check the quality of the powder. More than once there had been ugly incidents in which Klara had screamed and raved like a madwoman—even up on stage—and Bernhard was worried that she was truly losing her mind. Most of the time, guests thought that they had been rewarded with an especially daring show. When this happened, it almost broke Bernhard's heart.

He had to protect his wife. And the only solution was to make sure that she got good cocaine. Reputable pharmaceutical companies sold it, and he wanted to be sure that she was taking the real stuff, not some dubious powder procured from a backstreet laboratory. Surely they understood that? Bernhard was pleading again.

Wanda and the others just looked at one another in confusion. Protect her? That wasn't how they saw it . . .

They didn't even need to encourage Borowsky to tell his story; he was talking as though his life depended on it.

Sometimes there wasn't enough money to pay for Klara's addiction. Then they had to resort to other means, such as picking customers' pockets. Their thefts had gone unnoticed until last summer, which Bernhard thought was sheer luck but which Claire attributed to skill. The fact was that most of the Blue Owl customers weren't sober enough to recall where they might have lost their wallet. Nobody suspected the half-naked dancer who readily sat on his lap. Or the stupid-looking cloakroom attendant who helped him into his coat at the end of the evening.

But one evening Klara picked the wrong target . . .

Wanda and the others traded glances.

Friedhelm Strobel!

Borowsky nodded. Strobel could be very convincing once he had his claws into somebody, he said with a hint of irony. It hadn't taken them long to agree to the terms; he was to come to the Thuringian Forest and perform a task for Strobel, after which he and Klara would owe the man nothing.

That was just the confession they needed! David leaned forward. "What happened to the money that you took from the glassblowers that day?"

"What do you think?" Borowsky said. "I gave it to Strobel, of course. That was part of the deal."

"That bastard!" Karl shouted, clenching his fist.

"Can anybody con . . . confirm that you gave Strobel the money?" David was so on edge that he began to stutter.

Borowsky thought for a moment. If he remembered correctly, the maid opened the door for him, but he and Strobel had been alone when he handed over the money . . .

They knew the rest of the story, he said. All in all it had been easy work—the glassblowers had practically thrust the money into his hands, he said.

It had been hard-earned money, Karl said. Benno added that it was the life savings of simple souls who believed that they were getting their money's worth with the shares. Borowsky must have known right from the start that the whole story stank!

He had suspected as much, Borowsky admitted. He shrugged. He was sorry, of course—now.

Wanda and the others knew that he didn't really mean that. Everything that Bernhard Borowsky said or did was for Klara—even now he barely seemed to register not only that his action had been criminal, but that he had brought misery to countless families.

Borowsky was confused. He was worried about Klara wandering the streets of Berlin, and he was scared of these complete strangers who showed no signs of letting him go. He saw now that

Friedhelm Strobel had gotten him mixed up in a much more serious offense than mere pickpocketing. As he came to realize that he would no longer be able to protect Klara—that he would be spending a long time behind bars—he began to cry bitterly.

Bernhard Borowsky didn't know how Strobel had gotten hold of the forged certificates or where they were printed. All he knew was that there were some genuine shares as well as the fakes. He had shown the genuine certificates to David Wagner when they first met. Then he had taken them straight back to Strobel, who had switched them for the fakes.

Once it was clear that the man had said everything he had to say, David called the police.

At two o'clock in the morning, Bernhard Borowsky signed a full confession naming Friedhelm Strobel as the mastermind behind the whole swindle. The police officers mostly dealt with drunk and disorderly behavior, pickpockets, and other small fry; they were more than a little surprised to have such a big case on their hands. They promised to have a certified copy of the confession sent to Sonneberg in the morning. It was good that the glassblowers had already lodged a complaint with the local police there against "parties unknown"—the Berlin officers reckoned that their colleagues in Sonneberg would probably arrest Strobel the next day. If a personal statement from Borowsky was needed at the trial, there would be no problem transferring the prisoner.

CHAPTER FIFTY-SEVEN

Nobody thought of trying to get even a few hours of sleep that night—it was all too exciting! The group set out for the railway station before it was even light, so they could be on the first train. Almost as soon as they had taken their seats on the hard benches they fell asleep, one by one. All of them except for Christoph Stanzer slept through the long train journey; he had gotten plenty of sleep in Berlin and was now in charge of waking the others when the time came to change trains.

They were still tired and sore when their train finally pulled into Lauscha that evening. David Wagner had gotten off the train in Sonneberg, so he could be there the next day when the police came for Strobel.

They had collected enough evidence to prove that Strobel was implicated in a crime! They felt drunk with elation and wanted to run down to the Black Eagle despite their exhaustion to tell everyone the good news and to celebrate.

But they decided to keep their secret for one more night. The news should strike Lauscha like lightning the next day. Not one day later, but not a moment too soon, either. They wanted it to be a thunderclap.

* * *

"Child, you don't know how happy I am . . ." Johanna didn't let go of Wanda's hand as she blew her nose with her other hand. Tears ran down her cheeks. She had come out of the workshop as soon as she heard the front door of the house open. By the look of her, she had just been applying glitter powder to Christmas globes.

"From now on I will truly be able to look to the future, without always looking back." She sobbed again, harder now.

Wanda was touched. She had not expected Johanna to react quite so strongly. She was glad she had come with Anna instead of going to her father's so she was here when Johanna got the news.

"Mother . . ." Anna cleared her throat and hesitantly stroked her mother's back.

Johanna blew her nose again noisily. "Oh, my girls, I'm only crying because I'm so happy," she sniffed. "Strobel is going to pay for his crimes at last! Forgery and obtaining money by deception—I don't even know what the law books call all that. But I can well imagine that such offenses carry stiff sentences. We're not just talking about stealing a few sticks of firewood or a chicken. This was a swindle that cost the glassblowers eleven thousand marks!"

Wanda and Anna nodded emphatically.

"He sits there like a king on his throne in the Gründler foundry—how can a man be so wicked?" Johanna gazed into the distance. "Sometimes, especially since Marie died, I've been close to losing my faith in a just God. Good people die too early and bad people can go about their evil business without fear of retribution. But now . . ." At last a smile spread across her face. Johanna took a deep breath.

"Children, I can hardly wait to see Friedhelm Strobel being led away by the police!"

"And who made it happen?" Anna looked from her mother to Wanda as she asked the question.

They both shrugged, uncertain. What did Anna want them to say? That she, and she alone, deserved credit for their success?

Anna looked at their faces and laughed. "The Steinmann girls, all of us!" She put her arms around Johanna and Wanda. "Mother, haven't you always told us how you and your sisters always stuck together? Through good times and bad?"

Johanna nodded in silence. Yes, she had always told those stories.

Anna raised her eyebrows. "Well, nothing's changed, don't you see? The Steinmanns are still a force to be reckoned with! A man like Friedhelm Strobel has no chance against women like us, not in the long run!" She looked at Wanda and fell silent for a moment.

"Wanda, what's wrong? For Heaven's sake, why are you crying, now of all times?"

"Because . . ." Wanda said, "because I'm so happy."

* * *

"As for these pipes—you can take then back to your brother tomorrow!" Karl swept his hand across the table and gathered dozens of porcelain tobacco pipes onto a tray that already held little vases and figurines. "Tell him he can find someone else to paint flowers and garlands on them!"

Barefoot in her nightgown, Martha Flein looked from the pipes to her husband. It was ice-cold in the house, but she had gotten up as soon as she heard him come in. She wasn't sure now that had been such a good idea. Was Karl drunk? Instead of telling her about the trip, he had gone straight to his workbench and started behaving like a bull in a china shop.

"Here—the brushes, the paints . . . Take them all back to him. And tell him I can't bear to look at the things a moment longer! This has nothing to do with art."

"But Karl . . ."

"Don't you 'but Karl' me! Starting tomorrow, I'll be a glass-blower again! As I should be! You'll see . . ."

* * *

"Another glass of wine, Mr. Wagner?" Gerhard Grosse was already waving his hand to beckon the waiter over as they sat together in the Swan Tavern.

Another glass of wine—why not? David nodded. He had to celebrate his victory over Friedhelm Strobel somehow, didn't he?

After the long journey he had been too worked up to go straight back to his rented room. When he had seen the lights in the windows of the Swan and heard the laughter from inside, he had spontaneously decided to go inside and have a drink. A glass of wine in one of Sonneberg's finest hostelries. Like one of the gentry. Just as he had always dreamed of. Now he had really earned it!

It was by sheer coincidence that he ran into Gerhard Grosse of all people. As he stepped into the tavern, the weekly meeting of Sonneberg's most important businessmen was just breaking up. When Grosse spotted his employee, cheeks flushed with excitement, eyes roving around, he knew that he had been right to give David the time off to go to Berlin. Had the young man found out something about Friedhelm Strobel? Was Strobel mixed up in fraudulent dealings, as Wagner had suspected?

Grosse had called David over to his table. As he listened in astonishment to David's story, he began thinking feverishly: How could the Grosse bank be sure of securing repayment on its loan if Strobel was about to be arrested, as seemed almost certain to be the case? He would have to consult his lawyer first thing the next morning, though he was confident the matter could be resolved in the bank's favor. After all, Strobel had several accounts, and taken together they added up to a tidy sum. Gerhard Grosse wasn't quite sure why the man had wanted to take out a loan for the foundry at all. He could only suppose that Strobel had intended to keep some of his money free for other deals. Now he was going to be in prison, and for a long time at that. What a scandal!

He put a hand on David Wagner's shoulder. "You've done very well, young man! Not everybody would have thought things through the way you did and done what was necessary . . . Our bank needs people like you. Believe me, what you have done for us will not go unrewarded. If there's anything I can do for you . . ."

"As a matter of fact there is . . ." David cleared his throat. "I . . . um . . . it's like this. I intend to propose marriage in the near future. The young lady—is from a very good family, and if she agrees to marry me, I want to be able to offer her a real home to live in. Do you understand me?"

Gerhard Grosse nodded.

David looked relieved. "At the moment I live in an unheated attic room. It's hardly luxurious. However, I don't have capital of my own, or other securities, and if the Grosse bank were to offer me a loan to buy a house, I couldn't back it up with anything but my name . . ."

"That's good enough for me!" Gerhard Grosse said. "Consider your loan underwritten. And of course the bank will help you look for a suitable property. I can already think of a few houses that will be on the market soon."

He looked at the young clerk and shook his head. Who would have thought that David Wagner would set his sights on Wanda Miles? This Wagner fellow was going to go far! Gerhard Grosse resolved to keep a close eye on him in the future.

* * *

Monika picked up her pillow and punched it so hard that a seam split audibly.

She glared over at the next bed, where her husband was already bundled up under the covers. Benno was simply impossible!

When he came home, he had gone over to the beer pump, pulled himself a beer, and then drunk it as calmly as if he'd never been away. When she asked whether the trip to Berlin had been a success, all he did was shrug.

Was she supposed to take that for an answer? Was that all she got in return for her tireless work? She'd been run ragged the past few days.

Monika wondered if Martha Flein had to put up with no sort of answer at all from Karl too. Or was it just Benno who was so tight-lipped? When she had run into Martha on the street the day before, she had known as little as Monika about the reason for the men's trip to Berlin. "It costs money, that's all I know! We can hardly get by on what we have anyway," Martha had said.

Monika stared up at the ceiling, deep in thought. Her Benno gave nothing away. It was almost as though he had something to hide. Just like the last time he had gone to Berlin!

What did it all mean?

There was probably another woman behind it all. She would talk to Benno about it first thing tomorrow. If he thought that she was going to work her fingers to the bone for him here while he had his fun with some little lady in Berlin, he had another thing coming!

Monika snorted and rolled over in bed.

* * *

How the paper shone! And how thick the pages were. There were no creases or folds, even though he had leafed through them time and time again. Gotthilf Täuber had truly spared no expense on the exhibition catalog. Richard ran the palm of his hand over the open pages as though he were handling the finest lace. There was a thick red check mark next to almost every item description.

Sold! Sold! Sold! Richard laughed.

Everything had sold except three pieces—he could hardly believe it. He had never had so much money in his life. Granted, Täuber was taking a hefty commission—twenty percent! And Richard had to bear the costs for renting the rooms for the reception and for various smaller expenses. When he added that all up, the bottom line didn't look quite so dazzling . . .

Lost in thought, he swirled the champagne in his glass and took another sip. It was the last day of the exhibition and Täuber had given him the bottle.

"With my very best wishes—you can drink it with your young lady!" he had said. Although Richard had accepted the gift, he hadn't told Gotthilf Täuber that he no longer had a young lady to celebrate his success with him.

The bubbles in the champagne prickled on his tongue, cool and refreshing, but at what should have been a sparkling moment in his life, it tasted somehow . . . flat. Richard sighed and shoved the cork back into the bottle. He should just have had a beer instead!

He got up and began to get ready for bed. In the morning he would think about the next step in his career.

After all, he was a highly regarded artist now.

CHAPTER FIFTY-EIGHT

"Have you written everything down?" Friedhelm Strobel asked, looking critically at his foreman. He had hired the man from the Unterneubrunn foundry specifically for the job and was quite satisfied with his work so far, though of course he did not say so. Why should he?

The man leafed back through his notebook.

"The breakfast break will be reduced from one hour to half an hour starting on December 24. Any worker who infringes on these rules will be fined. Likewise for the lunch break, which will also be reduced to thirty minutes beginning on the same date."

Strobel nodded. Very good. He waved his hand impatiently for the man to go on.

"This week Gustav Müller will have one-fifth of his wage docked as punishment for carrying out work without instructions."

"Tell him that next time he can take his hat and leave. For good!" Strobel said curtly. He simply could not understand Gustav's impertinence. Instead of blowing Christmas decorations as instructed, he had gone to help the glassmaking team the day before. Strobel had happened by chance to look through his office window and observe this, then he had asked Gustav what he was doing. The man had replied, honestly enough, that he had noticed that the glassmakers were falling behind with their work and he wanted to help them.

Strobel could hardly believe his ears. "Since when does every Tom, Dick, or Harry get a say in how the work is carried out here?" he had shouted.

The foreman shrugged. "If you say so. But to be honest, it wouldn't hurt to have another pair of hands at the furnaces. I was wondering whether to assign an extra man—"

Strobel raised a hand. "Please spare me the details. God knows I have plenty of other things to attend to today." He pointed to the pile of lists in front of him on the desk. There were lists showing the rising production figures. Lists showing which worker had been docked how much of his pay and for how long. Lists showing the figures for production costs and sales prices for various lines, and lists of the best-selling items.

The foreman cleared his throat. "Siegfried Braun has to have his pay docked for being absent without leave. One week's wages . . . ?"

Strobel nodded. He had noticed the unspoken question in what his foreman said, but he decided to ignore it. Even if the business was mostly running smoothly, it would do no harm to set an example every now and then. This Siegfried Braun would serve that purpose just fine. Otherwise the place would descend into anarchy.

The foreman left. Strobel knew that he would follow his instructions to the letter. He had been a good find. At first, some of the workers had tried to test the limits of the new foreman's authority. Strobel could understand that—the foundry workers wanted to know how far they could go. But they had soon discovered that the man from Unterneubrunn was much stricter than Karl Flein had ever been.

Yes, they were beginning to learn . . .

A moment later, Strobel leapt to his feet and hammered on the window from which he could observe almost everything that went on in the foundry. He had had the window put into his office the very first week he was there, and now he could hardly imagine life without it. He frowned and raised the index finger of his right hand.

Jockel, who was just holding up a vase at the sorting table, flinched and gave a hasty nod.

Strobel turned away from the window. So, that was working well enough . . . He still wasn't sure that Jockel was the right man for quality control. He didn't pick out many wares as rejects, and Strobel was very happy with the quality of the foundry's wares overall—which must have something to do with the sorter and his work. But there was something insolent about the man. They had clashed early on when he had questioned one of Strobel's new regulations. A trifling matter. Since the foreman had been busy elsewhere at the time, Jockel had come straight to Strobel. He had puffed himself up like a fighting cock and demanded that Strobel eliminate one of the new rules. Strobel had just laughed.

Then Jockel had said that he who laughs last in Lauscha, laughs longest. With a sly look on his face, he asked whether Strobel hadn't heard about the arsonist who had been causing trouble in the village lately. If a fire broke out in the foundry, that could really mean trouble . . .

Strobel had been furious. How dare the man threaten him?

The grin was soon wiped off Jockel's face when two policemen from Sonneberg turned up later that same day. After spending a long night in the station answering questions about the fires that had broken out in Lauscha, he had returned to work cowed and quiet.

Strobel had been very relieved that his sorter was no longer a suspect in the matter of arson. He had explained of course that given certain remarks that Jockel had made, he had been afraid that he had the arsonist right there in front of him, and had felt obliged to inform the police . . .

Strobel leaned back in his chair, laced his fingers together behind his head, and sighed. After that little episode nobody else had dared protest—or at least Strobel hadn't heard any complaints. As for what people said about him behind his back, he couldn't really care less . . . There were some things, however, that he did care about.

Wanda Miles, for example.

Friedhelm Strobel was not the least bit happy about how his plans for Wanda Miles had turned out. He nervously bit off a hang-nail on his right thumb and licked at the blood that seeped out.

Why had he heard nothing more from that young lady? He had assumed that she would come to see him to put in a good word for the workers—he had given her plenty of reasons to do so. But no, it was as though she had vanished from the face of the earth. Did she not care about these people at all?

Damn it, he had had his chance when she came to visit him in his shop, but he had squandered it!

Strobel sighed deeply and burst into such a violent fit of coughing that his chest hurt. Curse the dry air here in the foundry! Strobel slapped himself on the chest until the coughing fit subsided.

Why was he even wasting his time thinking about that girl? Granted, it hadn't gone quite as he had planned—he should have taken out the key when he had locked the door. Then she would never have escaped.

But hadn't plenty of things gone just right?

Strobel took a tentative deep breath.

To think of all the money he'd made in the past few months! He had 30,000 marks in his Hamburg bank account from that shares transaction. And then the 11,000 marks that he kept in a cardboard box under his bed at home.

A cardboard box—like a little old lady who saves up coins in an old stocking? *Strobel, are you becoming eccentric in your old age?* He chuckled at the thought.

More than 40,000 marks profit—all thanks to the Schlüter lines shipping company of Bremen . . .

He could have paid off his loan with the Grosse bank in cash. But he had chosen not to. He had to keep up appearances, after all. So far nobody suspected a thing, and that was how it should stay.

By now Strobel had teased away the hangnail on his right index finger enough to bite it off altogether. He shut his eyes and enjoyed the fleeting pain that shot through his finger.

The Christmas trade was going very well. His customers had been more than a little surprised when they learned that Strobel now had his own foundry. He had told them nonchalantly that he had to change with the times. Sometimes he shrugged modestly and remarked that it was all a matter of organization.

And Strobel was a master of organization. His shop in Sonneberg was in good hands with the new salesman. Strobel himself had been surprised to see how good the man was. The customers accepted him, and he knew how to fill order books—what more could anyone ask for? Strobel hadn't even caught the man embezzling any money yet. Which meant that he could devote his own time to the foundry.

Yes, it was all going nicely . . .

What did Wanda Miles matter? Or that bitch aunt of hers? He should forget about the Steinmann women, all of them! They were irrelevant.

Friedhelm Strobel was so lost in thought that he didn't notice the knot of people gathering in front of the foundry. He only looked up when his office door opened and two policemen came in.

"Friedhelm Strobel?"

"Yes?" He straightened his cravat. "If you are here because of Jockel—that's all sorted out now. He's not the arsonist . . ."

"We're not here because of any of your employees!" one of the policemen said gruffly. "Mr. Strobel—you are under arrest! You are accused of forgery and fraud, and you have serious charges to face."

"What—how . . . ? But I . . ." Before Strobel knew what was going on, the policemen took him by the arm and dragged him outside.

CHAPTER FIFTY-NINE

The news that something was happening at the foundry spread quickly through Lauscha. Nobody knew quite what was going on, but the rumors sprang up everywhere like mushrooms on the forest floor after rain.

Whenever anybody asked Benno whether he knew anything about it, he raised his eyebrows meaningfully and told them that it would do no harm to go down to the foundry sometime that day. No, he couldn't tell them exactly when. And he wasn't going to say just what would happen, either.

By noon everybody in the village had gathered at the foundry. The workers were all there, of course. And Karl Flein and his wife, who had been in such a hurry that she had put on her winter coat over her apron. Christoph Stanzer, now fully recovered from his migraine. Everybody from the Steinmann-Maienbaum workshop— all led by Johanna, who stood hand in hand with her daughter. Thomas Heimer, and Eva with Sylvie. Neither of them knew what was going on—all Wanda had told them was that her inquiries over the last few weeks were about to bear fruit that day. David Wagner stood next to Thomas Heimer, with a green silk handkerchief peeping out of the pocket of his suit. Benno stood next to him. He had said nothing to his wife, who was sweeping up the fallen leaves behind the Black Eagle. Richard wasn't there, either—he had set off that morning to go visit Gotthilf Täuber.

When the front door of the foundry opened and two policemen appeared leading Friedhelm Strobel between them, a murmur ran through the crowd. This was more than they had dared hope for! What was going on?

Benno, Karl, and Christoph told the onlookers about the serious charges against the owner of the foundry, and how they had spent the last few weeks investigating the matter. Even the American girl had joined in the hunt, and Anna as well! Indeed, it was Wanda who had set the whole thing in motion. And Johanna had financed the whole investigation. Nobody knew quite why she had done such a thing, but it seemed that she had a score to settle with Strobel. Benno mentioned he had furnished the vital clue— this ensured that nobody overlooked his part.

A buzz of conversation broke out. People were confused, and they were angry as well. Strobel was behind the forged share certificates? The man who had been sitting in the middle of Lauscha like a worm in an apple? It was incredible! How in the world . . . ?

David Wagner had already spoken with the bank's lawyer that morning, and he could add several more details to the story. Forgery carried a jail sentence of several years. In Strobel's case it was a particularly serious charge since it had led to considerable loss of money. Then there was the additional charge of fraud.

"Thief!" called out someone from the crowd. "Swindler!" called another voice. "Miserable swine!" called a third. "How can you cheat honest folk out of their money that way?"

The police were having trouble making their way through the crowd. Although they tried to push people back to make way, they could not prevent them from lashing out at Strobel with fists, elbows, and feet. The air was thick with curses but the policemen acted as though they heard nothing. When the three of them reached the place where Karl Flein stood, his wife, Martha, suddenly blocked their path. Before anybody could pull her back, she slapped Strobel in the face so hard that the sound was heard by all. Without saying a word, she wiped her hand on her apron and disappeared back into the crowd. Karl turned to look at her in astonishment. "Would you rather I slapped you for not telling me a thing?" she snapped at him, but he saw a grin flit across her face as she spoke.

The policemen eventually took Strobel away, but people were far too excited to go back to work. They stood around in little groups, talking and gesturing wildly.

"What now?" David asked, taking Wanda's hand.

She gave a start—she hadn't seen him approach. She felt as though she were seeing everything through a fog. She opened her mouth, but before she could say anything, a man spoke up next to her.

"Yes! What now?" said Jockel. "What happens to us next? It looks like that villain's not coming out of the clink any time soon! So who does the foundry belong to?"

"Yes, who do we work for from now on? Who's going to pay our wages?" asked yet another man.

"I assume that the whole purchase will be annulled," David said. "Starting with the loan that our bank made to Friedhelm Strobel—after all, he bought the foundry dishonestly. He certainly won't remain the legal owner, so the foundry will revert to Otto Gründler. He'll have to be told, of course, but I believe our bank has his new address, so that won't be any great problem. As for the money that Strobel cheated you out of . . ." He shrugged. "I think there's a good chance the money will be found and can be returned to its rightful owners."

Another murmur traveled through the crowd at these words. What wonderful news!

"Then you can get the money back that you paid people in compensation," Thomas whispered to his daughter, but Wanda simply waved a hand.

People fell quiet again, as though hoping to hear something that would help them make sense of all this confusion. But it wasn't David who spoke next.

"Do you remember what happened nearly ten years ago?" Christoph Stanzer looked around expectantly. When nobody spoke, he went on. "It's only another three weeks until December 31. On that day"—he paused for effect to be sure that he had their attention—"in 1901, the old village foundry closed its doors forever. That was ten years ago!"

"Ten years . . ." "A dark day . . ." "How time flies . . ." A hubbub of voices broke out once more.

Christoph Stanzer raised his hand for silence. "Lauscha has never been the same since. Perhaps you young folk can't understand it . . ." He glared at Jockel and a couple of the others. "But for those of us who've been around for a while, it was as though the heart had been torn out of the place!"

"That's all well and good," Jockel said. "But what does that have to do with us? With the problems we have here and now?"

"I can tell you that, young man!" Christoph Stanzer said. "If we all stick together and help one another, then starting on December 31 the Gründler foundry can belong to the glassblowers! Just the way the investors planned back in the summer. Just imagine: the Gründler foundry could be what the old village foundry used to be, once upon a time!"

"Then Lauscha will finally have a beating heart again!" Karl called out, and his wife nodded.

"And we'll have steady jobs!" Siegfried Braun shouted out.

"The new foreman can pack his bags and go back to Unterneubrunn!" another man shouted.

"Yes, we'd be our own bosses! Just the way the master glassmakers used to be in the days of the old foundry. My word, didn't we always envy them!" Gustav Müller's eyes gleamed.

Martin Ehrenpreis, standing next to him, put his arm around his shoulder. "You fancy being a master glassmaker, then?" Both men laughed.

Jockel frowned. "Could you be serious for a moment? It all sounds like a very pretty dream, but how's it supposed to work? Isn't it enough that you've come to grief once already?"

Wanda was following the exchange breathlessly. David, still standing beside her, winked at her.

"Our chances are a lot better this time!" Christoph Stanzer called out. He had been a master in the old foundry all those years ago. "This time we'd hold all the best cards!" He walked over to where David stood, took his hand, and held it in the air like a trophy. "We have among us today a very capable banker who can help us get a good loan!"

David and Wanda looked at each other. Was this really happening? David shook his head, baffled, as people began to applaud.

"And we've got the American girl!" By now Christoph Stanzer had to shout to be heard. "She did everything right the first time around, and her advice was a great help. If it hadn't been for Strobel . . ." He waved his hand as though shooing away a fly. Then he took Wanda's hand and held it up in the air too. "Wanda, we're counting on you this time as well!" And the crowd cheered again.

"But how . . . ?" Startled, Wanda looked past Christoph at David, who shrugged his shoulders as though to say, *We'll just have to go along with it!*

"So? What do you say to that?" Christoph asked, looking at Wanda expectantly.

She laughed, though it sounded a little hysterical. "Well, I might have one or two ideas about how to organize the new company . . ." she said.

"That's lovely! Looks like Wanda won't have as much time for you in the future, but don't worry, my little angel. Together we will all take care of you," Eva whispered into Sylvie's ear, loud enough for Wanda to catch every word. But before she could say anything, Eva squeezed her arm. "You've done everything right, my girl! Marie would be proud of you, just as we are."

Wanda could hardly believe her ears. Had Eva really paid her a compliment?

Eva then turned her attention back to the baby in her arms. "They do make a racket, don't they, eh, those glassblowers? You'll just have to get used to that . . ."

There was a lump in Wanda's throat as big as a dumpling, and she was so moved that she couldn't say a word.

"I still can't believe we've gotten rid of Strobel!" Karl Flein called, whooping loudly.

"Free beer today!" Benno shouted. "Off to the Black Eagle, one and all!"

"Here's to the Gründler foundry and December 31, 1911!" Christoph said.

Wanda stood where she was, utterly perplexed and rooted to the spot. David put an arm around her shoulder. A smile played on his lips.

"It looks as though the whole story's starting again from the beginning . . ."

She beamed at him. "It looks as though I'll have to delay my visit to Lake Maggiore for a while!"

AFTERWORD

This story is a work of fiction. The Gründler foundry did not exist, and no glass foundry was sold or closed in Lauscha in 1911. Historically, the decline of the foundries began much later.

I hope that the Lauschaer Sparkasse bank, founded in 1883, will forgive me for the fact that it played no part in my story—in real life, I am sure that it would have been more than ready to help the glassblowers with a loan.

A paper mill really did burn down in 1909 in Obergurig. However, there are no records that any of the paper stock was saved from the fire.

The Schlüter lines shipping company of Bremen never existed, and there was no fortune to be made on their shares. But the Bremen jutes mills did exist and were well known for employing a number of Thuringian workers.

ACKNOWLEDGMENTS

Nothing is further from the truth than the idea that an author simply sits in a room and writes! As always, a great many people helped me write this book. First of all I must thank Lothar Birth from Lauscha, who went to great lengths to check details for me. Thomas Müller-Litz, a glassblower in Lauscha, read my glassblowing scenes and likewise has my thanks. I would also like to thank the Lauscha tourist office, which has always been very helpful and supported me and my books over the years. I thank Dr. Peter Puff of Jena for his efforts in checking the manuscript for all matters related to the history of Thuringia. Any mistakes that have crept in are mine alone. My thanks as well to my assistant Kirsi Eiting, whose specialized knowledge of banking was a great help to me, and who has done a great deal else besides! As with all my books, my friend Gisela Klemt read the early drafts, and has earned my heartfelt thanks for that. Thanks as well to my agent Ingeborg Rose for all our work together.

I would also like to thank my family and my husband, all of whom have given me the space I need to work and write.

—Petra Durst-Benning

ABOUT THE AUTHOR

Photo © Privat

Bestselling author Petra Durst-Benning has written seventeen novels. As a child and young woman, Durst-Benning frequently visited the United States, where she developed a passion for American fiction that has since inspired her own writing career. She now lives in her native Germany with her husband.

ABOUT THE TRANSLATOR

Photo © 2013 Maria Pakus

Samuel Willcocks was a prolific translator from Czech, German, Romanian, and Slovene into English in many genres, including science fiction and historical novels. He studied languages and literature in Britain, Berlin, and Philadelphia before winning the German Embassy Award (London) for translation in 2010.